HER INFINITE VARIETY

HER INFINITE VARIETY:

TALES OF WOMEN AND CRIME

B.K. STEVENS

WILDSIDE PRESS

DEDICATION

In memory of my grandparents,
Israel and Sarah Levow

The righteous shall be held in everlasting remembrance.
Psalm 112

ACKNOWLEDGMENTS

Putting this collection together has given me a chance to look back on my years as a mystery short story writer. It's stirred a lot of memories—editors I've worked with, friends I've made, experiences I've shared with my family. I have many reasons to be grateful.

Over twenty-five years ago, my first published mystery story appeared in *Alfred Hitchcock's Mystery Magazine.* My next story will appear there, too, and that's also where eight of the stories in this collection first appeared. Some mystery writers make a point of trying to place stories in all the major magazines. Unless I'm responding to an anthology call or have a particular reason for thinking a story belongs somewhere else, I always begin by submitting it to *AHMM.* During my early years as a mystery writer, I learned a great deal from Cathleen Jordan, editor of *AHMM* from 1981 until her death in 2002. Her successor, Linda Landrigan, continues the tradition of providing writers with invaluable guidance and always treating them with respect. Over the years, I've also enjoyed working with Emily Giglirerano, Jackie Sherbow, and others on the *AHMM* editorial staff. I feel incredibly lucky to have found such a wonderful home for my stories so early in my mystery writing career.

Now, I've been lucky again. I've loved working with editor Carla Coupe as we've put this collection together. When we first started to talk about a collection and were casting about for a possible focus, Carla suggested choosing stories with women protagonists. We worked together to narrow the list of possibilities, to try to come up with the right mix of whodunits and suspense stories, of lighter stories and darker ones, of women as detectives and women in other roles, of novellas, shorter stories, and flash fiction. I've enjoyed working with Carla during the editing process, too (though it's hard to keep up with her), and I appreciate John Betancourt's interest and support. For a long time, I've thought that if I ever wanted to do a short story collection, Wildside Press would be the ideal publisher. I was right.

I'm also grateful for the support I've received from the mystery writing community, especially the Sisters in Crime Guppies, the Mid-Atlantic chapter of Mystery Writers of America, the Short Mystery Fiction Society, and the Malice Domestic family. At conferences and over the

Internet, I've formed some wonderful friendships with other short story writers, who have been incredibly generous with their encouragement and advice. Even when we're competing with each other, I think we always wish each other well and take genuine pleasure in each other's successes. I can't possibly list them all, but I can't resist the temptation to mention Paula Gail Benson, Susan Furlong Bolliger, John Floyd, Kaye George, Barb Goffman, Terrie Moran, and Art Taylor.

As I said, working on this collection brought back many memories. As I was going through folders of old stories, I came across a multicolored, densely decorated note my daughter Sarah wrote when she was eight years old, congratulating me on my first sale to *Woman's World*. I'm tempted to frame that note, as a visual representation of my family's support for my writing. During the long, rejection-laden years before *Alfred Hitchcock's Mystery Magazine* accepted that first story, my husband, Dennis, kept me going when I felt like giving up. He's always read everything I write—usually, several drafts of everything—and spent endless, patient hours discussing everything from character development to bookmark design. When our daughters, Sarah and Rachel, became old enough, they joined in the reading and the discussions. I think working on the stories together made our family closer; I know it made the stories better. I still email drafts to our daughters, and they still respond with careful, perceptive comments and suggestions. For this collection, Rachel has taken on special responsibilities as proofreader, so I owe her extra thanks.

I have great affection for the stories in this collection, partly because of my affection and respect for all the people who helped make them happen.

SPOILER ALERT

Each story in this collection is followed by brief comments—about the story's origins, about its characters or themes, or about some other sort of background information. Some comments contain spoilers, so please always read the story first.

Published by Wildside Press LLC.
www.wildsidebooks.com

CONTENTS

THE DETECTIVES

In the 1980s and 1990s, mystery series about women detectives surged in popularity. In some of the most successful series, these women detectives were free of any binding family obligations—parents conveniently dead, husbands conveniently divorced, children conveniently nonexistent. These detectives could, if they liked, choose compatible mentors to serve as temporary parent substitutes, enjoy more or less fleeting relationships with men they found attractive, and occasionally take young people under their wings, straightening out their lives before the last chapter. These series offer readers many delights. Why not indulge, from time to time, in fantasies about women detectives as gloriously independent as Philip Marlowe and Sam Spade?

But it seemed to me that the personal lives of most women I knew were much more complicated, much messier. My friends and I struggled with guilt and resentment as we tried to care for aging parents and in-laws, to share responsibilities and joys with lifelong partners, and to provide continuing guidance and support to children who wouldn't set off confidently on their own after we gave them a few wise, pithy paragraphs of advice. I wanted to see if I could write stories about women detectives whose personal lives come closer to the lives of the real women I know, stories that still provide some of the satisfying wish-fulfillment of the popular series.

I ended up writing two series of stories about women detectives; *Alfred Hitchcock's Mystery Magazine* has provided the ideal home for both. When private detective Iphigenia Woodhouse makes her debut in the 1991 "Night Vision," she's single and childless. To that extent, she's like the central characters in those popular series. She does, however, have a mother—an extremely demanding mother. She also has enduring ties to an ex-fiancé who's still faithful to her, even though she broke their engagement off years ago. And in narrator Harriet Russo, her assistant, she has a protégée who becomes her Watson and, eventually, her daughter substitute and sister substitute.

Amateur sleuth Leah Abrams, introduced in a 1998 story called "Death on a Budget," has a more conventional family life. She's married to Sam, a remarkably patient and understanding husband (almost as patient and understanding as my own husband), and she has two daughters, Sarah and Rachel (coincidentally, so do I). Every story is framed by conversations with Sam, and the daughters usually make at least one appearance, sometimes frustrating Leah and sometimes providing her with unexpected inspiration.

"The Detectives" includes the first story and one later story from each series. (So far, there have been nine Iphigenia Woodhouse stories, five Leah Abrams stories.) As you read, please remember the early stories were written before everybody had cell phones, before Craigslist existed, and before people turned to Google rather than the library when they had to do research. And yes, in "Night Vision," Iphigenia smokes. Smoking was controversial back then—Iphigenia's mother definitely doesn't approve—but not yet as widely condemned as it is now. I thought an occasional cigarette might make Iphigenia seem more like a tough ex-cop. But she never seemed much like a tough ex-cop anyway, and as smoking became increasingly unpopular, I quietly dropped it from the series. I'm happy to report that both Iphigenia and Leah are still in good health, and both still show up in the pages of *Hitchcock's* from time to time.

NIGHT VISION

(1991)

"Your academic preparation is adequate," Iphigenia Woodhouse said. She was one of the biggest women I'd ever met—almost six feet tall, broad shouldered, and lean. Her hair was black and a little bit gray, sort of frizzy but sort of nice, except it was pulled back from her face too hard, caught at the nape of her neck with a thick blue rubber band. She frowned at my transcript again before flipping back to my resume. "What else have you got? A black belt, a marksmanship certificate—not relevant, except as indications of commendable but naïve enthusiasm. Our caseload is numbingly nonviolent. The secretarial experience, on the other hand, is extremely relevant. Now. One more thing." She took off her glasses and stared at me, managing to look both intense and almost bored. "Are you nice, Miss Russo?"

I blinked. "Nice? What do you mean, nice?"

She sighed. "Nice. You know. Kind. Considerate. Pleasant. That sort of nice. I had to fire my last five assistants for insufficient niceness. So. How nice are you?"

Back in Cleveland, I'd paid two hundred dollars for a Power Interviewing seminar. It hadn't prepared me for this. "I don't know," I said. "I try to be nice."

"Trying isn't good enough." She stuck her glasses back on her face. "This job requires a high, consistent level of niceness. Specifically, it requires extreme niceness toward Mother." She pointed to a mahogany rocking chair outfitted with red cushions. It was set against a bay window, ten feet from Miss Woodhouse's desk, and next to it was a table spread with brushes and oils and a large paint-by-number canvas of a lighthouse ringed by stormy seas. "Mother's napping now, but normally she sits there. If you get this job, you will always be nice to Mother. You will always treat her, and speak to her, with great respect. If she asks for any sort of assistance—*any* sort—you will provide it promptly and cheerfully. You will not chew gum in front of Mother. You will not smoke in front of Mother. You will not use foul language in front of Mother."

"But I *never* smoke or use foul language," I protested.

She scowled and lit a cigarette. "I don't give a hot damn about what you 'never' do. My sole concern is with what you do, and do not do, in the presence of Mother. Oh, yes. Clothing. No low-cut blouses, no short skirts, no tight slacks, no high heels. Mother doesn't approve."

When I'd come here, I'd been desperate to get this job. I'd run through five cities and all my savings without advancing one inch toward my dream of an apprenticeship at an East Coast detective agency. Annapolis had felt like my last chance, and Woodhouse Investigations had seemed ideal. Now, I wasn't so sure. What sort of private detective kept a well-cushioned mother rocking in the front office, painting by number and imposing a dress code? Would Philip Marlowe stub out his cigarettes and censor his language in deference to Mother? Visions of the Bates Motel flashed through my mind.

"Is your mother a detective?" I asked cautiously. "Your partner?"

She took a long drag on her cigarette. "Mother is my most trusted advisor, but she takes no professional interest in investigative work. She is a professor of classical languages and literature—or, rather, she was, until medical developments forced her premature retirement some sixteen years ago. I might as well tell you some people consider Mother eccentric. I assure you, however, she is an acute observer of human events, and her insights have been of incalculable value to me on countless occasions."

"I see," I said, and began to feel I really did. I'd done background research on Iphigenia Woodhouse—one of my Power Interviewing strategies—and learned that, until sixteen years ago, she'd been a successful, ambitious police detective, rising fast, regarded as likely to become the first woman to head the homicide division. Then, abruptly, she'd left the force, broken off an engagement to a fellow detective, and started Woodhouse Investigations. Now, I thought I understood why. "Is it Alzheimer's?" I asked gently.

She ground out her cigarette, so emphatically tiny sparks scattered onto her desk blotter and sizzled out harmlessly. "I'll thank you not to slap labels onto my mother. No, it is not Alzheimer's. She had a breakdown—the doctors don't know why—and in some respects she's never completely recovered. The doctors can't explain that, either. At the moment, however, our focus is on you, not on the failures of the medical profession. Tell me why you want to become an investigator—or perhaps I can guess. It was the library, wasn't it? You got bored with being a secretary, you started reading detective novels, and you decided you want to be exactly like Philip Marlowe and Sam Spade."

"Not exactly like them," I said, blushing because she'd come so close to the truth, and because it sounded so silly. "I wouldn't want to sleep around so much, or kill so many people."

That made her smile—the first smile I'd seen since the interview started. "You might do after all, Miss Russo. You and Mother might get along fine. Now. As to your duties. There'd be a lot of typing and filing and answering the telephone, and you'd also handle most of the legwork. Mother doesn't like me to go out. Anything requiring tact or real intelligence I would of course handle myself."

It occurred to me that she should maybe consider reassigning the tact work. "I'd like to do as much legwork as possible," I said. "I'm eager for field experience."

"I'm sure you are. Let's give you a trial assignment." She opened a desk drawer, rummaged efficiently, and pulled out a manila folder. "This," she said, tapping it with her index finger, "is the simplest of all possible assignments. If you can't handle this, you can't handle anything. The client is Christopher Sinclair, director of the Bay Club."

"Is that a country club?"

"An extremely exclusive one. Mr. Sinclair has a seventeen-year-old daughter, Jennifer. When Jennifer was three, Mr. Sinclair divorced her mother and cheerfully surrendered custody. The mother moved to California, and Mr. Sinclair evidently gave not another thought to his daughter's existence until last year. Then the mother died in a plane crash, and custody bounced back to Mr. Sinclair."

"And he wasn't delighted to receive it?"

She shrugged. "Jennifer is not the sort of daughter best calculated to inspire delight. Long orange hair with a bright green streak, tight skirts and thick thighs, lots of mascara, lots of acne, late nights, loud music, lousy grades. Plus the usual miniature messes at school. He was appalled, but he was stuck. So he assigned her a back bedroom and was remarkably successful at continuing to ignore her. Then, one month ago, she cut her hair and dyed it brown. She started wearing baggy clothes, she stayed home every night, she stopped getting in trouble at school, and her grades shot up. Her father thinks she must be on drugs."

"Drugs?" I echoed. "Now? Why would he think that *now*?"

She lifted a hand. "He read a pamphlet. 'Watch for sudden changes in your teenager's behavior. Changes in appearance, social habits, academic performance—these can be warning signs of drug abuse.' The standard wisdom on the subject."

"But that doesn't seem likely in this case, does it?"

"No. I told Mr. Sinclair that, the first time he came here, but he insisted it must be drugs. I'd guess he's *hoping* it's drugs, so he'll have an excuse to slap her into a residential rehabilitation program and forget about her for a few months or a few years. Even without the orange hair, she's a dumpy, pimply embarrassment to him."

"He sounds like a horrible person," I said. I couldn't help it.

"He's a charmer," she agreed, "but he pays his bills. And he wants Jennifer watched." She glanced at the clock. "She gets out of school in half an hour. All you have to do is to follow her while she walks home—about six blocks. You don't have to worry much about being spotted, because she never takes her eyes off the sidewalk. And you definitely don't have to worry about anything dramatic happening. I've followed her every day for a month, and she never goes anywhere racier than the orthodontist's office. Generally, she walks straight home. Once she gets there, Attila the Housekeeper takes over, and your job is done. Mr. Sinclair doesn't want a full-scale investigation—too much risk of scandal. So you're not to speak to Jennifer or to attempt to question her friends. Understand?"

"Yes," I said, sorry the job was so easy and unimpressive.

"Good." She wrote rapidly on an index card. "This may be our last day on the case. I called Mr. Sinclair again yesterday and told him he's wasting his money, and if he wants to know what's going on in his daughter's life, he might consider the heretofore untried technique of talking to her. He said he'd think about it."

"I hope he does." I looked up at her. "Why do you think she *did* change so suddenly, Miss Woodhouse?"

"At that age, who knows? Chances are she fell in love with the president of the Young Republicans' Club and decided to change her image. Or she got tired of being a junior delinquent, or she got religion, or she just plain grew up. Here." She handed me the card and a photograph. "The address of the school, and a picture of her. I took it last month, from my car. In the most recent photo her father had, she was in diapers."

"Thanks." I put the things into my purse. "You said this is a trial assignment. If I do all right, do I get the job?"

She sat back in her chair, looking me over. "If you botch something this simple, you *don't* get the job. I have a policy against hiring hopeless incompetents. If you don't disgrace yourself, you may meet Mother. Then Mother will decide about the job."

* * * *

If you've seen pictures of Annapolis, you've probably seen the city dock, or the state house, or narrow streets crowded with tiny, elegant houses and artsy shops and seafood restaurants. All that quaintness is packed into about two square miles called the historic district. After that, there's the business district, nice enough but nothing special. Then you cross the bridge, and it's just malls and discount stores and endless stretches of bland, expensive suburbs without centers. Annapolis calls itself a tourist center, but if you come, plan on a short tour. You can visit every spot with a shred of interest without using up half a tank of gas.

Woodhouse Investigations occupies the bottom floor of one of those tiny, elegant houses in the historic district, almost within sight of the dock; Miss Woodhouse and her mother live on the top floor. I was parked on one of those narrow streets, across from gracefully crumbling Calvert High School, waiting for students to make their daily escape. I took out the picture of Jennifer and studied it again. She looked drab and sad—short, chunky mud-brown hair chopped off in a thick fringe, a black skirt that drooped several inches below her knees, a bulky gray sweater. She was hunched over the stack of books she carried, eyes riveted on the ground. I had no way of knowing, but I'd guess she'd looked better with the mascara and orange hair—no prettier, maybe, but stronger, more cheerful. I propped the picture on my dashboard and wondered why any seventeen-year-old would do this to herself.

I heard the hollow echo of a bell, and the school began to empty. Spotting Jennifer wasn't hard. She was one of the last ones out, hanging back, not talking to anybody. She looked exactly as she did in the picture—graveyard outfit, back stooped, head down, books hugged to her chest like a shield, or like a security blanket. When she reached the sidewalk, her head popped up for a quick look in all directions. Then it snapped down again, and she took off down the block, plowing through the ambling, laughing crowd of students like a demented bulldozer. I eased into the flow of cars, anonymous among all the mothers, girl-friends, and boyfriends converging on the school to pick up passengers. Even if Jennifer had been looking for me—and she wasn't looking for anybody, she was studying the sidewalk—she probably wouldn't have spotted me. This job was an obvious cinch.

At the corner, she turned left. That made me perk up. Miss Wood-house had said Jennifer always turned right here. Chances were, she was simply making a detour to return an overdue library book or grab a mid-afternoon pizza. Then again, maybe she was finally on her way to make a drug buy. Maybe this assignment would turn into a chance to prove myself after all. I kept my eyes tight on her as she took one unpredict-able turn after another, straight into the heart of the historic district. She was walking faster, she never looked up once, she tunneled down Duke of Gloucester Street, and then, before I realized what was happening, she shot up a cobblestone walkway and disappeared into St. Michael's Church.

A church. Nothing Miss Woodhouse had said prepared me for a church. Still, what could be more innocent? And this kid had Troubled Teen written all over her. Probably, she was meeting sweet old Father Somebody for counseling. I searched frantically for a parking space, settled for one in a loading zone half a block away, and tried to figure out my next move. Should I follow her into the church, pretend to pray, and risk being spotted? Or should I sit here like a ninny and lose the chance to see sweet old Father Somebody pass her a dime bag? What would Travis McGee do? I chewed my lip, tugged at my hair, and couldn't decide.

At least I was bright enough to keep an eye on the rearview mirror, so I saw the silver Cadillac pull into a handicapped spot in front of the church, saw the man climb out, scan the street, and start up the cobblestone path. He didn't look handicapped, and he didn't look like sweet old Father Somebody. He looked like a pimp. He was maybe forty, short and wiry, lavender suit, black shirt, white tie, blond hair slicked back tight against his skull, designer sunglasses. My God, I thought. Human trafficking, and the world's least suspicious-looking pickup spot. I jumped out of my car and raced down the street to rescue Jennifer.

He made it into the church maybe a minute before I did. I tried to fling open the oversized oak door, found it too heavy to fling, strained to pull it back, and scrambled inside. The adjustment from sunshine to semi-darkness cost me another few moments. I was at the back of the sanctuary, and Jennifer was in a front pew, already struggling with the man in the lavender suit. He had her by the left arm, he was pulling her toward the aisle, he had something in his right hand. Her right hand was reaching for something inside her baggy sweater.

All this registered in about a second. Then, a shot—only one, loud. He lurched back, his hand still on her arm, his face stretched long with astonishment. He fell, and she screamed.

I didn't think. I just felt sick. "Oh, no!" I cried. "Jennifer!"

Her head jerked back—obviously, she hadn't noticed me before. But she noticed me then. I've never seen such pure terror in a human face.

She screamed again. Then she must've stepped over the body, or jumped over the body. Within seconds, she was charging up the aisle, howling—a deep, wild, hopeless howl. Whatever happened next, it was a disgrace to my years at Mr. Lee's Aerobic Kung Fu Studio. I don't think I even went into a stance. She ran straight at me, she smacked the side of my head with her gun, and then I think she must've run over me. I have a vague memory of falling down, hitting my head on the carefully preserved eighteenth-century floor, and feeling stupid.

* * * *

"Your first name is Harriet, is it not?"

Slowly, I opened my eyes. I was lying in a crisp, narrow bed, and for a second I thought the woman sitting next to me was Iphigenia Woodhouse. The gray eyes were right, and the thick, almost archless eyebrows, and the large-lean frame, and the your-opinion-doesn't-matter-much voice. But this woman's hair was white, gathered into a fat, neat braid descending almost to her waist, and her face was saggy and spotted. And would Iphigenia Woodhouse be holding an eight-inch square metal loom on her lap, or be busily engaged in weaving a pink-and-green potholder?

"My daughter told me about you," the woman said, frowning as she threaded a polyester loop through the haphazard maze she's constructed. "She didn't want me to come along—she never wants to take me anywhere. But I wasn't about to let her go to a hospital without me. It would be such a perfect chance for her, wouldn't it, to talk to the doctors and make her plans. She wants to put me in an asylum, you know. She wants them to lock me away, and feed me on bread and water, and then she can run straight to That Man, and stay out past midnight, and eat greasy food and smoke cigarettes. Well, I was too quick for her. 'Take me to that hospital with you, Iphigenia,' I said, 'or no allowance all month.' As you might imagine, she didn't have much to say to *that*."

I'm not a lucky person. But this time I said the perfect word, and it must've been luck that led me to it—I was wrapped in fog, and even at my clearest I wouldn't have been sharp enough to know what she most wanted to hear.

"Are you Professor Woodhouse?" I asked.

Groggy as I was, I could see the thrill shoot through her when she heard the word "Professor." The shoulders straightened, the old gray eyes danced, and the thick braid twitched with pleasure.

"I am," she said. "I am Professor Woodhouse. And you are Harriet—poor, sweet Harriet, who's had such a nasty bump on the head. Iphigenia said nasty things when she heard about it—she's always been a nasty girl—but don't worry. I'll make her be nice."

She walked to the door and looked down the hall. "Iphigenia," she called. "Come here this minute. Little Harriet's awake." She squeezed my hand and winked at me before sitting down again.

Iphigenia Woodhouse walked into the room, stood at the foot of my bed, crossed her arms across her chest, and scowled. The galloping pain in my head got worse.

"Well," she said. "How do you feel?"

"Not too bad," I lied. "What happened?"

She scowled again. "You may well ask. Let's review your progress on your first case, shall we? You were given the difficult assignment of watching a teenaged girl walk home from school. During the seven or eight minutes you had her under your surveillance, she killed a man in a church, assaulted you, fired three wild shots at a police officer as she ran down the street, and disappeared. Thanks to you, I had to call my client and tell him his daughter, who had never before been charged with anything more serious than smoking in the girls' room, is now a fugitive from justice, wanted for murder and a fistful of other felonies. How would you rate your performance, Miss Russo?"

Professor Woodhouse reached for her potholder loom. "Don't you dare blame poor, sweet Harriet, you nasty girl," she said. "This fiasco is *your* fault. You shouldn't have given her such a dangerous assignment on her first day."

Iphigenia Woodhouse's eyebrows popped up. I could see her scrambling to adjust to the fact that I'd become "poor, sweet Harriet." When she spoke again, her voice was so much gentler and more tentative that you'd have thought it was a different person. "I'm sorry, Mother," she said. "I didn't mean to upset you. I didn't think the assignment would be dangerous. Jennifer didn't seem violent or—"

"She'd smoked in the girls' room," Professor Woodhouse said. "That should have told you what sort of person she is. It's the sort of disgraceful offense *you* used to commit, you nasty girl. What were you thinking of, exposing dear little Harriet to someone who had smoked in the girls' room?"

Iphigenia Woodhouse sank into a chair. "Yes, she'd smoked in the girls' room," she said wearily. "And now she's killed a man."

"Six of one, half a dozen of the other." Professor Woodhouse kept weaving. "If anything, she's taken a step up. There's no legitimate excuse for indulging in such a filthy, unhealthful habit, especially not on school property. There are, on the other hand, any number of legitimate reasons for killing a man."

Iphigenia Woodhouse lifted her head, a look of wonder transforming her face. "You're right, Mother," she said.

"He *did* seem to be attacking her," I offered cautiously. "He was dragging on her arm, and she looked awful scared."

"You see?" Professor Woodhouse demanded. "When I finish this potholder, dear little Harriet, I will give it to you. Indeed, I will make you three matching potholders, and that will be very nice. Iphigenia, have the police identified the nasty man who was shot in the church?"

"Edmund Fox." Miss Woodhouse rubbed her forehead. "A fence, from Baltimore. The police figure Jennifer was planning to sell him something she'd stolen from her father, to get money for drugs. Then something went wrong, and she shot him—with a gun also, presumably, stolen from her father."

"The police seem to be making many unwarranted assumptions," Professor Woodhouse observed. "I'm sorry to see you guilty of the same mistake, Iphigenia. Thank goodness you have sweet little Harriet with you now, to guide you. Rest well tonight, little Harriet. In the morning you can go with Iphigenia when she apologizes to Mr. Sinclair."

Miss Woodhouse nodded meekly, and it was settled. Impossible as it seemed, I apparently still had a shot at this job.

* * * *

I'd figured Mr. Sinclair would stay home the next day, to pace by the phone and hope for news about his daughter. But no, he went to work. We found him in the Bay Club's restaurant, a big, sunshiny room with huge picture windows overlooking a quiet stretch of the Severn River. There were round tables with pastel linen tablecloths, and pale wooden chairs with slender backs. In the center of each table sat a bunch of flowers—real flowers, but so glossy and flawless you'd swear they were fake. It was elegant. So was Mr. Sinclair—slim, silver-haired, impeccably dressed. He stood near the hostess's station, talking to a very stylish, very thin, very blond woman who looked maybe thirty from across the room, maybe forty-five close up. She was flipping through pages attached to a clipboard, taking notes occasionally, nodding constantly.

"Lillian Dexter complained about the salmon again," he was saying. "She swears it was overdone. Mention it to Gunther, will you? And Bill Radford says he's bored with our salad dressings, wants us to try something lemony. We'll humor him. And—oh." He noticed us and frowned. "Miss Woodhouse. I'm surprised to see you here. This is my restaurant manager, Nancy Bracken." He tilted his head, slightly, in my direction. "And this, I take it, is the incompetent young person assigned to keeping my daughter out of trouble yesterday. Well done."

I felt like hiding behind Miss Woodhouse's skirt. The corners of her mouth tightened. "It wasn't her fault, Mr. Sinclair. I take full responsibility for what happened."

"Yes, I rather think you should." He took the clipboard and initialed something. "As you'll recall, I told you Jennifer must be on drugs. As I recall, you said my fears were groundless. I paid you to get me reliable information, and all you ever gave me were platitudes about learning to trust in and communicate with my daughter. Well, trust in Jennifer would have been a tad misplaced, wouldn't it?" He put the clipboard down. "As to communicating with her, at your urging I attempted that, yesterday morning. The results were not as heartwarming as you'd predicted. She went into hysterics, ran from the house, and, before the end of the day, committed murder. How much do I owe you for your professional services and advice?"

You could see how much she hated that, but she took it. "I'd like to help, Mr. Sinclair. I'd like to find Jennifer before she gets into more trouble. Could you tell me about your conversation yesterday, about why she got so upset? That might tell me where to start."

He gave her a sideways glare. "I did exactly as you'd suggested. I complimented her on the more positive aspects of the changes she's made in the last month, and I offered her the opportunity to become more a part of my life. I said, 'Jennifer, since you no longer seem intent on looking like a sideshow freak, perhaps you'd like to work toward dressing in a genuinely presentable way. I spoke to Miss Bracken, and she agreed to take you to a beauty salon and a clothing store tomorrow. If the results are tolerable, you may come to the club for a soft drink; if you behave in a reasonably civilized manner, perhaps some day you may stay for dinner.' Why should she be upset by a generous offer such as that?"

I imagined how I would've felt, and thought Jennifer had shown a lot of restraint by shooting only one person that day. But Nancy Bracken put a hand on his arm, her icy blue eyes thawing half a degree. "I'm sorry Jennifer didn't accept, Chris. I would have been delighted to help."

He patted her hand but didn't look at her. "Thank you, Nancy. Yes, I'd hoped you could be a positive influence, but clearly she was already beyond help. Only a fool could fail to perceive that." He looked at us. "However, Miss Woodhouse, I believe in giving people second chances. If Jennifer remains a fugitive much longer, the publicity will become unpleasant. If you can locate her and turn her over to the police quietly, I will pay you."

She scowled. "I will not accept payment. I will continue to work on this case, but only because I feel sorry for Jennifer, and responsible for what happened to her."

She turned away and stalked out. I did my best to stalk after her. I felt rotten, though, and I think maybe I shuffled. When we got outside, we had to stop stalking and idle under the awning while the parking lot attendant ambled off to get Miss Woodhouse's car. He had a Schwarzenegger build, curly blond hair, smoky blue eyes, and dimples. Miss Woodhouse was not impressed.

"This," she said, "is the definition of decadence. People come here to golf and swim and play tennis, to reap the benefits of fresh air and exercise. But can they walk the length of a small parking lot? No. That would exhaust them. So they stand about uselessly while some uniformed

Adonis parks and fetches their cars. Perhaps society matrons can work up a sweat simply by fantasizing about him caressing their keys."

"Maybe." I cleared my throat. "Miss Woodhouse, it was nice of you to take the blame in there, but I hope you don't really feel responsible. It was my fault. I should've—"

"No. You're new at this, and I told you it was a routine assignment. I was wrong about that, wrong about everything. I thought Sinclair's drug theory was idiotic, so I assumed there was no real reason to worry about Jennifer. A stupid mistake. All those changes in her appearance and behavior—maybe they weren't warning signs of drug abuse, but they were warning signs of something. And I shrugged them off."

Her car pulled up then, and the parking lot attendant eased himself out. I hadn't paid strict attention in high-school mythology classes, but I remembered enough to know Adonis was a pretty good name for him. He walked over, real slow, and pressed Miss Woodhouse's keys into her hand. Before he released them, he gave her a long head-to-toe look, letting his gaze wrap itself around her. Then he grinned, like he'd just had his thrill for the week, and gave me the same treatment. It was an act, I knew, a hokey, obvious act he probably used on all the ladies. But it pretty nearly took my breath away. Miss Woodhouse glared and didn't tip him.

We got into the car. "Do you think Jennifer was stealing things," I asked, "since the man she shot was a fence? You think she was messed up in a gang, a robbery ring, something like that?"

"Possibly. The one thing I'm sure of—and I should have realized it long ago—is that she was scared. I should have seen it in the way she walked, the way she carried herself. And the most obvious explanation for the hair and the clothes is that she didn't want to be recognized. Hiding out at home fits that theory, too, and so does bringing a gun into a church. She must have thought she might have to defend herself."

"Do you think she might've been scared of something connected to her father's club?" I suggested tentatively. "After all, she got hysterical when he invited her to go there."

Iphigenia Woodhouse lifted an eyebrow. "A surprisingly perceptive suggestion, Miss Russo. Now, we must try to move beyond guesswork. So I will make some calls and consult some sources, and you will go to the library."

"The library?" I felt disappointed. I'd been hoping she'd let me watch her grill suspects.

"That's right." She pulled up in front of a long, low concrete building. "Jennifer cut her hair and started dressing like a professional frump on Saturday, March 9. Whatever scared her into making those changes, it was probably violent, it was probably illegal, and it probably made the newspapers. Try to find some possibilities. Check a few days before the ninth, a few days after. Check the Baltimore papers as well as the Annapolis one. Check for homicides, robberies, assaults, anything lively. Make a list. Then take a nap—Mother's concerned about that bump on your head—and come to the house for dinner. Understand?"

"Understood." I wondered if the second assignment meant I had the job, or at least a chance to redeem myself. But I didn't ask. It'd be better, I thought, to wait until I'd impressed her by putting together the longest, goriest list I could manage. It would definitely be better to wait until her mother was around.

* * * *

The Woodhouses' kitchen is small, old-fashioned, and efficient—walls and cupboards and all the appliances white, crisp gingham curtains, utensils hanging in a symmetrical pattern on a pegboard, clear counters, no clutter. Next to the refrigerator, there's a large oil painting in a scrolled gilt frame. It's a portrait of Winnie-the-Pooh—the Disney character, just the face, slightly smudged here and there, slightly shaky, and you can tell it's paint-by-number. Still, it's cheerful, and she'd mostly stayed inside the lines. I glanced at Professor Woodhouse, who stood by the sink, slicing onions.

"What a nice painting," I said. "Is it your work, Professor?"

She looked up, smiling. "How clever of you to guess. It *does* brighten the room a bit, doesn't it? I like to have smiling faces around—and with Iphigenia so glum, I'm not likely to see smiles unless I paint them. Iphigenia, I shall need two more onions for this salad."

From what I could see, the salad consisted almost entirely of onions, but Miss Woodhouse fetched two more without commenting. Then she took a roast and baked potatoes from the oven, her mother added croutons and green olives to the salad, and we all walked into the dining room. It's a cool, lovely room, vaguely nautical but not cutesy, all dark woods and blue fabrics. The centerpiece is a big green Styrofoam cube dotted with colored pipe cleaners twisted into flower shapes and studded with sequins. I didn't waste much time wondering who the artist was.

"Would you mind if we discuss business at dinner, Mother?" Miss Woodhouse asked. "Miss Russo and I have—"

"Call her Harriet," the professor cut in. "Why must you be so cold and formal, Iphigenia? It's no wonder you have no friends. And no, I don't mind if you discuss business—not that it would make any difference if I *did*, since in either case you'd do exactly as you please, as you always do, you nasty girl. And if I so much as murmur in protest, it's off

to the asylum with me, and you'll run to That Man. Don't bother denying it. You don't fool me, and you don't fool Harriet." She turned to me,
crinkled her nose, and smiled. "Now, little Harriet. Mean old Iphigenia
made you work this afternoon, didn't she? She sent you to the library,
even though I *told* her you needed to nap. I'm sure you discovered exciting things. Tell us about them. And have some salad."

As she filled my plate with onions, olives, and croutons, I reached
for my purse and took out a thick stack of index cards. "Thank you.
Yes, I went to the library—I was happy to go—and looked through the
Annapolis, Baltimore, and D.C. papers for the last six weeks. I think I
caught all the significant crimes. Murders are in red ink, assaults in blue,
robberies in black. And one burglary, in green. It's not violent, but I think
it's interesting."

I handed Miss Woodhouse the cards, and I could see she was impressed—by the amount of work I'd done, if not by the color coding. I'd
put the green burglary card on top of the stack, and she skimmed it and
frowned. "March 12: Mr. and Mrs. William Radford return from a trip to
the Bahamas to find their Annapolis home stripped of jewelry, paintings,
appliances. Well, it's fine you took notes on this, Miss Russo—Harriet—
but I don't see why you consider it interesting."

"Because the Radfords belong to the Bay Club," I said. "Remember?
This morning, Mr. Sinclair told his restaurant manager Bill Radford had
complained about the salad dressings. I called the Bay Club to make
sure, and it's the same William Radford. And I thought maybe, if Jennifer was messed up with that fence she killed, she could've been keeping
track of when club members were out of town and passing names on to
him. Then they'd rip off the houses, and he'd fence what they stole. This
burglary wasn't discovered until March 12, but it could've happened
earlier, and maybe something went wrong."

Miss Woodhouse nodded. "And maybe Jennifer got scared, and
maybe that's why she changed her appearance on March 9. Intriguing."

"Better than intriguing," Professor Woodhouse said, and beamed. "It
is ingenious. I'd like to see *you* come up with something half so clever,
Iphigenia. Little Harriet has done a fine job. She has earned more salad."
She piled another helping onto my plate.

Miss Woodhouse's mouth twitched. "Harriet's earned all the salad
she wants, and then some. Now, the homicides. Two in Annapolis, both
domestic—probably not what we're looking for. Baltimore had thirty-
two—rather a slow six weeks for Baltimore. And forty-nine in D.C. Why
did you check the D.C. papers? I didn't ask you to."

"No, but I wanted to be thorough. And it's barely an hour away. I
hope you don't mind."

"Not at all. You've shown commendable initiative." She set to work, skimming the cards and sorting them into piles. "Excuse me while I glance through these. Enjoy your dinner."

The roast was so tender you hardly needed teeth to chew it, the potatoes were firm and rich, and the salad was interesting. Professor Woodhouse chattered steadily as I ate, telling me long, confusing stories about how her Uncle Ed had killed his father and married his mother; later, I think, his daughter got buried alive. It was pretty gruesome, but I'd read a little Sophocles in high school, and I figured maybe Professor Woodhouse had mixed up stuff she'd lived and stuff she used to teach. So I didn't let it bother me. I just ate, smiled, and nodded. Out of the corner of my eye, I watched Miss Woodhouse. She was concentrating on murders—I could see the red ink flash by every time she flipped a card—and making a big stack, a small stack, and a tiny stack.

Finally, she stopped sorting, picked up the top card from the tiny stack, and snapped it in the air. "This homicide interests me most. The victim was Clayton Davis, age seventeen, Black, high-school senior, resident of Fairfax, Virginia. Shot twice in the back, body found in a dumpster in D.C. at seven a. m. on Saturday, March 9."

"Exactly one month ago yesterday," Professor Woodhouse observed, spreading mustard on her potato.

"You're right, Mother—of course." She flashed me an I-told-you-so glance, as if I'd doubted her mother's intelligence and now they'd proven me wrong. "It exactly coincides with the change in Jennifer's appearance, too. And the one thing I've discovered about the night before she changed is that she went to a party with some friends and left, about midnight, with a Black teenager nobody had seen before." She ran a squared, unpolished fingernail under the bright red lines of my notes. "The police assumed the shooting was drug-related—what else would they assume?—but apparently there's no evidence he was ever involved with drugs. The dumpster interests me, too. Presumably, he wasn't shot there; presumably, the body was moved. He could have been shot anywhere."

"Like at the Radford house?" I suggested. "Maybe he helped her burglarize it, and there was an argument, and the fence shot him, and they dumped the body in a place nobody would associate with the burglary, so the police would assume it was just another drug-related shooting."

"Possibly." Miss Woodhouse frowned. "It doesn't quite fit the facts, but we're getting closer. I'll call friends in the D.C. police department and see if they've learned more about the shooting."

Professor Woodhouse sighed impatiently as she served me more salad. "That's all well and good, but hadn't you better find that girl? She must be frightened. Every time I turn on the radio, some police officer or prosecutor is jabbering about how much trouble she's in, and how much worse it will be if she doesn't give herself up. Dismal old things! As if threats would make that poor, frightened girl give herself up!"

"That's true, Mother. But what else can they say?"

"They can promise her something nice," Professor Woodhouse shot back. "That's what you should do, Iphigenia. Go on the radio and say you'll give her something nice if she calls you. A pony, perhaps—all girls like ponies. And I don't think she can be such a *very* bad girl, even though she smoked in the girls' room. She went to church yesterday, after all."

"She probably went there to meet the fence," Miss Woodhouse pointed out, reaching for the butter.

Her mother slapped her hand. "Did it ever occur to you that perhaps she went there to pray? Why must you always think the worst of people, you nasty girl? Now, send that poor thing a message. Promise to give her something nice if she calls you. Do as I say, Iphigenia. Now."

Miss Woodhouse froze, looking stunned and dismayed, like she wanted to obey her mother but didn't know how to manage it. Without speaking, she stood up and walked into the den. Ten minutes later, she came back, carrying a legal pad.

"I've written a message for her, Mother," she said, all meek. "I'd like to put it in the newspaper, if that's all right, rather than on the radio. If Jennifer's still in Annapolis—and she probably doesn't have either the money or the courage to run—she may be reading the paper for news about her case. And if she's desperately searching for a way out of town, she might check the classifieds." She grimaced. "It's a long shot, but if she *does* see the ad, it might appeal to her."

She handed me the pad. "This ad should appeal to her, all right," I said, reading quickly. "But also to every other teenager in the county. You'll get thousands of calls."

"That's why I'd like to put your telephone number in the ad," she said. "I'd like you to screen all calls, and let me know if you hear from any possible Jennifers. Can you handle that?"

"Of course she can!" Professor Woodhouse shimmered with delight. "That's the first good idea you've had in months. Dear little Harriet will find poor little Jennifer and clear this whole unpleasant business up, and you may both have some ice cream. Won't that be nice?"

"Very nice," Miss Woodhouse said. "Thank you, Mother." She turned to me, and I swear her eyes were all teary. "Will you take the calls?"

How could I say no?

* * * *

Miss Woodhouse pulled some strings, and our ad made the next day's newspaper. By late afternoon, my phone number had to be the most popular seven-digit sequence in history. The moment I set the receiver down, the phone shrilled again, and I went back into my act. After three solid hours, I'd gotten good at eliminating callers quickly, but I hadn't found any possible Jennifers. And I was exhausted. I left the phone off the hook, splashed cold water on my face, did thirty sit-ups, poured myself a stiff Diet Coke, and put the receiver back in place.

Of course, the phone rang instantly. I shoved two fresh sticks of gum into my mouth. "Rockbuster Productions," I drawled. "The bands we book really cook. Whaddaya want?"

"I—um, well, hi." Female voice, definitely nervous, maybe scared. "I'm um, calling about your ad. In the *Capital*, you know? About the job. Could you, um, tell me more?"

So far, promising. I snapped my gum. "It's like the ad says, kid. The Hot Rivets are leaving for a Midwest tour, and they're looking for a roadie. A roadie, not a groupie. So if it's sex, drugs, and rock and roll you want, forget it."

"No sex," she said quickly. "No drugs. Just rock and roll. That is, all I want is a job. But I love rock and roll, and even though I've never heard of the Hot Rivets, I—"

"Never heard of them?" I demanded. I was wearing jeans and my Paul Simon t-shirt, and I purposely hadn't washed my hair that morning, so it was easy for me to get into the part. "Don't you read *Rolling Stone*? The boys got a fabulous review, totally fabulous—said they bring new meaning to the term heavy-metal techno-funk. They just cut their second album, and we've got first-class gigs set every five inches, solid, from Columbus to Sioux Falls to Tucson. And you've never *heard* of them?"

"Sorry. I missed the last issue of *Rolling Stone*. But they sound great. I was wondering—um, the ad said it's an immediate opening. How soon will the band leave?"

"Day after tomorrow, kid. Could you swing that?"

"Yes," she said. "The sooner, the better. Does the—um, does the band travel in its own bus? Not on a public bus? Is it leaving from the depot?"

Strange question—except from someone who figured the cops might be staking the depot out, watching for her. I sat up straighter. "Nah, they're leaving from the bass player's house, on Riva Road. Now, there's no experience required, like the ad says, but it's heavy work. Setting equipment up, lugging instruments around, like that. It ain't no job for Miss Junior Petite. So if you're some Skinny Minnie—"

"I'm not," she said eagerly. "I'm not skinny at all. I'm sort of heavy. And I'm strong, and I'll work really hard."

"That's what it takes, kid—that, and a realistic attitude. This tour ain't gonna make you rich and famous."

"Fine," she said, her voice bleak. "I've been rich, and it stinks. And famous is the last thing I need. The ad says room and board and modest wages. That's plenty for me."

"Well, the wages are pretty damn modest." I cringed. I don't like saying that word. "One more thing. We don't provide transportation back. The tour ends in Tucson, and that's where we leave you. You gotta find your own way home."

"I won't want to come home." The voice was utterly flat now. "Tucson sounds great."

You sound great, I thought. I yawned to conceal my excitement. "Okay. Maybe you'll do. I'll check with the road manager, and if he's interested, I'll call you back to set up an interview. You can bring your parents—they'll probably want to check us out, make sure we're legit."

There was a pause. "No, thank you. I mean, I'm on my own. I'm twenty-one—I don't look it, but I am. And my mother's dead, and my father—my father's in prison. Sex crimes. Can I come to the interview alone?"

"Fine." It was hard not to bounce in my chair. This had to be Jennifer. Every other caller had been at least a little wary, had wanted to bring half a dozen relatives to the interviews. "Give me your name and number, kid. Maybe I'll get back to you."

She hesitated. "My name's Joan. Joan Mellancamp. My number's 544-9236. I really hope you'll call."

"If you're lucky." I slapped down the receiver and immediately called Miss Woodhouse.

* * * *

At 11:30 the next morning, I was back at the Bay Club. The parking lot Adonis took my keys, gave me one of his head-to-toe leers, and eased himself into my car. Miss Woodhouse was right. It's decadent to have valet parking at a country club. The man had style, though.

I sighed away his spell and headed for the restaurant. Nancy Bracken was tiptoeing about the room, aiming sly peeks and smiles at scattered early lunchers, occasionally hovering by a table long enough to drop a murmur. She stiffened when she saw me.

"Miss Russo, isn't it?" she said. "Are you looking for Mr. Sinclair? He's at the Rotary Club luncheon. Could I help you?"

"I sure hope so." I pushed my hair back from my forehead. "I'm in a jam, Miss Bracken. It's my first week on the job—I'm not even sure I *have* the job—and I don't know what to do. Miss Woodhouse is in D.C. working on another case, and she said to meet her there by noon, and already I'm not gonna make it, but I don't see how I can leave town." I glanced around the room and lowered my voice. "I found Jennifer."

She did a double-take, recovered, and led me to an empty corner of the room. "That's wonderful. What did she say?"

"Nothing that makes sense. She's a mess—hysterical, paranoid, incoherent." I lifted my hands. "She'd been hiding out in the basement of a friend's house. I won't go into detail about how I found her, but when she saw me, she freaked. She wouldn't tell me anything, just babbled about how people are after her, people want to kill her, that kind of garbage. I managed to get her to Miss Woodhouse's place, and then I slipped her some sedatives. She's out cold—I don't think she'd slept in days, so she's all right for a while. But what should I do? I can't reach Miss Woodhouse, and I don't want to call the cops until Jennifer sees her father and talks to a lawyer."

"That's very wise." Her eyes got squinty, and you could tell she was thinking it over. "So she's at Miss Woodhouse's. Alone?"

I shrugged. "Miss Woodhouse's mother is there. But Professor Woodhouse is—I wouldn't want to call her senile, but she's confused, you know? Thank goodness Miss Woodhouse gave me a set of keys to her house. There's a little attic bedroom, with a door that locks from the outside, so I put Jennifer there and locked her in. That sounds awful, but it seemed safest."

"I think you did exactly the right thing." She paused, and you could hear the gears churning again. "Mr. Sinclair should know about this. I'll try to phone him. Wait here."

She was gone maybe three minutes, and she looked all brisk and cheerful when she returned. "I couldn't reach him, but I'll keep trying. I don't see why you can't leave for D.C. now."

She had questions about Jennifer's state of mind, so it was another ten minutes before I went to get my car. Adonis singed me with his sultriest leer as he handed me my keys.

* * * *

One forty-five in the afternoon. I lay on my side in the narrow bed, my face to the wall, quilt pulled up snugly around my shoulders and neck. It was very quiet. I couldn't see her, of course, but in my mind I had a clear image of the ancient, hunched figure dozing in the rocking chair next to the bed—thick glasses sliding down her nose, afghan nearly enveloping her, fat braid descending down her back.

I heard the door pushed open cautiously, a male voice, soft. "Not locked," it said. Then a pause. "Damn. The old broad's in here."

A female voice—also soft, but ice-firm. "So we do them both. Old ladies fall all the time. This one can break her neck on the stairs. But first the kid gets her accidental overdose. Now, Frank. Nice, quiet, quick."

I lay absolutely still. Another second, two seconds, three, four. Then a rush of cold air as the quilt was pulled back from my shoulders.

Another second, and now the room filled with noise and motion—a scream, a thud, a startled obscenity, grunts, shouted orders, feet pounding up the stairs, a soft crash as the bed collided with the wall. I flipped onto my other side in time to see Adonis hit the floor. Already, Miss Woodhouse was on top of him, afghan thrown aside, braid swinging as she struggled to pin down his arm, to dislodge the thing grasped in his fist. I looked toward the door and saw Nancy Bracken, shrieking, kicking wildly at the police detective who held her. Two other officers crowded into the room, trying to help, making futile grabs at her.

Miss Woodhouse was still on the floor, grappling with Adonis. She knocked the syringe from his grip, but he got a hand free and punched her, hard, in the face.

"I'll help you, Miss Woodhouse!" I cried. I started to leap up, got tangled in the quilt, and landed on the floor, face down and useless.

It didn't matter. Bellowing, the police detective shoved Nancy Bracken away and bounded across the room. He grabbed Adonis by the shoulders, yanked him to his feet, and threw him to the side. It's a sturdy house, but I swear it shook when Adonis hit the wall. He sort of melted then, oozing to the floor, grinning. Even semi-conscious, he looked good.

By now, other officers had succeeded in handcuffing still-kicking, still-cursing Nancy Bracken. Miss Woodhouse sat cross-legged on the floor, rubbing her chin in an absent-minded way, looking content. She cast a reproachful, vaguely affectionate look at the police detective, who was easing wobbly Adonis to his feet.

"You didn't have to do that, Barry," she said. "I could have handled him."

The police detective grinned. "I believe you could have, Iphigenia," he said.

Instantly, I knew he must be That Man, the long-abandoned detective fiancé. Before I'd recovered from that jolt, there was another one—a clear, strong voice from downstairs, so loud it sliced through the floor.

"Let go of me, young ruffian!" Professor Woodhouse shouted. "This is *my* house, and I'll go where I please! No, don't tell me it's not safe—*I'll* decide when it's safe. My dear little Iphigenia's up there, and she may need me. Out of my way, you nasty boy!"

I heard a thud and a moan as some unfortunate young officer was knocked aside. Then the house shuddered again as Professor Woodhouse thundered up the stairs.

"Don't be afraid, little Iphigenia!" she cried. "Mummy's coming!"

Miss Woodhouse jumped to her feet. "I'm fine, Mother," she called. "I'll be right with you." She looked at the police detective one more time, with something that might have been regret; but when she turned to me, her eyes blazed with triumph. "You see?" she demanded.

* * * *

Nobody felt like cooking that night, and I've got to say I was relieved. We ordered a large pizza, with onions and olives and extra cheese, and ate in the living room so Professor Woodhouse could watch reruns of *Lassie* and *The Love Connection*. She frowned at her daughter.

"Don't think you're fooling me, Iphigenia," she said. "This whole business with Jennifer was an excuse. You simply wanted to see That Man again, to get him into the house so you could sneak into corners with him when my back was turned and do nasty things."

Tonight, there was nothing strained about Miss Woodhouse's smile. She had a bruise big as Cleveland on her chin but seemed utterly at peace. "We didn't do nasty things, Mother. All that ended years ago. But I couldn't turn to anyone else in this situation. Not many police detectives would bend the rules so much to get evidence against those two. And without evidence, no jury would have believed Jennifer."

"*I* believed her," I said tentatively. I still didn't know if I'd gotten the job, so I wasn't sure I had the right to an opinion. "Sure, it sounded crazy at first, when she realized the interview was a trap and got hysterical. But I thought her story made sense. She goes to that party last month, meets Clayton Davis, likes him, wants to impress him. She tells him her father runs a country club, and she knows how to sneak onto the grounds after hours. So they decide to grab a six-pack and take a midnight stroll on the golf course. That's not hard to believe. Lots of kids do crazy things like that."

"Yes," Miss Woodhouse agreed, "but the next part strains credulity, doesn't it? That they just happened to walk past the storage shed while Nancy Bracken, Adonis, and the fence were inside, dividing the profits from the Bradford burglary. That Jennifer and Clayton could hear them quarreling about how long to wait before the next burglary. And then poor Clayton happened to sneeze, at exactly the wrong moment—that sounds like something from a melodramatic thriller."

I nodded. But it had never sounded like a thriller to me. It had sounded sickening. I could still see Jennifer shaking as she told us about it—how she and Clayton raced desperately across the golf course, how she heard two shots explode behind them, how Clayton groaned and fell, how she looked back in terror, just once, and saw Nancy Bracken, her face grim and ugly in the glare of Adonis's flashlight, a gun in her hand. And then, somehow, Jennifer made it to the woods bordering the fourth hole, crashed through the bushes, and tumbled into a shallow gulley and huddled there, sweating and shivering and trying not to sob, until the footsteps and curses faded. Minutes before dawn, she went home and cut off her hair.

Miss Woodhouse reached for another slice of pizza, one with only a few traces of olive. While her mother was absorbed in watching a Tylenol commercial, she furtively plucked the olive bits off, rolling them up in a paper napkin. "Ironic, isn't it?" she said. "If Christopher Sinclair had been anything vaguely approaching a decent father, Jennifer would have been doomed. But he'd never let her come to his club and didn't have her picture on his desk. So Nancy Bracken had no reason to suspect the orange-haired punkster running across the golf course might be her employer's daughter."

"Not until you urged him to be friendlier to Jennifer," Professor Woodhouse put in. I almost choked on my pizza. I hadn't realized she was still listening. "That wasn't terribly bright of you, was it?"

"You can't blame her," I said. True, Miss Woodhouse's attempt to help had set off a chain of nearly disastrous events—Christopher Sinclair telling Nancy Bracken about the abrupt change in Jennifer, Bracken figuring out the connection and calling the fence, the fence following Jennifer to the church and trying to kill her. But it didn't seem fair to hold Miss Woodhouse responsible. "How could she possibly have known what would happen?" I asked.

"She fancies herself a great detective," Professor Woodhouse countered. "Great detectives should be able to deduce things—things far more unlikely than the pitifully obvious scheme those nasties were operating. I declare I'm ashamed of you, Iphigenia. It was right under your nose, but you never took the trouble to glance down and see it."

Miss Woodhouse nodded meekly. "You're right, Mother. It *was* obvious—Nancy Bracken chatting with club members to see when they'd be out of town, the parking lot attendant making impressions of their keys, the fence helping them pull the burglaries and dispose of the valuables. And the sudden change in Jennifer's appearance—I should have considered the possibility that she'd witnessed a crime and was afraid of being recognized by the criminals. I was culpably unimaginative."

"If you ask me, Mr. Sinclair's the one who's culpable," I said. "Didn't it rip your heart out when Jennifer said she was afraid to go to the police because they might not believe her, and afraid to go to her father because he *might* believe her, and might hand her over to Nancy Bracken to spare his club bad publicity? What a forty-carat creep! That was good advice you gave her, Miss Woodhouse, about keeping her grades up so she can go away to college next year. I hope she picks a school in California."

"Or, better yet, Alaska." Miss Woodhouse looked at her mother with a shy smile. "There are so many horrible parents in the world. That's one reason we must cherish the good ones."

The Professor gave her a cold stare. "Don't try to flatter me, you nasty girl. You handled this case clumsily, and no amount of sentiment can disguise that fact. You'll notice, by the way, that I was right about little Jennifer's reasons for going to church. She went there to pray. It was the one-month anniversary of poor little Clayton's death, and she felt guilty and frightened, in need of guidance and forgiveness. And she nearly got killed. All thanks to you, Iphigenia."

Miss Woodhouse nodded again, looking low and miserable. Maybe it was stupid to step between mother and daughter, but I couldn't stop myself. "She saved Jennifer, Professor," I protested. "The trap we set this afternoon—telling Nancy Bracken Jennifer was in the house, so she'd tell Adonis to make copies of my keys and they'd come here to murder the witness—all that was Miss Woodhouse's idea. Jennifer's safe now, the police believe every word of her story, and those two are on their way to prison. Doesn't your daughter deserve credit for that?"

Professor Woodhouse scowled. With great dignity, she took a last bite of pizza, then set her plate on the coffee table and reached for a tangled mess of knitting. "That will be quite enough from *you*," she said, thrusting a knitting needle into an immense knot of lilac and orange. "Why must you always take her side, you nasty girl?"

Miss Woodhouse sputtered loudly, only once, clapped her hands over her mouth, and turned her face aside, her body shaking with suppressed laughter.

Suddenly, I somehow felt sure I had the job.

When I began planning the Iphigenia Woodhouse series, I knew the relationships among the three women at the center of the stories would be crucial. I wanted to create a brilliant detective capable of making deductions worthy of Sherlock Holmes or Nero Wolfe. But maybe she wouldn't be quite as infallible as Holmes or Wolfe—maybe she'd have some blind spots, and she'd sometimes have to rely on the other women on her team to set her straight.

I thought of Jane Austen's Emma, of the relationship between Emma Woodhouse and Harriet Smith. Miss Emma Woodhouse is clever and sophisticated, but sometimes she's too confident in her mental abilities and overlooks the obvious. Sometimes, naïve little Harriet Smith sees things more clearly than her intellectually superior mentor does. That was my starting point for thinking about the relationship between Iphigenia Woodhouse and Harriet Russo, though Austen's characters and mine clearly don't match up exactly. And while Iphigenia's mother can be as demanding and eccentric as Emma's father, Professor Minerva Woodhouse is far more intelligent. Like Harriet, she plays a part in solving mysteries. After all, she gets her first name from the Roman goddess of wisdom.

Iphigenia Woodhouse's first name is significant, too. Like Iphigenia, the daughter Agamemnon sacrifices to get favorable winds for the journey to Troy, Iphigenia Woodhouse is a sacrificial figure. She gives up her professional ambitions and marriage plans to serve a parent. (In most versions of the Troy myth, though, Agamemnon's daughter survives the sacrifice. So does Iphigenia Woodhouse.)

TABLE FOR NONE

(2008)

"And he shows up every night?" Miss Woodhouse asked.

"Every night for three whole years," the younger of the two women said. She looked about twenty-five, reasonably pretty and resolutely slim. "Practically the whole time I've been working at Chez Cubbe."

"And he always shows up around eight," the man said. He looked mid-way through his thirties, but his hair didn't match his age—shaved to a pale orange shadow on the sides and back, slicked into tall, sharp, dark peaks on top. "And he always sits at the same table, always orders pretty much the same thing. He starts with a martini and a glass of water, and he nurses them for a solid hour—take a sip of the martini, pour a little water into the martini glass, sip, pour, sip, pour until both glasses are empty."

"Then he orders a cup of soup," the other woman said. She looked about fifty and had probably never been attractive, but she kept herself up—trim figure, careful makeup, studiously grayless brown hair cut sensibly short and combed into a just barely flirty arc that bumped up over her forehead. "Clam chowder, usually—it's the house specialty."

"Yeah, we got a real creative menu," the man said. He blew his nose disdainfully. "An Annapolis restaurant with clam chowder as the specialty—imagine that!"

"It's what people expect, Chuck," the young woman said, half-smiling. "Anyhow, he takes a long time eating the chowder—or the tomato-basil, he'll have that when it's soup of the day. The soup's served with a roll, but he wraps that up in a napkin and sets it aside. I bring him a basket of crackers, too. He'll eat those."

"And sometimes I'll bring him a little something from the kitchen," Chuck added, "just as a freebie—if I'm trying out a new appetizer, say. He enjoys that."

"Then he orders a sandwich to go," the young woman resumed. "A turkey club, usually, but sometimes it's chicken salad with fresh tarragon, or ham with Swiss and honey mustard. And coffee. He stretches the coffee out till closing time—that's 10:00 on weeknights, midnight on weekends. Then I bring him his check." She paused, clearly expecting to amaze us. "And every night, he pays with a crisp hundred-dollar bill."

"Then Brenda brings him his change," the other woman said, sounding impatient, "and he leaves a three-dollar tip—never a penny more or less—takes his sandwich and roll, and leaves. That's the way it's been, every night for three years."

"And you don't know anything about him?" I asked. "Not even his name?"

"It's Howard," Brenda said. "Terry finally asked him, and that's what he said—just Howard, no last name. At first, I tried to strike up conversations, because he seems lonely. But it made him uncomfortable: He always loves to hear about what I'm doing, but he doesn't like to talk about himself. He's old—seventy, maybe—and doesn't wear a wedding ring, but that's all we know. Except, of course, that he's rich."

Professor Woodhouse looked up sharply from the mounds of uncooked pasta on the small mahogany table next to her rocking chair. "Do you base that conclusion solely on his habit of paying with hundred-dollar bills? Or do you have solid evidence?"

It was the first time the professor had spoken, and all three of our visitors looked taken aback. They'd probably assumed she served a purely decorative function—the quaint, grandmotherly figure with her black shawl and long gray braid, musing serenely as she threaded manicotti and ziti onto long strands of dental floss.

"Well, gosh," Brenda said, tugging thoughtfully on her artfully highlighted hair. "I mean, what other evidence do you need? Plus he eats out every night, and he drives this great car—a classic Mustang, in mint condition. I mean, he's gotta be rich, right?"

With every word she spoke, I could see Brenda losing points with the professor. As I'd learned long ago, the professor has a low tolerance for chatty incoherence and a special disdain for "I mean" as an interjection. The professor couldn't have liked the way Brenda was dressed, either—low-slung jeans and a tight, sleeveless t-shirt that skimmed her tummy. Whenever she shifted in her chair, her navel peeked out coyly. Professor Woodhouse is not the sort of person who enjoys looking at other people's navels. She's never told me this. She doesn't have to. By now, I know the professor well enough to feel sure she doesn't particularly enjoy looking at her own navel.

Miss Woodhouse spoke up quickly. "There are other ways of interpreting the hundred-dollar bills, and the rest. But let that pass. I assume you have a specific reason for seeking help from a private detective at this point, that you're not simply troubled by the presence of an odd but exceptionally loyal customer."

"Hell, we're not 'troubled' by Howard," Chuck said. "He's a little weird, yeah, but he's a great old guy. The thing is, we're afraid he's in some kind of trouble. Three months ago, this other guy started showing up every Thursday around nine, joining Howard at his table, talking to him real low and making him unhappy."

"And he's creepy-looking," Brenda put in eagerly. "Tall and skinny, with a long pony tail, and piercings, and *way* too many tattoos. He always wears this crummy leather jacket, and carries this ratty-looking red knapsack. And all he ever has is coffee, and he always leaves just a fifty-cent tip, even though he stays a full hour. Not that I care about the tips. Sometimes he takes something out of the knapsack—a piece of paper, like, or a photo—and gives it to Howard. Sometimes Howard gives him an envelope. But Chuck's right. Whatever this guy's saying to Howard, it gets him all worked up."

"Last week," Chuck added, "Howard got so upset, he ordered a second martini."

"And he still left just a three-dollar tip," Brenda observed. "Not that I care."

"The point is," the woman called Terry said, "we're concerned. We've heard about con artists who prey on older people—we're afraid that might be going on. Not that I'm convinced we need a private detective. That was Brenda's idea, and she persuaded us to come along. What do *you* think, Miss Woodhouse?"

Miss Woodhouse sat back, thinking it over. As always, she looked imposing—almost six feet tall, broad-shouldered, lean, black-gray hair pulled back hard and caught at the nape of her neck with a thick blue rubber band. Part of the reason she looks so impressive is that she clearly isn't trying—she doesn't bother with makeup and wears boxy beige suits chosen for utility only. The other reason she looks so impressive is that that's what she, in fact, is. "That depends," she said. "What would you like us to do?"

Brenda leaned forward, and the navel made another appearance. "We thought maybe you could, like, send some big, scary guys to the restaurant tonight, and have them wait in the parking lot, and when this guy comes out, they could tell him to stay away from Howard or else, and—well, you know. Shove him around. Rough him up."

"Only a little," Chuck added. "Only enough to scare him off."

Miss Woodhouse grimaced. "I don't employ big, scary guys. And I'm not in the business of having people roughed up, not even a little. What I *can* do is come to your restaurant, pose as a customer, and observe this man. When he leaves, I'll follow him, find out what he's up to. If it's appropriate, I'll warn him off or notify the proper legal authorities. First, though, we should discuss payment. Have you consulted Howard about this plan? Is he willing to—"

"That's okay," Chuck said. "We'll probably never tell him about this. *We'll* take care of the bill. I've got a little stashed away, Brenda's been saving her tips, and Terry said she'd chip in. We might even talk Little Dave into parting with a few bucks."

"Little Dave?" Miss Woodhouse said. "Who is that?"

Terry pressed her lips together and made the corners twitch. I think she was trying for a smile. "David Cubbe," she said. "My husband. He owns the restaurant."

"Yeah, he inherited Chez Cubbe from his father," Brenda said. "And everybody called his father Big Dave. So naturally everybody calls Little Dave—well, Little Dave."

"Big Dave Cubbe," the professor said, nodding. "I met him. I ate dinner at Chez Cubbe on several notable occasions—my cousin's engagement, my parents' fiftieth anniversary, the day my tenure was revoked. Goodness! Such memories! Chez Cubbe used to be quite the spot—but isn't now, clearly. I thought it had gone out of business."

"Not yet," Chuck said sourly. "But Little Dave's working on it."

"That's enough, Chuck," Terry said sharply. "Shall we please just stick to business." She didn't inflect her voice at all, didn't put a question mark at the end of the sentence—it was an order, not a request.

"Very well," Miss Woodhouse said.

"I'll come to the restaurant tonight and—"

"You shall do no such thing, Iphigenia," the professor cut in. "I will not have you going to a place where alcohol is served. You know how little restraint you have. You would surely disgrace yourself."

Oh, brother, I thought. How do we defend Miss Woodhouse without admitting that while the professor's still sharp as ever in most ways, in other ways she's—well, confused? And once we admit that, how do we explain why Miss Woodhouse defers to her mother on business decisions and accepts all her insults meekly? Private detectives are supposed to be hard-boiled. We'd sound scrambled.

Miss Woodhouse would not blush. "I appreciate your concern, Mother, but I assure you—"

"Not another word, Iphigenia," the Professor said. "I will not have it. You may send little Harriet. She, at least, is sober and responsible."

Our three potential clients exchanged uncertain looks. No wonder. "But she's a secretary," Chuck said. "Isn't she?"

"I'm Miss Woodhouse's assistant," I said. "I've followed lots of people."

"Generally with little success," the professor put in cheerfully, "but always with a willing spirit. Do you remember, little Harriet, that afternoon when you attempted to follow a lime-green SUV from Duke of Gloucester Street to Porter Road, and ended up in Reston? Oh, my! How we all laughed on that occasion!"

"That was a long time ago," I said, blushing plenty. "Anyhow, Miss Woodhouse, I'd be glad to handle this—if you're too busy with other cases."

I'd hoped that would sound tactful. Judging from the look Miss Woodhouse gave me, it didn't. "I'm not sure," she said. "The situation might be too dangerous for you. We know nothing about this man. Suppose he carries a gun?"

"So what?" Brenda asked. "I mean, she carries a gun, too, doesn't she?"

"Not usually," I said. In fact, I've never carried one. "But I know how to use one. I took a class." I looked at Miss Woodhouse hopefully. "If you'd lend me *your* gun—"

"Absolutely not," Miss Woodhouse said firmly. "You're not licensed for it, you're a terrible shot, and you're not level-headed enough to be trusted with a firearm."

God. Why does anyone ever hire us? "Well, I won't need a gun," I said. "I'll just follow him at a safe distance." I turned to the woman called Terry—somehow, I knew she'd make the decision. "I'll come to Chez Cubbe tonight. Agreed?"

The three of them exchanged looks again. Then Chuck shrugged, Brenda nodded eagerly, and Terry sighed. "All right," she said. "But please understand, Miss Woodhouse, that if your assistant isn't able to follow this man—"

"If I lose him," I said, "you won't owe us anything. But I won't lose him."

That seemed to settle it. They all stood up, and Chuck drifted over to the professor's rocking chair and inspected her handiwork. "So you've got all this pasta, and all this dental floss," he said, "and you're making—what?"

Professor Woodhouse drew her head back and stared at him—incredulous, scornful, pitying. "Biodegradable wind chimes," she said. "Obviously."

"That's cool," Brenda said. "I design stuff, too—jewelry, purses, like that. I mean, I don't actually *make* them, but I draw pictures, and I figure out how much it'd cost to manufacture them, how much you could charge, how much profit you'd make."

The professor looked at her coldly. "A fascinating enterprise, I am sure."

Chuck jabbed his co-worker's arm. "Maybe you could lend Harriet *your* gun."

Brenda jabbed him back. "Stop giving me a hard time about my gun," she said, and turned to me. "It's only a *little* gun. See, my apartment was burglarized a few months ago—it's a first-floor apartment, near the city dock, cute neighborhood but not the safest. I wasn't home when it happened, so it was okay—I mean, the guy stole some stuff, but I didn't get hurt or anything, since I wasn't there, you know? But what if it happens again, when I *am* there? So I bought this little gun to keep next to my bed."

"And you've never had to use it," Terry said impatiently. "We should get back to the restaurant. Miss Russo, will you please arrive at 7:30 and come to the office first."

Once again, it wasn't a question. I saw them to the door, then rejoined Miss Woodhouse and the professor. "That warms your heart," I said. "Doesn't it? This Howard isn't their relative—he's not even a friend, really—but they're so concerned they're dipping into their savings and hoarding their tips to help him. Getting rid of that creep won't benefit *them*—they simply want to protect a lonely old guy. What nice people."

The professor, smiling, bit off a fresh length of dental floss. "*You* are a nice person, Harriet," she said. "Not a silly ninny, generally speaking, but so trusting, so eager to see the good. *That* warms my heart—and, simultaneously, chills my spine. Do be careful tonight, sweet child. What do you plan to wear?"

"What I'm wearing now," I said. "It doesn't sound like a fancy place."

"Nevertheless, you will be representing our firm, so you must look your best. Here." She struggled with the clasp of her cameo brooch, then pinned it on my sweater. "This was my mother's—it has always brought me luck. I trust it will do the same for you."

* * * *

Chez Cubbe is across the bridge from the Naval Academy, on a grassy bank of the Severn. It's sprawling and white and looks like it was once a private mansion. But it didn't look like a mansion now, and it wasn't just the driving rain that made it feel tired and shabby. The peeling paint, the sagging roof, and the weed-packed cracks in the parking lot all did their parts. Remembering Terry's instructions, I hurried to the back and knocked on an unassuming door. The man who opened it was five foot eight, looked in his mid forties, and had thinning reddish-brown hair parted sharply on the left, plastered down hard on the right. He wore loose white pants and a red shirt with a black collar.

"Are you Harriet Russo," he asked, "the private detective?"

And what if I hadn't been? What if I'd been Jane Doe the restaurant-robber? Wouldn't I have claimed to be Harriet Russo the private detective? This guy apparently hadn't considered that possibility. "That's right," I said. "And you must be Little Dave."

I hadn't meant to say that. I'd meant to say Mr. Cubbe. But this guy was so obviously a little one thing or another that the words rushed out. He didn't seem to mind. Probably, everyone called him little.

"Yup," he said. "Come in." He snatched the page that had just chugged out of the printer, stuffed it in his pocket, and exited from whatever site had been showing on the computer screen. "This guy who's bothering Howard," he said, "he's got a nasty look in his eye, like any second he could flip out, get violent. That doesn't scare you?"

It's my job not to get scared, I wanted to say. All my life, I've wanted to say something like that. But I imagined the look Miss Woodhouse would give me if she heard me say it. I held back. "Not really," I said. "Do you know what kind of car he drives?"

"A beat-up white Chevy," he said. "Dirty, lots of dents. Y'know, I don't like the idea of you going up against him alone." He opened a file cabinet drawer and took out a revolver. "I keep this handy, just in case. You could borrow it—just in case."

"No, thanks." Once again, the image of Miss Woodhouse's reaction held me back. I walked over to inspect an architect's drawing tacked to the wall. "This is your restaurant, isn't it?" I said. "I love the new entrance. And the landscaping!"

"Yeah, we're doing a major renovation." His eyes brightened. "Probably get started this spring. So, I'm supposed to show you around. What do you want to see?"

"I'm not sure. Where's your wife?"

"Terry?" he said, as if unsure of which wife I meant. He paused. "She's probably at the hostess station." He paused again. "She's the hostess," he added helpfully.

"Interesting." I cast about for a way to keep the conversation going. "And Brenda's a waitress, right? Is Chuck a waiter?"

"Sometimes," Little Dave said. "Mostly, he shops in the morning, sets up in the afternoon, buses tables, cleans up at the end of the day. Plus he's my sous-chef."

"Sounds like he keeps busy." I was relieved to hear the back door open and shut, to see Brenda walk in. She took off her dripping black raincoat and slung it on the coat rack, gave me a quick hug, gave Little Dave a longer one.

"Sorry!" she exclaimed. "Late again. I had an audition in the District—mostly dancing, and that's not my strength, but I did okay. Is Terry steamed?"

"Not too bad," Little Dave said. "It hasn't been real busy—she and Anne have managed. But you better get out there."

Pointing toward the dining room, he gave her a little swat on the behind. That didn't necessarily mean anything in particular. When I was a secretary in Cleveland, some of the men in the office gave me little swats like that when they told me to do something. I never liked it, but I knew it usually didn't mean anything in particular. But now, when he gave her that little swat, and she turned around half-way and met his eyes and giggled, I thought maybe this time it *did* mean something in particular.

The door from the dining room opened, and Terry stepped in, in time to see the little swat, the half-turn, the giggle. She, too, seemed to think it might mean something. "Finally," she said to Brenda. "Will you please get out there. Well, Miss Russo. You're here, too. I thought you'd want to look around. At 8:00, you can come in through the front door and be seated at a table. Will you please come with me."

"Hey, I can show Harriet around," Little Dave said. "I'm heading back to the kitchen anyway, to see if Chuck needs help with—"

"He doesn't," Terry said. "In the last two hours, we've had nine customers. Chuck has coped with the rush. Should a tenth customer arrive, I will alert you. In the meantime, will you please circulate in the dining room. Charm customers. This way, Miss Russo."

Without hesitation, he headed for the dining room; without hesitation, I followed Terry down the narrow hallway that led to the kitchen. In the center of the room, Chuck stood at a butcher-block table, sneezing, lethargically chopping shallots.

"Chuck, will you kindly show Miss Russo around," Terry said. "And will you please cover your mouth when you sneeze. You'll infect our customers."

With that, she was gone. Chuck, who seemed wrapped in gloom, glanced at me briefly before refocusing his attention on his shallots. I attempted a smile.

"Slow night," I said. "Well, it's Thursday."

"It could be Saturday," he said glumly. "It'd still be slow." Suddenly, he grabbed a small pot from the stove, thrust in a spoon, and handed it to me. "Taste," he ordered.

It was a cream sauce, specked with green and black and red. I tasted—hesitantly, then incredulously. "My God," I said. "This is good."

"Isn't it?" he demanded. "And it's my recipe. I'm going to ask Little Dave to let me drizzle it on his damned poached scallops. He'll say no. Know why?"

I shook my head. I didn't know. I didn't care. I just wanted more sauce.

"Because he didn't come up with it," Chuck said. "And as far as he's concerned, nothing I come up with can be good enough to serve, because I'm a sous-chef. Sous-chef! How the hell can I be a sous-chef? To have a sous-chef, you gotta have a chef."

"I guess," I said. "And you don't consider Little Dave a real chef?"

"Him? Please." He brought his knife down brutally, reducing the shallots to goo. "He's never come up with a decent recipe in his life, and he burns half the stuff he cooks, leaves the other half raw. You know the only thing he's good at?"

Maybe, if I humored him, he'd give me more sauce. "What?" I asked.

"Buying useless junk." He yanked a drawer open and started holding things up. "Just look at this stuff. A garlic press. A garlic peeler. A garlic pulverizer. A deluxe Sir-Chops-A-Lot. A Minute Marinater. A nutmeg juicer. He shells out good money for these stupid gadgets, then never uses them. You know the only thing a real chef needs?"

"What?" I asked, my eyes still on that little pot simmering on the stove.

"A good knife." Chuck held up the knife he'd used to butcher the shallots—broad grooved blade, bright orange handle. "With one good knife, a real chef can do everything he needs to do. But Little Dave—he leaves all the prep work to me, insists on doing the actual cooking himself, and botches everything." He shook his head. "*Big* Dave was a *real* chef, built this place up from nothing. I started working here when I was a teenager—I was like a son to him, and he taught me lots. But he left Chez Cubbe to Little Dave, and Little Dave's running it straight into the ground."

Brenda slipped into the kitchen. "Howard's here," she said, keeping her voice unnecessarily low. "Terry says Harriet should come watch him." She walked over to me. "Hey, cool brooch—nice vintage-y look. I design jewelry—did I tell you?"

"You mentioned it this afternoon. And you also audition for shows?"

"Yeah, well, most celebrities these days design stuff," she said, examining the brooch more closely. "So I figure when I finally get my break in acting or singing—I'm real good at both—I should have a few lines of merchandise ready to go."

"You'll get that break." Chuck gave her a look heavy with adoration. "You should've got it long ago. Those guys must be crazy. Crazy, and *blind*."

Brenda smiled at him—warmth, gratitude, real affection, no matching adoration. "You're sweet," she said. "Harriet, better get out there."

Obediently, I walked to the front door and entered as a customer. Doing a good job of pretending not to recognize me, Terry led me to a table a few yards away from the table occupied by a man who had to be Howard—seventyish, mildly gaunt, thinning gray hair, thick gray sweater, water glass and martini glass both still full. He had a sweet, trusting face, I thought, and a sad, quiet way about him.

After Brenda came to my table and recited the specials in a falsely casual tone, I gazed around the dining room. It was spacious—too spacious, making the few customers look like castaways in an ocean of threadbare carpet. Once, it might have been described as quietly elegant or subtly luxurious; now, the only phrase it brought to mind was "deferred maintenance." The figurines at the center of each table were intriguing, though. I picked mine up—eight inches tall, so heavy it had to be iron, polished to a grudging sheen. It was a lion cub wearing a chef's hat, holding a spoon aloft jauntily. It took me a minute to figure it out—Chez Cubbe, lion cub. Cute, I thought, and set it down.

As I worked my way through a limp salad, I kept sneaking glimpses at Howard, hurting my neck but learning little: He ate slowly, he looked gloomy, and that was all I could say about him. At one point, Chuck brought him asparagus topped with creamy sauce—that amazing sauce, I thought, and envied him. At another point, Little Dave came to his table to chat and slap him on the back. Finally, minutes before nine, just as I got my grilled chicken and Howard got his turkey club, the mystery man arrived. I perked up.

This guy looked like trouble, all right. He matched Brenda's description tattoo for tattoo, piercing for piercing, ratty red knapsack for ratty red knapsack. But she hadn't mentioned the constant over-the-shoulder glances, the fidgeting fingers, the general twitchiness. As he spoke to Howard in a low, urgent tone, he kept picking things up, turning them around, setting them down—fork, spoon, iron lion cub chef figurine, salt shaker, pepper grinder. Even at a distance, his jitteriness made me on edge.

What was he saying? I strained but couldn't hear. I couldn't blame Terry for not seating us closer together—in a mostly-empty dining room, it might've seemed odd—but it was frustrating. At least sawing off slivers of petrified chicken kept me busy.

Shortly before ten, the mystery man pitched his voice still lower, twitched still more sharply, and handed Howard a bedraggled sheet of paper. Howard glanced at it and put it in his shirt pocket. Fine. Brenda had already boxed up my nearly intact dinner, and I'd already paid and tipped. Casually, I strolled to the parking lot, got in my car, and waited. At least the rain had stopped. That should make my job easier.

Moments later, the mystery man came out, got into a dented white Chevy, and pulled onto the street. I counted to ten before following, pleased to see a Corvette and a Mitsubishi between us. He won't spot me, I assured myself. I'm being discreet as hell.

He crossed the bridge, heading for the historic district, and stopped at a mildly seedy coffee house. Luckily, a spot was open across the street. For nearly an hour, I waited in my car, sometimes nervous, sometimes bored. Finally, he came out and drove on. I followed. He crossed the bridge again and got on Ritchie Highway, heading toward Baltimore. Maybe, I thought, he's a commuting con man. When we reached Arnold, he got off the highway and drove to a waffle house with an "Open All Night" sign blinking sleepily in its window. He pulled into the lot in back. I parked across the street, wondered who'd want to eat waffles all night, and settled back for another long wait.

Then the door to my car was yanked open, and the mystery man stood inches from me, pale, shaking, furious. "Who the hell are you?" he demanded. "Why are you following me?"

Time for a tough, clever comeback. "Excuse me?" I said.

"Don't give me that," he shot back—though, as far as I could tell, I hadn't given him anything. His eyebrow ring quivered. "You were in the restaurant—you kept watching me. You work for Eddie Three-Ears, don't you? So he figured it out. Well, tell him it won't do him any damn good. She's not coming back—I won't let her. So he damn well better back off. And you—you back off, too, or I'll make you sorry you didn't."

He slammed the door and was gone. Good grief, I thought. It was a solid minute before I could calm down enough to think anything else. The next thought that did come was that I'd better call Miss Woodhouse and tell her I'd messed up.

I didn't have time to feel bad about that, though, because already someone was rapping sharply on my window. I shrieked, jerked forward so hard my seat belt nearly knocked the wind out of me, looked to my left, and saw Little Dave's face pressed against my window, Little Dave's fist pounding. "Hey," he said. "Come out."

Numbly, I got out of the car. "What are you doing here?" I asked.

"I told you I didn't feel right about you going up against this creep all alone," he said. "So I followed you—I been following you the whole time. You didn't spot me?"

I shook my head. Of course I hadn't spotted him. Idiotic excuse for a private detective that I am, I never spot anyone. Instead, people spot me.

"I was pretty cagey," he said, smugly. "Oh, man. When he ripped your door open, I thought you were dead for sure. But I brought you something. Here."

He stuffed it in my jacket pocket. "No," I said. "No guns. Miss Woodhouse—"

"That's not all," he said. "His car's parked behind the waffle house, beside the dumpster. I sneaked a peek while he was hassling you, and that red knapsack is in the back. Let's grab it—I bet that'll tell us what he's up to. I bet the car isn't locked."

"No," I said. "What if he comes out and—"

"Hell, he's been in that place two minutes at most," Little Dave said confidently. "Waffles don't cook that fast. We got plenty of time. Come on!"

He raced off. For a moment, I stood frozen. Call Miss Woodhouse and tell her how I'd botched things—let Little Dave get himself killed and feel guilty for the rest of my life—follow him into the parking lot and risk getting killed myself. On the whole, the last option seemed most attractive. I raced after Little Dave.

He stood next to the dirty white car, hissing into his cell phone. "Damn it, Terry," he whispered harshly, "I *told* you not to call me. No, I *won't* tell you where I am. Go home. I'll see ya when I see ya." He snapped his phone shut and yanked on a back door of the car. It didn't budge. He looked straight at me, grinning sheepishly.

That's pretty much the last thing I remember. I have some vague impression of something crashing down against me, of sharp pain and sudden darkness. But my next definite memory is of fading slowly back into consciousness—of hearing sirens blare, of feeling the cement against my back, of seeing Little Dave sprawled a few feet away from me, of spotting a small iron figurine next to him, of falling into darkness again.

* * * *

"I have some questions for you, Miss Russo," the man said.

Groggy as I felt, I knew who he was—Detective Barry Glass, the man Miss Woodhouse had dumped over a decade ago when the professor had some kind of breakdown and made her daughter give up her fiancé and her police career. I tried to sit up, didn't make it, and looked around.

I was on a cot in a small, white, nearly empty room with a heavy antiseptic smell. He sat next to the cot on a straight-backed chair.

"Is this a hospital?" I asked.

"Yeah," he said. "The doc says you're fine—probably not even a concussion."

I tried to sit up again and made it this time. "I should call Miss Woodhouse."

"I already called her. She's in the waiting room just outside." His whole face twitched hard, brow to chin. "With her mother."

Poor Barry Glass. The professor despised him, always treated him like dirt. I couldn't figure it out, nobody could figure it out, because he's an awful nice guy. I rubbed my forehead as memories came back. "Little Dave," I said. "Is he all right?"

Barry Glass shook his head. "He's dead. That's why I gotta ask you questions. How did you and him end up in that parking lot?"

"He followed me," I said. "I was working on a case—Miss Woodhouse probably told you. I followed this guy to a coffee house, then to the waffle house. But he'd spotted me, and he came to my car and threatened me. Then Little Dave rapped on my car window and said he'd been following me the whole time."

Wincing, Barry Glass shook his head. "Now, I know that's a lie. Try again, Miss Russo. Tell the truth this time."

"That *was* the truth." I stared at him, confused. "Little Dave followed me from—"

"No he didn't," Barry Glass cut in. "You and David Cubbe arranged to meet in that parking lot, didn't you? What was the plan?"

"There was no plan. I didn't *want* him to follow me. He just—"

"No." He handed me a plastic-wrapped sheet of paper. "We found this in his pocket—see? He did a MapQuest search at 7:28, had the route from Chez Cubbe to the waffle house all mapped out. He knew exactly where he was going—he didn't have to follow you. You knew exactly where you were going, too, didn't you?"

I remembered walking into the office at Chez Cubbe and seeing Little Dave grab a page from the printer. It must've been the map. "This doesn't make sense," I said. "Why hire me to follow this guy if he already knew—oh, no." A horrible thought came to me. "Little Dave stuffed a gun into my pocket. You said he's dead. Was he—"

"He wasn't shot," he said. "We found the gun—his prints on it, but not yours, and it looks like it's never been fired. Don't worry about that. Just come clean with me."

"I have. I was hired to follow this man, and that's all I did."

Barry Glass sighed. "You said this man threatened you. What did he say?"

"Crazy things," I said. "It was all, like, 'I saw you at Chez Cubbe,' and 'You must work for Eddie Three-Ears,' and 'Back off or else.'"

He straightened up. "He mentioned Eddie Three-Ears? You're sure?"

"Positive. Have you heard of him? Is he a real person?"

"He's real, all right," Barry Glass said grimly. "He's bad news—pimp, drug dealer, works out of Baltimore. So Stanley Carson's mixed up with Eddie Three-Ears."

"Stanley Carson? Is that the name of the man I was following? Is he the one who knocked me out and killed Little Dave?"

"That's his name," Barry Glass said. "We got it from the cook in the waffle house—Carson's his friend, stops by every Thursday night to visit for a few minutes. As to what Carson did—we're working on that. *Somebody* knocked you out and killed Little Dave. And stole some things, presumably. Little Dave's watch and wallet and phone were gone. What about you? Were you wearing a watch? Any other jewelry?"

I looked down at my wrist and realized my trusty Timex was missing. Carson must be hard up to steal a Timex. "Yes, I was wearing a watch," I said, "and a turquoise ring, and—oh, God. The brooch. The professor's brooch. Oh, no!"

His eyes filled with alarmed sympathy. "Oh, man. Professor Woodhouse lent you a brooch, and it's gone? That's a tough break. If you want, I'll tell her you *do* have a concussion. I'll tell her you almost died. Would that help?"

"Probably not," I said. "But thanks for the thought. Have you arrested Carson?"

"We can't find him. Best guess is, he did whatever he did, then took off in a hurry. He *did* call 911, though, from his cell phone, to report there were two people hurt or dead next to the dumpster. That's how we found you so fast."

"Handy," I said. "A criminal who calls in his own crimes. But Little Dave—if he wasn't shot, how *was* he killed? And do you know what Carson hit me with?"

"We're waiting for lab reports on Little Dave. As to what you were hit with, we found something—a little statue of a lion, iron, in a chef's hat. That could've been what your assailant used. Any idea what it is?"

"It's a centerpiece," I said. "When we were at Chez Cubbe, I saw Carson fiddling around with the one on his table. He could've stolen it, hidden it in his jacket."

He nodded. "That'd fit. The statue's covered with fingerprints. We'll know soon if they're Carson's. We got plenty of his prints on file.

Possession, car theft, all kinds of stunts he pulled, probably to support his habit. Nothing for the last five years, though—the cook at the waffle house said Carson sobered up and took a job at a halfway house in Baltimore. Guess he didn't get as sober as the cook thought. All right, Miss Russo. Let's go through your story once more. Give me the exact truth this time."

"That's what I gave you last time," I said, but went over it again, filling in all the details I could scrape up, making my head hurt even more fiercely. We'd started a third run-through when Professor Woodhouse burst in, an orderly clinging to her arm.

"Naughty man!" she cried, pointing at Barry Glass. "You have kept this poor child in here nearly two hours, despite the injuries she suffered. She is innocent of any wrongdoing and utterly without guile. I told you that before you began this merciless interrogation, and I tell you again now. Yet you persist. You, sir, are a bully and a fool."

Detective Barry Glass jumped to his feet, swallowed twice, and pointed, shakily, at me. "She lost your brooch," he said.

"And what if she did?" the professor demanded. "I am sure she did so in the pursuit of justice. Come, little Harriet. Your ordeal is over. I am taking you home."

Barry Glass took one timid step forward. "The doc says she should spend the night here for observation, in case—"

"And who is better able to observe her than I?" the professor countered. "My daughter and I shall gather her to our collective bosom. She shall sleep in the blue bedroom, and we will take turns sitting up with her all night. Harriet! Come!"

Barry Glass isn't an idiot. He knows when he's beaten. He bowed his head, the professor wrapped a mighty arm around me, and we were gone.

* * * *

I woke up the next morning to the soothing impression of sunlight warming crisp linen curtains, to the sight of Miss Woodhouse sitting in the Queen Anne's chair near my bed, her eyes fixed on the laptop perched on the nightstand.

She glanced at me. "Feeling better?"

"Much," I said.

She nodded. "The bathroom's down the hall to the left. You'll find towels in the cupboard, fresh clothes in the closet. Half an hour. Mother's making breakfast."

I don't know how she managed the fresh clothes, and I didn't press for details. It doesn't do to press the Woodhouses for details about how they manage things. I showered and changed, arriving downstairs just as the professor was setting breakfast on the table—tuna-macaroni salad, sweet potato casserole, olive-and-onion scones, Jell-O.

"Sit, little Harriet," she said, beaming. "Eat well, and tell us about last night."

I ate everything, told them everything, answered all the questions they asked me. When I finished, Miss Woodhouse folded her napkin. "Now I'll tell you what I know," she said. "I've spoken to the coroner's office and the police department—"

"Not to That Man, I trust," her mother said icily, buttering a scone.

Miss Woodhouse glanced away. "He's the officer in charge of the case, Mother. First, as to Little Dave's cause of death. Lab results are still pending, but he had a large, clumsy puncture wound on his neck. The coroner thinks it's from a hypodermic needle. He was injected with something—evidently not a street drug, more likely some household chemical—and that evidently killed him."

"Well, Detective Glass said Stanley Carson's been arrested for possession," I said, "and that he stole to support his habit. A drug addict, a hypodermic needle—that fits."

"That's the prevailing theory with the police," she said, "though Carson seems to have been clean for years, and though it's hard to say why an addict would carry about a hypodermic loaded with household chemicals. At any rate, those were indeed his prints on the iron lion chef figurine. Traces of your blood were found on it, too."

"So Carson's definitely the one who hit me," I said.

Miss Woodhouse shrugged. "It appears so."

Her mother looked at her and smiled. "But you don't think so."

"I think we've been manipulated," Miss Woodhouse said, "and I don't like that. Three people came to see us yesterday and said they wanted to get rid of a troublesome man. With our help—and Little Dave's—they are now rid of him. He's wanted for murder, and the police can't find a trace of him."

"So he's hiding out," I said. "That figures—it's what a guilty person would do."

"Or a scared person," Miss Woodhouse said, "who knows he'd be easy to frame."

"You think someone's framing him? Who?"

"I'm not sure," she said. "But yesterday afternoon might well have created the impression we'd be unlikely to detect an attempt to frame an innocent person, and might even be maneuvered into becoming unwitting accessories in such an attempt."

I thought of things Miss Woodhouse and her mother said when Brenda, Terry, and Chuck were here. After the show we'd put on, who *wouldn't* think Miss Woodhouse is an irresponsible drunk, and I'm too flighty to handle a firearm? And then Little Dave had promptly tried, twice, to put a gun in my hand. "Do you think Little Dave hoped I'd panic and shoot Carson? But Little Dave was the one who got killed."

"Perhaps the plan went wrong," Miss Woodhouse said, "or perhaps he knew about only part of the plan. Think about the computer map found on Little Dave's body. Clearly, somebody already knew Carson always went to the waffle house after leaving Chez Cubbe. Probably, somebody had followed him there."

"Could be," I agreed. "They've been wondering about this guy for three months. It wouldn't be surprising if someone decided to follow him."

"And managed to do so without being detected," the professor put in brightly, and gave me a friendly wink. I blushed.

"Be that as it may," Miss Woodhouse said, "I doubt Little Dave was the one who followed Carson. He wouldn't need a map if he'd already driven the route himself. Someone else must have followed Carson, told Little Dave, and drawn him into the plan. But this person must not have known Little Dave decided he needed a map—not if this person had been planning all along to kill Little Dave and frame Carson."

"So you think maybe Brenda or Terry or Chuck wanted to get rid of both Little Dave and Carson," I said. "Do they have alibis?"

"Not strong ones, according to the police. After Carson left Chez Cubbe, Little Dave and Terry had an argument. He wanted to follow you; she told him not to be a fool; he insisted. Then the restaurant closed for the night, and Brenda and the other waitress left, as usual, and Brenda went to a local bar. Normally, Chuck stays to clean up, but his cold had grown worse, so he went home. Terry remained at Chez Cubbe, did some cleanup, and got home shortly before midnight, when police came to tell her Little Dave was dead."

"Do any of them have anyone to back up their stories?" I asked.

"Brenda might," she said. "So far, the police have found several people who saw her at the bar, but no one who's sure she was there before 11:00. That makes the timing for her tight but possible. Chuck went to bed without seeing or talking to anyone. There's nothing to back up Terry's story—except the phone conversation you overheard."

"She could've lied about still being at the restaurant," I said. "And she's the one with a motive, right? With Little Dave dead, won't she inherit Chez Cubbe?"

"Presumably," she said. "But inheriting a failing restaurant isn't a strong motive."

"Well, Little Dave must've had cash, too," I said. "He was planning renovations. Anyhow, the other two don't have *any* motive. Little Dave and Brenda seemed to be on friendly terms—very friendly. Chuck didn't like Little Dave much, but—"

"Yes, you said you sensed ill will between them," the professor cut in. "Why?"

"Chuck thought Little Dave was a lousy chef," I said. "Always burning stuff, always wasting money on gadgets like a Minute Marinater, a Sir Chops-a-Lot, a—"

"A Minute Marinater?" the professor asked. "How oxymoronic. What is it—a compression chamber of some sort?"

"Not a chamber. It's a thing you hold in your hand. There's a thick tube—you must put the marinade in that—and a plunger, and a pointy thing you must stick into the meat, and—oh, my God."

I stared at them. They stared at me. "It's like a hypodermic needle," Miss Woodhouse said. "A large, clumsy hypodermic needle. Isn't it?"

"Exactly like that." I jumped up and looked around wildly for my purse.

* * * *

When Miss Woodhouse and I arrived at Chez Cubbe just before 9:00, we found Chuck in the kitchen. Cupboard doors stood open; most shelves were empty; pots, pans, bowls, and cooking implements crowded the countertops. Chuck greeted us perkily.

"Hey, Harriet!" he said. "Great to see you up and around. Nice to see you, too, Miss Woodhouse. Shame about Little Dave, isn't it?"

"It is." She looked around the room. "You seem to have to have major preparations underway. I would have thought the restaurant wouldn't be open tonight."

"It's not," he said. "Terry says we should stay closed a few days, outta respect. I had to come finish cleanup anyway, so I thought I'd use the time to reorganize the cupboards. I've been wanting to do that for a long time."

And now you have a free hand, I thought. "Your cold seems better," I observed.

"Yeah," he agreed. "Just a twenty-four-hour thing, I guess. You guys hungry?"

"No, thank you," Miss Woodhouse said. "But Harriet's description of your cooking gadgets aroused my curiosity. She mentioned a Sir Chops-a-Lot and a Minute Marinater—might I see them?"

"You can *have* them," he said, opening a drawer. "*I* don't want them. Here's the Sir Chops-a-Lot, and—that's funny. The Minute Marinater should be here, too."

"Perhaps Little Dave moved it," Miss Woodhouse suggested.

"Why? He never used it." Chuck scratched his head, shrugged, and opened the immense dishwasher, packed full with clean dishes. "Here it is," he said. "Little Dave must've used it after all. Weird. What the hell did he marinate?"

Or maybe, I thought, someone marinated Little Dave. A dishwasher-safe murder weapon—if it had been loaded with poison last night, there wouldn't be a trace left.

"If you don't mind, I *will* take this," Miss Woodhouse said, dropping it into her purse. "It intrigues me. Will Terry keep the restaurant going, do you think?"

"Doubt it," Chuck said. "She married into the restaurant business, but I never got the impression she likes it much. She'll probably sell."

"And will you buy?" I asked. "You said you have some savings stashed away."

"Not that much," he said, "not on the measly salary Little Dave paid me. Of course, if I could find a partner—who knows? Sure I can't fix you something?"

Miss Woodhouse agreed to omelets, probably to give us an excuse for sticking around. Watching the jaunty way Chuck set butter sputtering in the pan and cracked three eggs at a time and sliced small mountains of peppers and onions, I had to conclude he wasn't weighed down by grief. As he slid the omelets onto our plates, the door from the parking lot opened, and Brenda stepped in. I noticed how pale she looked, how weary.

Chuck glanced at her, then looked away. "I called you last night," he said, "after the cops came by my place. But you weren't home. Where were you?"

"Clubbing." She glanced self-consciously at Miss Woodhouse. "I went home for maybe like ten minutes, and then I went to a bar. I didn't get home till after two."

"On a Thursday? You must've been having a good time." He couldn't keep his tone light. "Meet anybody special?"

"Please," she said. "I just came to get my raincoat. I left it here last night—it was soaked. But it's my only black coat; I thought I might need it for—you know. Then I'm gonna go see Terry to, like, pay my respects. Have you gone yet, Chuck?"

"No, I been here since six this morning, and I'm sorta into stuff. I'll go later, talk to her about the wake. I think we should have it here, invite other restaurant owners, food critics, like that. I'll cook—I got great ideas for appetizers."

"Sounds nice," Brenda said, and headed for the office. It was several minutes before she came back, the coat belted tightly around her waist, her hands thrust deep into its pockets. She tossed her hair back, looked at me, and smiled.

"So, tell me about last night," she said. "The cops wouldn't give me details."

I didn't volunteer many, either. "That's all I remember," I finished.

"So this Carson knocked you out and killed Little Dave." Brenda's face looked flushed now, not pale. "That's it? He didn't, like, steal anything?"

"I forgot to mention that," I said. "Apparently, he took Little Dave's wallet and phone, plus jewelry from both of us."

"Really?" she said. "He took *all* the jewelry you had on? Everything? Too bad. Well, I've got errands to run before going to Terry's. See you later, Chuck."

"If you feel like it," he said, still not looking at her, "come back later. I'm gonna try out some recipes for the wake. You could sample them. If you feel like it."

"I'll call you," she said, and left. We lingered, savoring our omelets but not learning much from Chuck. Then Miss Woodhouse decided we, too, should make a sympathy call. I agreed glumly. Yesterday, when she'd had no reason to dislike me, Terry had been curt; today, when she might blame me for her husband's death, she'd be worse. But Miss Woodhouse was right. As detectives, as human beings, we had to go see her.

The house she'd shared with Little Dave bordered the historic district, not ten minutes from the restaurant. Like most houses in the area, it was old and small, with the automatic charm most old, small houses in Annapolis have. She opened her front door, lifted an eyebrow at the sight of us, and led us to a tiny living room decorated in shades of beige. She wore a widow-like black skirt and sweater, but every hair was in place, her makeup was as precise as it had been yesterday, her air was placid. She looked fine.

"I suppose," she said, crossing her legs, "you've come about payment. Will you talk to Brenda and Chuck about that. They may feel obligated to pay. I do not."

"We don't expect payment," Miss Woodhouse said, matching Terry's passionless primness exactly. "We came only to express our sympathy."

Terry lifted the other eyebrow. "I doubt that," she said.

When she's right, she's right. Miss Woodhouse nodded. "We also came to see if we can learn more about last night. A client was killed, my associate was injured, yet we don't know exactly what happened, or why. Can you tell us anything that might help us?"

"Nothing," Terry said. "I warned my husband not to follow Miss Russo. Later, when I called him just before I left the restaurant, I told him to come home. He wouldn't listen. Now he's dead. I must say, Miss Russo, I would have thought a private detective could do a better job of protecting a client."

It wasn't my job to protect him, I wanted to say; he wasn't supposed to be there. But that would be beyond tactless. "I'm sorry," I said.

She looked me over coldly. "I suppose," she said, and stood up.

Clearly, she thought it was time for us to go. Thank God, Miss Woodhouse agreed. As we walked to the car, we saw Brenda walking up the street from the opposite corner. She spotted us, waved, but didn't slow her pace. In another minute, she was in the house.

"Terry didn't seem grief-stricken," I observed after we got into the car.

"No," Miss Woodhouse agreed. "She could be being brave, but I'd guess it wasn't a particularly happy or loving marriage. That doesn't make her a murderer."

"It also doesn't give us any reason to think she's *not* a murderer," I said. "Brenda seemed more upset. But maybe it was an act—she says she's a good actress. Chuck didn't even try to act upset, and he didn't get defensive when you asked about the Minute Marinater. That could mean he's innocent, right?"

"Or very clever," she said, "or very, very dense. Our next task is to find Howard and ask why Carson was hounding him. That's our project for this afternoon."

It sounded tedious, possibly hopeless. Luckily, we didn't have to attempt it. When we got to Woodhouse Investigations, there was a classic Mustang in the driveway; when we walked into the east parlor, there was Howard, drinking tea with the professor.

"At last, Iphigenia," the professor said. "I hope you haven't exhausted Harriet. Allow me to introduce Mr. Howard Braxton. He came here minutes after you left. He heard a news report that Little Dave had been killed and a Woodhouse Investigations employee injured. He's eager to help but reluctant to go to the police. So he came here."

As simple as that. "I feel horrible about Little Dave," Howard said, shaking Miss Woodhouses's hand. "And to think I caused his death, by meeting Stan at Chez Cubbe! But I never thought Stan could kill anyone. I can still hardly believe it."

"Perhaps you don't have to," Miss Woodhouse said. "Perhaps that's not how it happened. Please, sit down. And tell me about Stanley Carson."

"I've already told your mother." Howard's face creased with shame and agony. "But I'll tell it all again—though I'm not proud of anything I've got to say."

It was a sad, terrible, ordinary story. Some twenty years ago, Howard had been a successful Philadelphia CEO with a comfortable marriage and an eight-year-old daughter named Amy. Then came the affair with a woman half his age—a mid-life crisis, he called it, with a wince that said he knew that didn't excuse it—and he'd left wife and daughter behind. Bitter and proud, his ex-wife refused alimony and moved to a distant state, taking Amy with her. She'd done all she could to discourage visits, and Howard admitted he hadn't tried hard to keep them up. Years later, when he learned of his ex-wife's suicide, he'd tried to find his daughter; but afraid of angering a new wife jealous of other claims on his affection or his money, he again hadn't tried hard. Amy had been lost in the foster-care system, just another rebellious teenager prone to running away, doing her best to alienate anyone who tried to help her, driven by hatred for the father she blamed for her mother's death. It wasn't until his second wife left him that Howard hired private detectives to track his daughter down. By then, the trail had frosted over.

"They found bits of information," he said, "none of it good. Drugs, jail, worse things. But they couldn't find Amy. I gave up. By then, I'd retired and moved here—I love the water, and Philadelphia held painful memories. Three months ago, Stan Carson called and said he could put me in touch with Amy. I didn't know anything about him, so I didn't want him to come to my apartment. I thought a public place would be safer."

"So you met at Chez Cubbe every Thursday," Miss Woodhouse said.

"Yes. He told me Amy was in trouble, hiding out. He wouldn't tell me where. She'd angered a man—a criminal who deals in drugs and in, well, other things."

"Eddie Three-Ears," I said. That was the man Carson had accused me of working for, the pimp and drug dealer Barry Glass had spoken of.

"That's right," Howard said. "Stan said Amy had worked for this man. But she'd hated and feared him, and finally found the courage to try to break away. He wanted her back—he said she'd stolen from him. Perhaps she had. Probably, he wanted her back so he could kill her, make an example of her. So Amy was hiding, and Stan was helping her stay hidden. At least, that's what he said. I don't know if it was true."

"Didn't Carson show you proof?" Miss Woodhouse asked.

Howard lifted his hands. "He showed me a picture. Maybe it's Amy. The last time I saw her, she was a little girl—happy, chubby, beautiful. The woman in the picture—she's skeletal, with this haunted look in her eyes." He paused. "But they're my wife's eyes. He's given me notes, too—angry, full of pain, still blaming me, not wanting to see me. But she needs money. So I've given him some, several times. Just small amounts—I don't know if it's really my daughter, you see. And I don't have much to spare."

"But you were a CEO," I said. "You eat out—you pay with hundred-dollar bills."

He smiled ruefully. "My second wife ran through most of my money while we were married, took the rest as a divorce settlement. At least she didn't get my car—I fought hard for that. I eat at Chez Cubbe to be around people. If I take my roll home for breakfast the next day and save my sandwich for lunch, I can manage on twenty dollars a day. The hundred-dollar bills—that's the vanity of an old man who used to be rich. Every week, I take my change to the bank, add what's necessary from my social-security check, and get a fresh stack of hundred-dollar bills. It keeps me from looking pathetic."

The professor looked up from the manicotti she was threading. "And, I imagine, it gets you better service at Chez Cubbe."

"What?" he said, startled. "Oh. But the people there are so kind anyway."

"People who rise to the level of CEO," the professor observed, "generally do not do so by relying on the kindness of strangers. Have you shared what you've told us with the people at Chez Cubbe? Does anyone there know about the loss of your fortune?"

"No," he said. "And I'm trusting you not to tell them. They respect me—they obviously consider me eccentric, but they think I'm a success. They tell me about their little hopes and dreams, and they ask for advice. It's one of the few comforts I have left."

"And you've never told any of them," the professor persisted, "about your affair, and your estranged daughter, and the reason for Carson's visits?"

He hesitated. "My infidelity was the worst mistake of my life," he said at last. "It's nothing I would brag about, and nothing I would ever be a party to again."

Miss Woodhouse toyed with a pencil, tapping its eraser against her palm. "Will you give this information to the police?" she asked.

"If I did," he said, "they'd look for Amy—if it *is* Amy. They might find her, and that might endanger her life. I'm hoping *you* can find her first. I can't pay much, but—"

"Payment is not an issue," Miss Woodhouse said. "I'm committed to investigating this case. If I fail to resolve it quickly, however, I'll insist on involving the police."

Reluctantly, Howard agreed. After he left, the professor ordered me to take a nap. By then, my car had appeared in the driveway—Miss Woodhouse must've had someone drive it over from the waffle house—so I drove home, eager for time to myself.

I didn't get it. Climbing the stairs to my apartment, I was absorbed in the task of shuffling through the bills that had stuffed my mailbox, deciding which had to be paid right away, which could safely be put on hold. I opened the door, stepped inside, and saw Stanley Carson standing in the middle of my living room, pointing a gun at me.

"Don't make a noise," he said, "or I'll shoot."

A gunshot would also make noise, but it probably wouldn't be tactful to point that out. I nodded. At the moment, it was the maximum response I could muster.

Seeming reassured, he lowered the gun to a less menacing angle. "It wasn't me," he said. "I didn't kill that guy—that David Cubbe—and I didn't knock you out."

"Your fingerprints were on the statue," I said. "On the iron lion cub chef."

"On the—was that what killed him? One of those centerpieces from the restaurant? His head didn't look bashed in."

It sounded innocent. It could have been a quick-witted response, but he didn't seem like a quick-witted guy. "It's not what killed him, but it's what knocked me out."

"Then somebody used it to frame me," he said. "Do I look dumb enough to leave behind something with my prints on it?"

Actually, he did. But I probably wasn't the only one who had noticed him fiddling with the statue. Somebody could've swiped it and planted it at the scene to incriminate him. "When you came out of the waffle house, did you see anything?"

"I heard something," he said. "I was coming out the back door when I heard this yelp in the parking lot. And I heard Cubbe yell something like, 'What did you do? Are you nuts?' Then there was a moan, and a thud. I waited a few minutes, too scared to move, then went out into the lot. There you were—you and him, next to the dumpster."

"So you called the cops, but you ran. Why? That made you look guilty."

He shrugged. "I've had bad experiences with cops. Whenever I've tried to talk to them, they've never believed me—not once."

"Were you telling the truth those other times?" I asked.

He shrugged. "No, but even so. They coulda been more trusting."

I let that pass. "Well, *I* believe you. My boss will, too—she's thought all along someone's framing you. Any ideas about who?"

"Someone from the restaurant, maybe. Nobody there likes me. I could tell. Especially that waitress, Brenda. I don't think she liked seeing me get friendly with Howard. I think she's got her eye on him—she's always real flirty with him."

"But he's old enough to be her grandfather," I said. Still, years ago, Howard had left his wife for a younger woman. Maybe he had a chronic weakness. Another thought hit me. "How did you get in here? How did you know where I live?"

"Credit card got me in. That's a crummy lock. And I got your address from a friend who works at the hospital they took you to last night. Don't ask me her name—I'm no snitch." He stepped forward. "I said what I had to say. You're the detective—you figure out the rest. Guess I'd better tie you up now, so you can't call the cops."

With effort, I convinced him that would be too melodramatic. I couldn't get him to turn himself in, though, so we compromised: He'd leave, and I'd count to three hundred before calling anyone. We shook on it, he left, and I counted.

"An interesting encounter," Miss Woodhouse said when I called her. "You still need rest, though. Come here at six. We'll have dinner and decide what to do next."

Rest didn't come easily—too many theories crowded my mind. I dozed raggedly, snapped awake before the alarm clock buzzed, knocked on the Woodhouses' door at 6:00 sharp, and spilled out my suspicions while the professor ladled out chili.

"I think it's Brenda," I said. "I think she killed Little Dave."

"Indeed?" Miss Woodhouse said, passing the onion muffins. "I have some new evidence that might support that theory. But tell us your thoughts first."

"You'd figure a murderer would try to arrange an alibi," I said. "Chuck and Terry didn't bother. Brenda stayed at a bar until 2:00—judging from Chuck's reaction, that isn't something she'd usually do on a Thursday. And she seemed eager to tell us about her alibi this morning. But the alibi doesn't cover the actual time of the murder—unless the police found a witness who can put her at the bar before 11:00."

"Not yet," Miss Woodhouse said. "They're still looking."

"So she *could* have done it," I said, "and run to the bar, and then gone home."

"She would have had to work in a stop at Chez Cubbe," the professor pointed out, spooning sautéed olives onto my plate, "to put the Minute Marinater in the dishwasher."

"That'd be easy," I said. "She said her apartment's near the city dock. That's close to the restaurant. She could wait till she'd talked to the police, then go back to Chez Cubbe and get rid of the marinater. The police weren't thinking of her as a suspect, so they probably didn't search her, right? And she must have a key to the restaurant. She came by this morning without calling first to make sure Chuck was there to let her in."

"Chuck has a key, too," Miss Woodhouse observed. "So does Terry, obviously. And they both live within minutes of the restaurant, which is in a rather isolated spot. Any of the three might have judged a quick trip to Chez Cubbe a reasonable risk. But continue with the case against Brenda. What motive did she have?"

"Ambition," I answered. "She wants to be a celebrity, but she hasn't gotten a break. Maybe she's been looking for shortcuts, for someone who could rent a theater for a one-woman show, manufacture her designs, whatever. Little Dave might've looked like a good prospect: He owned a restaurant, he probably had cash—"

"He didn't," Miss Woodhouse cut in. "I checked. He was in debt. The restaurant was his only asset, and it lost money every month."

"Oh." That stumped me, but only for a moment. "Maybe Brenda didn't know that. Or maybe she'd found out recently, and that made her decide Howard looked like a better prospect—a supposedly wealthy old man with a fondness for younger women."

"And you think Brenda knew about this fondness?" the professor said.

"Maybe Howard told her his story," I said, "to get her sympathy. When you asked him, he was quick to say he hadn't told anyone at Chez Cubbe about losing his money. But when you asked if he'd told them about other things, he hedged. He only said he'd never brag about his infidelity or do anything like it again. With Brenda, infidelity wouldn't be an issue—Howard's single now, and so is she."

Miss Woodhouse smiled. "Good observations," she said. "Sound logic."

I flushed—she doesn't hand out many compliments. "Then Stanley Carson comes along," I said. "That's got to make Brenda nervous. If Carson can get Howard together with his daughter, Howard might give his money to Amy, not Brenda. So Brenda's first scheme is to hire you and have Carson roughed up. When you say no, she decides to get rid of both Carson and Little Dave. If she's going after Howard, dumping Little Dave could be awkward. He might get mad enough to tell Howard she's been stringing them both along. So Brenda gets Little Dave to help her in some plan to scare Carson off. I don't know how she'd manage that—"

"Perhaps by promising to split Howard's fortune with him," the professor suggested. "Little Dave needed cash more desperately than Brenda did. Perhaps Brenda persuaded him she'd use Howard long enough to secure his money, then give Little Dave all he needed to save his restaurant—and renovate it."

"That's right," I said. "Little Dave was broke, but he was planning this big renovation. He must've been hoping to get cash from somewhere—probably, from Howard. No wonder he agreed to go along with Brenda's plan."

"If you're right," Miss Woodhouse said, "the plan was to put a gun into your allegedly unsteady hands and scare you into killing Carson. But Brenda double-crossed Little Dave, killing him instead. That would explain what Carson overheard. It's plausible. But we have no real proof. The police did, at my request, check Brenda's phone records. Last night, she received a 10:26 call from Little Dave's cell phone."

"That fits," I said. "It practically proves those two were conspiring."

"Practically—but not quite." Miss Woodhouse stood up. "Mother, I must ask you to excuse us. I think Harriet and I had better have a talk with Brenda."

When we got to Brenda's apartment building, we saw a row of four rusting metal mailboxes lying on the foyer floor. Miss Woodhouse gazed at the battered security door.

"Someone might have ripped the mailboxes from the wall and thrown them against the door," she said. "But the door didn't give way." She pressed the buzzer for Brenda's apartment several times, then stood back, aimed a precise, powerful kick at the security door, forced it open, and took out her gun. "Keep behind me," she said.

She had to kick open the door to Brenda's first-floor apartment, too. As instructed, I kept behind her, but even so I saw the devastation immediately—drawers dumped out onto the floor, sofa cushions slashed open, clothes ripped from closets. Then Miss Woodhouse took a step forward, and I saw the worst of it—Brenda, still in her black raincoat, crumpled face-down on the floor. A few feet away from her lay a small gun. I cried out and rushed to kneel by her side, to feel uselessly for a pulse.

Already, Miss Woodhouse had checked every corner of the tiny apartment. Sure we were safe, she called 911 and walked over to the broken kitchen window.

"We're supposed to think," she said, "a burglar broke the window, climbed in, and searched for valuables. When Brenda came home unexpectedly, the burglar panicked and shot her. But what burglar slashes sofa cushions? Don't touch anything, Harriet, but look around. The thing the killer was looking for might still be here."

Unlikely as that seemed, I did as I was told. Brenda's purse sat on the kitchen table, its contents spilled out. I crouched down to look at a thin sheet of yellow paper emblazoned with a bank logo and called Miss Woodhouse over.

"Look," I said. "A receipt for a safe-deposit box, dated today."

"Interesting." Miss Woodhouse reached into her own purse and took out a list of names and phone numbers. "Call them all, quickly—Terry, Chuck, Howard. Let's see who has an alibi this time. Don't tell them about Brenda."

Seconds before the police arrived, I finished the last of the calls. "Terry's at home," I reported. "I couldn't reach Howard. No answer at Chuck's apartment, but I got him on his cell—he's in his car, he says, on his way to Terry's house."

"Then we'll go there, too," she said, "as soon as we finish with the police."

We finished more quickly than I would have thought possible. When Detective Barry Glass arrived, minutes after the first uniformed officers, Miss Woodhouse took him aside, speaking to him urgently. He nodded, and we were free to leave.

She drove the short distance to Terry's house, so absorbed in thought that I hesitated to speak. "Do you still think Brenda murdered Little Dave?" I ventured at last.

"I never said I *did* think that," she said sharply. "*You* thought that. But no, I don't think she did. I think they were both murdered by the same person."

"But why? Who'd want to kill Brenda?"

"Figure it out," she said, her eyes hard on the road. "Think about the way Brenda acted when she first came to the restaurant this morning, about how her manner changed after she came back from the office. Think about the questions she asked you. And think about this: If Little Dave and Brenda weren't plotting a murder together, why did he call her at 10:26? Why did she then go to a bar and stay ridiculously late?"

I had maybe two minutes to try to sort it all through before we arrived at Terry's. A red Escort I recognized as Chuck's was parked out front, and a classic Mustang was pulling into the driveway. We got to the front door moments behind Howard.

"Good to see you," he said, not looking like he meant it. "I'm here to pay my respects. I'm not a personal friend, of course, but in view of the tragedy, I—"

Terry cut his fumbling short by opening the door. "Howard! What a nice surprise! How considerate of you!" she said, then saw us and grimaced. "Again?"

"We have news," Miss Woodhouse said. "May we?"

Standing aside with an air of aggrieved resignation, Terry let us enter the beige-on-beige living room. Chuck sat on the sofa, slumped and brooding; Howard hesitated a moment before sitting next to him. We remained standing.

"I have bad news," Miss Woodhouse said, managing to keep her eyes on all of them. "I apologize for announcing it so abruptly. Brenda has been murdered."

Terry gasped and put her hand to her mouth, Chuck stared numbly, and Howard looked, instantly, ready to cry. "Little Brenda? Oh, no. No."

"How did it happen?" Terry asked, her eyes downcast. "Where?"

"At her apartment," Miss Woodhouse said. "It seems she was shot by a burglar."

Chuck looked up. "At her—but I was there. Not an hour ago—I was there."

"Indeed?" she said. "You went into her apartment? You spoke to her?"

He shook his head. "No. She called this afternoon and said she'd come by the restaurant at six. I made a special dinner for her. When she didn't show up, I was steamed, so I went by her place, and I rang the damn buzzer again and again, and—oh, God! I didn't know—I didn't *know*!"

"You ripped the mailboxes from the wall, didn't you?" Miss Woodhouse said. "And threw them against the security door? Then what did you do?"

He wiped his eyes briefly. "I called Terry on my cell, to ask if I could come pay my respects." He looked down at the carpet. "I thought maybe Brenda was here."

Terry had gone to stand by Howard, to put a hand on his shoulder. "She had a first-floor apartment. That made her an easy target. It's happened before."

"Yes, a few months ago," Miss Woodhouse said. "Brenda spoke freely about that yesterday—and about the little gun she bought to protect herself and kept next to her bed. That's probably the gun the murderer used to kill her."

"A terrible irony," Terry said, sighing.

Chuck looked up sharply. "The cops are sure it was a burglar?"

"The apartment was certainly burgled," Miss Woodhouse said. "Ripped apart, in fact. And I'm sure some things were taken. Possibly, the person who took them has not yet had time to dispose of them—especially if he or she was forced to return home sooner than planned. When you called Terry, Chuck, did you call her home number?"

"I tried that first," he said, looking puzzled. "When that didn't work, I tried her cell, and she answered. Why?"

"It's good to know these things," Miss Woodhouse said. "And you should all know Detective Barry Glass is even now dispatching police officers to your homes, to make sure no items taken from Brenda's apartment are removed." She turned to face me. "Have you figured it out yet? You had the motive nearly right, didn't you?"

"But the wrong murderer," I said. "I knew Howard had a weakness for younger women. I should've realized that now that he's seventy, Terry's a younger woman, too. So *she* could be the one with a reason to see Carson as a threat—and Little Dave as an obstacle."

Terry's indignation was instant and fierce. "Will you stop this ridiculous speculation. How dare you imply I had anything to do with my husband's death. I was at the restaurant when David was killed. And I'd begged him not to follow Miss Russo. Chuck heard me—I *ordered* David not to go."

"Yes—and for perhaps the first time in his life, he stood up to you," Miss Woodhouse said. "That uncharacteristic defiance should have told me immediately the argument was staged. Harriet, what about Little Dave's 10:26 call to Brenda?"

"I'd guess he called to brag," I said, "to say he and Terry were getting rid of Carson. He probably wasn't explicit, just dropped hints to impress Brenda by making it sound daring and dangerous. But he probably alarmed her—she figured he was doing something risky, so she'd better have an alibi handy, in case things went wrong and she had to prove she wasn't involved. That's when she headed for the bar. And when she heard about Little Dave's death, she knew Terry must've had something to do with it."

"Nonsense!" Terry said. "Insulting nonsense! I won't listen to any more."

She started for the kitchen, but Chuck jumped up to block her path. "Don't," he said, his face rigid. "Take a seat, Terry. My God! If you killed her—"

A car door slammed outside; voices conferred. The police had arrived. "There's no time left, Terry," Miss Woodhouse said. "No time to hide whatever you took from Brenda's apartment. You didn't find what you were really looking for, did you? Brenda wasn't bright enough to realize it's dangerous to blackmail a murderer, but she wasn't foolish enough to hide the evidence in her apartment. She put it in a safe-deposit box."

"I'd figured out that much," I said, frowning. "But what *is* the evidence?"

The doorbell rang. Miss Woodhouse smiled at me before answering it. "Think of the black raincoat Brenda left in the office last night. Think of how convenient it must have looked to a murderer eager to find a quick disguise. Think of what deep pockets the raincoat has, of how many small stolen objects they might hold, and of the odd questions Brenda asked you this morning after coming back to the kitchen. And hope, just hope, you might soon be able to return that brooch my mother lent you."

* * * *

The brooch had been stuck to the lining of the raincoat pocket, thanks to the stubborn clasp that never closes properly. Terry must've been in such a hurry to dispose of evidence and get home that she missed it when she went back to Chez Cubbe to return the raincoat and toss the Minute Marinater in the dishwasher. But Brenda found it the next morning, tried to blackmail Terry with it, and died because of it.

The police found other evidence, too, most of it tied to Brenda's murder, not Little Dave's—the pieces of costume jewelry Terry took from Brenda's apartment and desperately tried to grind up in her garbage disposal, half a dozen other stolen items stashed behind a wheelbarrow in Terry's garage. Except for the brooch, the things Terry took from Little Dave and me weren't found—she'd had more time to get rid of those, and she'd done a better job. But there was the note Brenda left in the safe deposit box, describing the call from Little Dave, her discovery of the brooch, and Terry's promise to give her half the money from the sale of the restaurant if she kept silent. Poor Brenda. It makes sense to take precautions to protect yourself from a murderer. But if you don't tell the murderer about the precautions, what's the point?

Terry's denying everything. But Miss Woodhouse's friends at the prosecutor's office have given us enough hints to let us piece the story together. It's a pathetic, sordid story—four people devoting three solid years to scheming with and against each other, all chasing the mirage of an old man's money. Chuck was the most straightforward, trying to dazzle Howard with his cooking and convince him that opening a restaurant with Chuck as chef would be a good investment. If Howard had really been a wealthy recluse, rather than a retiree with an income stretched so thin he'd never turn down free food, Chuck might've succeeded. Brenda apparently tried a variety of unsuccessful tactics, from seduction to fraud, until Little Dave persuaded her he was inches away from getting Howard's fortune and would share it with her in return for the usual favors.

As for Little Dave's approach—evidently, it had been to use his wife to get Howard's money. Soon after the murders, Howard admitted to us that he'd carried on a flirtation with Terry for years. He thought her husband knew nothing about their secret meetings, but I'd bet Terry had Little Dave's blessing. She'd often tried to escalate the flirtation to an affair, Howard said, but his shame about his past wouldn't let him destroy someone else's marriage. Besides, if Terry got too close to him, she might discover the truth about his finances. Howard obviously preferred things as they were—keeping them all dangling, seeming to make half-promises from time to time but never delivering, enjoying the feeling of being an important, sought-after man again.

Then Stanley Carson came along. Terry was probably the only one who knew the full truth about him. Howard confided in her, and she'd undoubtedly followed Carson to learn his Thursday night routine. But all four of Howard's suitors considered him a threat. We guessed at the rest. Terry, convinced Howard would never have an affair with a married woman, resolved to become a widow. She talked Little Dave into some plan to kill Carson or scare him off, she orchestrated a phone call I was supposed to overhear so she'd have an alibi, and then she jumped from behind the dumpster, knocked me out, and sank the Minute Marinater into her husband's neck. It was a hare-brained scheme. If it hadn't been for the computer map in Little Dave's pocket, though, and his call to Brenda, and the stubborn clasp on the professor's brooch, it might have worked.

Terry had owned Chez Cubbe jointly with her husband, so there were no inheritance delays. To cover legal fees, she had to sell at a loss—to Chuck, together with two long-time customers eager to keep their favorite restaurant open. The notoriety from the murders was good for business, and word of Chuck's sauces spread quickly. Several months later, when the Woodhouses and I decided to have dinner at the restaurant, we had to wait forty minutes for a table. Anne—the only employee left from the old days—was our waitress. She let Chuck know we were there, and he came out to greet us.

"Nice and bustling, isn't it?" he said. "And we got big renovations planned. Not those retro plans Little Dave drew up. Our designer wants to give the place more of a bistro feel—traditional but trendy, minimalist but opulent."

"Sounds great," I said. Glancing around the crowded dining room, I spotted first one familiar figure, then another. "Oh, gosh. There's Howard. And isn't that Stanley Carson? And that very thin woman—is she Howard's daughter?"

Chuck's nose crinkled. "Yeah. They been coming here every night for weeks. Howard told me a long, boring story about it—his daughter was hiding from some creep with a weird name, but then some cop named Glass pulled a joint sting operation with the Baltimore police, and now the creep's headed for prison, and Howard's back with his daughter. And with Carson—him and the daughter are engaged. Howard hinted about having the wedding reception at Chez Cubbe. As if! He couldn't manage our prices."

The professor took a slow sip of water. "Perhaps you could give him a special rate. He has a long history here."

"*He* should be history here." Chuck snapped his fingers. "Anne! Stop refilling water glasses at table twelve. And hound them every two minutes—let me get this plate out of your way, may I box that up, do you want to see the dessert menu, here's your check. You know the drill. Move 'em along." He waited for her to walk away, then shook his head. "God, she's slow. I'm giving her notice tonight. And she's too tolerant of Howard and his crew. All they ever order is soup and sandwiches and one drink each, and they sit around forever. We can't afford to put up with that kind anymore—we need the table. Well, enjoy your dinners. And tell your friends."

"So Howard's losing his haven," I said after Chuck left. "That's too bad."

"Let's hope he'll build himself a truer sort of haven," Miss Woodhouse said, "with his daughter and her new husband—a haven based not on deceit and false hopes but on openness and true affection."

Professor Woodhouse gave her daughter a disdainful look. "Openness and true affection! Please do not assault my sensibilities, Iphigenia, by indulging in such blatant sentimentality. I should hope I raised you better than that."

Miss Woodhouse cast her eyes down. "You're right, Mother. I'm sorry."

"You should be," her mother snapped back, "you nasty girl. Besides, as I should not need to point out, Howard is not guiltless in all this. He knew what he was doing. Toying with people's dreams—that's a dangerous business, and a cruel one."

I sighed. "That's true. I guess no one involved in this case is admirable. I guess I shouldn't be surprised. But when Terry and Brenda and Chuck first came to our office, they seemed so unselfish, so kind. I should've seen through it, even then. Private detectives are supposed to be cynical; I was naïve. But I wanted to believe people really can be that—well, that *good*."

The professor glanced at me, then at her daughter. Miss Woodhouse still gazed down at the table, her eyes still dull with shame. Her mother reached out, briefly, to touch her hand. "You may continue to believe in that goodness, little Harriet," she said softly. "But you must look for it in the right places."

On a chilly February evening, my husband and I had dinner at a faded restaurant in Toledo. It had the feel of a place that had once been elegant—cloth napkins, centerpieces, soft-spoken servers—but most of the tables were empty now, and the food was two or three notches below mediocre. At a table not far from us, a gaunt man in his seventies sat alone, going through the rituals described in "Table for None"—taking a sip of martini and replacing it with a splash of water, eating his soup and crackers but wrapping up his roll, ordering something to go, nursing cups of coffee for over an hour as his eyes traveled from table to table. There's got to be a story there, I thought. So I made one up. And since I'm a mystery writer, it's a story that leads to murder.

But all Iphigenia Woodhouse stories combine murder with humor. Since this story centers on a restaurant, and since I'm a Food Network junkie, I incorporated some inside jokes for Food Network fans to enjoy. At one point, sous-chef Chuck brandishes his favorite knife, inviting us to admire its "broad grooved blade, bright orange handle." That should sound familiar to Rachael Ray's viewers—I have a set of those orange-handled knives in my kitchen. The restaurant's centerpieces, which Harriet describes as "so heavy they must be made of iron," are figurines of a lion cub wearing a chef's hat. Eventually, Harriet gets knocked out by one of these little iron chefs. (Harriet doesn't get knocked out in every story, by the way, only in the two in this collection. I didn't intentionally pick the two stories with this element—it just happened.)

As for the Minute Marinater, it's inspired by a gizmo I spotted in a cookware catalogue. (It had a different name; I don't remember what.) The minute I saw it, I knew it would make a great murder weapon. I ordered one and tested it—on a roast, not on a person. Frankly, it didn't do much for the roast. But the Minute Marinator in the story does an effective job on Little Dave.

DEATH ON A BUDGET

(1998)

"If you're sure it's what you want," he said. "We don't absolutely need the money. We could make do."

She stood on tiptoe to kiss his forehead. "We absolutely need the money," she said. "We *couldn't* make do. Besides, even if we didn't, even if we could, I'd want to. This is my work, Sam. It's important to me."

"And to me. But that place, Leah! Why *that* place?"

"Because it's a place. And I have to learn about as many places as I can." She picked up her purse and checked for her keys. "You can handle the kids?"

He shrugged. "What's to handle? I get Sarah and Rachel up from their naps at 3:30. I make them snacks and watch *Wishbone* with them. At 4:45, I put the chicken in the oven and make rice and salad. I feed the girls, I bathe them, I put them to bed, and then I don't have another thing to do until 11:45, when I warm up the chicken and rice and wait for you to come home and eat them."

She kissed him again, this time on the lips. "It's nice to be married to an organized man. Rats—where'd my notebook go?"

* * * *

Monday, March 9

Arrived at Budget Psychics at 2:20 p.m., went to manager's office. Bess Walker at her desk: mid-forties, thin, dress-for-success suit. Seemed mildly surprised when she saw my resume. "So you have an M.A. in communications," she said. "Why are you working as a temporary secretary?"

Note: Leaving the Ph.D. off the resume was the right decision. The M.A. makes people suspicious enough. "I haven't found a satisfactory teaching job," I said. "And my husband's an artist, so we can use any cash I bring in. And I enjoy secretarial work, and my skills are quite good."

"I can see that." She scanned my resume again. "Sixty-five words a minute—not that typing is the most important part of the job." She tapped the telephone on her desk. "*This* is the most important part. I need someone with smarts manning the phone lines. Maybe the communications will help. If it does, this could turn into a permanent job. Our receptionist's on maternity leave, but I'm not all that eager to take her back. She's pleasant but not sharp. If you're sharper, I'll make a switch. You don't mind the hours?"

"Not really," I said, shocked by her attitude toward her regular receptionist. Not a Nurturing Stabilizer, I decided. "Since my husband's self-employed, we can pretty much make our own hours. We'll adjust things so I still get plenty of time with the children."

"Oh. Children." She pursed her lips. "I suppose somebody has to have them. Now, your most important duty is routing calls. You work Prime Shift—3 p.m. until midnight. That's when we get most of our calls, so we have five psychics on duty. Regular clients always get their regular psychics—that's crucial. Our psychics work on commission, and they get steamed if you give somebody else one of their regulars. For new callers, refer to these notes."

I took the typed sheet from her. "Kids and flakes get routed to Phoebe," I read out loud.

"Right—because Phoebe's a kid and a flake, too. She relates well to crazies. Also, if you sense callers are on drugs, route them to Phoebe right away. Ditzy old ladies get routed to Harvey. He makes a big impression on them, but God knows he can't impress anyone else. Don't throw other clients away on him. Vince specializes in financial advice, but he's good at everything—he's our top psychic. Sean's first-rate, too, especially with people searching for spiritual guidance, the meaning of life, crap like that. And Delia's a solid, all-around little psychic. If Vince and Sean are busy, route new callers to her unless they're flakes or old ladies. Got that?"

"I think so." A Task-Oriented Designator, I decided—that described Bess best.

She nodded. "You have custodial chores, too. Plus you enter data into the computer." She handed me a stack of forms. "Our psychics fill these out whenever they get calls. There are spaces for identifying information—name, age, sign—plus headings for data about Love, Money, Past Lives, Angel Guardians, Alien Encounters. All the standard stuff. This way our psychics can punch up data about anyone who's called in before. They can't enter info, though. Only you and I have the codes for that. I used to give the psychics access, but they were always typing in false stuff, sabotaging each other's files."

I felt my eyes widen. "Sabotaging?"

"Yeah." Her tone stayed matter-of-fact. "After all, they compete for clients. And we *are* Budget Psychics. We charge a fraction of what major hotlines charge, so we have to keep overhead low. We advertise only in the tri-state area—most of our calls come from right in town—and we have no infomercials, no celebrity spokespeople. And no deadwood. If psychics can't meet their quota, they're out. Ready for the staff meeting?"

All five Prime Shift psychics were already crowded into the small break room. I smiled warmly—to succeed as a secretary, I've learned, one must be a Bridging Nurturer—and found a seat.

"I've got last week's totals," Bess said, not bothering to look up. "They're not great. Too many psychics sitting around during Prime with too few callers, and that increases overhead. So either you prolong calls and drive up call-backs, or we'll downsize. The end-of-month totals will decide it."

"But we work on commission," a twentyish woman protested. She wore a long paisley skirt and a floppy peasant blouse. Phoebe, I guessed. She drew a long, thickly fringed shawl around her shoulders more snugly. "Even if we don't get calls every minute, how does that cost you?"

Bess gave her a slow, bored look. "You still go to the bathroom. Every time you flush, it costs me. Grace has an offer from Psychics-To-Go. If she leaves, I'll move someone to Day Shift to replace her."

"But nobody calls between six and four," a plump, balding man protested. "You can't make a decent living on Day Shift."

"*You* can't make a decent living on Prime, Harvey," Bess said. "I don't see why it'd make much difference to you. Now, then. Vince, you get First Graveyard. Okay?"

"Fine." Vince was about fifty, dressed in a red silk shirt and sparkling white slacks. "I enjoy First Graveyard. Plenty of loonies are still awake midnight to three."

"Show some respect," a fortyish man said, frowning. He wore a buckskin jacket and jeans; his long hair was pulled back in a ponytail. "Maybe this is all a joke to you, but it's not a joke to *them*. Or to me. *I* don't consider them loonies."

"Vince doesn't, either," the young woman next to him said. It had to be Delia. She was delicately lovely and wore a trim pale blue suit and was obviously a Negotiative Clarifier. "That was just a figure of speech—right, Vince?"

Vince shrugged. "Whatever."

"*Anyway*," Bess said, "Harvey gets Second Graveyard."

"Again?" The soft, balding man looked down at his hands. "Three to six—I'm lucky if I get a single call. And you put me on that shift so often, and I *do* have a day job. If I'm not alert—"

"How alert do you have to be to bag groceries?" Bess put down her clipboard. "*Somebody* has to take Second Graveyard, and I won't waste Vince or Sean or Delia on a no-call shift. They consistently average above fifteen minutes a call—your average is six and a half. It makes sense for you to take the bad shifts. But if you won't cooperate—"

"No, no," Harvey said. "I'll take the shift."

"Fine." Bess stood up. "Vince gets the main office, and Sean and Delia get the small offices, as usual. Harvey and Phoebe take the cubicles. Oh, yes. This is Leah Abrams. She's filling in for Elaine. Leah, make sure everyone has a full water pitcher. Then I'll show you how to work the phones."

* * * *

8:45 P.M.: I'm in the break room, eating the fruit Sam packed for me. This is the first chance I've had to take notes since the staff meeting. It's been a fascinating first few hours on the job. I've gained several insights and faced my first communicative and ethical dilemmas. Around 5:30 I took a call from a woman who sounded distressed.

"This is Emma," she said. "I usually talk to Vince, but I need to talk to a woman this time."

I punched up Emma's file—for three months, she'd been calling Vince every night. Always route regular callers to their regular psychics, Bess had said. I glanced at the row of red lights near my phone, which told me which psychics were free. "Are you sure?" I said. "Vince doesn't have a caller right now. Perhaps—"

"No," Emma cut in. "Vince has helped me so much—*so much*—but I really need to talk to a woman. Please?"

"Of course." Emma didn't sound like a flake or a kid, so I connected her to Delia.

Minutes later, Vince strolled into the reception area. "Slow night," he commented, stretching his arms and settling into a chair next to my desk. "But both Sean and Delia have callers, I see."

Should I tell him about Emma? It might be helpful, or it might cause Conflict-Inducing Static. I smiled. "That's right."

"Well, they're both good." He picked up a magazine from my desk. "Delia's smooth. She knows how to work a call. And Sean—Sean is Sean. He was a monk once."

My first response, I admit, was sexist and ethnocentric—how could such a good-looking man have been a monk? "Really?"

"Yeah. Then he went to India and attached himself to a guru, then lived with aborigines in Australia, and at various points—I can't recall the sequence—became involved in acupuncture, spirit channeling, all-bran diets, like that. Then he became a psychic—or discovered he was a psychic, whichever you prefer. He had a lucrative practice on the West Coast, wrote a bestseller. Maybe you've heard of it—*Spirit Pure, Path Sure*?"

"I have. How did he end up here?"

Vince shrugged. "Sean says he was channeling the spirit of a Mongol warlord for some Fortune 500 CEO, and the warlord told him to bring psychic comfort to the masses. So he wandered highways and byways, seeking a way to share his gifts, and found Budget Psychics." Vince raised his eyebrows. "Either that, or he messed up and had to take any job he could get. Personally, I think everyone who works for Budget Psychics messed up."

Was this an invitation to Intimacy Building? "Including you?"

Vince grinned. "Definitely. I was a professor of psychology at a rather fine women's college. It enrolled many rather fine women. I got along with some of them extremely well. Then one went to a consciousness-raising workshop and decided I'd gotten along with her *too* well. So here I am. That's okay. Teaching bored me, my training as a psychologist helps me sense what our pathetic callers want to hear, and every job has perks. Now, let's talk about you. That ring tells me you're married. Not happily, I hope?"

"*Very* happily." My tone stiffened even though I'd been determined to achieve Total Receptivity. I was relieved when the hotline rang, and a new caller said she needed financial advice. "I'll connect you with Vince," I said, waving him to his office.

As soon as he left, Harvey slunk over. The poor thing—three of his regulars had phoned in tonight, but none of the calls lasted long, and that wouldn't do him much good in an office that makes its profits by charging by the minute. He gestured apologetically. "Might I disturb you, Leah?"

"Of course." I smiled, trying to radiate Maximum Reassurance. "How may I help?"

He sat down. "I've been listening to you handle calls—I haven't had much else to do. You seem very articulate. Perhaps you'd draft a note for me. I'd meant to ask Bess about something at the meeting, but considering her insinuations that I wasn't cooperative—and in short, I was afraid. I didn't dare speak, but I'd like to leave her a note. Could you help?"

"Of course." Classic, I thought. Bess's excessive Task Orientation had lowered her Nurturance Quotient so much workers feared to make basic Needs Clarification. This was a chance to demonstrate the contribution a Bridging Nurturer could make. I pulled over a legal pad. "What would you like to communicate to Bess?"

"I'd—that is, I'm grateful to work Prime Shift, but Thursday's my fortieth anniversary, and I'd like a little time off—6:00 to 8:00, say—so I can take my wife out to dinner. I wouldn't ask, except these last years have been so hard on Mary, on both of us."

I took notes, then paused—sensitively, I hoped. "Problems in the marriage, Harvey?"

"Oh, no. Mary's wonderful—she's suffered so, with never a complaint. But our daughter—our only child, the sweetest girl—was hit by a drunk driver on her eighteenth birthday, in a coma ever since, and that private hospital costs so much! Mary works in a shoe factory so we won't have to send Sharon to a state institution, and we managed while I had my little tearoom and my dear ladies came for their readings. But most of my dear ladies have passed on, I've lost my little tearoom, and Mary stitches soles all day, and I bag groceries at KostKutters and answer phones here, and still the bills aren't paid. I'd like to take Mary to dinner on our anniversary, but I don't know how to ask for time off without sounding uncooperative. Can you help?"

If I can't help with *this*, I thought, I'll ask the university to cancel my degrees. "I will," I said—and when a call from a young flake on drugs came in, I routed it to Harvey. Phoebe needed minutes, too, but all I could think about was a young woman in a coma, and a timid, faithful father, and a fading mother stitching wearily.

Phoebe herself wandered over to my desk not long after.

"Hey, Lisa," she said, smiling drowsily, "you got aspirin, anything like that? I've got a bitch of a headache."

"I'll see if Elaine has something." I checked drawers and rummaged through the decorative clutter on the reception desk—framed photos, scented candles, tiny ceramic kittens—until I found a bottle. "Tylenol—will that do?"

"Groovy." She shook half a dozen pills into her hand. "So, Lila. How do you like the job so far?"

"It's Leah," I said, "and I like it fine. Do *you* like it?"

"Pretty much." Her fringed shawl had drooped off her shoulders and trailed on the floor. She scooped it up and slung it around her neck. "Harvey's nice, Delia's cool, and Vince—oops. Your phone's ringing, Mia."

I answered it. "I need to talk to Sean," a carefully resonant male voice said. "This is Ethan Lawrence."

It couldn't possibly be *the* Ethan Lawrence. I checked my row of red lights. For almost the first time all evening, Sean was free.

"I'll connect you right away, Mr. Lawrence," I said.

Phoebe perked up. "Ethan Lawrence? *Again?* Wow."

I stared at her. "You don't mean it's *the*—"

She nodded. "*The*. The movie star, the producer, the incredible stud. I've talked to him myself sometimes, when Sean was busy. Ethan *worships* Sean. See, a bunch of years ago, Ethan was messed up—it was after his third divorce, and he got *really* heavy into drugs and booze, and he couldn't get roles, and he was broke and fat and all. You probably read about it."

"I think so," I said, hating to admit I read such stuff.

"That was when Sean was out West," she continued. "He met Ethan and became his personal spiritual trainer. He got him into bran and sit-ups, put him in touch with his angel guardian, helped him work through a conflict he'd had with his father in a past life. Ethan slimmed down *fast*, won an Oscar, and started a production company. Now he wants Sean to work for him, start a new psychic network, but Sean always says no, he's happy here. Geez! I mean, here's okay, but give *me* a chance to work for Ethan, and see what *I'd* do." She glanced at my row of lights. "Good—Vince is free. I gotta talk to him. See you, Maya."

That was my last significant communicative exchange. By 7:00, the calls were coming in more frequently, and most of the psychics were busy most of the time. I was relieved when Bess told me to take a break, and—

* * * *

11:07 P.M.: My shift ends soon. I've had two more exchanges and want to get down some notes while the details are fresh. Just as I was finishing up my notes about Phoebe, Sean came into the break room to refill his water pitcher.

"I'm sorry," I said, standing. "I forgot to refill the pitchers at 8:00."

He smiled, beautifully. "I don't mind doing it, and I don't like the way Bess turns secretaries into maids. She's too cheap to hire a janitor, so she makes you vacuum and empty trash and—"

"It doesn't bother me," I said, honestly. "All labor has dignity, don't you think?"

He beamed. "Absolutely. I *knew* you were a compatible spirit. So. Leah Abrams. Jewish?"

Sean, I thought. No way. "That's right," I said.

He nodded and sat down at the table. "I was a Jew once," he said. "Well, almost. After I returned from Australia, I met an amazing Hasidic rabbi and studied with him for over a year. When I was almost ready to convert, I discovered Native American spirituality. Reb Moshe wouldn't let me keep my totems in the synagogue. He was a dear, learned man, but narrow. So I left. I traveled to the Dakotas and—hello, Delia."

She smiled at us as she got her yogurt from the refrigerator. "It's a busy night. Any special calls?"

Sean shrugged. "Every call is special."

"Of course." She licked a fragment-of-an-ounce of yogurt from her spoon. "I had a splendid talk with one of my regulars. It was *so* exciting. We nearly accessed the spirit of her deceased dachshund. So, Leah, tell us about yourself. You're wearing a wedding ring—do you have children?"

I showed them pictures of Sarah and Rachel. Then Bess strode into the room. She was about to leave, she said, and wanted to know why water pitchers weren't refilled. Sean and Delia were still talking busily when I left. That's a definite Duad, I thought.

* * * *

Of course, Sam was in his attic studio when she returned. Leah stepped over the mounds of rosewood shavings and tapped his shoulder. "I'm back," she said.

He kissed her gratefully. "At last. I hate these hours. So? How was it?"

"Revealing." She leaned over to examine the flamingos. "Sam, they're lovely. I know this isn't what you want to do—you should be free to do your own work, you shouldn't have to carve custom-made lawn ornaments just so we can make our mortgage payments—but even so, these are lovely. The tall one seems to be laughing. It's Sarah's laugh, isn't it?"

He peered at it. "I guess it is. What do you know. The girls were playing up here while I was carving the face, and they were both laughing—I must've absorbed the expression."

She gazed at the shorter flamingo. "And this one—oh, Sam! It looks so despondent. Just *look* at how its neck droops, how limp its wings are. Were you alone when you carved it?"

"I was. I was thinking about all I'd hoped to achieve as an artist, I was despondent, and I guess that came through in the sculpture. It makes an interesting grouping, don't you think? And it confirms what I've said before. Whether they mean to or not, artists can't help putting their signatures on their works. Anyway, the chicken and rice should be hot by now. Tell me about your day. Did it support your theories?"

"Sort of. Delia has potential as a Transcendent Nurturer—she communicates well with everyone and resolves conflicts—but the office power structure keeps her from true Bridging. And I've identified two

Duads, but there must be more—there always are. It was only my first day. I'll learn more tomorrow."

"Of course you will." He put an arm around her shoulders. "But first, you'll eat."

* * * *

Tuesday, March 10

It's 7:50 p.m. I'm in the break room, waiting for the police, hoping I can stay calm enough to get some coherent notes down before they get here.

I arrived at 2:45. Bess told me to empty trash in all the offices, so I got plastic liners from the break room cupboard and made my rounds. I should mention one potentially significant wastebasket, the one in the main office, the office Vince always claims, the office all the psychics use when they're manning a graveyard shift. Two empty bottles were in that basket—a Windex bottle, and a Jim Beam bottle.

Someone's drinking on the job, I thought. I was sure that wasn't kosher but didn't think it was my place to say anything. So I cinched up the liner and carried it to the dumpster with the others. Now, I wonder if that was a mistake.

By the time I got back, psychics were gathering for the daily Prime Shift meeting—Phoebe, Sean, Delia, Harvey. No Vince. Bess paced until 3:15. "Vince seems to be late," she said. "Again. I see that last night the answering machine for the hotline was turned on from 2:15 to 2:55. Any comments, Harvey?"

Harvey blinked. "I arrived for Second Graveyard at 2:55 and found the office empty, the machine on. I'm sure Vince had good reasons for leaving early."

"I'm sure he did," Bess said. "So don't simper and imply he didn't. We'll cover for him until he arrives. Delia, you've got First Graveyard tonight. Harvey, you've got Second. Any complaints? Then get to work."

We all took our places, but the atmosphere was hardly conducive to Maximum Harmonious Output. Everyone seemed uneasy. After barely fifteen minutes, Phoebe came over. "You got more Tylenol? I've got a *super* bitch of a headache." She lowered her voice. "And Bess is *super* pissed. I can tell: I'm not psychic for nothing. Vince pulls stunts like this all the time, but she never dares to say anything because he's a part owner of Budget Psychics. He's really her boss more than she's his. So whatever he does, she has to take it. Talk about bad vibes. I'm *super* tense."

"I can imagine," I said, and then the phone rang. It was Emma, asking for Vince.

"I'm sorry. He's not available." I punched Emma up on the computer. That's right—she was Vince's regular, but yesterday she'd asked to talk to a woman, and I'd connected her with Delia. "You could talk to Delia again."

"That's all right." She sounded anxious. "I'll call back." She hung up.

I skimmed the data I'd typed into the computer after her conversation. Odd—she'd talked to Delia for thirty-seven minutes, but Delia had written just two vague sentences on the form: "Emma needed advice about relationships. I counseled her to be trusting." Puzzled, I picked up the three forms Vince had filled out during First Graveyard last night. Emma had called again, at 1:03 A.M. "I gave Emma advice about finances," Vince had written, and that was it. Delia and Vince might be skilled psychics, I thought, but they weren't communicating fully. A few workshops might help.

It was a slow evening. Bess paced in the reception area, glancing at her watch. At 7:30, she turned on me. "Do you enjoy sitting there twiddling your thumbs," she asked, "or would you like to *earn* your money? I'll watch the phones—they're not ringing anyway. You use this time to wash the windows. There's Windex in the supply closet."

"Right away," I said, and hurried down the hall and pulled open the supply closet door.

It's bizarre, but the first thing I noticed was the puddle on the floor. There was nothing ominous about the puddle—it wasn't bloody, just clear water—but there was a lot of it, and I took a step back to keep from getting my feet wet. Then I looked up and saw Vince hanging in midair, his eyes staring, his mouth gaping, Phoebe's long, fringed shawl wound tightly around his neck, a chair kicked to the side. I screamed, people came running, and now we're waiting for the police. God help us.

* * * *

10:40 P.M. My first chance to take notes since the police came. It's been hard. Phoebe cried hysterically, Bess seemed in shock, Sean seemed shaky—and the younger police officers kept cracking jokes, finding it funny that a body went undiscovered for hours in a building packed with psychics. Thank goodness the detective, a middle-aged man named Brock, is more sensitive. And thank goodness for Delia, who's been comforting everybody. As for Harvey—I don't know what to make of his behavior.

I'd better explain. Bess and Harvey took poor Vince down, hoping there was a chance of reviving him, but he was stiff and cold. When Detective Brock arrived, he looked at Vince, looked at the shawl still hanging there. Vince must have opened the access panel in the closet's ceiling and tied one end of the shawl around a beam in the crawl space. Detective Brock frowned.

"Can anyone identify that shawl?" he asked.

Phoebe burst into hysterics again, and Delia put an arm around her.

"It's Phoebe's," she said. "She must've left it here by accident. It was always drooping off her shoulders and falling on the floor, and Phoebe often forgets things. You left your purse in the office last week, didn't you, dear?"

Phoebe sobbed in agreement. "And my shoes," she said.

"That could explain it," Brock agreed. "Who was the last person to see the deceased alive?"

I cleared my throat. "Probably me. I'm the temporary secretary. Vince was working First Graveyard—that is, he worked alone here from midnight to 3:00 A.M.—and before I left at midnight, I refilled his water pitcher." I shrugged. "He seemed fine—cheerful, friendly, fine."

"I see," Brock said, taking notes. "And who was the first person to arrive at the office this morning?"

Harvey stepped forward, not looking as nervous as I would've expected. "I was. I arrived at 2:55 A.M. to work Second Graveyard. Vince wasn't here. That surprised me, but I assumed he had some urgent reason for leaving his shift early."

Brock nodded. "Did you see anything else unusual?"

Harvey hesitated. "I didn't *see* anything unusual. But I—I may have *sensed* something. I didn't mention it before because I wasn't sure, but now—perhaps it would help if we went to the office where Vince was working."

We trooped into the office. There wasn't much to see, just a small bookcase, a swivel chair, and a gray metal desk stocked with the usual necessities: telephone, answering machine, computer, blank caller forms, water pitcher, glass, pencils, tarot cards, Ouija board. Everything looked normal and tidy—sparkling, even.

Harvey walked slowly toward the desk, closed his eyes, and pressed one hand against his forehead.

"When I arrived this morning, I sensed a female presence. Not a woman who works here—an outsider. And I sensed—I sense even now—romance, liquor, a flickering flame. But I sense conflict, too, and heartbreak." He lifted his hands. "I sense—despair!"

"Interesting." Brock's voice stayed flat. "Are you sure you didn't *see* anything that helped you sense all that?"

Harvey opened his eyes. "Why, no. The office looked perfectly normal to the physical eye. But to the spiritual eye—ahh! So much was revealed, and will yet be revealed."

"That's good to know." Brock looked him over. "Make sure you share any revelations with me. You can all get back to work now, let my people do *their* work. They'll need some time in this office. Meanwhile, I'll talk to each of you privately."

He held the interviews in the break room. When he got to me, I told him about the bottles in the wastebasket. He asked if I knew of any tensions in the office, and I told him about yesterday's meeting, about what Bess said about downsizing. It can't be relevant—Vince was the top psychic and a part owner, so worries about losing his job couldn't explain his suicide—but investigators need to consider all the data when they're interpreting a situation. When we finished, Detective Brock thanked me and said we might talk again soon. I wonder what he meant.

* * * *

Sam brought her a hot water bottle wrapped in a maroon towel. "Put this behind your back, Leah," he said. "You know how your spine tenses up at times like this. I'll get you another glass of wine."

She sighed gratefully as she slid the water bottle into place but shook her head. "No more wine. I should go to bed."

He took her glass. "You need to unwind before trying to sleep."

"True," she admitted. "I *couldn't* sleep now. Poor Vince! I never guessed he was in such pain. I'm supposed to be an expert, but—damn! Who could be at the door at this hour?"

"I'll see," Sam said, and returned moments later with Detective Brock. Embarrassed, Leah wadded up her afghan.

Brock, too, looked embarrassed. "Sorry to disturb you so late. Your lights were on, so—"

"It's fine," she said. "Please have a seat. You've met my husband, Sam Abrams? How can I help?"

He settled into the rocking chair Sam had carved when Sarah was born. "I want to know why you're working at Budget Psychics. I know about the regular secretary's maternity leave. But in my job you get a sense for people, and I've got a feeling something's going on. When I talked to you earlier, I couldn't help feeling I was talking to a teacher. What gives?"

She glanced at Sam, and he nodded. All the data, she decided. "I *was* a teacher," she said. "A professor. I have a Ph.D. in communications. But I hated campus politics, I got tired of listening to students whine about grades, and I was wasting too much time in committee meetings instead of getting *real* work done. I'm fascinated by workplace communications, but I think most studies are flawed because the people being observed *know* they're being observed. I quit my teaching job and registered with a temporary agency so I could observe a variety of work settings in a more natural way."

Brock nodded. "So you're working undercover."

She didn't like the term. "I'm writing a book—the tentative title is *The Hermeneutics of Workplace Communications: Duadic Networking and Transcendent Nurturization.*"

"Wow," Brock said. "Quite a title. And it's only tentative! What does it mean?"

She hesitated. "The theory's rather involved, but I posit that all workers want to do their best, to make the workplace a success and enjoy meaningful relationships with coworkers. If they have good communication and conflict resolution skills, workers realize every situation is potentially win-win, so they find ways to cooperate rather than compete. Too often, though, people pair off. They form Duadic Networks with one person with whom they communicate well, and they view other Duadic networks as competitors. So every workplace needs Transcendent Nurturers to build communicative bridges between one Duad and another."

"Wow," Brock said again. "That's something. Of course, if you'd asked me, I woulda guessed some people are plain rotten no matter how well you communicate with them—the more you understand them, the more they make your skin crawl. I woulda guessed there are always winners and losers, and some people just wanna win and don't care who they hurt. But I'm just a dumb cop. If I had a Ph.D., I'd probably understand these things better. Now, here's the other thing I want to talk to you about. Vince didn't commit suicide. He was murdered."

Leah sat forward. "*Murdered*? You're sure?"

"Positive. The coroner says that shawl didn't kill him. He was strangled with something harder, like a telephone cord. He wasn't strung up until after he was dead. And he was hit in the head before he was killed—there's a bruise. I'm not telling anyone else at Budget Psychics yet. I'm telling you because you barely knew him and presumably didn't have any reason to kill him, and because I'm grateful to you for telling me about the bottles in the wastebasket and the threat of downsizing—nobody else mentioned any of that. So. Any ideas about who killed him?"

She shook her head slowly. "I'm sorry, Detective. I don't have any ideas. I can hardly believe he was murdered."

Brock stood up. "Think it over. And keep your eyes open and let me know if you notice anything suspicious. Okay?"

She stood to shake his hand. "Okay," she said.

* * * *

Wednesday, March 11

9:25 P.M.: My first break in over six hours, and I'm a wreck. I wouldn't have thought any day in a workplace could be more stressful than yesterday, but today proved me wrong.

It started as soon as I arrived. Bess, suit rumpled and eyes dull, took me by the arm. "Phones are ringing like crazy," she said. "I don't know why the news that a psychic committed suicide should make people call in, but it does. It'll be even worse during Prime. So I'll act as receptionist, and you fill in as a psychic."

I stepped back. "I'm not a psychic! I make no claim to extrasensory powers of any—"

"You'll do fine." She pulled me into the main office, the one where Vince had been murdered. "You've got an M.A. in communications. You should be able to lay on the bull with the best of them. Tell people whatever they want to hear. If you can add some mystical mumbo-jumbo, great. Between calls, empty wastebaskets. Damn—there's the phone."

She ran off. Seconds later she connected me with a college student who wanted to know whether majoring in theater would guarantee her a brilliant Hollywood career. I struggled with my conscience, then resigned myself to listening and making sympathetic noises. In the end, I advised her to get a broad background in the liberal arts regardless of her major and to make sure she had solid computer skills just in case. She was deeply grateful, impressed by my ability to see into the future.

There were other calls, constant calls. One, from an elderly gentleman who thought his garbage disposal was haunted, caused me profound ethical anguish. I put decisions about right and wrong on hold. Around 6:00, I got a call from Emma. I checked the computer. Yes—one of Vince's regulars, talked to Delia on Monday, called back yesterday asking for Vince again. Now, she needed my help.

"I need to find a lost object," Emma said. I could tell she was near tears. "Can you tell me where it is?"

Great, I thought. Where do I start with something like this? "Can you describe it?" I asked, stalling.

"It's valuable," she said. "And it's small and round and—special. If I can't find it, things could get bad. Can't you go into a trance and *sense* where it is?"

"I'm not all that good at trances," I admitted. "Can you remember the last time you saw this object?"

"Of *course* I remember the last time I saw it. The point is, I can't see it *now*. But you don't even know what it is, do you? You can't even sense that much."

"No. If you'll tell me where you've been since you last saw it, and—"

"I shouldn't *have* to tell you. What the hell kind of psychic are you, anyhow?" She slammed the receiver down. I scanned the records of her many conversations with Vince. Advice about her investments, her trips to Bermuda, her troubled marriage, her unfulfilled dreams. Three solid months of advice. Oddly, Vince's notes got less specific, not more specific, as time went on.

My phone rang again and again, and I got caught up in work. Then, around 8:00, there was a long lull. I was about to risk a run to the ladies' room when the door opened.

It was Bess, followed by Harvey and Phoebe, followed by a camera crew, followed by Detective Brock and two uniformed officers. Sean and Delia were in the procession, too, but hung back by the door, not stepping into the office.

"Get away from the phone, Leah," Bess said. "I've had to switch all the lines off. Harvey called the press and the police—without asking me—and now he wants to have some sort of demonstration. Detective, can't you stop this?"

He shrugged. "I didn't invite the press, but I got no right to throw them out. If *you* want to, go ahead."

"No," she said, wincing. "I have—that is, *we* have nothing to hide. Harvey, try not to make *too* big a fool of yourself."

He waited until the cameras were on and the reporter had given her opening spiel, and then he went into a trance. He was dressed spiffily—freshly pressed suit, crisp white shirt, broad red tie with an Aztec sun smack in the middle. He closed his eyes, pressed a hand to his forehead, staggered a bit, and spoke.

"It comes." He lowered his voice to a stage whisper. "The curtains of time draw aside, and it comes. A vision, revealed only to the spiritual eye. I sense a feminine presence, a stranger—beauty, intrigue, romance. I smell the heavy fragrance of liquor, and see a flickering flame. And I hear echoes of conflict. I feel heartbreak and despair!"

"You said all that yesterday." Bess tried to sound bored.

Harvey opened his eyes long enough to stare at her, then closed them again. "There's more. Can you feel it? Can you feel *him*? Yes, Vince is still here, and still in pain. He's trying to break through, to speak to me. Yes, Vince? What was that? You regret giving in to despair? And you're—could you repeat that? I didn't quite catch it. You say you're sorry for *her*? And you want to bring her peace, to restore to her the precious thing she lost? All right, Vince. Tell me where this precious thing is, so I can give it to her. No? Oh, I understand. You want to *show* it to me."

He opened his eyes, gazed at the ceiling, and spun around slowly, three times. Then he stretched out his arms and clapped his hands together, making a pointer of them. Zombielike, he strode forward until he reached the small bookcase stocked with back issues of *Modern Psychic*. He brought his hands down jerkily to point at the space between the bookcase and the wall. Dropping his arms to his sides, he came out of the trance and wiped his forehead, exhausted.

"There," he said.

Brock picked it up with a handkerchief. It was a gold bracelet studded with rubies. The reporter scurried over to ask Harvey to explain this amazing demonstration of psychic ability.

"I *can't* explain it," Harvey said, gazing modestly into the camera. "It's a power beyond all of us. But the spirits have been generous to me, and I'm eager to share my gifts. Call Budget Psychics, 555-0101, and ask for Harvey. I also do private consulting work and assist at weddings, funerals, bar mitzvahs. And I hope soon to reopen my little tearoom, located at—"

"That's enough," Brock cut in. "Miss Johnson, I need that film. It's possible evidence in a homicide. Now, clear the room." He pointed at Harvey. "Not you, though. You stay."

"That's not fair," Harvey said. "That film *has* to go on the air. People must learn—did you say homicide?"

"That's what I said. Your friend was murdered. I'm giving you one last chance to tell the truth about what happened last night, about what you saw and what you did, and then I'm arresting you."

"But I did nothing last night!" Harvey protested. "I saw nothing with the physical eye. Only through the spiritual—"

"Fine. I'll read you your rights." Brock took the rest of us in with a glance. "Clear out."

We waited in the hall, and moments later poor Harvey was led out in handcuffs. Phoebe was in tears again. "Harvey never *did* like Vince," she said, sobbing. "And now he's killed him!"

"Shut up," Bess snapped. "Harvey's no killer."

"That's right." Sean patted Phoebe's shoulder. "Harvey didn't approve of our late friend, but there's no violence in his soul. Bess, let's keep the lines closed down tonight. There's so much turmoil in this place—how can we give clear readings? We should go home out of respect for Harvey and the departed one."

Bess looked tempted, but Delia stepped forward. "Vince would want us to keep going. Think of his regulars. They're in special need—how will they feel if they get a recording? And there may be other special calls, Sean. We *need* to stay open."

He looked at her hopelessly, then nodded.

"*You* can stay," Bess said. "I'm going home to get drunk. Leah, take over the reception desk. Sean's got First Graveyard, and Phoebe's got Second."

Sean shook his head. "I can't. I'm too overcome by grief."

"I'll take both Graveyards," Phoebe said, wiping her eyes. "I want to sit in the big office, to feel close to Vince."

Bess shrugged and left. I'm connecting callers mechanically, jotting notes whenever I can, thinking of Harvey sitting in jail, wondering how his wife will take his arrest, wondering what will happen to their daughter, trying to figure things out.

* * * *

11:35 P.M. Half an hour ago, Delia came into the reception area. "Don't connect me to anyone for a while," she said. "I'm too on edge. God! Maybe it *was* a mistake to stay."

"Bess pretty much said staying was optional," I said. "I'm sure she'll understand if you go home now."

"Maybe soon." She glanced at the red lights near my phone. "Sean has a caller, I see. One of his regulars?"

"Ethan Lawrence," I said, happy to share some harmless gossip. "They've been talking for almost an hour."

"That's nice." She yawned. "When Sean finishes his call, tell him that I want to talk to him."

"Sure." I hesitated. "Delia, I wanted to ask you about Emma—you talked to her the night Vince died. Do you remember what you talked to her about?"

Her eyes narrowed. "I filled out a form about that call."

"Yes, I entered that in the computer. But you said only that you counseled her about relationships. Do you remember more details?"

"The details," she said coldly, "are confidential. We're like priests or psychiatrists, Leah. Information that's useful to share goes on the forms. The rest we keep to ourselves."

"I respect that, but Emma called today, asking about a lost object, and I wondered if there might be some connection—"

"You've got no business speculating about our callers," Delia said sharply. "Stick to answering the damn phones, or I'll tell Bess you're asking about confidential matters."

"I'm sorry." I realized I'd made a communicative blunder. This was no time to try to initiate Professional Trust Sharing. Delia was too upset—we all were. When she left with Sean minutes later, she barely glanced at me. *Note: Add chapter on Special Sensitivity Needs in Times of Workplace Crisis.*

* * * *

"Leah, I think you're onto something." Sam squinted at the base of the birdbath and started to sand it again. "I think you should call Brock."

"But how would he react?" she asked. "I think he'd *over*react and arrest the wrong person, just as he did tonight. How could anyone think Harvey's a murderer? He's so gentle!"

"Gentle people have been known to commit murder. And Harvey *does* have a motive."

"Yes, I handed Brock the motive," Leah said bitterly. "I told him about Bess's talk of downsizing. That talk wouldn't scare Delia or Sean—Bess sees them as stars. Harvey and Phoebe were the ones in danger of getting cut. And Harvey couldn't pay his daughter's hospital bills if he got fired, so if he could save his job by killing a rival—but Harvey wouldn't *do* that."

"Maybe not." Sam stepped back from the birdbath, surveyed it, and smiled. "*That* should hold water. So what do you plan to do?"

"I'm not sure," she said slowly. Water, she thought. What should I be remembering about water?

* * * *

Thursday, March 12

11:45 A.M.: Arrived at the jail. While I was waiting to be searched, Detective Brock came out of the visiting area.

"You here to see Harvey?" he asked. "Research for the book?"

"No, just a visit to cheer him up," I said. "Detective, you *must* be wrong about Harvey. He *can't* be the killer."

Brock shrugged. "If he'd tell us the truth—but he's lying. Spirits didn't guide him to that bracelet. My people searched that office the day after the murder. We've got a photo of that exact spot between the wall and the bookcase. No bracelet. So how did it show up there?"

"Harvey might've planted it," I admitted. "But not because he's a killer. He just wanted to score points as a psychic."

"Maybe. But he knew too much about the night of the murder, and don't tell me he learned it in a trance. He says he senses a feminine presence in the room, and sure enough, the coroner says Vince had sex shortly before he died. Harvey says he senses liquor, and the coroner says Vince's blood-alcohol level was sky-high—not to mention the bourbon bottle in the wastebasket, which Harvey claims he never noticed. Harvey says he never glanced at the wastebasket, but there was a burned-out match there, too. Fits with what he said about the 'flickering flame,' doesn't it? Then there's the empty Windex bottle."

"The Windex bottle? *That* can't be incriminating."

"It can if it indicates someone attempted to clean up evidence. That office was spotless and fresh-smelling. A few fingerprints from Harvey and the day shift psychic, but not one from Vince, even though he spent hours there the night before. There's no janitor, you didn't clean the office—so who did, and what was he hiding?"

"I don't know." I felt defeated.

Brock sighed. "I'll tell you how it looks. The coroner says Vince died around 2:00 A.M. So I figure Harvey got back to the office earlier than he says, maybe found Vince with a woman. That'd make Harvey mad—he's a straitlaced guy. After the woman left, he and Vince got into a fight. Vince was drunk, so Harvey won, and he strangled Vince with the telephone cord. He panicked, strung Vince up in the closet to make it look like suicide, went nuts with the Windex to cover up any trace of what he'd done. Later, when we seemed to buy the suicide bit, he figured he'd fake a trance on TV, become a famous psychic."

"Doesn't *anything* point in another direction?"

He pursed his lips as if trying to decide whether to tell me. "A phone call at 1:40 A.M.—not on the hotline, on the regular office phone. It came from a pay phone a few blocks away. Harvey claims he didn't call, but he could be lying. Or the call could be insignificant. Mrs. Abrams, I like Harvey, too, but things look bad. If you can get him to open up to us, you'll be doing him a favor."

"I'll try," I said, determined, and didn't flinch once as the matron searched me.

Harvey looked pathetic sitting behind the plate glass wall, dressed in an absurd orange jumpsuit, his face drawn. I smiled and picked up a phone.

"Hello, Harvey," I said. "How are you doing?"

"All right." He wiped his brow. "But my wife was here. She was weeping. I never meant to—oh, poor Mary!"

"And today is your fortieth anniversary," I said gently. "That must make everything harder. Have you gotten her a gift?"

He blanched. "A gift? No. That is, we don't have money to spare. She understands. She wouldn't expect—"

"But it would be wonderful to surprise her," I said, "to give her something to brighten all her years of sacrifice. The fortieth anniversary is rubies. Wouldn't it be wonderful to give her a ruby ring—or bracelet?"

He looked down at his hands. "I'm not a thief, Leah."

"Of course not. But with your fortieth anniversary coming, with all your wife has been through—if you were cleaning the office during Second Graveyard, and you saw a ruby bracelet and knew the woman who must've dropped it had no business being there and would probably never dare ask about it, I can see how you'd be tempted."

"She was a slut," he burst out. "One of Vince's many sluts. He preyed on women. He even took advantage of little Phoebe—she told me so. And these sluts! He'd seduce them over the phone when they called for guidance, he'd lure them to the office when he had a Graveyard shift, and they'd carry on disgracefully! *This* slut must be rich. She owned a precious thing, but she cared for it so little that she left it behind! Why should a woman like that have everything, and my poor wife have nothing?"

"But your wife *does* have something," I said. "She has a loving husband, and I'm sure all she cares about is getting him home. Tell me the truth, Harvey. I'll help you tell the police, and we'll get you out of here. Was the woman still there when you got to the office?"

He sighed, and his shoulders drooped. "No. The office was empty. The answering machine was switched on, and the desk was *filthy* and *sticky*, spilled liquor, I'm sure, and in the middle were a Windex bottle and a scented candle from Elaine's desk—your desk, that is. It was burning. Burning! Who'd leave a candle burning in an empty office?"

I nodded. "That must've made you mad."

"It made me *furious*. I knew what had happened. Vince had a slut up there, and he hadn't bothered to clean up. I went to the break room to refill the water pitcher—it was empty, he hadn't had the decency to refill it for me—and found two glasses in the sink. Did I need more proof of what he'd been doing? So when I went back to the office, I looked in the desk drawer, and there was a bottle of Jim Beam, half full. I emptied it and put it in the wastebasket, hoping Bess would find it and at least reprimand Vince. I didn't dare complain about him—he was a part owner—but she doesn't allow drinking on the job, and he *deserved* to be reprimanded."

Remarkable, how caught up Harvey was in the emotions of that night. He now knew Vince had been murdered, but was still offended that he hadn't refilled the water pitcher. "Then you cleaned up the office?"

"Of course. I can't work in a *sty*, the Windex was right there, and I had plenty of time. No one calls during Second Graveyard. So I put the candle back where it belonged, and when I was cleaning under the desk, I saw the bracelet, and, well, I took it. After Vince's body was found, and I thought he'd committed suicide, I decided to put it back and to try—oh, dear." He sighed. "I simply wanted to get my little tearoom back. Is that so terrible?"

"I don't think it's terrible, Harvey," I said. "Detective Brock won't think so, either. Let's go talk to him."

* * * *

1:05 P.M.: I'm at McDonald's, grabbing a quick lunch before heading to Budget Psychics—I want to get there early. The session with Detective Brock went well. I think he believed Harvey, but he hasn't released him. There's too much evidence pointing to him, Brock says. So I'll see if I can't find evidence pointing to someone else. I have a pretty good idea of what happened, but I need proof. No time to take more notes—I have to stop at the library on my way to work.

* * * *

Midnight. I'm alone in the office, working First Graveyard. Bess has pressed me into service as a psychic again. She's shorthanded with both Vince and Harvey gone. The day's gone well, I think. The next few hours will show if I'm right.

I got to Budget Psychics at 2:30 P.M. The day shift psychics were frantically trying to keep up with the unusual volume of calls, so I had no trouble doing what I needed to do. By 3:00, Bess, Delia, Sean, and Phoebe had all arrived, and Bess called everyone into the break room for the staff meeting. She frowned at the scented candle in the middle of the table. "What the hell is *that* doing here?" she demanded.

"It's Elaine's," I said, looking confused. "I noticed it on the reception desk. But I don't know how it got in here."

"Take it away," Bess said, "as soon as the meeting's over. Now, Vince's funeral is at 11:00 tomorrow morning, and I want you all there. There'll probably be press, so—"

"What's that smell?" Phoebe cut in.

Delia sniffed, tentatively. "I don't smell anything."

Bess gave them an exasperated look, then sniffed—only once, expertly. "Bourbon. Damn! Who's been drinking on the job?"

Sean shifted in his chair. "It can't be one of us, Bess. We just got here. It must be a day shift psychic."

"Carol, probably," Bess said, eyebrows quivering. "I've never liked that broad. And I *won't* sit here inhaling that stench. Phoebe, get some air freshener from the supply closet."

Phoebe scurried off, and Bess got back to business. Moments later, she was interrupted by a sharp, terrified scream. We all ran out and saw Phoebe huddled against the wall, shrinking from the open door of the supply closet. She gasped. She pointed. "Look!" she said. "Look!"

Delia stepped forward. "It's just a telephone cord, Phoebe. Did you think it was a snake?"

"But it's *hanging*!" Phoebe cried. "Right where Vince was hanging!"

Bess stepped forward to look. "Damn! Who'd pull a stupid practical joke like this?"

Delia shrugged. "If Carol's been drinking—"

Bess turned on Phoebe. "Or maybe *you* set this up. You were here last night, for both Graveyards, and you probably got high. You *do* get high sometimes when you work Graveyards, don't you?"

"I got a *little* high," Phoebe admitted. "But I didn't do *this*."

"You were probably so high you don't remember what you did," Bess said. "No more Graveyards until you straighten out. Sean, take First Graveyard. Delia, take Second."

Sean shook his head. "No. I can't. I have—I have a date."

"Cancel it," Bess said. "Damn it, Sean, I can't ask Delia to work both Graveyards, and I've got nobody else."

"I'll work First Graveyard," I said quietly. "I'd like to."

They all stared at me, and Bess frowned. "You don't have enough experience. Delia could work First, and you could work Second. Nobody calls during Second anyhow."

"I'd *especially* like to work First." I tried to sound modest but confident. "As I was handling calls yesterday, I began to feel I might *really* be a psychic. I felt I was helping people—feeling things, seeing things. And last night I dreamed about Vince, and he *asked* me to work First Graveyard."

Bess smacked her hand against her forehead. "Lord. Another nutcase. *Just* what I need."

"What if Leah's right, Bess?" Phoebe asked. "What if Vince *does* want her to work First Graveyard? It's the night before his funeral—his spirit may be restless. Maybe he wants to say something before he's buried, and he's chosen Leah—"

"Don't be silly," Delia said. "I'm sure Vince is at peace. And why would he choose Leah? He hardly knew her."

Bess held up a hand. "Everybody shut up. Leah wants First Graveyard. She's got it. Maybe she'll do fine—nutcases sometimes make the best psychics. Delia, you've got Second, and I don't want to hear another word about it."

That ended that. After Bess left around 10:00, I doubled as both receptionist and psychic, so I took the call from Ethan Lawrence when he
called Sean from California and once again talked to him for over an
hour. Minutes after that call ended, Mr. Lawrence called yet again, asking for Delia, and spoke to her for fifteen minutes. By then Prime Shift
was almost over, and Phoebe wandered into the reception area.

"You gonna work First Graveyard from here?" she asked.

"No, Vince told me to use his office. And he said he'd speak to me
around 2:00—he said that's when he died."

"Wow." Phoebe's eyes widened. "Say hi for me, okay? And say—
well, no hard feelings, rest in peace, like that."

"I'll tell him." I looked up as Sean and Delia came out of their offices. "Goodnight. If I make contact with Vince, is there anything you'd
like me to say?"

Sean shook his head. "Don't play games with this, Leah. If our departed friend is at peace, you shouldn't disturb him. And if he *isn't*—
well, leave him alone."

"He doesn't want me to leave him alone," I said. "That's why he
came to me in my dream. He told me to bring him this." I took a small
bottle of Jim Beam from my purse.

Delia snatched it. "So you were the one playing pranks today. What
did you do—splash this around the break room?"

"Of course not. As you can see, the seal on the bottle isn't broken.
Vince told me not to open it until 2:00 this morning." I snatched the
bottle back, picked up the scented candle from the desk, and walked to
Vince's office.

I heard them all leave. It's now 12:57—a good time for me to jot
down my theories about the murder. As I see it, on the night he died,
Vince—oh, there's the phone.

* * * *

I picked up the receiver. "Budget Psychics," I said cheerily. "What's
your name? What's your sign? How may I help?"

"Delia?" A woman's voice, slurred and heavy. "Is this Delia?"

She's drunk, I thought. "No, this is Leah. Who's this?"

"Emma." I heard ice cubes clinking in a glass. "I gotta talk to someone who can get me in touch with Vince."

It was the worst ethical dilemma yet. "Maybe I can help. You and
Vince were close?"

"Real close." Emma sobbed. "A few nights ago, right about this
time, we were real, *real* close."

"I sense that," I said, despising myself. "I sense the two of you in a small room. I feel close to that room."

"Hell, you're *in* that room," Emma said. "You're good, Leah. What else do you sense?"

"I sense love," I said, faltering. "And passion. And liquor. But do I—yes, I sense a bit of distrust."

"You're right," Emma said, sobbing brokenly. "I'd told him stuff about my husband's business. I'd said my husband was planning to buy this company, and that morning my husband was upset because someone had bought up all this stock and now the deal would cost more. And I wondered if Vince had used what I'd told him and bought the stock himself. So I called and asked to speak to a woman, and Delia said not to worry and Vince truly loved me, and I should see him that night and show my trust. So when my husband fell asleep, I called Vince on the hotline."

"I hear you calling," I said, wincing at my shamelessness. "I hear him telling you to come to him. And you came. I see you—you look so lovely, and you're wearing something beautiful. It glitters, it's red—is it a ring?"

"No, but you're close. Damn, Leah. You're good. It's a ruby bracelet my husband gave me, and it cost a ton. And I'm upset because—well, Vince and I had a great time, we made love and got *so* drunk. But the phone rang—not the hotline, the regular phone—and Vince answered it, and I was so plastered I couldn't stop laughing, but he got serious all of a sudden and told me to leave the room. When I came back, he said I had to go away, someone was coming. So I left, but I hurried so much I lost my bracelet, and I didn't realize it until the next day. And now I've *got* to find it. My husband's suspicious—he's been going over our phone bills and reading newspaper stories about Vince's death, and he's asking questions, and what if he asks about the bracelet? I'll have no Vince, no husband, nothing. Can you tell me where the bracelet is? Please?"

I made my voice ominous. "I see it. It's in a little box, in a big building, guarded by people in uniform. Is it a bank? No, it's—I'm sorry, Emma. It's in a police station."

Emma gasped. "Oh, God. I was afraid of that. The police found it, didn't they, when they arrested that little bald psychic? Did he kill Vince? Because of me?"

"No." I tried to sound entranced. "But the police think the little bald man killed him, and they plan to use the bracelet as evidence. Then your husband will know everything. Stop them, Emma. Save yourself, and save the little bald man. Tell the police everything. Then they'll know the bracelet had nothing to do with the murder, and they'll give it back to you."

"Will they really? They'll give it to me?"

"I'm sure they will." Of course they will, I thought—after they've used it to convict Vince's killer, and after your husband knows all about your affair. "Call the police and talk to—is it Bock? Rock? No—it's Brock. You must call Brock tonight."

"I can't. I'm too afraid. Can you call him, Leah? Have him call me—Emma Whitley, 555-9392."

"I will," I said, jotting down the number. "I'll call Brock, and he'll call you, and soon you'll feel better."

I was about to dial Brock's number when I felt—genuinely this time—a cold presence. I turned and saw Delia standing in the doorway.

"My God," she said. "What are you doing? Giving a policeman a client's name, getting her implicated in a murder? Do you know what a breach of ethics this is?" She strode to the desk. "Give me that name and number. I'll rip it up and take over the shift. You can go home and pray I don't tell Bess."

I clung to the paper. "I'm calling Detective Brock, and I am not going home. Emma's testimony can help clear Harvey—and I have to be here when Vince comes."

I lit the candle, ripped open the Jim Beam, and spilled some on the desk. "Come, wronged spirit," I intoned, closing my eyes, swaying in what I hoped was a mystical manner. "Come over water, come to the fire. It is cold in the land of the dead—come warm yourself by this flame."

"For heaven's sake," Delia said, voice heavy with contempt. "Stop that nonsense."

Then there was another voice, and this one wasn't contemptuous. It was scared. "Stop it, Leah!" I opened my eyes and saw Sean standing in the hall.

"I'll handle this, Sean," Delia said sharply. "Go away."

He looked too scared to leave. He still stood in the hall, not crossing the threshold. "No, Leah," he said. "It's dangerous. You don't know how angry spirits get."

"Vince isn't angry at *us*." I glanced at my watch. Only 1:13. Sam was coming at 1:30 as a witness and, if necessary, as my protector. How long could I stall? I'd have to do some guessing to fill up the time. I smiled. "Vince is angry at the murderer, not at us. Let's share happy news. Vince," I called, gazing upwards, "come enjoy this warm flame, this fragrant liquor. Come rejoice with us. Did you know Sean and Delia are going to California? They'll work with Ethan Lawrence and start a psychic network and become rich. It's the sort of thing *you* always wanted to do, and now your friends will have the chance. Aren't you happy for them, Vince?"

"Don't tell him that!" Sean said, his voice hoarse with fear. "And stop saying his name! You'll call him back!"

Delia wheeled around to face him. "Be a man, Sean. You don't really swallow that garbage, do you?"

He stared at her. "You never called it garbage before."

I swayed in my chair, wishing Sam would come. "Betrayal," I chanted. "She communicates, only to manipulate. She tells Harvey of Vince's affair with Phoebe, only to stir up enmity. She talks to Emma and learns Vince is sleeping with callers, just as he slept with students when he was a professor. He's milking them for financial information. She tells Sean. She wants Sean to get mad at Vince, to strike Vince, to lose his job. She wants Sean to be forced to accept Ethan Lawrence's offer, to take her away to sunny, smoggy skies. Sean is happy at Budget Psychics, but she cares nothing for Sean's happiness. She cares only for wealth. And she knows Sean has a temper."

Sean turned wildly on Delia. "She's right. She knows I told you about how I messed up in California, when I punched Martin Scorsese for giggling during a séance. You wanted me to mess up here, didn't you? That's why you told me about that call from Emma. That's why you dragged me to that pay phone and called Vince and held the receiver up so I could hear Emma laughing. You made me see what a slimeball he was, and you goaded me to confront him. You *made* me do it!"

She sank into the chair next to my desk and glared at him, furious but already bored. "I didn't make you do anything. I gave you information and hoped you'd use it sensibly. You were supposed to come here and tell Vince you quit. You were supposed to punch him, to make sure you'd never get your job back and would *have* to go to California. You weren't supposed to kill him. I never thought you'd overreact that much. You big baby!"

He roared and leapt. Suddenly, he'd knocked her chair over backwards, he was on top of her, his hands were around her throat.

I jumped to my feet. "Vince!" I cried. "Vince! Vince!"

That did it. Sean let go of Delia's throat and looked around, as if only now realizing that he was in the office, that he'd unwittingly crossed the threshold. Horrified, he looked in all directions, spotted the pitcher on my desk, and seized it.

"Away, angry spirit!" he shouted, and gave the pitcher a mighty heave. But the pitcher was empty.

He sank to his knees. "Oh, God! No water!"

"That's right," I said ruthlessly. "No water, no protection, and it's almost 2:00. I told him about your new job—he's jealous. He'll take his revenge unless you appease him with the truth. Did you kill him?"

"Yes." Sean hid his face in his hands. "I didn't mean to, but he was so drunk—he laughed at me, at everything I believe in. I hit him, and he fell back in his chair, and the telephone, and the cord—I strangled him. I took the life from him, and I haven't had a moment's peace since."

"You'll have more peace now that you've told the truth." I turned to Delia. "You're a witness. It's one thing to pretend you don't realize someone must've committed murder so you can continue to exploit him. It's something else to hear a confession and lie about it. You could go to prison for that."

She glanced at him, eyes burning with what looked like pure hatred. "I wouldn't bother to lie about it. He's no good to me now. He's a baby."

He was, at any rate, crying—crying and lying on the floor in a little ball, hugging himself with terror. I shook my head sadly, picked up the phone, and called 911.

* * * *

Friday, April 20

12:35 A.M.: My last entry about Budget Psychics. My six weeks there are over, Elaine comes back from maternity leave on Monday, and I'm free. Sam is in the kitchen warming the chili and opening the wine, and I can finally gather my thoughts.

That Thursday night was the hardest. I had to watch Sean get arrested—I despised what he'd done but felt he'd been driven to it—but also saw Harvey reunited with his wife, who probably hadn't looked that radiant even on her wedding day.

At 5:30 A.M., Sam, Detective Brock, and I sat down for a cup of coffee. "You did it, Mrs. Abrams," Detective Brock said. "You figured it all out and solved my case. *How* did you do it?"

"It was a lot of things," I said. "The calls from Emma, the calls from California, and something Sam said about artists leaving their signatures on their works, whether they mean to or not—I figured murderers leave signatures on their works, too. But mostly it was the water."

"The water?" he said. "What water?"

"The water on the floor of the supply closet. I remembered noticing it just before I looked up and saw Vince's body hanging. Finally, I made the connection." I glanced at Sam, embarrassed. "It was when my Great-Aunt Naomi died when I was a little girl. She was laid out in her bedroom, and when we went to see her, there was this puddle of water near the door. My grandparents were scandalized. They were immigrants, too, but they tried to be modern, and they thought Great-Uncle Jacob was being very old world, very retro. Very superstitious."

Brock squinted. "Great-Uncle Jacob put the water there?"

"Yes. It used to be a custom among some Jews, and other peoples have similar customs. When someone dies, you pour water on the floor. It's a symbol of mourning, and it's also supposed to form a barrier, to keep the spirit of the dead person from coming back to take revenge against anyone who's wronged him or her. It's primitive—most modern Jews have never heard of it. We don't believe in avenging spirits. But Sean had studied with a Hasidic rabbi, and when Harvey said the pitcher in the office was empty, I wondered. And there were other things."

Brock nodded. "Such as?"

"Such as the candle left burning, and the fact that after Vince died, Sean never referred to him by name—it was always 'our deceased friend' or 'the departed one.' I studied anthropology in college, and I remembered certain aborigine and Native American customs, and I knew Sean had spent time living in both cultures. I checked it out in the library, and it all came back. It's a custom to light fires after someone dies. Spirits warm themselves by the fire instead of coming after people who'd wronged them. And using a dead person's name can call the spirit back. So I guessed a superstitious person had killed Vince, and I guessed it was Sean, and this afternoon I did several things that might unsettle him."

"Like spraying Jim Beam in the break room," Sam supplied. "And putting the candle on the table and hanging the telephone cord in the closet. That was all designed to get to Sean."

"Or to whoever the murderer might be," I said. "I thought it was Sean, but I wasn't certain. Bess is a cynic, so I didn't suspect her, but Phoebe's a believer, and I wasn't sure about Delia. But I thought I could flush out the killer by faking those signs and making up a story about Vince appearing in a dream, saying he'd come back the night before he was buried. In some cultures, spirits are thought to be especially potent before the body's laid to rest. I guessed Sean left that Windex bottle on the desk, hoping Harvey would return it to the supply closet and discover Vince's body. It must've driven Sean crazy to come to work the next day and realize the body was still hanging in the closet. I'm surprised he could function."

"Maybe he's tougher than you think," Brock said. "Tough enough to be torn between fears of an avenging spirit and fears of getting arrested for murder. And Delia—she's plenty tough. What am I supposed to do with *her*?"

"Probably not much," I said. "She inspired a murder, but it's probably more than she meant to inspire. She wanted Sean to get fired and accept Ethan Lawrence's offer. Afterwards, she probably knew Sean must've murdered Vince, but you'd have a hard time proving that. You may have to just let her go."

He did. I told Bess the truth, though, and she fired Delia—she'd destroyed Bess's top two psychics, and Bess wasn't about to let her get away with that. So there was no cushy California job for Delia, not even a Budget Psychics job as consolation. But it's too soon to count Delia out. She's opened a consulting firm offering Stress Management and Leadership Development workshops. I have a sick feeling she'll do fine.

Budget Psychics is doing fine, too. Bess hired a whole new crew of Prime Shift psychics, and business is better than ever, even without Phoebe. Phoebe left for California three weeks ago. After Sean's arrest, she called Ethan Lawrence several times to console him about the loss of his favorite psychic, and they got close. So now Phoebe's going to star in the infomercials for Ethan's new psychic network. I wish her well.

As for Harvey, he hardly needs my good wishes. Once the film of his fake trance wasn't considered evidence anymore, the local television station ran it endlessly. I thought it would end his career—I thought the film would make it obvious that he's a fake, that he was pretending to find evidence in a suicide everybody now knew to be a murder. But it didn't work that way. That film made him famous. Budget Psychics was flooded with calls from people who wanted to tell everything to Harvey, trust everything to Harvey. Within days, he left Budget Psychics and reopened his little tearoom. He's doing fine. Last night he called to say he'd bought his wife a ruby tiara as a belated fortieth anniversary present.

Sam's calling me—the chili must be ready. Note: Tentative title for new book—*A Hermeneutics of Media Communications: Transgressive Credibility and Transcendent Celebrity.*

When I wrote "Death on a Budget," I don't think I intended to establish a pattern all the stories in the series would follow. But that's what I ended up doing. The title always begins with "Death." Each story has to land Leah in some implausible workplace—a party-planning outfit so short staffed it makes even temporary secretaries play in the band, the headquarters of a diet program founded by a woman who claims she learned the secrets to weight loss from Tibetan monks. In each story, the solution to the mystery has to be tied to Leah's current theories about workplace communications and also to Sam's latest lawn ornament project. And in each story, Leah has to figure out who the murderer is by applying some insight she's gained from her knowledge of Judaism—from her reflections on a Jewish holiday her family's observing, from her familiarity with a Jewish custom, or from her insight into Jewish teachings about the evils of gossip or some other topic. It can be tough to make all these elements come together in a coherent whodunit, but I enjoy the challenge.

Often, the Leah stories also contain a hint of social satire—nothing too heavy, but a few gentle pokes at some current foolishness. When I wrote "Death on a Budget," psychic hotlines were extremely popular—their commercials seemed to dominate late-night television. Since I tend to be skeptical about such things, I thought it would be fun to set a mystery at a psychic hotline staffed by sincere but deluded enthusiasts and also by flat-out frauds. I especially liked the idea of having a body go undiscovered for hours in a building full of people who supposedly have special powers to sense what can't be seen.

DEATH IN REHAB

(2011)

"I'm not so sure about this job," he said. "It sounds dangerous. You'll be surrounded by addicts."

"By addicts committed to overcoming their dependencies." She started to pour herself a third cup of coffee, paused, and decided she didn't need it. "That's not dangerous. That's inspirational."

"Maybe. But they're still addicts, and addicts do dangerous things. Did you read the local news this morning?" He found the right page and pointed to a headline. "'Gambling Addict Embezzles Millions, Disappears'—probably in Vegas by now, the paper says. Or this story— 'Small-Time Drug Dealer Killed Execution Style'—probably because he stole from his bosses, the paper says. Or this one—'Shooter Flies into Drunken Rage, Wounds Two'—the police haven't caught that one, either."

She sighed. "In the first place, I don't think people who fly into drunken rages are necessarily alcoholics, and I'm sure not all alcoholics fly into drunken rages. In the second place, there won't be any alcoholics at the center—no drug addicts, either, much less any drug dealers. It's not that sort of rehab center. The temporary agency said no one there has substance abuse problems."

"Really? What sorts of addictions *do* these people have?"

"The agency didn't say." She carried her dishes to the sink. "I probably won't have much contact with clients anyway—I'll be tucked away in an office, typing and filing. I'll be perfectly safe, Sam. So, you're meeting with the Hartwells today? What sort of lawn ornament do they want?"

"They're still arguing. She wants a bird bath; he wants a family crest. So I'll have to use my negotiating skills, steer them toward a compromise." He put the newspaper down. "Not exactly what I had in mind when I went to art school, Leah."

"I know." She walked back to the table and put a hand on his shoulder. "And I'm sorry no one bought any of your sculptures at the gallery show last week. Well, next time for sure. Want me to take homework duty tonight, so you can focus on your design?"

"That'd be nice. Last night, Sarah spent half an hour kvetching about her religious school assignment; I tried to explain it but didn't have much luck. And it *does* seem unreasonable to expect kids to do religious school homework every night."

"It's the counting of the *omer*," she said, looking through her purse. "Every night is part of the point. Now, I've got my keys, I've got my pencil—what am I forgetting?"

"Your notebook." He handed it to her. "As usual."

* * * *

Tuesday, April 26

1:05 P.M.: Lunchtime—my first chance to take notes. It's been a surprising morning. Some of my observations are bound to provide useful data for the book.

When I arrived, I was struck by how beautiful this place is. It looks like a resort, not a rehab center: An immense lobby with a marble floor, a courtyard with a sparkling fountain, broad corridors, walls lined with cheerful watercolors, a stunning variety of vibrant flowering plants everywhere. The director ushered me into his elegantly furnished office and insisted I call him Fred.

"We all use first names here," he said. "Guests, staff, visitors, everybody. It helps guests feel special. And it reinforces the idea that everything that goes on at the center is confidential, that the life guests live here is separate from the lives they live outside."

What happens in rehab stays in rehab, I thought, noting that he referred to the people who come here for treatment as "guests," not "patients" or "clients." "The name of the center reinforces that idea, too," I said.

He beamed. "Exactly. The Cocoon Center—a safe place for people to change and grow, to transform themselves into something beautiful. Our six-step program makes that possible."

"A six-step program? Don't most rehab centers have twelve-step programs?"

"We did some editing." He shrugged. "Our guests like fast results. We dropped the Higher Power stuff; some guests find that a stretch. And listing people one has harmed, making amends—that damages self-esteem. Our program is more positive and forward-looking." He handed me a slim pamphlet and a thick folder. "The pamphlet explains how it works. And skim through those files on the guests in your therapy groups."

"My therapy groups?" I said, confused. "Secretaries participate in therapy groups?"

"Oh, you're not here as a temporary secretary. Didn't the agency explain? You're here as a temporary therapist. You have a master's in communication, right?"

A Ph.D., actually—but I've learned to leave that off my resume, along with any references to my years as a professor. Most places don't like hiring secretaries who seem overqualified. "But I don't have much background in psychology," I said. "And I've never worked as a therapist."

"You'll do fine. It's all about helping people open up. Your background's perfect." His face grew somber. "And it's an emergency situation. I had to fire a therapist yesterday. I caught him smuggling contraband to a guest."

"Drugs?" I said, apprehension growing. "Alcohol?"

"Oh, no. Our guests have no interest in drugs. And they're all welcome to enjoy cocktails in the lobby at five and wine with dinner, so alcohol isn't an issue. Still, there *are* things some guests shouldn't have. This particular guest is addicted to video games and had been on the wagon for two weeks—until his therapist slipped him a portable play station. It's a heartbreaking setback."

I hid a smile. An addiction to video games sounded harmless enough. But if it grew into an obsession that interfered with work or family—yes, I supposed it might require treatment. "It must be upsetting to have one of your own staff members break one of your rules."

"It's a terrible betrayal of trust," Fred agreed. "And trust is central to our work. We trust our guests, too. Unlike most centers, we don't search guests' luggage when they arrive: We just have a friendly chat about what they should and shouldn't have, and they voluntarily surrender anything that seems problematic. But this incident left me no choice. Last night, for the first time in the center's history, I conducted a search of guests' rooms. Not an intrusive one—just a quick look to see if anyone else had bribed that therapist to smuggle things in. I did have to confiscate some items; I'm sure some guests are upset. Give them a chance to talk about that during your session this morning."

"This morning?" I looked at the folder in dismay. "I'm not sure I can be ready."

He glanced at his watch. "You have nearly an hour. All the guests in your morning group have been at the center less than a week—one is arriving today, in fact. After one week, guests are reassigned to their permanent groups; we like to keep people with similar addictions together. But this morning you'll have a variety."

"And this afternoon?" I asked, afraid I knew what the answer would be.

"You'll have two other groups. I'll put those files together for you." He stood and smiled. "I have complete confidence in you, Leah. I'll come back at ten and show you to the Caterpillar Room."

Seizing the folder, I read frantically, trying to absorb as much information as I could. Three minutes before ten, Fred returned to hurry me to a room that felt both spacious and cozy: walls painted a soothing light green, a dark green couch with two bright red throw pillows, pastel print armchairs, a mellow oak coffee table and matching end tables. At the back of the room I spotted a refrigerator, a microwave, and a bookcase stocked with paperbacks. All the comforts of home, I thought—if you come from a very nice home.

"This room is reserved for our first-week guests," Fred told me. "A place for both working and relaxing while they adjust to the center's routine. Your group members will be returning from their Independent Meditation Hour soon. As for our newest guest, he's still checking in— I'll bring him here in ten minutes or so. Enjoy your first session."

Before I could ask a single question, he was gone. I'm not qualified, I thought. I'll say something wrong, and someone will go into hysterics or commit suicide.

I had no time to indulge in such fears. A slightly chubby, slowly balding man in his early forties started to walk into the room, saw me, and froze, eyes wide with confusion.

No way to avoid it—I had to try to act professional. "Hello," I said, holding out my hand. "I'm Leah."

His eyes brightened, and he gave me a shy, warm smile. "What's a Hebrew name meaning 'weary?'" he said.

So this must be Felix. I remembered the description from his file: "*Jeopardy* addict—obsessed with trivia, speaks only in the form of questions." He'd been a *Jeopardy* grand champion about a decade ago, winning enough to start a highly profitable online investment company that he ran from his mother's basement. Quite a success story—except that his glory days had left him incapable of interacting with others in normal ways. "It's nice to meet you, Felix," I said. "Would you like to have a seat?"

But he couldn't respond to questions, only to statements that let him reply with a question of his own. He smiled silently, walked to the refrigerator, took out a bright blue thermos labeled "Felix," and chose a chair near the back of the room.

The other group members arrived together: a honey-haired woman of twenty or so, striking in a white pencil skirt and a silky red top; a lean, muscular man of about fifty, wearing sweat pants and a sleeveless orange tank top; and a gaunt woman in her thirties, dressed in a shapeless black skirt and a gray sweater worn thin at the elbows. They all took thermoses from the refrigerator and found seats. The gaunt woman immediately reached into the oversized purse slung over her shoulder, pulled out an embroidery hoop, and hunched over it, stitching furiously. The others stared at me.

I sat down and cleared my throat. "I'm delighted to be here," I said, hoping I didn't sound as insincere as I felt. "I'm Leah, your new group leader—your temporary new group leader. I understand you had a rather upsetting experience yesterday—"

"'Rather upsetting,' hell," the lean, muscular man cut in. "It was damn upsetting. Fred had no right to search our rooms. The brochure guaranteed our privacy would be strictly respected. I wouldn't have signed up here otherwise."

"Yes, that's the only reason I came to the center," the stylish young woman said, "because it promised our privacy would be guarded stringently."

Quickly, I matched the guests with their profiles. The lean, muscular man was Brian—wealthy entrepreneur, overweight since childhood, lost over eighty pounds in just six months, now so obsessed with diet and exercise that his doctor feared he'd endanger his health if his body fat percentage sank any lower. And the young woman had to be Courtney, a chronic plagiarist on final probation with her college, facing expulsion unless rehab made her change her ways.

"Damn it, Courtney," Brian said, "don't just repeat what I said. You do stuff like that all the time. Don't you have any ideas of your own?"

"I *didn't* simply reiterate your statement," Courtney protested. "I used different words, in a different order. And I have plenty of thoughts that originate with me."

"Is that so?" Brian said. "Then I guess it's a coincidence that during yesterday's session, the so-called reflections you shared matched up almost word for word with what Martha had written in her Recovery Journal. I bet you'd gone into her room the night before, snuck a look at her journal—"

"*Sneaked* a look," the gaunt woman said. "No matter what anyone thinks, 'sneak' is *not* an irregular verb—never has been, never will be. Get used to it."

So this must be Martha, the compulsive proofreader. I'd try to draw her into the discussion in a more constructive way. "Martha, how did *you* feel about the search?"

She looked up from her embroidery—a sampler, featuring cross-stitched words and an eagle soaring past a beautiful mountain. "I resented it," she said. "Fred confiscated my *Fowler's English Usage*."

"I can see why," Brian said. "You shouldn't dwell on that stuff so much."

"I don't 'dwell' on it," she shot back. "I just like to browse through it for an hour or so before bedtime. It helps me relax."

I tried to remember more details from her file. "As I recall, you used to be a copyeditor—is that right?"

Savagely, she thrust her needle through the taut circle of linen. "I'm *still* a copyeditor," she said, "and a tutor. I do freelance work now."

"She used to work for a publisher," Brian put in, "but she was fired last year. She got on her co-workers' nerves by correcting their grammar at staff meetings. I understand how they felt. It's not much fun when someone keeps pointing out your mistakes."

"Yes, their reaction is comprehensible," Courtney said. "Nobody enjoys having their grammar corrected."

Martha glared at her. "Nobody enjoys having *his or her* grammar corrected. 'Nobody' is singular. Good God! Don't you know *anything*? And for your information, some people *do* enjoy being corrected. Some people are eager to learn, to improve themselves." She let her needle rest a moment and fingered her bracelet—a clumsy, heavy-looking circlet composed of large red beads.

So far, the session was not going well. Maybe I should ask Courtney a question, to try to force her into saying something that was truly her own. "How are you enjoying your first week at the center, Courtney? Do you feel you're making progress?"

She looked around uncertainly, then shrugged. "It's all right. I mean, the massages are nice, the yoga's okay, and I like the hot tub. As for progress—who cares? I'm only here because my parents talked the dean into giving me another chance."

"Misplaced limiting modifier," Martha muttered, but nobody paid much attention.

"Courtney plagiarized eight times," Brian said helpfully.

Courtney smiled—a quick, secretive smile. "I got *caught* eight times. So the dean said he wouldn't let me back unless I went to rehab. Or Daddy could've given the college another building, I guess. But rehab's cheaper."

"Not much cheaper," Brian said. "They really fleece you at this place."

"Unstated antecedent," Martha said, and went back to stitching.

Courtney had gotten started now, and she wasn't stopping. "I don't see why my parents won't just let me drop out. I mean, college is so *stupid*. You've gotta spend *hours* writing all these dumb *essays*. My parents just want me to go so I can get the right kind of job for a few years and then marry the right kind of man and go to the right kind of parties. But I don't want that. I mean, ever since I was a kid, my mother's been dragging me to garden shows, and horse shows, and charity luncheons, and it's all so *boring*. I don't wanna waste my whole *life* doing that stuff."

"What *do* you want to do, Courtney?" I asked.

She sat forward. "I wanna be a personal assistant. I wanna go to Hollywood or New York, meet somebody famous, and, like, assist her. I could help her shop for shoes and purses, and drive her home from parties when she gets drunk, and bail her out, and stuff. I'd be *perfect* for that. I mean, I'm really pretty and really smart, and I've got great taste and a great personality. I don't see what else anyone could want."

"What is an interesting vocabulary?" Felix asked. He mumbled it; I don't think Courtney heard.

"Well, lotsa luck, kid," Brian said. "Your parents won't give you one penny for a hare-brained scheme like that. And you don't have money of your own, right?"

"I will," Courtney said, "as soon as I turn twenty-five and come into my trust. But that's so *old*—who'd want a personal assistant who's practically middle-aged? And who'd care if an assistant can write a dumb *essay*?"

The teacher in me couldn't let that go unchallenged. "College can be valuable in ways you haven't considered," I said. "Even if you don't think the skills and knowledge you're acquiring are relevant to your career choice, you're encountering ideas that can deepen your understanding of the world. And if you do your work honestly and independently, you'll develop work habits and discipline that can help you succeed in any field you enter."

She looked at me sourly. "Work habits and discipline. Oh, wow. *Now* you've got me excited."

Brian looked ready to hurl back an insult, but the door opened, and Fred walked in, accompanied by a tall, fit, thirtyish man with a mass of curly blond hair, deep blue eyes, and a half-shy, half-flirtatious grin. I think we all gasped at once.

"Hello, everybody," Fred said. "This is Roland. He arrived today, and he's joining your group. I have to get going, so Leah can handle the introductions."

I stumbled through them. Fred should have warned me, I thought. Both of my daughters have crushes on Roland. He'd first won fame as a stand-up comedian, a favorite on late-night talk shows. My daughters fell in love with him when he landed a role on a situation comedy, playing the easy-going coach of a hapless girls' soccer team. And now he was set to star in his first movie, a romantic comedy pairing him with one of the most famous young actresses in Hollywood.

But during the last few years, most of his publicity had come from his off-screen antics—rowdy behavior at restaurants, shouting matches with directors, a reputation for missing rehearsals, bounced checks, disputes with the IRS, arrests for reckless driving. I wondered which of those offenses had brought him here.

"It's great to meet all of you," he said when I'd finished the introductions. He grinned—an amazing grin, one that seemed to prove, all by itself, that he was smart, funny, friendly, thoroughly nice. "I'd like to say I'm glad to be here, but I bet you wouldn't believe me."

It wasn't funny, but we all laughed. Even Martha looked starry-eyed. "Why *are* you here, Mr.—but no." She remembered the first-names-only rule just in time. "Why are you here, Roland?"

He smiled at her, and her jaw went slack. How many years had it been since any man had smiled at Martha that way? "Little matter of a disagreement with a judge, Martha," he said. "I'd been doing maybe seventy—who knew it was a school zone?—and this fat, greasy cop wouldn't listen to reason. Then the court date slipped my mind. I've got lots of appointments—it's hard to keep track of them all."

"It must be difficult to remember everything," Courtney said eagerly, "when you have such a busy schedule."

He rewarded her with a smile. Probably, celebrities don't mind when someone echoes what they say; probably, they're used to it. "Damn straight," he said. "But the judge started spouting all this garbage about contempt. So my attorney and my shrink and some other folks got involved, and the judge agreed to suspend the sentence if I went into rehab. Not some fancy celebrity rehab center, she said—a real rehab center, far away from Hollywood. So my agent checked into it and came up with this place." He looked around the room and shrugged. "Not too bad."

"The judge must've figured you have an addiction, right?" Brian said. "To what?"

Roland sighed; his shoulders slumped; his grin drooped. "I'm addicted to failure, Brian. I have a crippling fear of success. Every time my career seems ready to take off—like with the movie I'm doing—I get scared, and I screw up somehow, just to derail things. I can't stand the thought of being too rich and famous, I guess. My shrink says deep down, I'm terrified that it'd turn me into a phony. But I have to get a handle on this fear. I'm determined to do it; with your help, I *can* do it."

He smiled again—a brave, humble smile, aimed at all of us. For someone with a crippling fear of success, I thought, he's done pretty well—a popular comedian, a television star. But I'm no psychiatrist. If that's the official diagnosis, fine. "We're delighted to have you join us, Roland," I said. "Do you have questions about the center—about its philosophy, for example, or its rules?"

He shrugged again. "Fred gave me a brochure. I think I pretty much got everything down." He looked around the room again. "What's with the thermoses?"

"They're one of the homey touches here," Brian said, sounding honored by the privilege of informing a celebrity. "See, the kitchen staff fills the thermoses by 9:00 in the morning and puts them in the refrigerator, so we'll have something to drink during therapy sessions and free periods. You can have just about whatever you want—just tell the staff. Me, I always have mineral water."

"Tasty," Roland said. "What's in *your* thermos, Martha?"

"Sweet tea," she said, blushing—with pleasure, I thought. "When I was a little girl, we'd visit my aunt in Georgia every summer, and she'd make sweet tea and serve it to us on the front porch. It's a precious memory, because—"

"Yeah, and I bet your aunt's dead now," Brian cut in, perhaps upset because Martha had drawn Roland's attention away from him. "All that sugar! Before you know it, you're obese, you're diabetic, you're dead. I used to have a sweet tooth—I admit it. No more. I quit cold turkey six months ago and haven't had a grain of sugar since. I don't even *want* it any more."

"Well, *I* always ask for diet soda in my thermos," Courtney said, with an arch look at Roland. "No calories."

"Loaded with artificial sweeteners, though," Brian pointed out. "Worst possible thing for you. They throw your whole metabolism off, make you digest food less efficiently. You'll be fat before you're thirty, Courtney."

"I can't imagine *that*." Roland gazed at Courtney with a frank appreciation that made her look ready to swoon. He turned around in his chair. "What about you, Felix? What're you drinking?"

I'd almost forgotten Felix was in the room—he's so quiet that he melds into the furniture. Now, he looked deeply flustered, clearly wanting to respond but not able to manage it. At the risk of feeding his addiction, I decided to help. "The beverage in Felix's thermos," I said.

He sighed with relief. "What is skim milk?" he asked.

Brian guffawed. "Milk. That figures. You gotta make allowances for Felix, Roland—nice enough guy, solid businessman, but sorta odd. And sorta secretive. It took me a long time to get him to admit he's never had a real date with a girl."

"You, by contrast, immediately announced you've been divorced three times," Martha said, stitching viciously. "I suppose that makes you feel superior to Felix."

"Hey, at least I've been married—more than you can say, Martha. And at least I know how to talk to women." Brian's eyes twinkled mischievously. "Felix does have *one* woman in his life, though. Let's see— how should I phrase this?" He thought for a moment, then turned to face Felix. "The category is Millionaires Who Have Never Had Houses or Apartments of Their Own. And the answer is Felix."

Felix hung his head. "Who still lives with Mother?" he said, his voice barely audible.

Clearly, it was time to take control of the session. I asked the guests to get out their Recovery Journals and share their reflections, and that took up the rest of our time. Brian accused Courtney of copying ideas from his journal—her reflections *did* sound remarkably similar to his— but that was the only moment of tension. I sent the guests on their way and hurried to the office to read files for my afternoon groups.

After half an hour, feeling uneasy about the conflicts that surfaced during the morning session, I decided to check on the group members, who had a free period now. Passing through the courtyard, I spotted Brian and Roland locked in conversation; Brian was talking about the profits one of his companies had garnered during the last quarter, probably trying to persuade Roland to invest. Unfortunately, Brian was punctuating his sales talk with push-ups, and I had to tell him to stop—he's not allowed vigorous exercise while he's in rehab.

I found Courtney and Felix in the Caterpillar Room. Courtney was reading a well-worn copy of a Sue Grafton novel, probably borrowed from the room's small library; Felix was trying to look interested in the paint-by-numbers landscape he was completing. Poor man—he's not permitted to read in rehab, for fear he'll add to his store of trivia. I asked about Martha, and Courtney said she'd decided to take a nap before lunch. All that seemed normal enough.

And now I really should have something to eat myself. I've used up most of my lunch hour taking these notes, and I need some nourishment to give me strength to face my afternoon groups.

* * * *

"So I never got a chance to take notes about my other two groups," Leah said. She rinsed the last plate and handed it to Sam. "I didn't get another free minute all day."

"Too bad." Sam dried the plate and placed it in the cupboard. "How did your afternoon groups go? Any problems?"

"Not really. Some people in the Verbal Addictions group were hard to take. I didn't mind the rapper so much, and the rhymer was sweet. But the punster and the insult addict! I enjoyed the Compulsive Hobbyists group, though. I learned a lot about coin collecting. And did you know there are hundreds of Civil War reenactments every year, in over thirty states? Did you know there are American Civil War reenactments in Italy and Australia?"

"I'll store the information away carefully," Sam said, "in case I ever go on *Jeopardy*. This Felix sounds like a pretty sad guy."

"I don't think he is, actually." Leah plunged the skillet into the suds and started scrubbing. "I think in his own weird little world, in his own weird little way, he's happy. His mother pressured him to go into rehab—she loves him dearly, she says, but she's worried about what will happen when she passes away. She's got a point. So, how did the meeting with the Hartwells go?"

"Brilliant," Sam said. "Genius. I did some Internet research and found out 'Hartwell' means 'well of the stags.' So I did a sketch of a well with big bucks standing on either side, just lousy with antlers—it's a bird bath *and* a family crest. Both Mr. and Mrs. loved it. They signed a check big enough to cover our mortgage payments for two months. So if you don't want to go back to this center tomorrow—"

"Of course I do." She stopped washing dishes and turned to look at him. "I made a commitment to Fred, to the people in my groups. Why wouldn't I want to go back?"

"I guess I'm the one who doesn't want you to go back," Sam admitted. "I still worry about your being around all those addicts. Did you listen to the noon news today? It turns out that gambling addict had been embezzling for years but hiding it so cleverly no one caught on to it before. The police followed a trail that seemed to lead to Atlantic City, but it turned into nothing—who knows where that embezzler's holing up? And that small-time drug dealer shot execution style, Arnold Belmont—did you know he was only nineteen? An informant told the police his suppliers killed him for stealing $200,000—but they didn't find the money. As for the person who wounded two people in a drunken rage, the police have no leads. I don't like it, Leah. All this crazy, violent stuff going on, and it feels like you're in the middle of it."

"I'm in the middle of silly squabbles between plagiarists and proofreaders. There's absolutely no connection between that and those scary stories in the news. Well, that's the last of the dishes. Go finish your design. I'll play homework police."

She quizzed Rachel on her multiplication tables, then turned to Sarah. "How are you doing on that history essay?" she asked.

"It's done," Sarah said. "Math's done, too. So all I have left is religious school. I still don't get it, Mom. Why is Mrs. Goldberg making us do this every night?"

"It's part of counting the *omer*. Remember? It's a way of marking the forty-nine days between Passover and Shavuot, between the exodus from Egypt and the giving of the Torah at Sinai. And during those days, it's traditional to study *Pirkei Avot*. Mrs. Goldberg wants you to take a few minutes each night to think about one saying from *Pirkei Avot*. I think it's a wonderful assignment."

"That's because you don't have to do it," Sarah said, pouting.

"Watch your tone, please," Leah said, not too gently. "That's no way to speak to your mother."

"I know. Sorry. Okay, then. *Pirkei Avot*—I keep forgetting what that even means."

"There are several ways of translating it," Leah said. "My favorite is 'Ethics of the Sages.' It's a book of moral teachings that some great rabbis of the past have handed down to us. What saying did Mrs. Goldberg choose for tonight?"

Sighing, Sarah opened her notebook. "It's a saying of Rabbi Ben Azzai: 'Be as quick in carrying out a minor *mitzvah* as in carrying out a major one, and flee wrongdoing; for one *mitzvah* leads to another *mitzvah*, and one wrongdoing leads to another wrongdoing; for the reward for a *mitzvah* is another *mitzvah*, and the reward for a wrongdoing is another wrongdoing.' I don't get it."

"I bet you will," Leah said, "if you think about it. You know what a *mitzvah* is, don't you?"

"Yeah, sure," Sarah said. "It's a commandment."

Rachel twisted around in her chair. "No, it isn't. It's a good deed."

"You're both right," Leah said, "because the commandments teach us to do good deeds. And when we do good deeds, we're honoring the commandments."

"But this saying doesn't make sense," Sarah said. "We should be as quick about doing minor *mitzvot* as about doing major ones? So clearing the table is as important as, like, saving someone's life?"

"Ben Azzai doesn't say they're equally important," Leah said. "I think his point is that doing minor *mitzvot* helps us develop the habit of doing the right thing. Then, when an opportunity to do a major *mitzvah* comes along, we'll be ready. See? 'One *mitzvah* leads to another *mitzvah*.' And 'the reward for a *mitzvah* is another *mitzvah*.'"

Sarah scrunched up her nose. "So the reward for clearing the table is that I get to clear the table again?"

"In a way," Leah said, smiling. "Every time you clear the table, you take a step toward becoming a helpful person who will be ready to help in lots of ways, both big and small. Ben Azzai also says the opposite is true—'one wrongdoing leads to another wrongdoing.' If you get into the habit of doing things that are wrong, even just a little bit wrong, you're more likely to become someone who does lots of wrong things, including things that are very wrong. Does *that* make sense?"

"I guess." Sarah picked up her pen. "I guess I can write a paragraph about that. You think it's okay to use clearing the table as an example?"

"I think it's fine," Leah said, and kissed her on the forehead and went downstairs.

* * * *

Wednesday, April 27

2:47 P.M.: I don't know if I'll be able to take notes or not. I have plenty of time—afternoon groups have been cancelled, and we're all sitting around, waiting for news. But I feel so numb that it's hard to hold onto my pencil. Still, I think I should try to write things down. Somehow, I think that's important.

From the moment I got to the Caterpillar Room, I should have sensed something was wrong. When I arrived five minutes early, Brian was already there, looking flushed, doing crunches.

"Oh, Brian," I said, "you know you're not supposed to do that sort of exercise. You should conserve your calories. Why don't you get your thermos and take a seat?"

"Maybe that's a good idea." He walked slowly to the couch. "I don't feel so great."

He'd forgotten his thermos. I opened the refrigerator door, spotted the purple thermos labeled "Brian," and set it on the end table next to him. "Maybe you worked out too hard and got dehydrated. Have some water."

"In a minute." He sat hunched forward, pressing one of the three bright red throw pillows against his stomach. "I'm not thirsty right now."

Felix scurried in next, managed a slight, silent smile, got his thermos, and sat in the same chair he'd chosen yesterday. A minute later, Martha arrived, found her thermos and a chair, and immediately took out her sampler. I walked over to admire it.

"'Fools hate reproof,'" I said, reading the cross-stitched words, "'but the wise love correction'—that's from Proverbs, isn't it? The translation I know is slightly different."

"I edited it," she said, adding several quick, hard stitches to the eagle's tail feathers. She took a sip from her thermos, frowned, and set the thermos down.

"It's certainly an appropriate verse for a copyeditor," I said, "or a tutor."

She winced. "Yes. I'd planned to give it to someone, but now I suppose I'll keep it." Without setting down her needle, she reached over to touch the bracelet on her left wrist. The oversized red beads were shaped like apples, I noticed. That was clever—ugly, yes, and gaudy, but clever.

Roland strode in next, and the whole room seemed instantly brighter. "Hey, who's always late for rehearsal?" he said. "Ten o'clock on the dot, and here I am. This place is helping me already—I bet I'll be all the way rehabilitated within a week. Let's see if they remembered my thermos." He flung open the refrigerator door, found the yellow thermos labeled with his name, sipped, and smiled. "Orange juice. Just what I requested. Now, if I can get them to add some vodka—but that's probably against the rules."

Why was I laughing? He hadn't said anything even vaguely amusing. But I couldn't help it. "It might be a bit much to expect in the morning. Well, as soon as Courtney gets here, we'll start."

Seven or eight minutes passed. I was about to go look for her when she stalked in, looking peevish. "Sorry. My mom called, and she would *not* shut up."

"I'm sorry, Courtney," I said, "but there's a rule against receiving outside calls at the center."

"Fred waived the rule for me, since I'm under twenty-one. My parents can call me—that's it." She grabbed her thermos and hurled herself into an armchair. "Next time you see Fred, tell him as far as I'm concerned, he can waive his damn waiver."

I decided I didn't need to respond to that. "All right. Today, you're all supposed to work on your personal inventories. Who'd like to start?"

Thank goodness for Roland. Immediately, he launched into an enthusiastic description of his mistakes and shortcomings, mixing sometimes startling confessions with charming little jokes and side comments reminding us that he was basically a great guy. Nobody else contributed much. Felix, of course, said nothing—I'd gotten used to that. Twice, Martha corrected Roland's grammar; beyond that, she too stayed silent. Courtney stared at her clenched hands, not making eye contact with anyone. And Brian—Brian's silence was the most puzzling. Yesterday, he'd chimed in constantly, always ready with a complaint or a criticism or a revelation designed to embarrass someone else. Today, he sat hunched over the pillow, breathing heavily, his face visibly damp with sweat.

Midway through Roland's account of a wild spending spree, I glanced at Brian and saw his shoulders were shaking.

"Excuse me, Roland," I cut in. "Brian, are you all right?"

"I dunno," he said. "My stomach's cramping up something awful, and my heart's racing like crazy. It can't be the crunches—I only did thirty-seven."

"Another misplaced limiting modifier," Martha said. "You mean, 'I did only thirty-seven.'"

"Maybe you should lie down," I said. "Roland, could you help him to his room?"

But Brian didn't make it that far. Even with Roland's strong arms to support him, Brian took only two steps before collapsing to his knees, retching miserably. Martha got a wastebasket to him just in time, and I raced down the hall to the nurse's station.

By the time we got back to the room, Brian was stretched out on the couch, panting rapidly. The nurse crouched next to him. "Did you feel sick when you got up this morning, Brian?" she asked.

He was too wretched to answer. "He seemed fine," Martha volunteered. "I saw him walking through the courtyard during Independent Meditation Hour—he looked perfectly healthy."

"So it started suddenly. Could be food poisoning," the nurse said. "It would help to know what he had for breakfast."

"What is oatmeal?" Felix supplied. He stood at the end of the couch, looking pale.

"I had the same thing, from the same serving dish," Roland said, "and I had four times as much as he did. The only other thing he had was water."

"That pretty much rules out food poisoning," the nurse said. "Let's get him to his room. I'd better call the doctor. Leah, inform Fred."

For reasons I didn't exactly understand, I grabbed Brian's yellow thermos. It felt light. Later, after the doctor arrived, I opened the thermos and saw it was almost empty. I hadn't noticed Brian drink anything during the therapy session, but maybe he'd had some water during Independent Meditation Hour—the thermoses would be filled by then, and guests can go wherever they like to meditate. Could someone get food poisoning from mineral water? It didn't seem likely, but I didn't know enough to rule it out. I went to Brian's room and told the doctor about the thermos.

"I doubt that has anything to do with it," the doctor said, "but I'll take the thermos along and have the water tested, just in case. We'd better get this man to the hospital. His heart rate's completely erratic." He looked down at Brian, who lay on his bed soaked in sweat, seeming oblivious to everything, his whole body shaking. "I checked his file. Losing over eighty pounds in six months—that can put a strain on the heart, just as gaining weight rapidly can. And if he's still been pushing too hard on diet and exercise, that might well bring on this sort of attack."

It was a reasonable explanation, but I felt uneasy. After the ambulance took Brian away, I went to check on the other guests in the group.

I found them all gathered in Martha's room. Martha sat at her desk, staring fixedly at a small antique clock that looked like a family heirloom; Felix stood nearby, holding a large plastic file box labeled "Cooking with Flair," flipping idly through the dozen or so laminated recipe cards it contained, stealing anxious glances at Martha. Both Courtney and Roland stood by the window. He gazed out at the Cocoon Center's lush grounds; she spoke to him softly, her hand resting on his arm. When I said Brian had been taken to the hospital, Roland turned around sharply.

"But he'll be okay, right?" he said. "Even if it's a heart attack, people survive heart attacks all the time. And he's in basically great shape, and they got him to the hospital quickly—they'll know how to take care of him there."

"Yeah, heart attacks often aren't fatal," Courtney agreed. "Plus Brian's receiving prompt medical attention from knowledgeable experts, and his overall fitness level is good. He'll be fine, won't he?"

"I hope so." I glanced at my watch. "It's your lunch hour. You may not feel like eating, but it's probably good to stick to the schedule."

Obediently, they filed out. Not knowing what else to do, I walked back to Brian's room and found Fred locking the door—standard procedure when a guest left the center unexpectedly, he said, to protect personal possessions. In view of what had happened, Fred had decided to suspend all planned activities for the afternoon while we waited for news. So I grabbed a sandwich and came to the staff lounge to take these notes.

4:15—Moments after I wrote the last sentence, Fred came to the lounge to deliver sad news. Brian is dead.

* * * *

"If you feel that strongly about it," Sam said, "call him."

Leah propped her elbows on the table and held her head in her hands. "He'll think I'm an idiot."

"Probably. But if you think there's even a chance it's murder, you should call." Sighing, Leah took the well-worn business card from her wallet and dialed the number. "Lieutenant Brock? It's Leah Abrams. You won't believe this, but I think it's happened again."

Within the hour, Lieutenant Brock sat at their kitchen table, listening to Leah's narration while Sam poured coffee. She gave quick descriptions of the Cocoon Center and of the people she'd met there, a more detailed description of what had happened that morning. When she finished, he stirred his coffee slowly.

"I can see why you're upset," he said. "Watching a guy who seemed strong and healthy get so sick all of a sudden, having him die—I'd be upset, too. And after what you went through those other four times, it's no wonder you expect somebody to get murdered whenever you take a temp job. But I stopped by the hospital on my way over here, and it sure looks like a natural death this time. The doctors agreed on that, and nobody from our department is giving them an argument. The guy was fifty-two, he'd been obese all his life, he lost so much weight so fast, he was still starving himself and overdoing the exercise even though his doctor warned him to slow down—all adds up to a heart attack."

"I know," she said. "But so many things seem so odd. What about the water in his thermos? The doctor said he'd have that tested—did he?"

"Yup. Pure mineral water. No trace of poison of any kind."

"Oh." Leah rubbed her forehead. "Will there be an autopsy?"

"No reason for one," Brock said. "Cause of death seems clear. The guy's only heir—an estranged son from his second marriage—flew in from Chicago to arrange the funeral. He hasn't requested an autopsy."

"But *you* could request one," Leah said. "Couldn't you? Lieutenant, I really think this man was poisoned."

Brock sighed. "Testing for poisons is expensive, Mrs. Abrams, especially since we don't have any idea of which poisons to test for. Let me ask you this. If this guy was poisoned, it pretty much had to be by someone at the Cocoon Center. Now, nobody there will profit from his death—his son's gonna get everything. Can you think of any other reason why anyone at the center would want this guy dead?"

"I can't," Leah said. "He wasn't a nice man—he insulted almost everyone in our group. But none of the insults seemed harsh enough to provide a motive for murder. And I don't know how the poison could have been administered. It wasn't in the oatmeal he had for breakfast, evidently, or in his thermos. Maybe it was in a medication—he probably took vitamins. You could have *those* tested, couldn't you?"

"I could," Brock said, "if I had any justification for it. And we've got a lot of other stuff on our hands right now—trying to find that embezzler and figuring out who killed that small-time drug dealer and tracking down that drunk who shot two people." He paused, drumming his fingers on the table. "Well, hell. You've helped us solve four murders. You've got damn good instincts—you've proven that time and again. I'm gonna request that autopsy, Mrs. Abrams. If the captain gives me a hard time, I'll weather it—and if the autopsy reveals anything interesting, I'll call you. Why don't you see if you can get into this guy's room at the center, check out his medications?"

"I think I can manage that." Her shoulders sagged with relief. "Thank you, Lieutenant."

"No problem." He took a last sip of coffee and stood up. "Say, what's happening with that book of yours, the one about impactful disclosure through nonarticulate signifiers? Is it coming out soon?"

"I didn't find a publisher for it, actually," she said. "An intern at a university press seemed enthusiastic about my proposal. Unfortunately, he couldn't get it past marketing. I'm working on a new book—*A Hermeneutics of Workplace Communications: Contra-Experiential Expectations, Obfuscated Infrastructures, and Exertion-Intensive Behaviors.* I feel sure this one will have wider commercial appeal."

"No doubt about it," Brock said. He winked and left.

* * * *

Thursday, April 28

When I volunteered to pack Brian's things, Fred accepted gratefully. Just as I'd expected, I found several bottles of vitamins. There wasn't much else to pack—only toiletries, sweatpants, tank tops, underwear. As I was rolling up socks, I heard something crinkle. Odd, I thought, and reached into the toe of a thick white sock, and pulled out two crumpled Snickers wrappers.

So even our dieting fanatic cheated sometimes, I thought, smiling sadly—the cheating made Brian seem more human, and that made my task feel more poignant. I started to throw the wrappers away, then paused.

Brian had boasted he'd conquered his sweet tooth. He'd said he hadn't tasted or even craved sugar in months. That, obviously, had been a lie. Sometimes, obviously, he'd sneaked sugar. What if the sugar craving had hit him again? When I'd walked into the Caterpillar Room yesterday morning, he'd been doing frantic crunches. Had he been working off calories he'd just indulged in on the sly?

Sitting on the bed, I pictured Brian's almost empty thermos, pictured Martha taking a sip of sweet tea, frowning, and setting her thermos down. Had Brian come to the Caterpillar Room early to guzzle down most of Martha's tea? Had he covered up his theft by pouring most of his mineral water into her thermos? Unlike other guests at the center, Martha hadn't been pampered all her life. If her tea tasted too weak, she probably wouldn't complain. She'd probably just frown and stop drinking.

I pressed my hand against my forehead. Last night, I'd lain sleepless for hours, trying to figure out why anyone at the center would want to kill Brian. Should I have been trying to figure out why anyone would want to kill Martha?

Immediately, the inconsistencies started hitting me. "Martha hadn't been pampered all her life"—a ludicrous understatement. She'd been fired. She'd been subsisting on freelance copyediting and tutoring. She probably didn't have health insurance. How could she afford this place? Maybe she was independently wealthy. But her sweater was worn at the elbows, and she didn't act like an heiress. She acted like a bitter woman used to being treated shabbily. I looked around Brian's room again. He'd brought only a few things here—only clothes, vitamins, toiletries. Only the sorts of things one would expect someone to bring to a rehab center. Martha had brought an antique clock and a recipe file. Why?

My cell phone rang. "We got lucky, Mrs. Abrams," Lieutenant Brock said. "I put a rush on that autopsy—the coroner owes me a favor—and the first test he did turned up positive. Oleander poisoning. Probably ingested in liquid form, the coroner said—that's probably why it acted so quickly, especially since this guy didn't eat much and his stomach was always mostly empty. Probably, someone stuck oleander stems in water, extracted the poison that way, slipped it into something he drank. Only problem is, the coroner says the water would taste really sweet. And this guy didn't drink anything but water, right? You'd think he'd have noticed—"

"Actually, he may have had some sweet tea yesterday. It's too complicated to explain now, but would adding the poisoned water to sweet tea hide the taste?"

"I'd think so, yeah. Now, you said there are lots of flowering plants at this center. Any oleander?"

"I don't know what oleander looks like. I'm sorry."

"That's okay. I'll head over to the center now and check. Just sit tight till I get there. Don't confront anyone. Looks like we're dealing with a killer, Mrs. Abrams."

I closed my phone and glanced at my watch. Almost 10:00. I had to go meet my group. And someone in that group might be a murderer.

When I got to the Caterpillar Room, Felix sat in his usual chair near the back of the room. Martha sat in a pastel print armchair, working on her sampler, not looking up. Did she suspect someone tried to kill her yesterday? Probably not—she looked tired, but not frightened. Both Roland and Courtney sat on the dark green couch, rather close together. He'd piled up all three of the red throw pillows and was leaning back against them as he told Courtney about his movie.

"It's not a standard romantic comedy," he said. "My character has an arc. At first, he's cynical, doesn't believe in love anymore, because he's divorced. His turning point comes when he meets the Amber Andrews character. She's cynical, too, because she just got dumped by the guy she dated in the last movie."

"A sequel." Martha pursed her lips. "Too bad. Sequels are always disappointing. Name one sequel that won an Oscar."

"What is *Godfather II*?" Felix said, eagerly.

Martha smiled. "Quite right, Felix. That was a sequel, and it was excellent. Well. Half of it was excellent."

"Yeah, fifty percent was good," Courtney said. She seemed out of her depth.

"True," Roland said. "The part about Michael was lame, but the part about young Vito getting drawn into a life of crime—fantastic. *There's* a character with an arc. Vito's turning point comes when a small-time gangster asks him to hide some guns—"

"Who is Clemenza?" Felix sat forward, his face pink with excitement.

"Right," Roland said. "Vito doesn't realize what he's getting into, but now he's guilty, too, because he helped Clemenza."

Courtney nodded vigorously. "Vito's not innocent any more. He's a criminal, just like Credenza." I don't think she had any idea of what she was talking about.

"That's enough movie trivia." Martha's face had gone pale. "Leah, could we please move on?"

"In a minute," Roland said. "I wanna develop the parallel with my character some more. See, there's no turning back for Vito. He sinks deeper and deeper—"

"Oh, for heaven's sake!" Tossing her sampler aside, Martha stood up and stalked out of the room.

Roland lifted both hands in a helpless, uncomprehending gesture. "Hey, what'd I say? I was just describing Vito's arc."

I didn't understand it, either. Picking up Martha's sampler, I gazed at the image of an eagle soaring past a beautiful mountain. Slowly, things started coming together—Martha's bracelet, Martha's room, even the stories Sam had been following in the news and the lawn ornament he was making for the Hartwells. "Felix," I said. "The meaning of the name 'Arnold.'"

His face clouded with confusion. "What is 'eagle?'" he said.

I nodded. "And the meaning of 'Belmont.'"

His eyes darted to the sampler; his voice dropped to a whisper. "What is 'beautiful mountain?'"

I nodded again. "Please take a break, everyone. I need to speak to Martha."

Taking the sampler with me, I found her in her room, sitting at her desk, staring down at her bracelet. "I'm sorry I made a fuss," she said. "I got upset by all the talk about guns and crime."

An odd response from someone who evidently enjoyed *Godfather II*, I thought. But it was time to stop noting inconsistencies, time to start explaining them. "Those are interesting beads," I said. "Shaped like apples—apples for the teacher? Was that bracelet a gift from a student?"

Her back stiffened visibly. "From a young man I tutored for a while, yes."

I set the sampler down on the desk. "Was this supposed to be a gift for the same student?" I paused. "For Arnold Belmont?"

She looked up at me, her face stretched taut with fear. "Oh, my God—they found me. They sent you to kill me. Please, I'll give it back, every penny of it. And I swear I didn't know what was in the box—I didn't open it until I heard he was dead."

"It's all right." I sat down on her bed. "I'm not a drug dealer, and I don't work for drug dealers. I'm just a temporary secretary with a husband who reads newspaper stories about local crimes. The symbolism on your sampler helped me see the link with Arnold Belmont. Were you creating a family crest for him?"

She nodded slowly, watching me, probably still not sure if she could trust me. "He didn't like the name 'Arnold.' He called it 'a sissy name.' I was trying to show him it's a beautiful name, a noble name."

"But he died before you could give it to him," I said. "Was it like the scene in *Godfather II*? He came to you one night and gave you something and asked you to keep it for him. He must have feared that his suppliers suspected him of stealing the money. He didn't want them to find it in his possession; he thought he'd be safe that way. But they killed him anyhow."

"He was only nineteen." A tear started down her cheek, and she rubbed it away. "In so many ways, he was such a nice young man—so respectful, so eager to learn. *He* didn't mind when I corrected him. He hoped to go to college some day, to change his life. He was eager to embrace the opportunities so many young people despise and resent. He'd never told me what he did for a living, but I suppose I'd always sensed it was something—well. Not quite kosher." She managed a wry smile. "Even so, I agreed to keep the box. When I heard he was dead, when I opened the box, I had to face the truth."

"And you must've feared that he'd told his killers where the money was before he died," I said. "You must've feared they'd come looking for you. So you decided to hide in a rehab center while you figured out what to do, and you took your most precious possessions with you in case it never felt safe to go home, in case you decided you had to disappear somehow. Why didn't you go to the police?"

She lifted her shoulders. "I was afraid that they wouldn't believe me, that they'd think that I must be involved in illegal things, too, that they'd think I was Arnold's accomplice. I was afraid they'd arrest me." She paused. "And I wanted to keep the money. I've worked so hard, I've been treated so unfairly, I've struggled so much—I felt I deserved it. So I used some of it to pay for a two-week stay here. I hid the rest."

She'd chosen her rehab center wisely, I thought—one that promises complete confidentiality, one that doesn't search guests' belongings when they check in, one that doesn't mind accepting payments in cash. Had Fred suspected something about Martha was, in her phrase, not quite kosher? Had he been too eager to fill his luxurious rooms to care? "Has someone taken the money, Martha?" I asked.

She looked startled. "No—that is, I haven't checked today, but I don't think so. Why would you ask?"

I gestured toward the recipe file. "It's a large file but contains only a few cards. I thought you might have hidden the money there, and someone might have taken it."

Again, she smiled wryly. "Very observant. Yes, I did keep it there at first. But when Fred searched our rooms the other night, I got nervous. I don't want the money found in my possession—I'd rather risk losing it. So I moved it." She hesitated, then looked at me directly. "I moved it to a very safe place, Leah. I'm sure it's still there. And there's a lot of it. I'll give you half if you—"

"No," I said. "A policeman's on his way here. When he arrives, tell him everything."

She let out a sound that was halfway to a sob. "You called a policeman? He's coming to arrest me for keeping the money?"

"Not to arrest you," I said. "To figure out who tried to kill you."

Before Lieutenant Brock arrived, though, I'd just about figured it out myself. It had made no sense to me that anyone would want to murder either Brian or Martha—there didn't seem to be a motive. Now that I knew about the money, the motive seemed clear. Someone had found the money, and wanted it, and figured stealing it would be safer if Martha weren't around to report the theft. Of course, she *wouldn't* have reported it—she'd have been too afraid of getting in trouble herself—but the would-be thief didn't know that. And then Martha prevented the theft by moving the money to a new hiding place, and Brian messed up the murder by drinking Martha's tea. That must be one frustrated wrongdoer, I thought.

But who was it? It might be a guest or staff member I hadn't met. My thoughts, though, focused on our group. Not Felix—he evidently had plenty of money and very few wants. If a new biography of Alex Trebek came out, Felix might be tempted to splurge, but he could manage that without stealing from Martha. And Courtney came from a wealthy family, and Roland probably made more in a week than most people do in a year. But Courtney yearned to pursue a path her family would never support, and Roland had IRS troubles and lavish spending habits. Either might covet a hefty stack of cash. Which one had found it? Which had schemed to steal it?

There was a knock on the door, and I stepped into the hall to talk to Lieutenant Brock. "What's going on?" he said. "I told you to sit tight, not to confront anybody—and I find you holed up with a patient. Is she the one you suspect? You trying to interrogate her all on your own?"

I shook my head. "Martha's not the murderer, Lieutenant. She's the intended victim. Did you find any oleander?"

"Whole bunch of it, right in the courtyard. What do you mean, intended victim?"

"I have things to tell you," I said. "So does Martha." I took a deep breath. "And then I think you should talk to someone named Courtney."

* * * *

"So where did Martha hide the money?" Sam asked. "The second time, I mean."

Leah poured lemonade first for Lieutenant Brock, then for herself. Sam had made sweet tea, too, but no one seemed interested. "She hid it in a throw pillow in the Caterpillar Room. I should have known. On my first day at the center, there were two throw pillows on the couch—I mentioned that in my notes. The next day, there were three. You see, after Fred conducted his search, Martha got nervous, took a pillow to her room, and sewed the money into it while pretending to be napping during the free period. Then she put the pillow back where it belonged. I noticed that there were three pillows the next day, but the change didn't really register. And naturally Martha chose a hiding place that let her use her sewing skills. I feel foolish about not making those connections."

"You made plenty of connections," Brock said. "I still haven't figured out all of them. What made you sure it was Courtney, not Roland?"

"Several things," Leah said. "Brian accused Courtney of sneaking into Martha's room the night before the search and copying ideas from her recovery journal. I'm sure he was right—Courtney copied ideas from

Brian's journal, too, the next night. While she was in Martha's room, Courtney must've looked in the recipe file."

Sam frowned. "Why would she do that?"

"Probably because it looked so out of place. Why would anyone bring recipes to a center where all meals are provided? Felix was looking through the file, too, after Brian got sick—anybody would be curious. Anyway, Courtney saw the money, but she didn't take it right away."

"She took three hundred dollars," Brock put in. "We found it under her mattress—serial numbers matched ones we had for the drug money. She probably figured that much wouldn't be missed, and she was right. Then, after Roland came to the center, she started itching to take the rest. He told us she flirted with him, talked about going to Hollywood with him when he left the center, having him introduce her to celebrities who need personal assistants. He admitted he encouraged her, also admitted he wasn't especially serious about it—mostly, he was thinking about getting some action to brighten up his days in rehab. Anyway, Courtney would need money to keep her going awhile once she got to Hollywood. I bet that's when Martha's stash started looking good to her."

"I bet you're right," Leah said. "So she poisoned Martha's tea the next morning—I hope you can prove that, Lieutenant."

"Well, when I arrested her, she said I couldn't charge her with murdering Brian because she'd never meant to murder him. She'd meant to murder Martha, and Martha was fine. She said it wasn't *her* fault that Brian drank Martha's tea. Not the world's strongest defense. But now her parents have her lawyered up good—I'm not holding my breath waiting for more confessions. We found a custodian who spotted her clipping oleander, though, and a vase with traces of oleander in the back of her closet—we're getting closer. And maybe *you* can come up with more evidence, Mrs. Abrams."

"Probably nothing that would stand up in court. There's the fact that she was late to therapy on the day of the poisoning. She said she'd gotten a phone call from her mother—did you check on that?"

"Yup," Brock said. "Her mother was getting a tummy tuck then, definitely not talking to her daughter. You figure Courtney was late because she'd been searching Martha's room, going nuts when she realized the money was gone?"

"Yes," Leah said. "She'd definitely want to grab the money before Martha got sick. Afterwards, the room would be full of doctors and nurses, and then Fred would lock it to protect Martha's possessions. Also, not everyone would be able to recognize oleander—I can't. But Courtney said her mother 'dragged' her to garden shows for years. I bet Courtney learned a lot about plants, just by osmosis. I also bet a jury wouldn't be impressed by that." Leah smiled ruefully. "They probably also wouldn't be impressed by evidence from *Pirkei Avot*."

"From *Pirkei Avot*?" Sam said. "From Sarah's religious school homework? *That* helped you realize Courtney tried to kill Martha?"

"It did. 'Flee wrongdoing,' Rabbi Ben Azzai says. Even minor wrongdoings are dangerous, because 'one wrongdoing leads to another wrongdoing.' Not that plagiarism's a minor wrongdoing—it's a serious academic offense—but Courtney's spent years breaking rules and thinking only about what she wants, not about what's right. When the temptation to commit a major wrongdoing came along, she didn't have the character to resist."

"Yeah, character isn't something you develop overnight," Brock said, "or in six easy steps. Even a sweet tooth isn't easy to overcome quickly—Brian found that out. That reminds me. Did Courtney's arrest get you in trouble at the center?"

Leah sighed. "Fred fired me. And he complained to my agency, saying I'm a meddler who stirs up trouble. He would have preferred to let Courtney get away with murder, I suppose, to protect the center's reputation. Oh, well. There are other temporary agencies. And I've developed reservations about The Cocoon Center. I'm sure some rehab centers do fine work, but Fred's emphasis on quick results, on avoiding unpleasantness—I'm not sure that's the right approach. Human beings aren't caterpillars. Retreating from the world and sealing oneself up in a safe, comfortable place for a short time isn't necessarily the best way of transforming oneself. I wish everyone there the best, though. What about Martha? Will she go to jail for withholding evidence?"

"No chance," Brock said. "I got no interest in charging her—she basically panicked and blundered into this. And she's cooperating fully now."

"I'm glad," Leah said, "especially since I think she and Felix may have a future together. Did you notice, Lieutenant? After you arrested Courtney, when we were all in the Caterpillar Room, Felix walked over to Martha and said, 'I hope you're not real upset, Martha.' And she said, 'Thank you, Felix. I'm fine.'"

Leah smiled brightly. The two men stared at each other. "So they made polite chitchat," Sam said. "So what?"

"Don't you see? He initiated a conversation with her—and he didn't put it in the form of a question. And he made a grammatical error—he modified an adjective with another adjective, not with an adverb—but she didn't correct him." Leah's eyes got dreamy. "They must be in love."

"Definitely." Brock covered his mouth with his hand. "Romance is in the air, all right. Now, what you said about one wrongdoing leading to another—I got that. But Roland's an old pro at wrongdoing, too—picking fights, cheating on taxes, speeding. How did you decide Courtney was the murderer, not him?"

"One final piece of evidence," she said. "Again, nothing you can use in court. On my first day at the center, during the free period, Courtney was reading a well-worn copy of a Sue Grafton novel—a copy of Sue Grafton's very first Kinsey Millhone novel. *A Is for Alibi*."

Sam breathed in sharply. "You're kidding. *A Is for Alibi*—oleander poisoning. Courtney even plagiarized her murder method."

"Talk about consistency of character," Brock said. "Hey, I bet you can get a book out of all this, Mrs. Abrams—something about micro-transgressive behaviors eventuating in macro-transgressive behaviors, maybe. I bet you could find a way to link that to workplace communications."

Leah smiled. "I'm already working on the title," she said, and poured him more lemonade.

Mystery series about amateur sleuths have some built-in problems. People who aren't police officers, lawyers, or law enforcement professionals of some other sort usually don't have access to inside information about crimes, so how can they figure out what really happened and who really did it? And most of us go through life without becoming involved in a single murder investigation. If an amateur gets caught up in not just one but several investigations involving interesting murder methods, a limited number of suspects, and ambiguous clues that require clever interpretation, that's pretty implausible.

When I decided to write the Leah Abrams series, I looked for ways around these problems. How would Leah get her inside information? Like many mystery writers, I decided to use a friendly police officer. Often, when the amateur sleuth is a woman, she has a romantic relationship with the officer. But Leah is happily married, and Detective (eventually Lieutenant) Brock is, too—his wife never appears in the stories, but he sometimes mentions her. (So she's like Mrs. Columbo in that respect—I love everything about the Columbo mysteries.) I thought it would be interesting to have a relationship between a female amateur sleuth and a male police detective who like and respect each other but never get romantically entangled. And I think Leah and Brock make a good team. She's sharp and observant, but she can be naïve, and she's often so caught up in her theories about workplace communication that she can't see what's right in front of her. Brock's far more sensible, far more realistic about human nature. He's not as imaginative as Leah, though, not as quick to see how seemingly unconnected bits of evidence might be related. Together, they have just about everything a detective needs.

As for the chances of an amateur continually stumbling across bodies and getting embroiled in murder investigations—that's just plain implausible, no way around it. Might as well admit it and pray readers willingly suspend their disbelief. When Brock encounters Leah at yet another workplace where a murder has been committed, he often makes a sardonic comment, such as joking about advising the temporary agency to put a warning sticker on her resume. Leah sometimes responds with an embarrassed rush of words. "I know it's the third time," she says in "Death of the Guilty Party." "I know it must seem like a coincidence. But I've had plenty of other temp jobs in between. I've worked at plenty of places where people weren't murdered."

VARIETY

Age cannot wither her, nor custom stale
Her infinite variety.

Antony and Cleopatra, Act 2, scene 2

Nancy Drew, Miss Marple, V.I. Warshawski—when we think of tales of women and crime, most of us think first of the detectives we've admired, of the pleasures we've found in reading about their deductions, their daring, their triumphs. We know, though, that not all women who become involved in crime are detectives. Some are victims. Some are accomplices or accessories, witting or unwitting. Some inspire crimes, and some commit them. Some play more than one role in a single story. For example, some begin as victims but find ways of striking back—sometimes justified ways, sometimes maybe not. Sometimes we sympathize with these women, and sometimes they appall us. Sometimes we're not quite sure of how to feel.

The women in the stories that follow all appear in stand-alone stories, most first published in *Alfred Hitchcock's Mystery Magazine*, a few first published in other magazines or anthologies. The women's ages vary, and so do their professions—librarian, administrative assistant, housewife, trophy wife, personnel director, college professor. Some are single; some are married, happily or unhappily. Often, relationships with sisters or female friends are significant elements in these stories—but some friendships turn treacherous. Romance is an element in some of these stories, too, but never the primary one. Always, the primary focus is on the connection between a woman and a crime.

Mystery short stories offer both readers and writers many different sorts of pleasures. A series of short stories lets us keep returning to characters we've come to like—characters with flaws, yes, with quirks and limitations and foibles, but characters so smart and basically decent we want to read about them, or write about them, again and again. Some characters in stand-alone short stories are also smart and basically decent, but other characters surprise us. Sometimes, we reach the end of a stand-alone story and discover the protagonist isn't at all what she at first seemed to be. Maybe she's so repellant or so passive that we wouldn't want to read a second story about her. Once in a while, the protagonist doesn't survive the story. Even if we'd like to read about her again, that's not an option. She's gone, or she will be soon.

As a writer, I've enjoyed the freedom these stories have given me. I've had fun experimenting with different sorts of mysteries—whodunits, suspense stories, psychological studies, very short stories, novellas. And I've loved beginning to explore the many entanglements of women and crime, in all their infinite variety.

THE LISTENER

(1995)

The universal confidante—that's what my college roommate called me. It didn't start in college, though. Ever since I can remember, people have wanted to tell me their secrets. When I was a little girl, cousins, aunts, even my grandparents would drift toward me at birthday parties and Christmas gatherings. They'd work their way over to the quiet corner where I stood watching, they'd chat pleasantly for a few minutes, and before long they'd be assaulting me with tales of their petty dishonesties, their drinking problems, their adulteries.

It's been that way ever since. My friends, teachers, strangers sitting next to me on planes, people interviewing for jobs at the company where I'm personnel director—they've all wanted to tell me things, private things, embarrassing things. My roommate used to say it's because I have a sympathetic way about me, because I seem more interested in hearing about other people's problems than in boring them with my own. It can't be because people want my advice. I don't give advice. I tried to, a few times, but it never worked out. So now, when people tell me secrets they wouldn't share with a psychiatrist or a priest, I don't tell them what to do. I listen.

It was that way when I went to see Will Ramsey at his office a few months ago. He's our vice president for marketing, and I'd just placed a new receptionist with him and wanted to see how she was doing. My first glimpse of Paulette at the reception desk wasn't reassuring. She was sorting mail efficiently enough, but meanwhile she was twitching her shoulders and snapping her gum to the beat of the music pumping discreetly through her portable CD player. Her makeup was a bit too much, her neckline a bit too low, her hair a bit redder than it had been at her interview. I didn't say anything about it. Some might think that, as personnel director, I have the right to tell employees how to dress. But I mean it when I say I don't give advice. I smiled at Paulette and walked past her to Will's private office.

"Jenny!" he said, looking up from his computer. He's forty-two, tall and blond, reasonably broad shouldered and still more or less lean. "This is a treat. Checking on the new girl?"

I nodded and sat down. "Any problems?"

"No, she's working out fine. Oh, Mrs. Jackson says her word processing isn't great, but you know Mrs. Jackson—automatically suspicious of anyone under sixty. Anyway, Paulette doesn't have to do much word processing. Mostly, she just has to establish a friendly atmosphere, brighten the place up—and she sure does that."

I peered out through Will's doorway and saw Paulette as she walked toward the file cabinets, her hips still gyrating to the music. "She does. I *was* concerned that she might be too young for the job—only nineteen, after all. But she seemed mature at the interview. She's been through a lot."

"You can say that again." Will glanced at his new receptionist. "She finally tracks down her birth father, moves all the way to South Dakota to be with him—and then, three weeks later, he drops dead of a heart attack, leaving her all alone in that house on Custer Ridge. Poor kid."

"She told you about that?"

"You bet. You're not the only person people tell things to." He grinned, and I tensed. A revelation was coming. I've learned to sense it. "Yeah, Paulette and I have had some good talks. But then I made the mistake of telling Valerie about them. When Valerie dropped by this morning and got her first look at Paulette, you can guess how Valerie reacted. You must know Valerie pretty well from working out with her every week. I'm sure you've figured out how she feels about Other Women. Has she ever said anything about that secretary back in Minneapolis?"

I shrugged. "A little."

"I'd love to hear that 'little.' She's never talked to me about it straight out. We'd been married five years, and I got this new secretary. A real looker—a little flashy, but a nice girl. Same type as Paulette. I guess you'd say we took to each other. But hell, we never did anything much. A little flirting, a drink now and then—it never went beyond that. I wouldn't have dared. Valerie's always been clear about her opinions on that subject, and there's always been something a little strange about her—you know?"

I did know, but what could I say? I shrugged again.

"Yeah," he said. "You know. Then one night somebody breaks into my secretary's apartment and crushes her skull with a fireplace poker. The police called it a burglary, even though nothing was stolen. We were never even questioned. And Valerie's never said one word to me about it.

That's odd in itself, isn't it, that she's never said one word? One way or another, it's kept me in line ever since."

I shifted in my chair. "I'm sure that's not the only thing keeping you in line. Valerie's a very—dynamic person. And a devoted wife."

He grinned. "What tactful adjectives. But dynamic and devoted get exhausting after a while. You know?"

He obviously wanted to say more, but I didn't want to hear more. I stood up. "I'm glad you're satisfied with Paulette's work. I'll check back in a few days, to make sure everything's still going smoothly."

He stood, too. "Check back any time, Jenny," he said.

I stopped by Paulette's desk on my way out. She was switching the disks in her CD player—from *Born in the U.S.A.* to *The River*. At least she had good taste. "How's it going?" I asked. "Job working out?"

She smiled. "You bet, Miss Ford. Mr. Ramsey's sweet as can be, real encouraging and all. Mrs. Jackson's always after me about my typing, but she's basically okay." Paulette lowered her voice and leaned forward over her desk, her blouse sagging to reveal more of her assets than I really needed to see. "That Mrs. Ramsey, though! She stopped by this morning, and I could see she didn't like me *at all*. It was like she was jealous or something. And I mean, like, *why*? Is she weird, or what?"

"She's a little possessive," I admitted. "How are you handling the adjustment to the Midwest?"

"Oh, I *love* it here. People are so *friendly*. They say hello to you right on the street—it's not *at all* like Jersey. I get nervous, though, when I'm all by myself in the house. I mean, there are some pretty weird murders in this part of the country."

"They're rare," I said, and watched as she applied another thick layer of lipstick. I noticed the label—Righteous Ruby. That sounded like a shade she'd choose. "I'm glad you like it here. If you run into any problems, don't hesitate to come by to talk."

"I won't," she assured me, and I knew it was true. Nobody ever hesitates to come by to talk to me.

Paulette did come to my office, several times, during the next few months, to tell me how much she was enjoying her job and to pour out her little anxieties. She talked, and I listened. We didn't really become friends—I'm almost twice her age—but we got to be friendly. She was calling Will Ramsey by his first name now, I noticed.

I saw her several times at her own office, too, when I stopped by to confer with Will about personnel matters. He'd been right about Paulette's ability to brighten a place up. The whole office seemed livelier now. Once, I even caught Mrs. Jackson smiling.

One person wasn't smiling much lately, and that was Valerie Ramsey. I could see her mood darkening week by week when we met at the gym. She always asked questions about Paulette—casual questions, but I felt resentment behind them. I gave her vague responses and shrugged a lot. Then, one Tuesday in April, her resentment shot to the surface.

"I wish you'd never hired that Paulette," she said. We'd just showered and were the only two people in the locker room. Valerie was toweling her hair too vigorously, as usual. "She's nothing but trouble."

I shrugged. "Oh, she got on Mrs. Jackson's nerves at first, but not lately. Her typing has really improved."

"That's not what I mean." She threw her towel down and faced me—a sharp-faced, stridently thin woman, only a few years older than her husband but aged by anxiety. "Tell me the truth, Jenny. What's going on between her and Will?"

"Nothing," I said, not sounding very confident. "She respects him, and they get along, but I don't think—"

"Well, I *do* think." She placed her hands on her carefully angular hips. "It's just like that time in Minneapolis, and it all started about three months ago, right about when you hired her. He's distant, he doesn't look me in the eye, and he's always staying out late and coming up with flimsy excuses. Last night, he didn't come home until after midnight. He said he was entertaining an out-of-town client. Does Will even *have* any out-of-town clients right now, Jenny?"

This was awkward. I knew for a fact he didn't. "I'm in personnel, Valerie. I don't always know what's going on in marketing."

"You know everything that goes on at that company. Everybody tells you everything. And when I was sorting laundry this morning, I found lipstick on his collar. Lord!" She shook her head. "He can't even be original. Lipstick on his collar—is there any more flagrant sign a man's having an affair? A big, bright red lipstick smear."

"Righteous Ruby." I said it under my breath, to myself. But she heard.

"Righteous Ruby? Is that the shade she wears? And you know what else I found? Here." She pulled a CD out of her gym bag. "*That* was in the CD player in his car—*Human Touch*. A *Springsteen* CD, of all things! You know Will never listens to rock and roll. So where did he get this? Does Paulette listen to this kind of trash?"

I thought of the Springsteen CD I'd seen her put into her portable player. "I wouldn't call his music trash, Valerie. I think—"

"Don't bother. You've never been good at evading questions. That gives me my answer right there. And Springsteen's from New Jersey, and I noticed Jersey plates on Paulette's car when she moved here. It all adds up."

I stared at the floor. "Valerie, it might all be coincidence."

"It's no coincidence. He's sleeping with that slut, she's giving him CD's with pornographic titles, and he has so little respect for me that he's leaving them right where I can find them—and not even bothering to wipe her filthy lipstick off his shirts!" She cursed under her breath, maybe more about Will's lack of "respect" than about the affair itself.

She'd convinced herself—there was no point trying to talk her out of it. "What will you do? Confront him?"

"What good would that do? He'd just deny it and be more careful to hide the signs. But I'd know. I'd *know*! And it would drive me crazy."

She didn't seem far from crazy now—pacing up and down the row of lockers, still naked after her shower but seeming not to realize it, slamming a fist into an open palm, her hair damp and wild. "So you'll file for divorce?" I asked.

"No!" She paced more rapidly, her face creased with rage. "Never. I'd rather kill him than let him go. I've told you that, and I've told him that, a million times. No." She turned to face me, a fierce resolution new in her eyes. "But it's not *his* fault. I know that. He's weak. And he's so handsome, and when these sluts throw themselves at him, he can't resist. Well, I've fought for him before. I'll fight for him again."

"Not the *way* you fought for him before." My voice sharpened with alarm. "Not like the other time you told me about, the time in Minneapolis—Valerie, no! It's wrong, and you might not get away with it this time."

"I'll get away with it." She pulled her clothes on methodically. "No one even suspected me last time. Except Will. I thought the suspicion would be enough to make him behave, but it obviously wasn't. So this time I'll do it in front of him, to *really* teach him a lesson. He said he has to entertain that client again tonight. You think he'll be with her?"

I should just listen. I should never give advice. It never works out when I do. "I don't know. But you can't—"

"Don't give it another thought." She picked up her gym bag and slung it over her shoulder. "You'll hear about it on the news tomorrow."

* * * *

I heard about it sooner than that. It was nearly midnight when the phone rang in my kitchen. I ran to answer it and heard Paulette's hysterical voice.

"Jenny, it was *awful*!" she said. "I've called the police—she broke into my house, and she had this fireplace poker in her hands, so it was obviously self-defense. I don't think I'll be in trouble. But I'm scared! Can you come over?"

"Paulette, calm down," I said. "What happened? Who broke into your house?"

"Valerie Ramsey." Her voice nearly broke. "Thank goodness you came over tonight and warned me that she wanted to kill me. Thank goodness I followed your advice, and sat up and kept my gun ready! But why, Jenny? Where did she ever get the idea I was sleeping with Will?"

"I can't imagine," I said. "So you shot her? You're sure she's dead? What a tragedy. But you'll be fine. Just explain everything to the police. I can back you up, tell them about her obsessive hatred of you and the threats she made. I can't come over now, though. I have a guest."

It took me five minutes to calm her down and get off the phone. Solemnly, I walked back to the bedroom.

Will Ramsey was sitting up in bed, relaxing against the pillows and smiling as he listened to "Hungry Heart." "Man, is that a great song," he said. "That's only one of the things I have to thank you for, Jenny. I never used to give this kind of music a chance. But who on earth was that, at this hour?"

"Paulette," I said, trying to look upset as I slid back into bed. "With shocking news. It's terribly sad. But at least you won't have to worry about getting Valerie to give you a divorce anymore." And at least I won't have to keep smearing your collars with this cheap stuff, I thought, reaching onto the bed stand and dropping the tube of Righteous Ruby into my wastebasket.

If it had worked out the other way, if Valerie had murdered Paulette and gone to prison for it, that would have been all right, too. But this was better. It was neater. And I rather like Paulette.

So I had good reasons to be satisfied. I'd broken my rule this once, I'd given Paulette advice this once, and just this once I'd gotten what I wanted. Now, I could slip comfortably back into my usual role. When I told him about Valerie, Will would be torn by guilt and regret for a while. He'd need to talk.

And me? I'd be ready to listen.

In 1994, Family Circle *sponsored a suspense-writing contest judged by Mary Higgins Clark. My mother, a regular* Family Circle *reader, told me about the contest and urged me to enter. I didn't have much hope of winning, but the contest sounded like fun, and the thought that Mary Higgins Clark might glance at one of my stories was reason enough to try. The contest had a lot of rules—I don't remember them all, but I do remember the clues in the story had to include a lipstick, a license plate, and a Bruce Springsteen CD. So my love of The Boss gave me another reason to enter. I wrote "The Listener" in what was, for me, a remarkably short time—it's not a whodunit, so it didn't require the painstaking plotting most of my stories do—and sent it off, and pretty much forgot about it.*

Months later, I got a call from Family Circle, *telling me my story had won. To say I was stunned would do scant justice to the state of numb disbelief that followed the call. In fact, the next time the editor called, I said, "Excuse me, but did I understand you correctly the other day? Did you really say first prize?" The prize money paid for a much-needed fence for our backyard (our dog had gotten big enough to literally step over the miserable excuse for a home-made fence my husband and I had rigged up), and it was fun to see my story in the August, 1995* Family Circle. *Best of all was a sub-heading someone had added—"Mary Higgins Clark's Favorite Mystery." I'm sure an editor or an intern wrote that; Mary Higgins Clark may well have winced when she saw it. But I felt ridiculously thrilled anyway.*

HONOR AMONG THIEVES

(2000)

The first time it happened, it was just barely a crime. It started as an honest mistake, and she simply didn't correct it.

Mary had noticed the woman standing at the Gourmet Meats counter. A walking cliché, she'd thought—ankle-length leather coat, salon-sculpted hair, piled-on rings and bracelets that'd be too much for an opera house, let alone a grocery store. And the loud, strident voice scolding an apologetic butcher because the chops he'd sold her last week had been too fatty, the steaks too lean. She's a parody of a rich woman, Mary thought—an arrogant, overdressed, overbearing parody. And she's buying steaks and chops. Mary felt resentment rising. On another day, she'd have forced it down; today, she couldn't be bothered. She looked away and considered her choices. No, the eighty percent lean ground beef cost too much. She chose a sausage-like roll of Hamburger Plus—traces of beef ground with soy beans and artificial colorings and God knew what else—and moved on.

A box of rice, a jar of generic peanut butter, a loaf of day-old bread, and she checked out, pleased she'd managed to fill three bags for only $37.54. A teenaged clerk pushed her cart to the pick-up spot while she went to get her car. There was the leather-coated woman, standing next to a BMW, chatting with a man who'd stepped out of a Lincoln. She glanced at Mary, surveying her from scarf to shoes. Then she smirked, shrugged, and turned back to her companion. Bitch, Mary thought, and got into her car. Pulling up to the pick-up spot, she noticed no one was on hand to help customers with their groceries. On such a cold day, she couldn't blame employees for staying inside.

She spotted the cart with three bags, opened her trunk, and started loading up. Only as she picked up the last bag did she notice packages wrapped in butcher's paper. This can't be my cart, she thought, and started to put the bag back. Then she glanced at the parking lot and saw the leather-coated woman still locked in conversation. There were no other carts at the pick-up spot—these must be her groceries. Later, Mary couldn't remember making a decision, only the phrase "screw it" flashing through her mind. She set the last bag next to the others, slammed her trunk, and drove away.

Panic seized her a block from the store. God, she thought. What have I done? She checked her rear-view mirror, expecting to see police cars bearing down on her. But there was no one. I'll turn around, she thought. I'll go back to the store, apologize, say I made a mistake and realized it only now. But who would believe she'd realized such a mistake while driving away, and how could she tell such a lie without blushing? She'd be arrested for attempted robbery, or larceny, or whatever it was she'd done. Her apartment building was now only minutes away. She turned down a side street to give herself time to think—and, she realized, to throw off pursuers.

She'd paid cash for her groceries, so no one could use a credit card charge to track her down. And she seldom shopped at that store, so none of the clerks knew her. Probably, the leather-coated woman was screaming at the managers right now. Probably, they'd already offered to let her replace her groceries for free. Probably, Mary could get away with this.

Did she want to? She drove for another fifteen minutes, turning down streets almost at random, forcing herself to think. It might be safe to go back now—she could say she discovered her mistake when she got to her apartment, and that should sound believable. But even if the store didn't press charges, people would suspect the truth. It would be humiliating, unbearable. And how much could three bags of groceries be worth? Maybe forty, fifty dollars more than the bags Mary left behind. The store could absorb the difference; it probably overcharged customers anyhow. And after all, it should be more careful about having someone watch the pickup spot. This whole thing had been the store's fault more than Mary's. Maybe now it would be more responsible. All in all, it made sense to go home and deal with the guilt—and, she thought, almost smiling, to put the groceries to good use.

When her sister came by for dinner, the kitchen was warm with rich, unfamiliar aromas. "Goodness," Ginny said, sniffing. "What are you cooking?"

"Oyster stew." Mary turned away from the stove, wooden spoon held aloft. "Fresh oysters, real cream, real butter. And there's a standing rib roast in the oven and fresh asparagus in the fridge and a bottle of pinot noir on the table—I don't think you're supposed to chill red wine, are you?"

Ginny looked stunned. "Roast, oysters, wine—Mary! Congratulations! You got the promotion!"

"No." Mary's smile faltered. "I got passed over again, for that boot-licking Mark Hanson. Mark Hanson! You can't talk to him five minutes without realizing what a dope he is, all he does all day is play up to Mr. Boyd and laugh at his jokes, and *he* gets promoted. Mark's got leadership potential, Boyd says. Mark gets noticed. I'm a hard worker, Boyd says, but I don't have pizzazz. I'm better off in a support position."

Ginny frowned. "I don't understand. If Mark got the promotion—oh, no. You quit and blew your severance check on all this stuff, didn't you?"

"No." Mary took a tray from the refrigerator. "Much as I'd have loved to, I didn't dare quit. And I didn't exactly buy all this stuff. I'll pour you some Absolut—did I mention we have Absolut?—and explain. Don't skimp on the caviar. That's the problem with these big cuts of meat—they take forever to cook. We'd better load up on appetizers. Now, where *did* I put those quails' eggs?"

When Ginny heard about what happened at the store, she needed a second drink. "I don't believe you, Mary. You actually stole that poor woman's groceries?"

"She isn't a poor woman. She was wearing a leather coat, and practically every inch of her that wasn't covered with leather was layered with jewelry. And poor women don't spend two hundred three dollars and eighty-six cents on gourmet treats. Would you have *believed* anyone could spend that much on three bags of groceries? Anyway, I'm sure the store made it up to her. It can afford to. You should see what it charges for eighty percent lean hamburger."

"And now we know one reason prices are so high," Ginny said. "Because stores have to cover what they lose to thieves. Besides, it isn't so much a question of what that woman can afford, or what the store can afford. It's a question of what you did, of the kind of person you are. You stole, Mary, and that isn't right. You've always been an honest person, and honest people don't steal."

Mary's shoulders drooped. "I know. But it was so tempting. The stuff was right in my hands, and no one was looking. And I was so angry—I don't know exactly why, but I was—and it happened so fast. I didn't even think about what I was doing. I just did it. Afterwards, I felt awful. I kept expecting cops to start pounding on the door. I threw the butcher paper in the incinerator and rewrapped the meat in tinfoil, to hide the evidence. And I cried. I felt so guilty I broke down and cried."

But she'd also gasped with delight, Mary remembered, when she'd unpacked the groceries, stacking one wonderful thing after another on the counter, hardly able to believe it all belonged to her. And she'd laughed out loud when she'd found the cash register receipt. Two hundred three dollars and eighty-six cents worth of groceries! She'd never had anything like it in her apartment before.

Ginny looked at her closely. "You'll never do it again, will you?"

"Of course not!" She was amazed Ginny could ask. "Believe me, I was never so scared in my life. I'll never dare go to that store again, and of course I'll never steal again. I gave in to temptation once, but I'm still an honest person."

"I hope so. You don't want to end up like *that*." Ginny pointed to a newspaper on the coffee table.

Mary laughed. "The Vincenti trial? Come *on*, Ginny. I half-accidentally take some groceries, and you think I'll end up a mobster? Thanks a bunch. I'm not beginning a life of crime. Fearless young District Attorney Jim Newgate will have no reason to prosecute me for racketeering."

"I didn't mean that," Ginny said, blushing. "But sometimes one thing leads to another, and—oh, forget it. I *am* sorry Mark Hanson got the promotion. Was he obnoxious about it?"

"He's obnoxious about everything." Mary drained her glass. "Naturally he lorded it over me all day. He's throwing a big party Friday night to celebrate. He's invited the Boyds, of course, and everyone else from the office. He was even gracious enough to include me. I'm not going."

"You'd better. You don't want to look like a poor sport. And it's a chance to get to know Mr. Boyd better."

"To play up to him, you mean, and tell him how smart and funny he is. No. I will not try to get ahead that way. I may not be above lifting groceries, but I'm definitely above *that*."

* * * *

She did go to Mark Hanson's party, though—Ginny convinced her it was the prudent move. So she accepted a glass of Mark's imported Champagne, joined in toasts to his success, made herself smile politely at Mr. Boyd's lamely off-color jokes while everyone else roared and chortled. Then she retreated to a corner and eyed Mark's living room enviously. Look at this place, she thought. Look at these carpets, that furniture, those paintings. Mark didn't even *need* this promotion. He must be from a rich family. The extra three hundred a month won't make a noticeable blip in his bank account, and it would've meant the world to me. And I *earned* that promotion. I work harder than Mark, I work better, I—

"Hey, Mary." Mr. Boyd wedged himself next to her, his breath thick with something stronger than Champagne. "Here you are, hiding in a corner again. It's the same mistake you make at work. You're a pretty girl—*very* pretty in your mousy little way—but you always manage to fade into the background. You should put yourself forward more. You should be more like Mark."

He pointed, and she looked. There was Mark Hanson in the middle of the room, back-slapping, hand-shaking, head-nodding. She forced her mouth into a near smile. "Mark and I have different personalities. But I *did* come up with the concept for the Bradford account. If you look at the figures from last quarter, you'll—"

"I'd rather look at *this* figure." Mr. Boyd let his gaze slide over her frankly, bust to waist to hips. He nudged against her, laughed when she jumped back. "Mary, Mary, Mary. You're a steady little worker, but if you wanna get ahead, you gotta have something extra, or *do* something extra. You don't have Mark's personality? Find another way to get noticed." He lowered his voice. "My wife's been upstairs the last half hour. She was plastered when we got here; by now, she's probably set in concrete. I bet she passed out on the bathroom floor. So how's about you and I go to the poolroom, discuss your future with the company? I'll sneak us a bottle of—"

"Excuse me." She darted out of the corner and backed away. "I'd love to discuss my future with the company on Monday, but I have to leave. My sister has a cold, and I promised I'd stop by her place."

"Mary, Mary, Mary," Mr. Boyd said, looking after her regretfully before transferring his attention to a receptionist.

She fled upstairs. Mark had carried coats off as guests arrived; probably, he'd piled them on a bed. Still fuming about Mr. Boyd, she peeked into an elegantly tiled bathroom, a den of some sort, a dimly lit chamber with bordello-like mirrors and draperies. Yes, this was the bedroom, that was the bed, those were the coats. And that was Mrs. Boyd, open-eyed and open-mouthed but deeply unconscious, spread-eagled on top of her mink. Pathetic, Mary thought, tugging to dislodge the coat she'd bought six years ago at an off-season sale. Then her eyes strayed to Mark's bureau. Look at that handcrafted, antique ivory jewelry case, she thought; look at those silver-plated mugs; look at—good heavens. Was that actually a money clip? Was that actual money in it? What kind of idiot would leave money sitting out on his bureau when his house was full of guests?

A cocky idiot, she thought. An ostentatious idiot, eager to show everyone how well off he is, how careless he could afford to be with sums his inferiors slaved weeks to earn. An arrogant idiot, sure no one would dare steal from him.

Another minute, and the money was in her pocket. Oh, no, she thought in horror. I've done it again. But she didn't undo it. Instead, she hurried downstairs, thanked Mark for the lovely party, and drove away.

* * * *

"I don't believe it," Ginny said. "You *promised* you'd never steal again. And now, only four days later—"

"I know, and I'm sorry. But it's only two hundred sixty-five dollars. That's thirty-five dollars less than the extra three hundred he'll earn every month, in the job he stole from me. And he can afford it. You should've seen his house, his furniture, his—"

"I don't care how rich he is. It's still wrong to steal from him. And what will you say when the police show up, asking how you all of a sudden managed to pay for your root canal?"

"They won't show up." Somehow, Mary had known this even before she took the money, though she couldn't remember thinking it through. "Mark won't report the theft. How could the police trace cash stolen from his bedroom? Besides, if he goes to the police, they'll question every guest at the party. Does Mark want the police to embarrass Mr. Boyd by questioning him? Does he want the police to question *Mrs.* Boyd—who, by the way, is probably his top suspect? She was passed out on Mark's bed for who knows how long. If I were Mark, I'd figure she stumbled around his room before collapsing, slipped his cash into her pocket without realizing it. Would a simpering sycophant like Mark Hanson report *that* crime to the police?"

Ginny considered it, then nodded. "You're right. He probably won't report it. But that doesn't change the fact you stole—again. You committed a crime. Don't let yourself become a criminal."

"Like Louie Vincenti?"

Mary glanced at the television screen. There was Vincenti being led away from the courthouse in handcuffs, and there was District Attorney Jim Newgate, speaking to the press, vowing this time Vincenti would pay for his crimes. Not very impressive for a district attorney, Mary thought idly—soft-spoken, too ordinary, too thin, too short. But he kept his eyes hard on the reporter, speaking with quiet, unblinking authority. The camera stayed locked on him for a full minute.

Mary looked up again. "Don't worry. I won't send a job application to the Mafia. But it's interesting to think about what Mr. Boyd said to me. I fade into the background, he said. I never get noticed. That's a handy quality for a thief to have, don't you think?"

"But you're *not* a thief," Ginny said. "You're an honest person. And you won't ever steal again, will you? Promise?"

Mary stood up and shook her hand. "I promise," she said.

* * * *

"I had every intention of keeping that promise," she said the next week. "But that clerk, Ginny! If you'd met her, you'd understand."

Ginny pressed the sofa pillows against her ears and moaned. "I don't want to understand. Don't tell me."

"You *have* to hear." Mary pulled the pillows away. "It was the watch Aunt Joan gave me for my college graduation. Of course I knew it wasn't expensive, but you know how much I love Aunt Joan, how much that watch means to me. So when it broke down, I wanted it repaired by an expert. I went to Rutherford's Jewelry. And that clerk—that wretched teenaged clerk—glanced at my watch and flat-out sneered and said, 'We don't deal with that quality of watch. Perhaps a discount store can help you.' She turned away like I was dirt. I was *so* mad."

"So why didn't you tell her off? Why didn't you say she has no right to treat customers that way?"

"I couldn't. She was so well-dressed, so confident. I didn't have the nerve to talk back to her."

"But you had the nerve to steal." Ginny touched the necklace tentatively. "This has *got* to be worth ten times what the watch is worth."

Mary sighed. "It's not the money. It's the *principle*. And the—well, the opportunity." She paced, trying to explain it to Ginny, trying to understand it herself. "It's strange. I never used to notice opportunities to steal. Now I do, all the time. Even before that clerk spoke to me, I noticed her take the necklace out to show it to another customer, I noticed her leaving it on the counter instead of putting it away, I noticed where the security camera was pointed. I had no idea of stealing anything, but I noticed. Isn't that interesting?"

"No, it's terrifying," Ginny said. "Your thoughts are turning in a dangerous direction. You're noticing things no honest person has any reason to notice."

Mary sat down. "I know. And it *is* terrifying. But it's intriguing, too. I seem to have an instinct for this—a gift. All my life, I've worked hard, I've done well, but I've never seemed to have a gift for anything. I've never gotten ahead. Prizes at school, promotions at work—they've always gone to other people, even when I've had higher grades or better ideas. Maybe I've finally found my gift. The people at the grocery store didn't pay attention to me, Mark doesn't pay attention to me, the clerk didn't pay attention to me, nobody pays attention to me. As Mr. Boyd said, I don't get noticed. Maybe I've found a field where that pays off."

Ginny looked at her uneasily. "But it's not *your* field. You're not a thief."

"Of course not." But Mary couldn't help thinking about how well she'd handled things. Moments after that clerk snubbed her, Mary started to reach for the necklace when something told her to wait. Sure enough, the clerk turned around, checking Mary over, before turning away again.

Now, Mary thought, and covered the necklace with a casual hand, absorbing it with one deft movement. Resisting the temptation to run, she lingered to gaze at an earring stand, to squint at price tags, to sigh, to walk slowly away. She'd been perfect.

"I hope this really was the last time," Ginny was saying. "And I hope you didn't get that clerk fired."

"I hope I did." Regrets evaporated as anger returned. "I didn't want to steal again—it was *her* fault for tempting me, leaving that necklace out on the counter. How irresponsible! And so snooty—she's probably alienated lots of customers, cost Rutherford's tons of money. I did that store a favor."

Ginny shook her head. "Louie Vincenti probably has lots of rationalizations, too, for all the money he stole and all the people he killed. And the end result is, you both committed crimes."

"It's hardly the same thing. How's the trial going, anyhow?"

"Pretty well." Ginny glanced at the newspaper. "It looks as if Jim Newgate will get a racketeering conviction—though that covers only a fraction of the crimes Vincenti's committed." She looked up. "I'm more concerned about the crimes *you've* committed. There won't be any more, will there? You think you're in control, but things like this can get out of control in a hurry."

"I realize that," Mary said, "and that's one reason I won't ever steal again." She almost believed it.

It was almost true. Except for the woman at the restaurant—the loud, obnoxious woman abusing the waitress and scolding her meek little husband. When they went to the salad bar and she left her purse sitting on the table, it seemed foolish not to take her wallet. Obviously, a woman that careless with money could afford to lose it. Maybe this would teach her to take better care of her things; maybe it would give her husband a chance to scold *her* for a change. And Mary was proud of her even, confident steps as she walked past the table, of the subtle movement of her hand as she plucked the wallet from the purse, of the steadiness of her voice as she paused by the cash register to chat with the hostess. It was neatly done, and it earned her sixty-four dollars.

And she couldn't feel guilty about taking the Music Mart bag a teen-aged boy left behind at a bus stop several days later. He and his friend had whispered about drugs while they waited for the bus, making plans to score some cocaine. Clearly they had more money than was good for them. Maybe now they'd use it to replace the Walkman and CDs in the bag instead of buying drugs; maybe she'd saved them from a fatal overdose. She'd let them push past her, shaking her head at the driver and stepping back, pretending she was waiting for another bus. After the bus pulled away, she'd yawned and stretched, letting her purse slip from her shoulder, scooping up the Music Mart bag effortlessly as she bent to retrieve the purse. A dozen people hurried by. No one noticed a thing. Unfortunately, she didn't much care for the CDs. But the custodian at work loved country music—she could give him a generous Christmas present, without spending her own money.

"And I pulled it off," she thought, half-delighted, half-ashamed, smiling to herself as she stuck a bow on the package of CDs. "I actually pulled it off *again*!"

Then Mr. Boyd decided to send her to an Assertiveness Training workshop in Philadelphia. Maybe, he hinted, since he was showing such an interest in her professional development, she'd find a way to thank him when she got back. Mary didn't want to go to the workshop, didn't want to think about what kind of thanks he expected, but didn't dare refuse. Maybe I *do* need assertiveness training, she thought, and packed her suitcase.

The workshop was worthless, the flight home an hour of boredom followed by fifteen minutes of terror. They hit turbulent weather, the plane rocked and jolted and seemed ready to buckle, and Mary clenched her teeth and prayed, repenting frantically for the five thefts she now could scarcely believe she'd committed. In the first-class cabin, a man screamed, and a brandy-bearing flight attendant risked injury as she lurched down the aisle to calm him. Then the plane steadied, landing with one last stomach-wrenching bump. I need to stop all this, Mary thought as she staggered away from the gate. This last month has been crazy, stupid, wrong. I need to clean up my act. I need to straighten out my life. But first, I need a drink.

Apparently, she wasn't the only passenger with that thought. The airport bar was crowded by the time she got there; she was lucky to find a place next to a moist-faced, middle-aged man.

"Dewar's, please," she told the bartender. She'd narrowly escaped death and felt entitled to brand-name scotch. She'd put it on her expense account and see if Mr. Boyd noticed it.

The moist-faced man turned to her, leering. "Dewarsh," he said. "I like that. Like a woman who likes real booze. Most women drink fruity stuff. But not *you*, sweetheart, huh? You on the Philadelphia plane?"

"That's right." Mary bet this was the screaming man from first class, the man who'd had to be quieted with brandy and now was numbing himself with bourbon. He was tall and lean and had close-cropped, rust-colored hair, and he was evidently in the mood to make friends. Mary kept looking straight ahead.

He put a hand on her knee. "Me too. Hate flying. Only thing that really scares me. But in my business gotta fly all the time. No flying, no business, y'know? I got *real* special business here. Local talent can't handle it—all being watched. *I* can handle it fine, boom boom boom and gone again. Y'know?"

"Yes," Mary said, appalled, looking at the pasty hand on her knee, wondering what to do about it.

"So that's why I fly," he said. "All I need is a little help from my friends—brandy, bourbon, all my friends. *You* wanna be friends—with brandy and bourbon and me? You know that song? Get by with a little help from my friends. Gonna fly with a little help from my friends. Ain't gonna die with a little help from my friends—yeah, yeah, yeah."

He started singing, right there in the bar, almost oblivious to her now. Mary swept his hand from her knee, swallowed her Dewar's, and got ready to leave. Then she noticed the carry-on bag her companion had stowed near his feet. Leather, for sure.

Swiftly, she thought it over. Rich enough to fly first class, obnoxious enough to put his hand on a stranger's knee and desecrate not one but two Beatles songs in public—yes. It would be a sin, but just barely. She'd repented sincerely on the plane, but if God kept throwing these opportunities at her, what could He expect? She took a last glance at the man, who was now urging other patrons to join him in "Hey Jude," slipped his carry-on bag into her hand, and strolled off.

* * * *

"This is a disease," Ginny said. "Kleptomania, maybe. You need help. I'll find you a counselor."

"Like the counselor you found to help Grace with her eating disorder?" Mary unzipped the carry-on bag. "How much did Grace weigh the last time we saw her? Three hundred fifty pounds? I don't have much faith in counselors, and I can't feel much guilt about ripping off a drunken, lecherous—what a nice Polaroid camera! And—Ginny! Look at this!"

She'd found a cheap-looking cigarette case. But instead of cigarettes, it contained tightly folded hundred-dollar bills. Incredulously, she counted them. Seventeen, eighteen—two thousand dollars! Who on earth put that much cash in a carry-on bag? "Look," she said, holding out the bills. "This guy must be incredibly rich."

"Maybe not now," Ginny said. "For all you know, that's every cent he has in the world. Mary, how *could* you? He said he's a businessman, right? Maybe he came here to make investments that would've insured his future, and you've robbed him of that chance. You *have* to find him and return his money. Look in that manila envelope. Maybe it'll tell us who he is."

"He's rich. He doesn't need the money," Mary said, but shook the envelope's contents out on the coffee table. Newspaper articles about the Louis Vincenti trial. Photographs of district attorney Jim Newgate, who'd won enough convictions to send Vincenti to prison for ten years. And a photocopy of a page from Newgate's week-at-a-glance calendar.

Ginny leafed through the stuff and frowned. "So Mr. Obnoxious is interested in Vincenti and Newgate. Maybe he's a journalist."

"No," Mary said, suddenly cold. "He said he'd come here for a special job. Local talent couldn't handle it because they're being watched, but he could do it boom boom boom and gone. He's a hit man, Ginny. He's been hired to kill Jim Newgate, and he'll do it some time next week!"

"You're jumping to conclusions. Who'd be reckless enough to kill a district attorney?"

"A specialist," Mary said promptly. "Someone hired to show the world it's a mistake to prosecute anyone in the Vincenti family. He could do it, Ginny. I bet he could do it and get away with it." Mary herself had gotten away with half a dozen crimes she wouldn't have dreamed of a few weeks ago. It wasn't hard to believe a real professional could get away with much more.

"So what now?" Ginny demanded. "You put your stolen money in the bank and wait to read about Jim Newgate's murder?"

"No." Mary pressed her eyes shut. Prison. That was a definite possibility. Prison, disgrace, an end to all hopes of ever making anything of herself. But she couldn't be a party to murder. She'd been angry, she'd been infatuated with unexpected skills, she'd yielded temptation again and again. But not this. She opened her eyes. "I'll go warn Jim Newgate tomorrow," she said. "I'll stop this."

* * * *

Getting into Jim Newgate's office was easier than she'd expected. "I have to see Mr. Newgate right away," she told a receptionist. "I have vital information about the Vincenti case."

The receptionist looked dubious but picked up her receiver, murmured a few words, nodded. "Jim says it's okay," she said.

He looked more impressive in person than on television. His thinness now made him seem intense, not slight, and something compelling in his eyes made her forget how ordinary the rest of his face was. *He's* the kind who gets noticed, Mary thought. That's why he's district attorney.

He did a double-take when he saw her. "*You* have a connection to the Vincenti case?"

"Only an accidental one." She sat down, wondering if she'd be able to get through the speech she'd rehearsed with Ginny, if she could turn over her information without confessing to a crime and getting arrested. "I'm Mary Firth, an administrative assistant at Boyd Advertising. I flew home last night on the 9:30 plane from Philadelphia. It was a rough flight, and I was shaky, so I stopped at the airport bar for a drink. I sat next to a man—middle-aged, tall, lean, rust-colored hair—who'd been on the same flight. When I left, I reached for my carry-on bag and mistakenly picked up his. At home, when I discovered my mistake, I looked through the bag to try to identify its owner. I found some things you should see."

She spread the things out on his desk—camera, money-stuffed cigarette case, manila envelope and its contents. He looked at each carefully, frowning when he got to the photocopy of the page from his calendar. He looked up. "So, Ms. Firth. How do you interpret all this?"

"At first I thought he might be a journalist doing an article about the Vincenti case." Ginny's theory had an appropriately innocent sound, so she adopted it. "Then I got worried. We talked for a few minutes in the bar, and he said he'd come to town for special business local talent couldn't handle because they're being watched, but he could handle it and be gone again, boom boom boom. It occurred to me—it sounds melodramatic, but what if he's a hit man, and the Vincentis hired him to—you know. Kill you. And since he has a copy of a page from your desk calendar, that might mean someone on your staff—but this must sound silly."

"No." He stood up and paced. "I wish it did, but it sounds all too plausible. After the judge passed sentence, Vincenti shouted some threats, and—damn."

He stopped pacing and looked at her closely. "You picked up his bag by accident?"

"Yes." She blushed. She couldn't help it. "My carry-on bag is similar—it's navy, not black, but the bar wasn't well lit, I'd had a drink, and I'd put it under the bar, probably right next to his. And he was drunk, and he'd put his hand on my knee, and he was singing Beatles songs. I was in a hurry to leave, so I barely glanced at the bag—"

"Ms. Firth." He sat down again and looked straight at her. "I want to trust you. I don't want to suspect you're working for the Vincenti family, tricking me into some embarrassing mistake. But if what you say is true, I can't trust even the people on my own staff. And you didn't take that bag by mistake. Did you?"

Oh, God, she thought. I'm going to prison. She covered her face with her hands and took a deep, half-sobbing breath. "No. I knew it was his—I don't even own a carry-on bag—but I saw he was drunk, and he made me angry by putting his hand on my knee. I'm not a professional thief—at least, I wasn't until a month ago. But I've started seeing opportunities—just six, just small—and when I get angry, I can't stop myself. I started with three bags of groceries. But you don't want to hear about that."

"I do, but maybe you'd better not give me details." He sat back, smiling. "I knew you were lying about something, and now that I know what it is, I can believe you about the rest. As for the other thefts, any crime is serious, but if these were fairly petty—"

"They were," she said, then hesitated. "They were big enough to make a difference to me. Legally, they'd probably be considered petty."

"Good. If I don't find any evidence aside from your confession, and if you'll swear you'll never steal again—"

"I swear it." This time, she meant it.

"—and if you'll help me with this Vincenti thing, I suppose there's no compelling reason for me to prosecute you for the thefts. I take it you looked through that bag carefully. Did you find the man's name?"

"Not his name," she said, taking a magazine from the bag, "but the name of a hotel. There, written on the back cover—Carrington Hotel, 51st Street. Do you think that's where he's staying? I could call the airport Lost and Found, ask if anyone's reported losing a black leather carry-on bag, and see if he's staying at the Carrington."

"Good idea." He handed her the phone.

Yes, the Lost and Found clerk said. Mr. Frank King of Philadelphia had come by last night, upset about a carry-on bag that disappeared from the airport bar. Yes, he was staying at the Carrington.

The clerk urged her to return the bag to the Lost and Found, but Mary, at a signal from Jim Newgate, said no. She'd picked up Mr. King's bag by mistake; he probably had her bag. She'd handle the exchange.

"Good job," Jim Newgate said. "Before you call Frank King, I've got some calls to make. I must have a mole on my staff—I have a theory about who it is, but I can't be sure, so I can't trust anybody. Except my Uncle Paul. He runs a private detective agency. I want to get him over here to give you some protection. And I've got an idea about your Mr. King. I want to send for some pictures."

When the pictures arrived, Mary had no trouble picking out the man she'd seen at the airport last night. His real name was Rick Banks, Jim Newgate told her. He'd long been suspected of being a freelance hit man, of doing jobs for the Vincentis. Jim would love to get him on an attempted murder charge. More than that, he'd love to use Banks to get the Vincentis.

"So far, I've only been able to get Louie," he said, "and only on racketeering. But he's done much more, and old man Vincenti—God. He must've ordered this hit, and it's far from his first. If we could prove that, we could send him away forever. But Banks is a professional. He won't talk. He knows it'd be death to talk."

"So you'll just arrest him?" Mary said.

Jim Newgate shrugged. "Arrest him for carrying pictures of me? We can't prove anything more. But if you return his bag and put on a convincing innocent act, maybe he'll go ahead with his plan. Uncle Paul and I will be ready. If we catch him in the act, we can take him off the streets. That's not as good as getting old man Vincenti, but it's something."

The plan sounded risky but feasible to Mary until she met Uncle Paul. He was useless—flabby, balding, inappropriately jovial, dim, old. She could imagine the sort of detective agency he ran—a one-man, one-room deal where windows were always grimy and rent always past due, where losers who wanted their spouses followed wandered in because they couldn't afford anyone better. If this was Jim Newgate's only defense, he was dead.

"Uncle Paul will go to the Carrington, see if King's in his room," Jim was saying. "If he is, go there and call him from the lobby. Give him the story we worked out. Say you'll meet him downstairs. Uncle Paul will be there. Whatever you do, don't go anywhere private with him. We can't protect you if you do."

You can't protect me no matter what, Mary thought, if you're relying on Uncle Paul. "So I return Frank King's bag," she said. "I play dumb, and I'm on my way. Then I've done my part? I'm clear?"

"With my thanks," Jim Newgate said, and shook her hand.

The call went smoothly. "Mr. King?" Mary said. "We met in the airport bar after the Philadelphia flight—remember? I accidentally picked up your carry-on bag, and you must've accidentally picked up mine. It's black vinyl, with a copy of *Gaudy Night* inside, and a half-finished needlepoint pillow with sunflowers and butterflies and—"

"Hold on," the man cut in. "You saying you got my bag? You picked it up by accident?"

"That's right." She made her tone apologetic. "I left before you did, so the mistake is all mine. I'm sorry. I called the airport Lost and Found to get your name, and the lady said you were at the Carrington. So I asked my boss to let me take an early lunch, and I'm here in the lobby with your bag. If you'll bring down *my* bag, we can—"

"Hey," Frank King said. "Hey, hey. I'm sorry, lady, but I don't got your bag. I don't know nothing about gaudy night or sunflowers. But you got *my* bag?"

"Yes." She made her voice sink in disappointment. "Are you *sure* you don't have mine? I've worked *months* on that needlepoint pillow. It's my Aunt Joan's birthday present. It's—"

"I'm sure it is, but I don't got it. I'm real grateful to you for returning *my* bag, though. Look, I'll be right down, and I'll buy you lunch, okay, as a thank you? Maybe that'll make you feel better about the sunflowers."

She met the rust-haired man in the lobby, turned over his carry-on bag, and made only a token show of reluctance before agreeing to lunch. Uncle Paul was settled in a corner booth, halfway through his first beer and already calling for a second. Some protection, she thought. But she wasn't scared. Frank King might be a professional hit man, but he'd hardly dare to harm her in a hotel restaurant, and he'd have no reason to. Besides, all this felt strangely exciting. She felt charged, confident, bold. Maybe she *was* meant for a life of crime.

Frank King seemed charmed. He protested when she ordered tuna fish and Diet Coke, talked her into having a steak sandwich and Dewar's instead. And he looked busily through his bag.

"There's my camera," he said, then held up the cigarette case. "You open this?"

"Why, no," Mary said, pretend-flustered. "I don't smoke. Besides, it's yours. I wouldn't—"

"Yeah, sure." He flipped open the case, smiling at the tightly folded bills. "You're an honest person—I see that. You open this envelope?"

She nodded. She shouldn't play this *too* dumb. "Yes, I was hoping to find your name or your hotel—stupid me, it wasn't until hours later that I thought of calling the Lost and Found. You seem very interested in the Vincenti case. Are you a journalist?"

He gaped blankly, then nodded. "Yeah, right. A journalist. That's me. Freelance, y'know? I'm doin' a big story on that brilliant district attorney of yours. Gonna sell it to *Time, Newsweek, Hustler*, some classy operation, y'know?"

"Oh, yes." Mary fawned openly. But this wasn't like fawning to Mr. Boyd. This was fake. This was fun. "How impressive!"

He ate it up. "You bet it's impressive. You're impressive, too. Classy looking, y'know? Not supermodel classy, but quiet-classy. Like a school-teacher or a librarian."

She shook her head. "I'm an administrative assistant."

"Administrative assistant, sure," he said, sounding delighted. "That woulda been my third guess. Look, I like you—so honest and classy-looking and all. Wanna have dinner at Brewster's tonight? I hear it's petty good."

Brewster's. She remembered the name from the photocopied page from Jim Newgate's desk calendar. He was attending a Bar Association lunch at Brewster's next Tuesday. God, she thought. Frank King must be casing places listed on the calendar page, picking the best spot for a hit. And Jim can't trust his staff and doesn't have anyone but Uncle Paul to protect him.

She smiled brightly. "Thank you, Frank. I'd be happy to have dinner with you."

* * * *

Jim Newgate was adamant when she called him. "Mary—Ms. Firth," he said. "Thank you for your concern, but you've done your part. This man's dangerous. I don't want you to have any further contact with him. Cancel the date."

"I'm sure I'll be safe," she said. "It's a public place, and I'm meeting him there—I'm taking my own car. I won't be alone with him at all. Besides, he has no reason to hurt me. He thinks he's got me fooled and I believe he's a journalist."

"He thinks he's got you fooled *now*," Jim said, "but he's got to be worried you'll figure things out afterwards. He knows you've looked in that envelope. If you go to Brewster's with him, and then he picks that as the spot for the hit—well. He won't want to risk leaving a witness behind. That could be why he wants to see you again, to learn more about you so he can get rid of you when the time comes."

"That may be part of his reason." Strangely, the thought hardly frightened her. She knew she could handle this. "But I'll bet he's also using me for camouflage. A man sitting alone in a restaurant attracts more attention than a couple does. People at Brewster's might be more likely to remember him if he goes by himself. And I have this—this quality about me. People never notice me. I always fade into the background."

"You're being unfair to yourself," Jim cut in. "You look quiet and respectable, but that's not a bad thing. It's nice."

She was really starting to like this man. "It helped me as a thief," she said. "I bet King thinks it will help him, too—we'll fade into the background together, and after the hit, no one will remember he was there. Also, I may be able to sense whether he's chosen Brewster's as the place. And if he gets tipsy, he might say something you can use against the Vincentis."

He was silent, obviously tempted. Then he spoke firmly. "No. It's too dangerous. I can't let you go."

His assumption that he could order her around made her angry. "It's not your decision. I'm going. I'll call you tomorrow and tell you what happened."

She hung up. Not until later did she realize what she'd done. She'd stood up to him. A few weeks ago, she'd been afraid to talk back to a rude teenaged clerk, and she'd never had the nerve to talk back to Mr. Boyd, though she knew a hint about sexual harassment would probably make him leave her alone. Now, she'd defied a district attorney. She'd been angry, but she hadn't swallowed her anger or let it tempt her into doing some stupid, self-destructive thing. She'd simply stood her ground. I must be changing, she thought, amazed. Maybe I'm learning.

Brewster's was about ten minutes outside of town, a yellow brick and dark wood structure that was probably supposed to look vaguely Tudor. When Mary arrived, Frank King was squatting in the parking lot, snapping Polaroid shots of a side entrance.

Grinning, he walked over to her. "I'm an architecture buff," he said. "Restaurants especially—I'm nuts about restaurant architecture. Wherever I go, I take pictures of restaurants, put 'em in a big scrapbook I got back home. You hungry? I saved us a nice table."

It was a very nice table, in a dark corner—and as Mary noticed, it gave them a clear view both of the main dining room and of a side room probably used for banquets, and for Bar Association luncheons. Frank chatted steadily about his love of restaurants, his fear of flying, his high opinion of the moderately low-cut dress she'd chosen. Casually, eyes constantly darting about the room, he picked up his paper cocktail napkin, took out a pen, and began drawing. He's sketching the room, Mary realized, probably noting exits and waiters' stations and anything else that might help him make a neat hit and a quick escape. Brewster's must be a serious contender.

Abruptly, he stood up. "I'm gonna check the restrooms."

She blinked. "Excuse me?"

"Oh, yeah." He shook his head, seeming amused by his mistake. "What I mean is, I gotta go to the men's room. Be right back."

He slid his cocktail napkin under his plate and left. That napkin's evidence, Mary thought. I want it. She slipped it into her purse, took out a pen, scrawled random lines on her own napkin, and knocked over her water glass. When Frank returned, she was dabbing ineffectually at the mess.

"Clumsy me," she said, smiling apologetically, holding up a sodden, inky wad of paper. "I spilled my water and had to use your napkin to clean it up. The waiter will bring you a new one."

He looked dismayed, then shrugged. "No big deal. You want steak or lobster or what?"

It wasn't until they'd ordered dessert that Mary spotted Uncle Paul at a small table across the room, absorbed in chasing down the last traces of his lasagna with a hunk of garlic bread.

So, she thought. Jim decided I need protection, and he sent Uncle Paul. Good plan. If Frank King emptied a machine gun into me, it's possible Uncle Paul would notice by the time the paramedics arrived.

Frank walked her to the parking lot. "I had a great time, Mary. You sure you won't come to the hotel?"

"I'd love to, but it's been a long day." She blushed and looked down. The part of timid maiden came to her naturally. "You understand."

"Yeah, sure." He patted her back. "You're a nice girl. I respect that. Some of my best friends are virgins. Look, tomorrow's Saturday. You don't work, right? Let's spend the day together. I hear this town's got a great art museum."

The art museum. Jim was going there next Wednesday for the dedication of the new wing. Evidently, Frank hadn't settled on Brewster's as the spot for the hit—he was still casing other locations. "That sounds lovely," she said.

"Great." Frank took a notebook from his coat pocket. "I'll pick you up at ten, and we'll make a day of it. Maybe we'll stop by the courthouse, see if there's a tour. I hear the architecture's real interesting. What's your address?"

She felt a chill—but what, really, would she lose by telling him? He already knew her last name, so he could find her address by looking her up in the phone book. And she'd have to get in his car tomorrow, but they'd be on public roads—they wouldn't really be alone. She could handle it.

He kissed her cheek before she got into her car, and she thought she saw affection in his eyes. But what sort of affection could a hit man feel?

"You're a peach, Mary," he said. "You're helping me lots, making this trip a real pleasure."

* * * *

It was almost midnight when she heard pounding on her door. She looked through the peephole and saw Jim Newgate.

She opened the door, and he walked in, shoulders rigid with indignation. "You promised you wouldn't be alone with him at all," he said. "But you let him walk you to your car, even let him kiss you. And what's this about the art museum?"

She got him to sit down and poured him a cup of tea. "How did you know about the kiss?"

"Uncle Paul told me. He was in his car, parked right next to you—didn't you notice him? The point is, King could've strangled you in that parking lot. And you've agreed to spend the day with him. You'll be alone in the car with him, completely at his mercy. Why?"

"Because we're going to the art museum and the courthouse. You'll be at the museum Wednesday night, and you're at the courthouse constantly. He's scouting out more locations. I already picked up valuable information tonight. He took photographs of a side entrance at Brewster's, and look at this napkin. I stole it from him. Isn't it evidence? Doesn't it prove something?"

She handed him the napkin. He looked at it and shrugged. "It *suggests* something. It's not proof. Anyway, I don't want you alone with him tomorrow. It's dangerous."

"I'll be fine." She stirred her tea. "But I'd like to get my sister out of town. If you'll lend me two hundred dollars, I'll get her on a plane tomorrow. We're giving our Aunt Joan a diamond necklace for her birthday. Ginny can deliver it in person. Now. Tell me more about the Vincenti case."

* * * *

Frank King was in a fine mood when he picked her up the next morning. "Man, am I ever up for seeing some art. I may take some pictures. Got a brand-new roll of film."

Mary looked at the Polaroid camera in the backseat. "I don't think you're allowed to take pictures, except in the sculpture garden."

"Then I'll leave the camera in the car. Speaking of the sculpture garden, I'm meeting a fellow journalist there at 10:30. Our talk's gonna be real boring, professional stuff. So make yourself scarce awhile."

"Okay." He's meeting his contact, Mary thought. Someone from the Vincenti family is paying him off, or giving him a gun—he probably couldn't bring one on the plane. I need to get evidence about this meeting.

So when Frank pulled into the museum lot and reminded her to lock the car door, she nodded obediently and clicked the lock—twice. Unlocked, and a convenient Polaroid in the back seat. Now, if she could only manage the timing.

As they wandered through the museum, Frank took out his notebook and made casual jottings. Exits, balconies, staircases. She'd love to steal that notebook but didn't dare. And photographs of his meeting with the contact would be even better.

At 10:25 he steered a path toward the sculpture garden. "There's my fellow journalist," he said. "How's about you check out the snack bar?"

"Good idea." She turned away promptly, ran to the car, grabbed the camera, ran back past four security guards. Not one seemed to notice she was running; not one seemed bothered. She ran to an alcove overlooking the sculpture garden, stationed herself in a corner, and took a rapid series of pictures: a nervous-looking, fair-haired young man handing Frank an eelskin briefcase; Frank smiling in satisfaction; Frank and the young man shaking hands. And a flabby, balding man wandering through the sculpture garden, gazing vacantly at a jagged granite hulk before shaking his head and wandering off again. Could it have been Uncle Paul? No, probably just some man who looked like him. In any city, you could find thousands of men who looked more or less like Uncle Paul.

She snapped her last picture, ran to the gift shop, bought more film, ran to the ladies' room. Quickly, she made the switch, slipping pictures and used film into her purse. Now, she thought. If I can just get to the car, leave the camera on the back seat, lock my door, and get back again.

But Frank was waiting when she came out of the ladies' room, briefcase in his hand. "Hiya, sweetie," he said. "We finished our business. Wanna check out more art?"

"Absolutely," she said, and shoved the camera into her purse.

Even if Frank had a genuine interest in art, he could not have prowled those corridors more slowly. Mary was in agony, constantly aware of the extra weight in her purse, sure she could never get the camera into the back seat unnoticed.

The gift shop, she thought. It's my only hope. She pretended to fall in love with some portraits of eighteenth-century ladies, declared she had to stop by the gift shop to buy prints, then begged for coffee. She left the bag containing her prints on the floor next to her chair. People sometimes leave packages behind—hadn't she learned that from the boys who left the Music Mart bag at the bus stop? As she and Frank walked into the parking lot, she stopped suddenly, slapping her hand against her forehead.

"My prints!" she cried. "I must've left them in the snack bar. Could you get them, Frank? Please?"

He grumbled but turned back, as if used to performing chores for scatterbrained women. By the time he returned to the lot, the camera was in the back seat, the car door was locked, and Mary was leaning against the hood, smiling. "Thanks," she said. "Where would you like to have lunch?"

"The Garden Spot." He half-snarled it. It didn't sound like a place he'd usually favor, but Jim was scheduled to lunch there Monday.

Obviously, Frank was still scouting for the perfect place for a hit. Obviously, Mary still had to stick with him.

* * * *

Jim Newgate showed up at her door minutes after Frank left. "You brought him up to your apartment," he said. "After all your promises, all my warnings, you brought him up. How the hell do you expect me to protect you if you do things like that?"

I *don't* expect it, Mary thought, not if the best you can offer is Uncle Paul. But she smiled pleasantly. "I was never in danger, Jim. I can handle Frank. And after I'd spent the whole day with him, it would've been rude not to offer him coffee. I think I got some valuable evidence today. I saw him sketching or taking pictures of four possible hit locations. I took some pictures, too. Do you recognize this man?"

Jim looked at the Polaroid shots and took a deep breath. "Yes. He's a junior partner in the law firm that represented Louie Vincenti at the trial. So Alan Moore's running errands for the Vincentis now. The whole firm may be in on this."

"Could you confront Alan Moore with these pictures? Could you do it now, tonight? You said Frank King wouldn't talk because he's a professional criminal. Moore's no professional—he looked very nervous. You could break him down, make him tell you about the whole scheme."

Jim shook his head. "I'm sure he doesn't know the whole scheme. The Vincentis put a dozen people between the top man and the hit man, and no one knows more than he or she has to. Moore probably knew he was doing something un-kosher, but he probably didn't know exactly whom he was meeting or why. If I confront him, he'll stonewall and call the next person in the chain. The plan will be called off, and we'll be back where we started. We'll have a better chance if he gets really scared later, after the attempted hit."

Mary sat forward. "You can't be sure it'll just be an *attempted* hit. You'll be on your guard, but that might not be enough. I can't believe that Monday you'll start walking into these places Frank's cased, making yourself a target."

"I'll be all right. I'll have Uncle Paul watching out for me." He put the pictures in his jacket pocket. "Thank you, Mary. I'm glad to have these pictures, even though you probably took too many chances to get them. But that's it. We're getting too close to the crucial time. Tomorrow, you get on a plane, join your sister in—"

"No." She looked down at her hands. "You could end this whole thing now by confronting Alan Moore or arresting Frank King on suspicion, but you won't play it safe. Neither will I. If there's any chance I can get enough evidence to make you take action before Frank takes a shot at you, I'm going to try. You need me. You don't have anyone else you can trust."

"I have Uncle Paul."

"Uncle Paul!" She stood up and walked a few steps away from him. "Jim, I'm sure he's a nice man, but he isn't up to this job. He's old, he's out of shape, he's absent-minded and unfocused, he—"

"—and you always fade into the background," Jim said. "Uncle Paul is like you in some ways. Maybe that's why you underestimate him. I don't. If anyone can keep me safe through this thing, he can. I'm grateful for all you've contributed, but there's nothing more you can do at this point."

"I can go to Brewster's again Monday night," she said quietly. "Frank's asked me to have dinner with him. I think that's the place, Jim. He plans to shoot you at the Bar Association lunch on Tuesday—that'd be a dramatic public statement, wouldn't it? And he wants to check the place out one more time. I want to go with him. I'll watch him, and maybe I can figure out his plan—where he plans to stand, how he plans to get away. Maybe he'll plant the gun in advance, and I'll see him do it."

She'd stunned him. He sat silent and motionless, hands resting on his knees, as if knowing the precise time and place had made the hit more real to him. "Monday night," he said. "You're not seeing him tomorrow?"

"No. He said he has other things to do. Maybe he's seeing that lawyer again. Maybe you should have Uncle Paul follow Alan Moore." Uncle Paul can't do much harm that way, she thought.

Jim nodded. "Good idea. Moore might meet *his* contact tomorrow, to report on his conversation with King—maybe we can follow the chain up another link or two. On Monday night Uncle Paul will be at Brewster's. Take your own car. Don't spend even a minute alone with King. And I'm buying you an airplane ticket for Tuesday morning. Promise me you'll use it."

"I'll think about it." She knew she wouldn't. How could she run away on the day Jim might need her most?

* * * *

At 6:15 Monday night Frank showed up at her apartment. "I got to thinking," he said cheerfully. "Why take two cars when we can both go in mine? And I gotta make a stop on the way to Brewster's, and I want you with me. Okay?"

"Okay." At this point, any change in plan was unnerving, but maybe she'd see something when he made his stop. Maybe he'd meet that lawyer again, and this would be the break that'd convince Jim to arrest Frank King before the hit was attempted. She followed Frank to his car.

He turned north on Thirty-seventh. Brewster's was south of town. "I love this town," Frank said. "Great restaurants, great art museums—and great people." He patted her knee before turning his attention back to the road. "Great stores, too. I did some shopping yesterday, got some great stuff."

She noticed the Croft's shopping bag in the back seat. "You went to Croft's, I see. The one at the mall?"

"Yeah, I got a great shirt. I wanna stop back there tonight, see if I can get a great tie to go with it."

The mall, she thought, her body clenching. Jim will be at the mall tonight. The page from his desk calendar came back to her—Monday night, 7:00, judge at safety poster contest, Center Court at mall. God, she thought. The hit isn't tomorrow at Brewster's. It's tonight, at the mall. Frank must've cased it yesterday, when I wasn't with him and Uncle Paul was following that lawyer. And now Uncle Paul is at Brewster's, waiting for me to show up—Jim won't have even him for protection. All he'll have is me, and I can't do anything.

She smiled weakly. "You know, the Croft's downtown is even nicer than the one at the mall. Why don't we—"

"Nah." Frank didn't take his eyes off the road. "I don't like downtown stores. Too stuffy. I like malls. And there's a nice jewelry store there, too. Rutherford's. I wanna get something for you." He smiled at her again. "You been so sweet, so friendly. I got something *real* nice in mind for you."

I'll bet you do, Mary thought, chilled. Jim had said Frank wouldn't want to leave a witness behind. He must plan to kill us both tonight. Will he kill us both at the mall? Maybe he'll fire wild shots so he can escape in the confusion and—dear God. The poster contest. All those children in Center Court, and a ruthless professional killer firing who knows how many bullets.

He pulled into the parking lot. "Help me remember where we're parked," he said. "These mall lots get awful confusing, since they're so big and all. See? I'm parking three rows to the left of the Croft's entrance, five cars down. Can you remember that?"

"Yes," Mary said numbly. Why does he want me to remember where the car's parked? What's his plan?

He reached for the Croft's bag as they got out. "I got the shirt I bought yesterday in here, in case I wanna check the color against a tie, y'know?" But the bottom of the bag sagged. He had something heavier than a shirt in there.

The gun, Mary thought. He got the bag yesterday so he could put the gun in there. He'll look like an innocent shopper as he wanders through Croft's, walks into Center Court, positions himself to shoot Jim. And he'll have me on his arm. We'll fade into the background. No one will notice us.

She had to do something, but she was too shocked to think, too scared to act. She could only walk stiffly as he led her through Croft's. He stopped at a rack of ties, briefly pretending to examine them. All the time he was gazing down the long aisle leading to Center Court. Already Mary sensed a new tension in him, a tightened focus. Do something, she told herself fiercely. Do *anything*.

Only one thought came to her, and she did what she could. She did it well, as she always did, without hesitation or unnecessary movements. Frank took no notice of her. No one did. That's something, she thought, but not enough. I'll have to think of something else.

She didn't have time. Frank's body stiffened, and she followed his gaze toward Center Court. The judges were walking onto a temporary stage, and people were clapping. Jim, smiling in his quiet way, chatted with a gray-haired woman, leaned over to shake hands with a little boy.

Frank turned to her abruptly. "Nah, I don't like these ties. And I'm getting hungry. I still wanna stop by Rutherford's, get you that little something. Tell you what. To save time, you get my car. Remember where I parked?"

"Yes." She tried to keep her voice steady. "Third row to the left, five cars down."

"Good girl." He couldn't give her more than a brief, rigid smile now. He was too intent on what came next. "You take my keys, get my car, drive around to the entrance near Rutherford's. I'll meet you there in five minutes. Okay?"

"Okay," she said.

So that was the plan. Not, thank goodness, a massacre in Center Court—probably one quick bullet for Jim, enough noise and panic to let Frank slip away to the car she'd have ready for him. Then he'd kill her on the way to Brewster's and leave her body by the side of the road. It was a good plan, better than the one she'd imagined for him. But she had a plan of her own now. Her hand closed around his car keys. "See you soon," she said, and walked away.

He'd told her five minutes, but that was probably to make her hurry—he wouldn't want to stand around waiting after the hit. He'd wait at least ten minutes before shooting to make sure she'd be ready. That was enough time to get to Jim and warn him, except she couldn't get to

Center Court from Croft's without walking past Frank. She needed help. Quickly, she scanned the shoppers as she hurried past them.

A petite young mother trailed by two toddlers, glancing anxiously at her watch; a distinguished white-haired man frowning at a display of men's colognes; a moderately burly, pale man in his early twenties, hardly noticeable in the rush of more dynamic shoppers, lounging near a stack of pajamas—yes. A good bet. She walked over to the young man and smiled nervously.

"Excuse me," she said. "Are you a security guard?

"Yes." He seemed dismayed she'd spotted him. "Is there a problem?"

"I saw a man—tall, lean, rust-colored hair, grey slacks, navy jacket—slip several ties into a Croft's shopping bag. He must be a shoplifter. Can you stop him?"

Instantly the young man came alert. "There's no point stopping him until he leaves the store. He'll say he was planning to pay for them. But those ties are tagged, so—look, come point him out, and if he tries to leave, I'll get him."

She didn't want to go with him. She wanted to leave Croft's, run to another entrance, and re-enter the mall in time to warn Jim. She definitely didn't want Frank King to spot her siccing a plainclothes security guard on him. But there didn't seem to be any way out of it. She sighed. "This way," she said.

She grabbed his arm, pulling him toward the racks of ties. Frank was striding toward the Center Court entrance, the shopping bag heavy on his arm. As parents clapped and beamed, Jim crossed the banner-strewn stage to pin a red ribbon on a Firearms Safety poster. She pointed; the security guard looked. Casually, Frank stepped out of Croft's and into Center Court.

She'd been expecting it, but even so the strident blare of the store alarm made her jump. Frank looked around, startled by the sound, at a loss. In seconds the guard had a firm hand on his arm.

"Excuse me, sir," the guard said. "I need to look in that bag."

Frank looked at him and blinked, still not understanding what had happened. Then things began to dawn on him, and his eyes took on a desperate look. Wildly, he swung at the guard with his free hand, hitting him squarely in the face, knocking him on his back.

Mary stepped forward. "Jim, get down!" she shouted. "It's him!"

Frank saw her—and now he seemed to get it, now anger filled his eyes. He knocked two shoppers aside, pushed over a display, and grabbed her, locking his arm against her throat, driving his gun into her back. The security guard struggled to stand, Jim raced toward the store, shoppers screamed and backed away. None of them could help her in time.

She still had his car keys in her hand. With her last burst of courage, she flung them far into Center Court.

"There," she gasped. "You scum! There!"

That startled him, but only for a moment. He was dragging her backwards now, away from Jim and the security guard, past cowering shoppers and clerks, toward the parking lot entrance.

"I'll get a car," he whispered, his breath harsh on her ear. "If I have to kill ten people to do it, I'll get a car, and I'll deal with you. Then you'll wish you'd let me shoot you clean. You'll be sorry you made me mad."

She had never heard anything more evil than his voice. She clawed at his arm, but it was no good. He was too strong, moving too fast. It's over, she thought. I'm dead.

And then she was facedown on the floor, an immense weight on top of her. Shouts, grunts, a sharp blast of noise—she couldn't see anything. Then part of the weight was gone, then all of it. She was free. Curses, more shouts, cheers. She got to her knees.

Jim crouched next to her, arms firm around her. And Frank King lay facedown on the floor, hands cuffed behind his back. Uncle Paul stood above him, sweating, wiping his red face with a handkerchief, panting.

"Sorry to give you that scare, Jim," he said. "You told me to wait for her at Brewster's, but I figured I'd better wait outside her apartment and follow her there, in case our boy tried something funny. Sure enough, he did. I tailed them here and saw what he was up to, but she had things pretty well in hand. That was a neat trick, miss, slipping those ties into his shopping bag. So I figured I'd just stick around, tackle him if worse came to worst. When it did, I did. Hope I didn't hurt you, miss."

"Not at all," Mary said. Jim was still holding her, and it felt very nice. She looked up and smiled. "Thank you, Uncle Paul."

* * * *

"That creep Boyd fired you?" Ginny said incredulously. "You saved the life of a district attorney, and he fired you?"

"Mr. Boyd hates bad publicity." Mary finished writing the check for two hundred three dollars and eighty-six cents and slipped it into the envelope addressed to the Food Bank. "So when I said I'd be testifying at the trial of Rick Banks, alias Frank King, Mr. Boyd realized I'd have to admit I'd been associated with what he calls 'an underworld type.' He thought that might hurt Boyd Advertising's reputation. I tried to reason with him. Alan Moore and three other lawyers at his firm have turned state's evidence—old man Vincenti's been charged, too. This time, Jim might be able to bring the whole Vincenti organization down. And a Boyd employee helped. I argued the publicity might bring in new accounts. Mr. Boyd didn't buy it. I'd associated with 'an underworld type,' and that's all he cared about."

"That's so unfair. You didn't do anything wrong. You were one of the good guys."

"I got to be a good guy," Mary said, "only because I'd been a bad guy. I *did* do something wrong. I stole a carry-on bag from a drunk, and I'll have to admit that on the witness stand. Jim won't tolerate perjury. Neither will I, not now. He won't press charges, but I stole, and everyone will know it. The publicity *might* hurt the firm." She wrote out a check for two hundred sixty-five dollars and addressed the envelope to the Girl Scouts of America. Mark Hanson would never donate a penny to any organization for girls.

Ginny sighed. "At least Boyd gave you severance pay. You can use that to support yourself while you look for another job."

"No, I'm using it to make amends for the first two thefts. As soon as I can, I'll make amends for the others, with donations to whatever charities seem appropriate. I don't have to worry about supporting myself. I start my new job Monday."

Ginny sat up straighter. "You found something already? Another advertising agency?"

"No, I'm bored with advertising. Uncle Paul's giving me a job. He says I'm a natural as a private detective. I fade into the background, and that's a plus in a job where it doesn't pay to get noticed. And he says I'm resourceful and daring and—well, I won't tell you all the things he said. Anyway, he showed me my office. Did I tell you he runs the biggest detective agency in the city, with fifteen operatives and a whole floor in the Bradford building? I'll have my own administrative assistant."

Ginny lifted both palms. "Incredible. You steal, you repent, you do a few measly good deeds, and you end up with a dream job and a private office and an administrative assistant. What's next? Is Prince Charming sweeping you off to his castle?"

"Don't be silly." Mary walked to the mirror and surveyed herself contentedly. This was a new dress, a red dress, slightly more low-cut than the dress she'd worn on her first date with Frank King. "But Jim Newgate *is* taking me out to dinner tonight."

Sometimes, a story starts with a sliver of experience, followed by the question "what if?" When our family lived in Annapolis, we bought groceries at a store with an asking-for-disaster pickup system: Shoppers left their carts in a designated area outside the store, got their cars, and drove up to retrieve their groceries. Usually, a store employee was on hand to supervise. When the store got busy or the weather got bad, though, customers were on their own. One night, my husband and I drove up to the pickup area, spotted what we thought was our cart, and started putting bags into our trunk. Then I glanced into a bag and noticed some item I knew we hadn't bought. So we put the bags back, found our own cart, loaded up, and drove away.

Not exactly an adventure, but it got me thinking. What if someone who couldn't afford to buy nice groceries got an unexpected chance to leave her bags of rice and peanut butter behind, and to drive off with bags stuffed with caviar and rib roast instead? She's never stolen any-thing before, but she yields to temptation—just this once, she tells her-self. What might happen next?

I thought of a book I'd taught several times over the years, one of the contenders for the title of first true English novel—Daniel Defoe's 1722 Moll Flanders. *The book's probably best known for its lusty account of Moll's romantic adventures—the full title describes her as "Twelve Year a Whore, five times a Wife (whereof once to her own Brother)"—but I'd always been even more interested in her career as a thief. Moll never intends to steal. The first time, she does it on impulse, almost against her will, when she's in desperate circumstances and an opportunity is practically thrust upon her. Afterwards, she's overwhelmed by guilt and the fear of getting caught. As time goes on, however, and she yields to temptation again and again, guilt and fear diminish, and she finds ways to rationalize what she's doing. It's a fascinating psychological portrait. If you haven't read* Moll Flanders *yet, I heartily recommend it. (I should warn you that Moll doesn't become a thief until almost two-thirds of the way through the novel—but the lusty parts aren't bad, either.)*

I decided to use Moll as a model for the protagonist who was be-ginning to take shape in my mind. I named my protagonist Mary Firth, which is an alias Moll uses at one point. Just for fun, I named a couple of other characters after places mentioned in the novel; Defoe fans may be able to spot them. Like Moll, Mary eventually declares she's repented and will never steal again. Readers will have to decide which protago-nist, if either, is telling the truth.

THE SHOPPER

(2014)

The worst part was knowing that she'd been in the house when it happened, that she'd slept through it. Compared to that, the loss of her purse and of the other things he'd taken hardly mattered. Yes, it was a nuisance—she'd have to clean up the mess he'd left behind, call credit card companies, replace her driver's license, replace so much else. It'd be costly, too, since she had never bought renter's insurance, had never thought anyone would bother to burglarize her house. And it was sad, since so many of the things he'd taken had been gifts from people she loved. But the worst part was the sense of violation, the chill of knowing a criminal had been in her house, had handled her belongings, had seen her lying in bed.

"Be glad you're a sound sleeper," Detective Foley said as he sat in her kitchen that morning. He was a heavyset man of about sixty, his still-black hair now thinned to a shadow. "You're lucky you didn't wake up while he was here."

"Do you think he might have hurt me?" she asked. The question had haunted her all morning. It was a relief to say it out loud.

Foley shrugged. "Most burglars aren't violent types. True, this guy's bolder than most. He almost always breaks in when someone's home. But he's never come face to face with anyone. If he did, chances are he'd just take off. On the other hand, he might not want to leave a witness behind. And, of course, you're an attractive young woman. Be glad you weren't the one to find out how he'd react."

She shuddered. "You know who the burglar was, then?"

"Not his name, no. But I know his pattern. We think he's pulled over two hundred burglaries during the last few years. I'll tell you everything we know about him, Ms. Hartman, if you'll make me a cup of coffee."

"Of course," she said. "And please, call me Diane."

But she couldn't make him coffee. When she opened the cupboard, her coffee filters were missing. For some reason, that made her start shaking. Foley got her to sit down, brewed tea, and told her about her burglar.

This guy, Foley said, always picked middle-income houses like hers, ones that didn't have security systems. He concentrated on volume, hitting two or three houses a week, taking only as much as he could carry. As to why he broke in when people were home, Foley couldn't say. Maybe it was so he could get purses and wallets—burglars who break into empty houses usually don't find cash. Or maybe he found it more exciting this way.

The corners of Foley's mouth nudged up. "He's gotten to be a legend in the department. We call him The Shopper."

"The Shopper? Why?"

"Two reasons. First, he always takes about enough to fill two shopping bags. Second, he almost seems to be shopping when he goes through a house. He never misses small valuables, but he also takes things he couldn't fence. Probably, they just catch his eye, and he uses them himself."

"That certainly seems to be what he did here." Diane looked around the room and sighed. "I'm amazed at some of the things he took."

"He's an amazing guy. Well, let's go over the list again, see if you can think of anything else." Foley picked up his notebook. "Your purse—about fifty dollars, credit cards, cell phone, all that. A watch. A jewelry box—mostly costume jewelry, but a ruby ring, two gold chains, a silver locket. A clock radio, a Kindle, two silver candlesticks, a college diploma in a brass frame, a flute. Right so far?"

"Right." Diane nodded glumly, thinking of the memories she'd lost, of how much it would cost to replace even this modest store of treasures.

"Next comes the weird stuff." Foley half-grinned. "Four hand towels. Sewing shears. A hairbrush. A bottle of Scotch. A pan of brownies, half a pound of salami, an eggplant, raspberry jam, a pint of ice cream." He grinned. "That's why I told you to check your kitchen. The Shopper always raids the refrigerator. The hairbrush, though—that's unusual, even for him. We'd better add coffee filters. You'll probably notice other things missing, too, over the next few days. Keep a list and e-mail it to me. And get your locks changed. The Shopper's never hit a house twice, and he's cleaned you out pretty good—I don't think he'll be back. But he's got your keys, and there's no point taking chances."

He gave her a few more bits of advice, she thanked him, and he left. Now came the dreary business of undoing some of the damage, and of trying to adjust to the rest. She made half a dozen phone calls, put away things The Shopper had tossed aside, watched bleakly as the locksmith did his work. It wasn't until after lunch, as she was getting ready for a half-day at work, that she broke down and wept. She couldn't be satisfied with the way she looked, because her favorite makeup had been in her purse. She didn't know if the Summer Reading Committee met today, because her appointment calendar had been in her purse. And her reading glasses—she'd be sure to have a headache after an afternoon of squinting at computer screens and call numbers.

It isn't fair, she raged, wondering if any man could imagine how much he hurt a woman by stealing her purse. And she felt like a stranger in her own home now, constantly reaching for things that were no longer there, every ten minutes discovering fresh evidence of The Shopper's intrusion—a bottle of aspirin missing, a box of tissues moved. She'd been so proud of this house, had felt so safe here. It was tiny, and only rented, but it was her symbol of security and independence, her proof she could take care of herself. And now some stranger called The Shopper had destroyed all that. Her privacy had been denied, her contentment sneered at. She felt suddenly vulnerable.

* * * *

It helped to go to work, to tell her little story while the other librarians gasped. Lori said she'd help with cleanup, Paula started planning a burglary shower to replace some of the stolen things, and Kaye, the head librarian, took her aside and offered to lend her money. By the time Diane got home, she felt cheerful and determined. She hardly flinched when she opened her door and saw the desk drawers still dumped out on the floor. Another few hours, she thought, and I'll make this place mine again.

She walked over to her phone to check her voicemail—she'd really be relying on her landline now, until she could get a new cell—and was startled to hear a deep, raspy voice.

"Diane Hartman," it said. "Look under your doormat."

She was half-afraid to do it, but she took a deep breath, opened the door, and picked up the manila envelope hidden under the doormat. Hands shaking, she slammed and bolted the door, then peered tentatively into the envelope. Her driver's license, the pictures from her wallet, her keys. She stared at them, then grabbed the phone and called Detective Foley.

"Don't touch anything," he said. "I'll be right over."

He arrived with a technician who dusted everything in the envelope for fingerprints and found none. As Foley played the message back, Diane served them lemonade, feeling almost joyful.

"What a nice surprise," she said, handing Foley his glass. "My friend was going to drive me to the DMV tomorrow to get a new license, but now she won't have to. And it's wonderful to have my pictures back. I guess I should be grateful to The Shopper."

"I guess." Foley took a long sip of lemonade. "Look, I don't wanna scare you, but I don't like this. The Shopper's never returned anything before. He's not the compassionate type. Now he's made personal contact with a victim, and he's taken a risk to do it. That's disturbing."

She tilted her head to the side. "What do you mean?"

"I mean he's taking an interest in you, and that makes me nervous. Look through your pictures. Did he return all of them?"

She spread them out on the coffee table. "No," she said, feeling her stomach clench. "One's missing—a picture of my sister and me. Dear God."

"See what I mean?" Foley said. "He chanced being seen by coming here to put that stuff under your doormat. Leaving the message was a risk, too, even though I'm sure he disguised his voice. And he's holding onto a picture of you."

She felt small and cold. "What should I do?"

"Don't panic. Maybe it's just his idea of a joke. But I'd like to put a tracer on your phone, and we'll have patrol cars check your street often. Also, be extra-careful about locking up, going out alone at night, everything. And if anything else happens, call me."

* * * *

Something else did happen, when she arrived at the library the next morning. Lori was waiting for her, holding out another manila envelope.

"We found it when we emptied the book-deposit box this morning," she said. "See? It has your name on it, with letters cut from magazines. What can it be?"

It was her reading glasses. She called Detective Foley and again watched the careful, useless search for fingerprints. Then she shivered until her co-workers' jokes and the comforting normalcy of library routine calmed her down. Lori thought it was terribly exciting, and Diane had to admit it would be a great story to tell over drinks one day. Probably, The Shopper was a meek little man who felt guilty about stealing a librarian's eyeglasses, and she'd never hear from him again.

By Story Hour, she'd pushed the whole thing out of her mind. This was her favorite part of her job—sitting in the big rocking chair in the children's room, gathering the preschoolers on the floor around her, delighting them with silly voices and exaggerated gestures as she read well-loved stories out loud. The parents were almost as much fun as the kids. Always, a small group of mothers stood in the back of the room, listening and smiling and sneaking cookies from the tray set out for the children. Today, two fathers had shown up as well. That's nice, Diane thought. I love seeing fathers take an interest in their children's activities.

These two were definitely interested. The thin, dark one hung back a little, probably feeling out of place in a cluster of women. But his eyes stayed on Diane the whole time, and he laughed out loud when she got to the quacking parts of *Make Way for Ducklings*. The blond, broad-shouldered one mingled with the mothers more, munching occasional cookies. When Diane took a sip of water before beginning *A Chair for My Mother*, he caught her eye and smiled at her directly.

They both seemed so pleased that she expected them to introduce themselves afterwards, but they left so quickly she didn't see them go—she was too distracted by the rush of children crowding in for hugs and a closer look at the pictures. Too bad, she thought. She'd been curious about which children were theirs.

As she walked home at the end of the day, she felt herself go tense, and she couldn't help checking under the doormat. Nothing. There, she thought. It's over.

When she looked through the mail, though, she found a plain white envelope—no return address, her own address written in large, clumsy capitals. She dropped it on the desk, called Detective Foley, and watched as he opened it. It could be a thank-you note from one of the children, she told herself, but didn't believe it.

It was the heart-shaped silver locket her parents had given her for her sixteenth birthday. The Shopper had returned the picture of her parents, but kept the picture of her. And he'd written a note. She gasped as she read it over Foley's shoulder.

> YOU LOOK SO PRETTY WHEN YOUR ASLEEP. PRETTY GIRLS SHOULD HAVE PRETTY THINGS.
> IT WAS HARD NOT TO TOUCH YOU. I LOOKED FOR A LONG TIME, BUT I DIDNT TOUCH.

"I don't like this," Foley said again. "He seems obsessed with you. Probably, he won't come near you—too afraid of being spotted—but we can't be sure. Maybe you should stay with a friend for a few days."

"No," she said. "I won't let him drive me out of my home. You don't really think I'm in danger, do you?"

He paused, then shrugged. "Not really. But be careful."

She was very careful, checking several times to make sure all the windows were locked, checking the chains and bolts on the doors even more often, lying awake for hours listening for noises downstairs. Nothing happened. At least, she thought as she yawned through breakfast, he's stopped calling and coming to the house. He's probably smart enough to figure on the phone tap and the extra police patrols. If he sends a few more things back through the mail, will that be so bad? And how much more is he likely to return? Probably nothing really valuable—and will he mail back half a pound of salami? Soon, she assured herself, he'll lose interest, or run out of things he feels like returning. He's a nasty, cowardly creep who probably gets some sick thrill from playing games with me. But I will not let him terrify me into moving out or changing my life.

Later that morning, as she sat at the circulation desk, she noticed the blond, broad-shouldered man who had come to story hour the day before. Today, he seemed to be looking for a book for himself, browsing for half an hour before settling into a chair near the back windows. Odd, Diane thought—I never noticed him in here before, and now I see him twice in two days. Odder still, the thin, dark man from Story Hour showed up, too. He found the Sunday *Times*, made a photocopy of the crossword puzzle, sat down at a table, and set to work. A coincidence, she told herself. Once you notice people, you start seeing them everywhere.

Even so, it felt strange to see them both sitting only a few feet away from each other, only a few yards away from her. I wonder what The Shopper looks like, she thought, and found herself stealing glances at them. Both seemed to be in their early thirties, about her own age. Both were conservatively dressed. And both, to her, started to look suspicious. The blond one—wasn't there something menacing about his blandly boyish features, the methodical way he chewed his gum? The dark one's facial features were too sharp, and the foot tapping constantly in the air seemed like a sign of excess energy, or maybe of a guilty conscience. And why were they here on a weekday morning? Didn't they have jobs? Or did one of them make a living by breaking into houses at night and brooding over women as they slept?

I'm being ridiculous, Diane thought. I'm doing them an injustice. They've been laid off, or they're taking breaks, or they work night shifts. I can't start suspecting every man who comes here during the day. A librarian should be glad to see people using the library.

She made herself concentrate on her work. But she couldn't help noticing when the blond man turned down the corner of the page he was reading, left his book on his chair, and went to the men's room. Minutes later, he came back, picked the book up briefly, set it down, and left the library. So he decided not to check it out, she thought. Or maybe he didn't want me to see his name on his library card. Shaking her head at her own silliness, she walked over to re-shelve the book. *An Illustrated History of Aviation*. That was certainly innocent enough.

As she walked back to the circulation desk, she passed the dark man, who was working steadily on his puzzle. Fifteen minutes later, he finished it, smiled, folded it, put it in his jacket pocket, and left. Did he keep a scrapbook of every crossword puzzle he completed? Or didn't he want her to see a sample of his handwriting, to have her ask the police to check it against the printing on the note he'd sent her? Good grief, she thought. I'm getting hopelessly paranoid.

As she was about to leave for home, a skinny, dark-skinned boy ran up to the desk, carrying a package wrapped in brown paper. "I found this near the bike stand, Ms. Hartman," he said. "It has your name on it. Did you drop it?"

She called Detective Foley before opening it. This time, The Shopper had returned the makeup from her purse, along with a bottle of cologne he'd taken from her dresser. And he'd written another note:

> I HOPE YOUR NOT TO MAD AT ME FOR TAKING YOUR THINGS. I DIDNT TAKE ALOT, JUST WHAT I NEEDED.
> YOU HAVE PRETTY EYES. THAT NIGHT, I WONDERED WHAT COLOR YOUR EYES WERE. NOW I KNOW.

"He's getting chatty," Foley commented. "And he's seen you, or says he has. He could be bluffing, to scare you."

Diane fought the impulse to tell him about the library's two newest patrons. She was probably imagining things, and Foley might over-react. It would be a shame to see two innocent men hauled in for interrogation because they'd used the library. Really, it *couldn't* be one of them. It would be insane for The Shopper to risk coming to the library. I have to calm down, she told herself.

Calming down proved hard. At 4:00, the blond man came back, flipped through magazines for about an hour, and left. Twice in one day, she thought, almost stapling her finger to a summer reading list. Probably, he was out of work and restless. Then, as she walked home, she saw the dark man sitting on a bench in the park near her home, reading a newspaper and drinking Diet Coke. Probably, he was out of work, too. These days, lots of people were out of work.

She didn't really feel like going out that night, but she and Lori had a long-standing date for dinner and a movie. It'd be embarrassing to admit she was scared to go out, and the company would do her good. But when she got to the restaurant, she spotted the blond man sitting in a booth, eating a slab of pie. He has a right to eat wherever he likes, she thought; but the minute Lori arrived, Diane grabbed her arm, pulled her to a table at the other end of the restaurant, and sighed with relief when the blond man left after a second cup of coffee.

The relief didn't last long. As she and Lori walked out, she saw the dark man sitting at the counter, picking at a salad. He must have come in after she had—had he followed her? She couldn't stand it anymore.

She turned to Lori and grabbed her arm. "Can we forget the movie," she said, "and go to your place? I need to talk."

* * * *

Lori poured her a glass of Merlot, listened to the whole story, and had a definite opinion.

"Call the police," she said. "It's too much, Diane. Maybe one guy could be a coincidence—you never noticed him before, but you're extra-sensitive now, so you get nervous when you happen to run into him a few times. But two guys? Right after the burglary? And The Shopper says he's seen your eyes. Call the police. Here." She held out her cell phone.

"I hate to do that." Diane shrank back from the phone. "At least one of these men has to be innocent. Probably, they both are. After all, neither has approached me. I hate to get innocent men in trouble with the police because I'm paranoid. Think of it—they'd be suspected of a crime because they came to the library. That'd be great public relations, wouldn't it?"

"This is no time to think about PR," Lori said, "but all right. If you won't do the really sensible thing, do the semi-sensible thing. Wait here."

She ran up to her bedroom and returned a few minutes later, carrying a small automatic pistol. "Do you know how to use one of these?"

Diane winced. "Sort of. A guy I used to date took me to a shooting range once. But I don't want to buy a gun."

"So don't buy one. Borrow mine. One of those jerks might attack you. You should be ready to defend yourself." She picked up Diane's second-best purse and shoved the gun inside.

Diane stared at her purse as if it had become a monster. "Is it legal to carry a gun if I don't have a license?"

"Don't worry about that. If you never have to use it, the cops will never know. And if you *do* have to use it—well, would you rather be dead, or in a little legal trouble?"

"What if I panic," Diane said, "and shoot the wrong man?"

"Then you'd better not panic," Lori countered. "And you'd better figure out who the right man is."

* * * *

That, Diane thought later, was the best suggestion Lori had made all evening. She took the gun home, carrying it with her as she double-checked doors and windows, shower stall and closets. Then she put it under her pillow. It'll be easier to sleep tonight, she thought.

She didn't take the gun with her in the morning. She'd never looked up the laws about carrying a concealed weapon, but she knew there *were* laws, and the idea of bringing a gun into a library shocked her. Besides, she decided, she should focus on figuring things out, not on arming herself. Lori was right. Two men suddenly showing up constantly—it couldn't be just a coincidence, not for both of them. One had to be The Shopper. But which one? Before she called Detective Foley, she had to be sure.

She was still struggling with the problem the next morning as she re-shelved a cart of books. She didn't feel surprised when the dark man came in, did a quick computer search, located a book, and sat down. *Evidence*, she thought. *I need more evidence. I can get it by confronting them and seeing how they react.* She marched over to him and rapped her fist on the table.

"I've had enough," she whispered fiercely. "You've been here three days in a row, and I know you're watching me. You were in the park near my house last night, and in the restaurant where I ate dinner. Why are you following me?"

He blushed. "I'm sorry. I don't understand. I haven't been following you. I just like to come to the library. You must be mistaken."

"Is that so?" she demanded. "Well, don't *you* make a mistake. If you keep bothering me, I'm calling the police."

His blush grew deeper, hotter. "I'm sorry," he said again. He stood up, re-shelved his book, and practically jogged out of the building. *There*, Diane thought. *If he's some innocent jerk I've been running into by coincidence, he'll make a point of avoiding me now. I may have lost the library a patron, but I've got a right to preserve my sanity. And if he's The Shopper, maybe he'll decide he'd damn well better shop somewhere else.*

The blond man arrived an hour later, strolled over to the magazine display, and surveyed covers. *The same tactics*, Diane decided, *and almost the same words. That way, I can compare their reactions.* She walked over and folded her arms.

"I've had enough," she said. Again, she kept it soft and made it sting. "You've been here three days in a row, and I know you're watching me. And you were at the restaurant where I ate last night. Why are you following me?"

At first, he didn't react. Then he shrugged. "You're crazy. I haven't been following you. And I got a right to come here whenever I want."

"*I've* got a right to my privacy," she shot back. "I intend to protect it. If you keep bothering me, I'll call the police."

"You're nuts, lady," he said, and turned back to the magazines. He couldn't seem to find one that interested him, though, because he left minutes later.

Good, Diane thought. I got rid of them both. If either complains to the head librarian, I'll know he's innocent. And if either shows up in the next few days, I'll know he's The Shopper.

Actually, she was pretty sure she knew already, but she was too jittery to trust her own judgment. I'll sleep on it, she decided, and call Detective Foley in the morning.

When Lori came to Diane's house for dinner that night, bearing a baked ziti casserole, she was not pleased. "You took a chance," she said as she shook more red pepper flakes onto the salad. "A really, really stupid chance. You should've told Foley about what's been going on, and you definitely shouldn't have spoken to them. You might've made The Shopper desperate."

"He didn't come back to the library, did he?" Diane broke the seal on the new bottle of Scotch she'd bought that afternoon. Tonight, she really needed a drink, to quiet the uneasy feeling Lori might be right. "If one of those guys actually *is* The Shopper. Anyway, I think I intimidated them both. And I didn't get any notes or packages from The Shopper today. This is the first day since the burglary that I haven't heard from him."

"Maybe," Lori said darkly, "he plans to deliver today's message in person."

* * * *

And that, Diane thought later that night, is exactly the sort of hysterical fear I have to avoid. After my assertive behavior today, The Shopper is probably cowering in a corner. As she double-checked doors and windows, shower and closets, she thought through all the evidence again. Really, she felt almost sure she knew the answer. Maybe she could call the police now. But it was almost midnight, Detective Foley probably wasn't on duty, and she'd hate explaining everything to a stranger. She'd call first thing in the morning. She decided to put the gun under her pillow and went to bed.

Two hours later, she snapped awake. Had there been a noise downstairs, or had she dreamed it? She lay still in the darkness, paralyzed with dread, straining to hear. A noise—she was sure this time. Maybe only a branch scraping against a window, but a noise. And her landline was downstairs, and the replacement cell phone she'd ordered hadn't arrived yet. She could stay here and wait to be attacked, or she could go downstairs and confront whatever it was. Silently, she eased out of bed, pulled on her bathrobe, and slipped the gun into her pocket. Her hands were shaking so much she was afraid she'd drop it if she tried to carry it.

She crept down the stairs, giving her eyes time to adjust to the darkness. She heard a soft crash, and a groan. When she reached the bottom of the stairs, they were both there—the dark man and the blond man, at the far end of the living room, grappling with each other. She stood frozen as they struggled, as the blond man landed a powerful punch, broke free, grabbed the dark man by the lapels, and heaved him against the wall. The dark man moaned and slid to the floor.

She gasped, and the blond man spun around. His face softened when he saw her.

"Diane," he said, walking toward her. "Don't be frightened. I just want to—"

She had her right hand in her bathrobe pocket, ready to pull out the gun. But he was close enough now. She wouldn't need it. She brought her right foot up and kicked him in the stomach, hard. When he hunched forward, crying out in pain and surprise, she snapped her foot up again to kick him in the face, knocking him off his feet, spilling him onto the floor on his back. Out cold, she thought, and glanced up at the dark man. Looking dazed, he got to his feet slowly. His head jerked back when she pointed the gun at him.

His eyes widened. "Don't shoot. I'm—"

"Shut up," she said. "Don't move. Put your hands up and clasp them behind your neck, or I swear I'll kill you."

He did as he was told, keeping his eyes fixed on her. "Calm down," he said. "I'm not The Shopper."

"I'm perfectly calm," she said, "and obviously you're not The Shopper." She looked at the unconscious form at her feet. "*He's* The Shopper. But who the hell are you? A police officer, or a pervert?"

"A police officer," he said. "Sergeant Gary Carson. If you'll let me reach for my badge—"

"Don't reach for anything, or I'll shoot. If you're an officer, you can prove it in a few minutes. I'm calling the police right now. Until they get here, don't you dare so much as twitch."

She edged toward the desk, picked up the receiver, and dialed 911, keeping her eyes on the dark man. By the time she hung up, he looked more at ease. But he was still careful not to move, and she still kept the gun pointed squarely at him.

"I really am a police officer," he said.

"Probably, but I'm not taking chances. Until tonight, I thought you were just someone with too much spare time. When I saw you in my house, fighting with The Shopper, I figured you had to be either a police officer or a pervert who's been stalking me."

"How did you know I'm not The Shopper? How did you know it was him?"

"Lots of things." She kept her gun poised but let herself relax a little. "The way you both behaved in the library, for example. Both days, you knew what you were looking for, but The Shopper browsed through the stacks and the magazines, looking for something that caught his eye. That fit Detective Foley's description of the way The Shopper goes through the houses he burglarizes. And when he was reading an expensive book, he turned down the corner of a page to mark his place. That fit, too—I figured a burglar wouldn't respect other people's property. You were more careful. When you did a crossword puzzle, you photocopied it instead of marking up the library's copy. That told me you probably weren't The Shopper."

He smiled slightly, shook his head slightly. "Not really proof. You can't judge people's characters by the way they treat library materials."

"I'm a librarian," she said. "Of *course* I judge character by the way people treat library materials—and believe me, I'm almost never wrong. And when you finished the crossword puzzle, you smiled, so you must've done well on it. The Shopper misspelled words in both the notes he sent me, and he's apparently never heard of apostrophes. I'd like to see *him* do a *Times* crossword puzzle and have any reason to smile. Besides, that wasn't the only evidence. The Shopper stole brownies, jam, and ice cream from my house, so he must have a sweet tooth." She looked down at the blond man again. "*That* guy wolfed down half a dozen cookies at Story Hour, he was chewing gum at the library yesterday, and he had pie at the restaurant. But you didn't have any cookies at Story Hour, you were drinking a Diet Coke in the park, and you had a salad at the restaurant. Are you dieting?"

"Diabetic," he said, grinning now.

"I see. There was something else, too. That creep arrived at the restaurant before I did yesterday, so he must've had my appointment calendar, the one that was in the purse he stole—I'd marked down the place and time. You didn't get to the restaurant until later. Did you follow me there? Did Detective Foley tell you to do that, to protect me?"

"And to try to catch The Shopper. Foley was afraid he might be watching you. So he told me to keep an eye on you whenever I could, and to watch out for any suspicious characters. But you spotted The Shopper before I did."

"That embarrasses you, doesn't it?" She couldn't quite keep the smugness out of her voice. "You were embarrassed this morning, too, when I confronted you. It makes sense that a plainclothes officer would blush when he realizes he hasn't been fading into the background as successfully as he thought. Don't feel bad. I know all the library's regular patrons by sight. So it's easy for me to spot newcomers, especially at

Story Hour, since not many men come. Why didn't Detective Foley tell me about you?"

He blushed again. "He thought you'd panic if you knew how worried we were about you. He thought you wouldn't be able to act naturally, and we'd miss our chance to catch The Shopper."

She threw her shoulders back. "I don't panic. You should've told me. I could've helped. Anyway, if you were so worried, how did The Shopper get into my house tonight? How did he get past you?"

"I'm not on duty now. The patrol cars are supposed to watch your house at night. Tonight, though, I couldn't sleep. I felt too on edge. So I drove over, checked the house, and saw the broken pane of glass in your back door. I should've called for backup, but for all I knew he was killing you right then. So I rushed in like a fool. He must've heard me, because he jumped me the minute I got in the living room. Knocked my gun right out of my hand." He nodded toward the bookcase, and she saw the gun on the floor. "You're safe, Ms. Hartman. I'm not armed. You could let me put my hands down."

She looked at the gun, thought it over, but shook her head. "No. We'll wait until the police get here—regular police, with uniforms. I think I believe everything you've said, but I can't be sure, not yet. Do you know what The Shopper was doing before you got here? Was he burglarizing my house again?"

"I think he was sitting on your couch," the dark man said. "Look at your coffee table."

For the first time, she looked. The bottle of Scotch, now half-empty, sat in the middle of the table. Beside it lay her largest kitchen knife.

"My God," she said. "He was going to kill me?"

"It looks that way. Looks like he decided to have a few drinks first—to steady his nerves, or just to enjoy being near you. He's obviously much more dangerous than we'd thought. And I obviously didn't do much of a job of protecting you. It's a good thing you know how to protect yourself. Where'd you learn to kick like that?"

"In tae kwon do class." She still felt numb, still couldn't take her eyes away from the knife. "I've got a black belt. But if you hadn't come in and made a noise, if he'd attacked me when I was sleeping—my God."

At last, someone pounded on the front door. Diane opened it, and two uniformed officers stepped inside. "Quick," she said, pointing at the dark man. "Do you know him?"

"Yeah, sure," an officer said, keeping his eyes on her gun. "Sergeant Carson. What's going on here, anyway?"

"Thank goodness." She sat down on the couch, put the gun on the coffee table, held her head in her hands, and breathed deeply, in and out.

Sergeant Carson, blushing more deeply than ever, put his hands down and retrieved his gun.

Detective Foley arrived moments later, a suit jacket pulled over his pajama top. Diane offered explanations as the uniformed officers hand-cuffed the still-unconscious Shopper and half-dragged, half-carried him outside.

"I can't complain about the way this turned out," Foley said, looking up from his notebook. "But I've gotta ask if you've got a license for that gun."

"No, I borrowed it from a friend. I know that's probably illegal, and I'm sorry. It isn't loaded, if that makes a difference. I took the bullets out last night."

Sergeant Carson's shoulders slumped. "It isn't loaded?"

"No. I didn't want to risk shooting an innocent person. I thought I might be able to use the gun as a bluff. And I was."

Foley chuckled. "So, Carson, you were held at bay by a librarian with an unloaded gun."

"I wish," Diane said severely, "people would stop stereotyping librarians as weak and helpless. If you'd had more respect for me, if you'd taken me into your confidence, we could've avoided a lot of danger and worry."

After that, nobody asked more questions about the gun. As Foley was making a phone call, Sergeant Carson came to stand by the couch.

"How are you feeling?" he asked.

"Much better," she said. "Fine, in fact."

"That's good." He smiled at her. "You know, I'll never live this down. Everyone at the station will make jokes about it for months."

"I'm sorry," she said, smiling back. His features weren't really too sharp, she decided. Really, they were very nice features. And he'd been so worried about her that he couldn't sleep, he'd rushed into danger to help her, and he'd probably saved her life—if only by stumbling around in the darkness and making a racket.

"You could make it up to me, though," he said. "What would you say to dinner tomorrow night?"

"I'd say yes." She smiled again. She had, of course, noticed he didn't wear a wedding ring.

If someone burglarized your house and then anonymously returned some stolen items, you'd be relieved—or would you? The idea for "The Shopper" came from an experience a co-worker told me about years ago. At the grocery store, she carelessly left her purse sitting in her cart while she walked down the aisle searching for an elusive something. When she returned to the cart, her purse was gone. Quite a quick, bold thief—and, as it turned out, a compassionate one. When my co-worker got home and opened the mailbox at the end of her driveway, she found the reading glasses that had been in her purse. Immediately, she called the police, afraid the thief might be in the house, waiting for her. After all, her keys had been in her purse, too. The police rushed over but found no one in the house, no sign anything had been taken or disturbed.

That's the end of the story. My co-worker spent a nervous few days wondering if the thief would make contact with her in any other way, but it never happened. Apparently, the thief couldn't use the glasses, felt bad about stealing them from someone who depended on them, and decided to take a risk to return them—again, pretty bold.

I decided to see if I could turn this slight but unusual experience into a story. To do that, I drew on one of my own experiences, too. One night, when I was in high school, our house was burglarized. No one was home when it happened, so no one got hurt. The burglars took many things that belonged to my parents (including a fair amount of the cash my mother kept hidden in odd spots around the house, since she'd grown up during the Depression and never completely trusted banks—the burglars found a surprising number of her hiding places). They didn't take much from me, though. After all, I was a teenager. I didn't have much worth stealing.

But they'd gone through my room—undoubtedly, a frustrating experience for them. I still remember how I felt as I cleaned up that night, constantly coming across more signs that strangers had been in my room and touched my possessions: my jewelry box sitting open on the bureau, a framed photograph on my desk knocked over, the worthless contents of an old purse dumped out on the closet floor. Not much was missing, but even so I felt unsettled, violated, vulnerable. I tried to get that feeling across in "The Shopper."

I also tried to make "The Shopper" a simple but solid whodunit: only two suspects, a generous number of clues woven in so quietly that readers may not recognize them as clues, and a librarian as the amateur sleuth—unpretentious, but confident she's interpreting the clues correctly, confident she can take care of herself. I've got to admit I think I pulled all that off pretty well.

ADJUNCTS ANONYMOUS

(2009)

"The one thing we *haven't* tried," Maureen said, "is a life of crime."

She was joking, of course. At least, mostly joking. At least, I thought so at the time.

We were sitting, as usual, at a back table in Monty's, dampening our Friday-afternoon sorrows in a pitcher of beer. I say "dampening," not "drowning," advisedly. One pitcher of Bud Lite will not drown sorrows such as ours.

"That's right," Inez said. She was the newest member of our group, still in her twenties, still in her first year as an English adjunct at Edson University. Dark-haired, olive-skinned, and lovely, she looked too petite to have ever borne a child, let alone the twin boys who had grown into irrepressible two-year-olds. "You've started several businesses over the years, haven't you? A resume-writing service, an editing service—"

"And a consulting service," added Julian—only five years older than Inez, but he'd been in the adjunct business much longer, had tried to leave, and had returned in defeat. He was short and trim and kept his blond hair down to crew-cut length; in many ways, he still looked like the soccer player he'd been in college, not like a Ph.D. who'd published two articles on Spenser's sonnets. "I was around for that one. We tried to talk companies into hiring us to give their employees business-writing workshops. How many takers did we get, Amy? Three?"

"Two," I said. "Turns out the business world isn't clamoring for the skills English teachers can offer."

"The academic world isn't clamoring for them, either," Maureen pointed out. "Not when there's such an inexhaustible supply of us. Twenty-some years ago, I thought that by knocking myself out in the classroom, and publishing, and serving on committees, I could work my way into a real job. I took me a long time to realize the university would gain precisely nothing by hiring me full time. Why give me a decent salary or benefits or job security when it can save a bundle by keeping me in adjunct limbo forever?"

A fine rhetorical question, I thought, and wished I could use it as an example in English 102. But I didn't dare. Adjuncts—part-time professors—never complain in public about the way colleges and universities exploit them. Maureen's right: There *is* an inexhaustible supply of us, at least in English. Anyone who makes a fuss can easily be replaced. Even as the wife of a dean, I couldn't risk it.

Maureen definitely couldn't risk it. Like Julian, Inez, and me, she'd come to Edson as a faculty spouse. All four of us could tell nearly identical stories: A willingness to make a sacrifice for a husband or wife offered a full-time teaching job in this remote college town, a yearning to spend more time with our children, a decision to put our own careers on hold temporarily, to step off the academic fast track and teach part-time for a few years. As we'd all discovered, stepping back on the fast track was the hard part.

At least Julian, Inez, and I still had our spouses, still had someone to provide a full-time income and health insurance. Maureen got divorced twelve years ago, and her attempts to find a real job in another city failed—colleges tend to hire bright young things fresh out of graduate school for full-time positions, not middle-aged women dulled by decades of adjunct service. So she was still here, still patching a living together by teaching part-time at Edson, at the community college, and for an online university she'd have scorned as a diploma mill in her less desperate days. This semester, she was teaching a total of seven classes—all composition, all generating stacks of essays for her to grade. For Maureen, even more than the rest of us, adjunct limbo was a brutal place.

"So, a life of crime," I said lightly. "Good idea. You're my mentor, Maureen—you always have been, ever since I moved here, and now you've quite possibly identified our only option for ever making real money. What do you suggest? Bank robbery?"

Julian shook his head. "Too risky. And too intimidating—too many memories of getting turned down for loans, and getting lectured about bounced checks, and watching tellers snicker when they see how low my balance is."

"We'll start smaller, then," Inez said, pouring herself another half-glass. "How about knocking over a convenience store?"

"Still too risky," I said. "Convenience stores have hidden cameras—the cops would listen to a tape of a grammatically correct demand for cash and know the robber had to be an English teacher. Home burglary's safer."

"Not safe enough." Julian counted off the perils on his fingers. "Dogs, home owners returning early, home owners with handguns, home owners with rifles—"

"And this," Maureen cut in, "is why criminals are richer than English teachers. Criminals know one can't make money without taking risks. We can't be so fussy about which crimes we'll commit. If we're serious about this, we'll have to take risks."

"We're *not* serious about this," I said. "But if you don't want to rule out risky crimes, I'll play along. Let's go all the way. Let's murder somebody."

"Not much profit in murder," Inez said regretfully. "Not unless the murderer is in the victim's will." She looked around the table hopefully. "I don't suppose we have a Jack Hanson in the group, do we?"

Jack Hanson—the mention of his name made us limp with envy. Like us, Jack was an English adjunct; unlike us, he was a retired public-school teacher. Even before the inheritance, he'd had luxuries beyond the reach of most adjuncts, such as a pension and a savings account. Then, last month, he'd driven to campus in a sleek BMW and announced a second cousin he barely knew had died and left him everything she had.

"We could trick Jack into putting us in *his* will," Julian said, not sounding optimistic, "and then murder Jack."

"No murdering fellow adjuncts," Maureen said. "Not even Jack. True, he loves hearing himself talk, and especially enjoys trumpeting his political opinions at top volume. But murdering any adjunct is ethically unacceptable."

"Now *you're* being fussy," I complained. "Well, fine. We won't murder Jack. But we should target *someone* on campus. Face it—we don't know anything about banks, or much about convenience stores. But we know the university intimately. Criminals should stick to their areas of expertise."

"Great," Julian said. "We can rip off the petty cash box in the mailroom. How much will *that* get us? Enough for another pitcher of beer?"

His last phrase reached the waitress slouching past our table. She slowed to a halt and looked us over languidly. "You guys want another pitcher?" she asked. The lilting rhythm of her syllables revealed that she didn't come from any place near this Midwestern town, that she'd grown up in the South.

Julian thought it over. "Sure. We need the inspiration. As they say, malt does more than Milton can."

The waitress stared at him, then shrugged. "Whatever," she said, and slumped off.

Maureen glared after her. "'You guys,'" she repeated. "She's one of my students, and she calls us 'you guys.'"

"An Edson student?" Inez said. "And she's old enough to work in a bar?"

"Oh, we get some non-traditional students," Maureen said. "Not that Danyelle's very non-traditional—she just turned twenty-one, I think. That's her name—Danyelle, with a 'y.' The spelling alone tells you volumes."

"Her parents may have saddled her with that spelling," I said. "Not that I have much to say in defense of Danyelle Travis. I had her in 101, and she sat there like a lump—never said a word, never opened a textbook. She just stared at me slack-jawed as I ran the education past her, as if she were daring me to interest her. And she always had her hands under her desk, playing with her cell phone, checking text messages."

"You had her in 101?" Maureen said. "And you *passed* her? She's half a notch above illiterate."

"I know that," I shot back. "And of course I passed her. I pass all my illiterate students, to keep them from giving me bad evaluations and from running to Nina Dixon and saying I abused them. When the time comes, you'll pass Danyelle, too."

Maureen scowled but couldn't deny it. "Damned if I give her anything higher than a B-minus," she muttered.

"Nina Dixon," Julian said reflectively. "Now, *there's* someone on campus with real money. When I worked in the grants office for those two brain-numbing years, I saw salary figures. Did you know she makes more than a full professor? And all she has is a master's in student development."

"Plus quickie certificates in developmental education and academic assessment." I turned to Inez to explain. "Nina started as an academic advisor. Whenever the university decided an area needed beefing up, she ran to some institute, took a six-week program—at the university's expense—and came back a certified expert on whatever it was."

"So now she directs the Office of Academic Excellence," Inez said, frowning. "I know she directs the writing center, and supervises us, and coordinates workshops for public-school teachers. But how did her salary get so high?"

"For one thing," Julian said, "she gets herself written into every grant proposal the university sends out. Grant-making agencies always want programs assessed, and Nina's our expert on assessment. So she gets five thousand for devoting ten percent of her time to assessing one program, ten thousand for devoting twenty percent of her time to assessing another—she must have two hundred percent of her time committed to various grant programs by now. She doesn't do much with any of them, but she always gets her money. Plus there's her slush fund."

Danyelle lumbered back with our new pitcher, sloshed a small pool of beer onto the table, and left without looking at us. While Julian mopped up, Maureen poured herself a full glass. She hadn't spoken since Nina's name was mentioned, but her mood had darkened noticeably. Once, Maureen made a few thousand extra a year by coordinating the schedules of the adjuncts who tutored at the writing center. When Nina became director, she decided to use student tutors, cutting all the adjuncts out completely.

"Somebody on campus has a slush fund?" Inez said. "Sounds like something out of *All the President's Men*. Where does the money come from?"

"From the workshops for public-school teachers," Julian said. "That's a steady source of income—teachers have to earn continuing education credits to keep their certification current, and the university can offer one-credit weekend workshops for practically nothing by having adjuncts teach them. You teach some, don't you, Amy?"

"You bet," I said. "Writing across the Curriculum, mostly. It's a way to boost my semester total to eleven credits." Full-time faculty teach twelve credits per semester, so university regulations ordain that adjuncts can teach no more than eleven—a convenient fiction that makes it possible to pretend that paying us a fraction of a full-time salary is ethical. That means adjuncts can teach just three three-credit courses per semester, and have to depend on Nina for the last two credits. Eleven credits at $650 a credit—just over $7,000 a semester. Not an extravagant income, but without workshops, it'd be even lower. Maureen knew this, all too well. Nina hadn't let her teach a workshop in six years.

"Anyhow," Julian told Inez, "when Nina took over the workshops, she worked out a special deal—don't ask me how. The university provides rooms for the workshops and pays for printing, mailing, everything—right down to water to flush the toilets. But it doesn't get the tuition money. That goes into the Academic Excellence account. It's a special account—called a restricted account—and Nina can use it for just about anything she wants. One year, she used it to buy herself a home computer— said she needed it to work on Academic Excellence programs on weekends. She also used it to attend professional conferences—two in California, one in Florida, one in Hawaii."

Maureen set down her empty glass. "So that's what we do. We get Nina to empty her slush fund, snatch the cash, and split it four ways. At the end of the month, when the treasurer checks all the accounts and sees zero dollars in Academic Excellence, Nina gets fired. That's our crime."

"'Good, good,'" Julian said. "'The justice of it pleases; very good.'"

"*Othello*, Act IV," Inez said mechanically, and turned to Maureen. "Look, you're just joking, right? You'd never actually do that?"

"Of course she's joking," I said. "It's only—well, it's therapy. We're venting our frustrations by fantasizing about a life of crime, plotting revenge on Nina. But we'd never do it. Among other things, we *couldn't* do it. We'd never get Nina to empty her account."

"We could kidnap her damn Chihuahua," Julian suggested. "I swear, it's the only thing on earth she loves. Then we cut letters out of magazines for a ransom note and—"

"We have to play on her weaknesses," Maureen said abruptly. "On her character flaws. She's got plenty. For example, she's ambitious and greedy and unscrupulous. If we could make her think she'd profit by withdrawing the money, she'd do it."

"And she's not bright," Julian added. "God knows, she's not bright."

I hesitated before joining in. It's only therapy, I reminded myself. "Plus she's a snoop," I said. "Remember when she smelled smoke on Charlie's jacket? She searched his desk while he was in class and found a pack of cigarettes. He swore he never smoked on campus, that he kept the pack there to ward off panic attacks—but she made sure he never taught at Edson again. She'll do anything to play up to President Swanson."

"Swanson didn't like Charlie?" Inez asked.

"I don't think Swanson ever met Charlie," Julian said. "But Swanson's a fanatic about health and fitness. That's why Nina's become a fanatic about health and fitness. She took up jogging and yoga the day Swanson signed his contract."

"So that's why she pressures us to play in those stupid volleyball games." Inez looked at her watch. "Yikes—I'll be late picking the twins up from daycare."

"And I'd better collect my kids from soccer practice and music lessons," I said. "We'll have to finish plotting Nina's destruction another time."

"Sounds good," Julian said. "But let's not tell anyone about our therapy session, okay? Not even spouses. If Nina found out, she'd be steamed."

Maureen stood up suddenly. "We have to take a solemn vow," she said. "Not one word about any of this, not to anyone. Agreed?"

She wasn't smiling. I glanced uneasily at Julian and Inez. "Ooh," I said. "A solemn vow. Should we slit our pinkies or spit over our shoulders?"

"A handshake should do," Maureen said, and actually held out her hand.

Julian and Inez got the giggles; then Maureen and I joined in, and we all kept laughing as everyone shook hands with everyone else. Then

Julian raised a fist and intoned "Destruction to Nina Dixon" in a low, awful tone, and we laughed again and left.

* * * *

At home, I found my husband in the kitchen, debating the wisdom of adding red pepper flakes to the marinara sauce. He asked if we'd had a nice time at Monty's.

Usually, I tell him everything. But the hand-shaking ritual, silly as it was, held me back. "Just a typical meeting of Adjuncts Anonymous," I said. "The usual foursome, the usual moping and whining—our weekly self-pity plunge."

"Sounds like fun." He turned to face me. "Amy, you don't have to keep doing this—all those composition classes, all those essays to grade every night, all the slights and insults. At least take a semester off—finish that article on *Persuasion*, start the new book. We could manage on my salary."

"We could," I said, leaning past him to sample the sauce, "if deans made as much as people think they do. I know my pay's pathetic, Craig, but it covers a few bills each month. Without it, we'd have to stretch to pay those bills. And with three kids to put through college in the next ten years, it's no time for me to take a semester off."

"We could manage," he insisted. "And it worries me, sometimes, to see how bitter you're getting. I don't want you turning into another Maureen Fahey."

"I won't turn into Maureen Fahey," I said, "if you don't turn into Roger Fahey." Maureen's husband had left her for a psychology professor—a full-time psychology professor. I think it would have hurt Maureen less if he'd left her for a student.

"Not a chance," Craig said. "But Maureen wasn't simply a victim. I've heard Roger's side. She pushed him to take this job—she was wild for more time with the kids. But when she started itching to teach full-time again, she turned on him. Every night, it was, 'I gave up tenure for you, and you dragged me to this God-forsaken town, and now I'm miserable, and what are you going to do about it?' Roger couldn't take it."

"I know," I said. "Even Maureen admits that, in her more reasonable moments. Well, I won't turn on you—even though you've been so brilliantly successful here that my wretched excuse for a career looks even more wretched by comparison."

"I have not," he said, "been brilliantly successful here."

"Sure you have," I said. "Swanson took just six months to promote you to dean. More important, he invites you to play in his Thursday afternoon basketball games. At Edson, that's the surest sign of success."

"That's a sure sign," he said, "that I'm one hell of a guard. Nobody gets past me."

"True," I agreed, "but that's not why he invites you. Anyway, I won't turn into Maureen." I started gathering salad ingredients, then paused. "Why this sudden concern?"

He winced and took both my hands. "The Curriculum Council approved a course proposal from the English Department today. For a Jane Austen seminar."

That hit me hard. I'd written my dissertation on *Emma*. "Who's teaching it?"

He let go of my hands. "Phil Hanson," he said.

"Phil *Hanson*?" I echoed. "Craig, that's absurd. He wrote his dissertation on Upton Sinclair. What the hell does he know about Austen?"

Craig gave the sauce a mournful stir. "He says he'll read up on her this summer. Look, I could take this up with the department chair. I could—"

"Don't," I said. I still felt the sting of my last meeting with the chair, six years ago. I'd put on my best suit and gone to her office and explained that, much as I enjoyed teaching composition, I thought I could serve the department more fully by teaching some literature courses as well—Introduction to Prose Fiction, perhaps. She'd looked shocked. Oh, no, she'd said. Potential majors take Introduction to Prose Fiction. We can't have a course for potential majors taught by an adjunct—by a faculty wife.

My degrees, my publications, my years of teaching advanced courses—none of that counted any more. I was an adjunct and a faculty wife, and that meant I wasn't fit to teach anything but basic composition.

"Fine." I smashed a garlic clove. "Having courses taught by the most qualified faculty available isn't a priority—not at Edson. The only priority is pampering full-time faculty and giving them the most desirable classes. And the smallest ones. How many students will Phil get in that seminar? Six? Seven? Maybe, if you add up all his classes, he'll have thirty students next fall. And I get sixty students every semester, and they all write essays every other week. And *he's* full-time, and *I'm* part-time? Please."

"It's not right," Craig said. "But it's not just Edson. Almost every college and university in the country employs an army of adjuncts now, just to make ends meet."

I knew it was true—Maureen said that at the community college, over seventy percent of the classes were taught by adjuncts. And I wondered how parents would feel about writing tuition checks if they realized how often their children were being taught by part-time faculty—some highly qualified, some recruited out of desperation and barely qualified at all, and some, like Maureen, so weighed down by low pay and heavy workloads that they were constantly exhausted, frazzled, and angry.

"Anyway," Craig said, "at least take a break from composition. You could still bring in some money by doing workshops for Nina Dixon."

"Ah, yes," I said, reaching for a tomato. "For my dear friend Nina Dixon." I smiled a grim, secret smile. Already, I was looking forward to the next therapy session.

* * * *

It took place sooner than expected, on the following Wednesday. Julian and I both had 10:00 classes in Beumler Hall, and afterwards we walked to the adjuncts' office together. It's a long, dark, narrow room, stuffed with rusty metal desks and dented file cabinets deemed no longer worthy of full-time professors. When we walked in, Nina was standing by Inez's desk, pawing through some envelopes.

She put them down hastily when she spotted us. "Oh, hi," she said. "I'm expecting a report from the registrar, but I didn't get it. I thought maybe Felix put it on Inez's desk by mistake."

Felix is a mailroom clerk. Since adjuncts don't rate the locked mailboxes assigned to full-time faculty, he brings our mail to the office and sets it on our desks. In nine years, I've never known him to misdirect a piece of mail.

"Really?" I said, icily. "But you didn't find the report?"

"Nope," she said. "Maybe the registrar didn't send it. He said he did, but you know how that goes. 'The check is in the mail.'"

It wasn't funny, but Nina laughed. My spine tensed. Few things on the planet horrify me as much as Nina's laugh. It's if as some other being has possessed her, making a sound no merely human body could produce—my husband says it reminds him of a scene in *Alien*, when a space creature bursts out of a man's chest and screeches.

Finally, it ended, and she left the office, and my spine sagged in relief.

"Can you believe that?" Julian said. "Wait till we tell Inez."

She walked into the office minutes later, chatting with Maureen, and was instantly indignant. Seizing her mail, she held up a manila envelope. "This must be what caught Nina's attention—it's from my dissertation director. My God! If you hadn't walked in, she might've taken it to her office and steamed it open."

"She's done worse things," Maureen said, nodding sharply toward the far end of the office. She, Julian, and I retreated to the ancient coffee urn, tactfully busying ourselves with mugs and sweetener. A missive from a dissertation director is too important to set aside: Inez needed some time, and some privacy.

She joined us in a few minutes, sighing. "He wants me to rewrite the chapter. I *knew* I should've developed the comparisons more fully. Thank goodness Nina didn't see the letter. Not that it's such a disgrace—rewriting chapters is part of the process—but if she spread it around campus and made it sound bad, she could hurt my prospects here."

You poor baby, I thought. Haven't you realized yet? None of us has any prospects here. "That Nina," I said, to fill the silence. "Always snooping, always gossiping—"

"We could use that," Julian said suddenly. "Remember what Maureen said about playing on Nina's character flaws? We could use her snoopiness to bring her down."

Maureen pounced on it. "How?" she demanded.

He looked taken aback by her urgency. "I remembered a story my grandfather told me. He was in the Navy during World War II, and this guy on his ship was always snooping, looking for dirt on people so he could report them. So my grandfather and his buddies got the camera used to show movies on the ship, attached some gizmos to it, took pictures of it, and labeled them 'Atomic Camera.' Then they put the pictures in envelopes, stole a 'Top Secret' stamp, stamped the envelopes, and left them in places where this guy was known to snoop. Sure enough, the next day he went to the captain and confessed, 'Sir, I've seen the Atomic Camera.'"

Inez and I laughed; Maureen didn't crack a smile. "That's good," she said. "So we plant false information that will mislead Nina into emptying the Academic Excellence account. If we put the information in places where she has no business looking and stamp it 'Personal and Confidential,' we can be sure she'll find it, and read it."

"Plausible," I conceded. "But what kind of false information would we plant?"

"Information that fools her into thinking she can make a profit," Inez said promptly. "She's greedy, right? So we tempt her with a phony get-rich-quick scheme. We make her think if she invests money from the account in this scheme, she can make a bundle for herself and replace the money before anyone notices it's missing."

I shook my head. "No get-rich-quick scheme works that fast."

"Does Nina know that?" Maureen asked. "She's not bright—we're all agreed on that. We just have to devise something that will befuddle and tempt her."

"We could mail letters to ourselves," Julian suggested, "from some make-believe investment firm. We could congratulate ourselves on making huge profits and—oh. That won't work, will it?"

"Definitely not," I said. "Nina knows we don't have money to invest and haven't made huge profits. We wouldn't be scrambling to teach composition classes if we had."

"True." Julian stirred his coffee gloomily. "I'll keep working on it."

He wasn't the only one. The next day, Inez unveiled an improvement on the plan. "I thought of a way to make the investment-firm scheme sound more plausible," she said.

She, Maureen, and I were in the women's locker room at the old gym, reluctantly suiting up for a volleyball game. Edson has a new athletic center on the edge of campus but still leaves the old gym open all day. Secretaries power-walk here on their lunch hours, students shoot hoops between classes, and informal staff teams sign the place out for games. The old gym's central location compensates for its starkness: one big room with a scuffed wooden floor, locker rooms, and that's all. It has charm, though—even President Swanson uses the old gym, for his weekly basketball games.

Maureen glanced around to make sure we were alone. "What's your idea?"

"We have to make Nina think this firm helps people make lots of money quickly," Inez said. "And we just happen to have in our office someone who came into lots of money quickly." She lowered her voice. "Jack Hanson."

"That was an inheritance," I pointed out.

"That's what Jack says," Inez said. "But how do we—or Nina—know that's true? This whole long-lost-rich-second-cousin bit sounds fishy anyway. It's probably true, but it's almost easier to believe Jack found a way of making huge profits but doesn't want to spread the wealth too thin by telling other people about it."

I dug through my gym bag to find my combination lock—the old gym's lockers don't have locks, so we bring our own. "That means bringing Jack in on the plan," I said.

"He'd never have to know," Inez said. "We address an envelope to Jack but put a mailing label addressed to one of us—to me, say—over Jack's address. Felix puts the envelope on my desk, we peel off the label, and voila—a postmarked envelope addressed to Jack. When Jack goes to class, we rip the envelope open and put it on his desk. Then we make ourselves scarce, give Nina time to read the letter, and take letter and envelope away before Jack gets back."

"That could work," I admitted. Nina's office is across the hall from ours, and she drops by often to make sure we're keeping our office hours. "And if Nina asks Jack about his investment firm, he'll say he doesn't know what she's talking about, and she'll be sure he's keeping a valuable secret. But we'd have to put a check in the envelope, to make Nina believe this firm pays off. That means opening a phony bank account."

"No," Maureen said. "That would leave a trace. After the money disappears, the university—and the police—will accuse Nina of stealing it, and she'll break down and tell them everything. We have to make sure the police can't trace the investment firm to us. We have to leave Nina with absolutely no evidence to support her story."

Just then, Nina stuck her head into the locker room. She wore hot pink sweats with a matching sweatband that pushed her short, reddish hair up into a thorny peak. "Hurry up," she ordered. "We shouldn't keep the Admissions Office team waiting."

"Admissions," I said dismally, after Nina left. "Another guaranteed defeat. Admissions counselors are disgustingly enthusiastic. They probably enjoy these games."

"Maybe we won't have to endure them much longer," Maureen said, and patted my shoulder as we headed into the gym.

* * * *

We held our next therapy session on Friday, when we met at Monty's. Again, Danyelle was our waitress; again, she expended the minimum possible energy and didn't condescend to making eye contact. These days, most students don't bother playing up to professors. Students know that even if we dislike them, we won't dare give them the grades they actually deserve.

Pushing those thoughts aside, I helped Maureen and Inez fill Julian in on our locker-room talk. "You're hung up on the check?" he said. "It's better without a check. We put a sentence in the letter—'As usual, to avoid tax complications, we've enclosed your dividend in cash.' She'll assume Jack pocketed the money. He might leave a letter lying on his desk, but not cash."

"But what investment firm mails out dividends in cash?" I objected. "That makes the whole business seem shady."

"Shady is good," Maureen said. "It makes the impossibly big, impossibly quick profits more plausible. Maybe the firm makes huge profits in a hurry because its operations aren't quite legal. Nina won't care. She's unscrupulous, remember? And if this firm conducts all transactions in cash, she won't be surprised when she's asked to hand over a stack of bills when she makes her investment."

"But how do we invite her to invest?" I asked. "We could probably produce reasonably convincing letterhead on a computer. But what address do we put on the letterhead? What telephone number? Nina would want to check this firm out. How?"

"Maybe through a website," Julian suggested. "Those are easy to set up, and to take down. Letterhead with just the firm's name and a web address—that fits the shady ambiance we want. If the site's sort of basic, that's okay. A shady firm that keeps a low profile wouldn't put bells and whistles on its website."

I shook my head. "Before she withdraws the cash, Nina will want to talk to someone. If this is supposedly an out-of-town firm, we'll have to provide an out-of-town phone number and have someone waiting to answer her questions. How?"

"I have a cousin in Vermont," Inez said. "She could—"

"No accomplices," Maureen said. "Only stupid criminals take accomplices. Accomplices make mistakes, they panic, and in the end they make a deal with the police and testify against you."

"Wait a minute," Inez objected. "You're talking about my cousin."

"I'm sure she's a lovely person," Maureen said, "but it would leave a loose end. If the police trace the phone number to your cousin, we're in trouble."

"Let's not get stalled on that," Julian said. "Maybe we could use a public phone, or steal a phone. Let's assume we can solve that problem and move on."

"Fine," I said. "It's just therapy, after all. Who cares if there are holes in the plan? So let's say we find a way to communicate with Nina. Now what?"

"Now we set up a meeting," Inez said. "We tell her to bring $10,000 in cash—"

"More than that," Julian said. "She must have over $100,000 in that account."

"But we can't ask for all of it," Maureen said. "Nina's greedy; we're not. I know we said we'd get her to empty the account, but that's unrealistic. She wouldn't do it."

"So we ask for $40,000, or $80,000," Julian said. "We've got to make it so high she can't take it from her personal account, or use her own savings to cover up the improper withdrawal when the money disappears. Then we say an officer from the firm will pass through town on a certain day and is willing to meet with her if—"

"You guys want another pitcher?" Danyelle asked.

We all jolted back in our chairs. "No, thank you," I managed.

Danyelle slouched away. "My God," Inez said. "Do you think she heard what we were saying?"

"Danyelle's never more than vaguely aware of anything in her vicinity," Maureen said. "Her cell phone's her only means of making contact with the outside world, and she makes a special point of not listening to teachers. We're safe. So, we say this officer will show Nina documents proving she'll make huge profits in weeks, and we tell her to bring cash to the meeting. Where will it take place?"

"In a restaurant, maybe," Julian said, considering. "The mythical investment officer could offer to buy her dinner. Investment officers do that—I saw it in a movie. We pick a restaurant next to a dark alley, and when Nina walks down the alley, one of us jumps out from behind a dumpster, knocks her over the head, and grabs—"

"No violence," I cut in. "I don't approve of it, and we're not up to it. I've never knocked anyone over the head, Julian. Have you? Has anyone?"

They all looked down at the table, ashamed.

"I thought so," I said. "So no more talk about knocking people over the head. I refuse even to fantasize about it. It's too silly. Not to mention the fact that I can't think of a single restaurant in town with dark alleys and dumpsters so conveniently located."

"You're right," Julian admitted. "I got carried away. Sorry."

"We could drug her," Inez said, refusing to give up. "One of us meets her in the restaurant, cleverly disguised—"

"Oh, good grief," I said. "Disguised? How could we possibly—"

"Please," Inez said. "Grant me this one point. One of us, cleverly disguised, meets Nina in a restaurant, at a table in a dark corner—some restaurants in town *do* have dark corners, Amy—and he or she orders drinks. Then he or she slips Nina a Mickey Finn."

"A Mickey Finn?" Maureen said, looking puzzled. "Oh, yes—I've heard that expression. In a Bogart movie, perhaps—or was it a *Seinfeld* episode? It's a drug, isn't it, to render someone unconscious? Do you know where to get it?"

"I think one generally *makes* a Mickey Finn," Inez said uncertainly, "by mixing various ingredients. We'd have to find a recipe. We could Google it."

"So we do some preliminary research," Julian said, "and slip Nina a Mickey. When she passes out, we grab her briefcase stuffed with cash—"

"I'm sorry," I said. "Fascinated as I am by this utterly convincing narrative about clever disguises and Mickey Finns, I have to pick up my kids."

"I should go, too." Maureen stood up. "My son's driving home from college for the weekend, and he's requested meatloaf—I'd better get started."

Together, we walked to the poorly lit hallway where both customers and employees at Monty's stow their coats. "That was fun," Maureen said. "I'm glad you challenged the children about their less realistic ideas. It's a better intellectual exercise if we don't make things too easy on ourselves."

"As long as they remember it's only an intellectual exercise," I said. "You don't think they'd actually—"

"Of course not," Maureen said. "Now *you're* being unrealistic."

Maybe. Still, odd things started happening. On Tuesday, while Inez was asking me for advice on confronting a plagiarist, Nina sidled over and oh-so-casually asked if we knew the name of the second cousin who supposedly left Jack all that money. When we said we didn't, she nodded curtly. "And did Jack ever," she asked, "mention this cousin to you *before* he got this so-called inheritance?"

When we said no, Nina nodded again and sidled away. We looked at each other.

"'Supposedly?'" Inez said. "'So-called?' Is Nina having doubts about where Jack really got that money? It almost sounds like—"

"Nina's gossiping," I said. "She always gossips. It's nothing." But on Wednesday, when we had our weekly English adjuncts' meeting, relations between Nina and Jack seemed frosty. Jack is Nina's pet: Usually, she lets him ramble on endlessly, because he's the only adjunct who doesn't despise her, and she knows it. At this meeting, she cut Jack off twice. The second time, he stalked out.

Nina glared after him. "Selfish bastard," she said.

When the four of us met at Monty's on Friday, I think we all felt uneasy. Nobody alluded to therapy sessions, or Nina, or the advantages of a life of crime. Instead, Maureen asked if we had new ideas about designing rubrics for comparison essays, and we stuck doggedly to that topic for a full hour.

Then Danyelle brought our second pitcher. "Hey, you guys," she said, "did any of you notice, like, a cell phone laying around anywhere? Because when I got here, I'm pretty sure I put my cell phone in my jacket pocket, but when I went to the coatroom to check my messages, I couldn't find it. So I thought maybe it, like, fell out of my pocket or something, and landed on the floor or somewhere. So have you guys seen it?"

We exchanged awkward glances. "I'm sorry, Danyelle," I said. "Would it be expensive to replace?"

She shrugged. "It's no biggy. I've lost phones, like, three or four times, and the company always replaces them. I mean, like, maybe they charge my parents extra or something—I'm not sure. The thing is, it takes about a week to get a new phone, and that's a long time to go without messages. So if you see it, let me know."

After she left, Inez turned to Julian. "You said we could steal a phone."

"I was joking," he said. "Anyway, Amy's the one who said we'd need an out-of-town phone number. And Danyelle's got a Southern accent—her phone probably has an area code from Georgia or somewhere like that. That fits perfectly with Amy's plan."

"Amy's plan?" I demanded. "I don't have a plan. You two kept coming up with plans; I kept saying they wouldn't work. Don't *you* accuse *me* of—"

"No one's accusing anyone," Maureen said. "It was only therapy, and I think we're all agreed it went far enough. Now, on my rubrics, I stress topic sentences. Do you?"

During the next week, the atmosphere in the office was more brittle than usual, less chatty. On Thursday evening, while I was breading chicken cutlets, Craig came home still sweaty from his weekly basketball game at the old gym.

"What the hell," he asked, "is wrong with Nina Dixon?"

"Do you want a list?" I asked. "Or do you have something specific in mind?"

He set his gym bag down. "She must be cracking under the strain of not doing much. First, a little after five, she bursts into the gym, resplendent in those hot-pink sweats, and bellows, 'Here I am!' As if we were expecting her—and believe me, we weren't. I wish you'd seen Rick Swanson's double-take. But nobody wanted to be rude, so we let her play. About an hour later, we called it quits. So we're changing in the men's locker room, and we hear a shriek. Naturally, it's Nina."

"She shrieked?" I said. "Was she hurt?"

"No. She was robbed. We ran back into the gym, and she was racing around, screaming, 'Someone stole something from my gym bag! Catch them!' We fanned out, searched the building, ran off in all directions. Nobody saw anything. So we came back to the gym, and she's sitting on the floor, moaning, 'I've been robbed!' Geez! What did she have in that bag, anyway? Diamonds and rubies?"

The olive oil in the pan started to smoke. I slid in the first cutlet. "Had her bag been in a locker? Was it locked?"

"Yeah," he said. "She swore she'd put her combination lock on her locker and clicked it shut, and said it was still locked when she came back from the game. So Rick said he'd have security check into it; she just had to give the chief a description of what was stolen. Then Nina turned—wait a minute. Is 'white as a sheet' a cliché?"

I nodded. "I'm afraid so."

"Nina got pale," he said. "Then she glanced at her watch, gasped, and ran back into the locker room—said she had to get dressed for an appointment. It was strange."

"It sure sounds strange." I flipped a cutlet. "Maybe I'll find out more tomorrow."

I didn't find out much. Nina called in sick, and nobody else seemed to have much to say. When our foursome gathered at Monty's, I had to start things off. "So," I said, "someone stole something from Nina's locker yesterday. Did you hear about that?"

Everybody nodded. Everybody had heard.

"Apparently, Nina was frantic," Maureen ventured. "She must have lost something valuable. Does anyone know what was stolen?"

No one said anything. Then Julian grinned. "Whatever it was, someone got it away from her without knocking her over the head or slipping her a Mickey."

"I heard," Inez said, "she ran an off-campus errand late yesterday afternoon."

Maureen sipped her beer. "Where do you suppose she went? To the bank? To make a withdrawal?"

"Possibly," I said. "I heard when she got back to her office, she found a typed note from Swanson's secretary on her door, inviting her to join his basketball game. But Cheryl says she never sent such a note, and Swanson says he never made such an invitation."

"They don't have much reason to lie about that," Julian observed. "More likely, someone who knows how ambitious Nina is knew she couldn't resist an invitation to that game—it's the biggest status symbol on campus. And if that someone had spent time in the women's locker room with Nina—before a volleyball game, say—she might have glanced over while Nina was unlocking her locker, memorized the combination—"

"Slow down," Inez said. "It's not easy to see the numbers someone's turning on a lock, not unless you stare in an obvious way. And we all use Yale locks, and they all look similar. It'd be easier to sneak into Nina's office—she doesn't lock it when she steps out during the day, and her gym bag's always next to her desk. If one took Nina's lock and slipped one's own lock into her bag, she probably wouldn't notice the difference. Then one could wait until Nina left the locker room, open up one's own lock, take whatever one wanted, put Nina's lock on the locker, skulk away—"

"You've given this a lot of thought," Julian commented "Anyway, the thief got into and out of the women's locker room. Therefore, the thief was a woman."

Maureen looked at him sourly. "Or a short, slim man, wearing baggy sweats and a jacket with a hood. There's no reception desk at the old gym, no one guarding the locker room entrances. And on late Thursday afternoons, there are no stray students or staff around, because everyone knows Swanson has the gym reserved for his game. A man could slip into and out of the women's locker room, as easily as a woman."

"Look, let's be frank," I said. "Some things that have happened are uncomfortably reminiscent of things we discussed during our therapy sessions. So we're all feeling a little suspicious of each other; we're all wondering if one of us carried out the plan the others regarded as a joke. Let's clear the air. This theft took place between 5:00 and 6:00. I'll admit I don't have an alibi. I don't have carpool duties on Thursdays: Other mothers brought my kids home from practice and rehearsals, starting around 6:00. Until then, I was home, alone, grading essays."

"And I was at the office until 7:00," Maureen said, "grading essays. I was alone, too. You know how that place empties out late in the afternoon. Inez?"

Inez sighed. "At home, grading essays. Not alone—my kids were there, making it hard to grade three sentences in sequence. But two-year-old witnesses wouldn't help much in court. If people think I'm such a terrible mother that I'd leave my kids home alone, I'm doomed. What were you doing between 5:00 and 6:00, Julian?"

He shrugged. "Grading essays. My wife watches the kids on Thursday afternoons, so I found an empty classroom and sat there all by myself from 4:00 until about 6:00, finishing a stack of essays. Great alibi, huh?"

"As good as ours," I said. "We all isolate ourselves to get our grading done, and that's hell on alibis. Now, the hard question. Suppose—just for the sake of argument—the story Nina eventually tells bears more resemblance to our crime-as-therapy scenario. Do we tell the police about our therapy sessions and say one of us is probably guilty?"

"Absolutely not," Maureen said. "In the first place, even if what happened yesterday resembles our plans, it might be a coincidence—"

"Oh, come on," Julian said.

"It's possible," she insisted. "Or someone could have overheard our plans and decided to carry them out. We can't *know* one of us did it." She looked at all of us, hard. "*I* certainly didn't do anything wrong. Would anyone else like to confess?"

We were all silent, possibly because we were all wondering exactly what the definition of "anything wrong" would be in this context. Maureen nodded.

"All right," she said. "No one confesses. So we'll wait and see what happens."

* * * *

Quite a bit happened. On Monday morning, Nina went to President Swanson's office. Moments after the closed-door session ended, rumors started darting around campus. Nina had admitted to "an error in judgment," all the gossips agreed. Some gossips talked about letters she'd found on Jack's desk, about an investment firm, about an e-mail she sent to a website, about a call from a woman with a "deep, dusky" voice and a Southern accent, about an invitation to meet an investment officer at a restaurant at 7:30 Thursday night. Nina admitted to withdrawing funds from the Academic Excellence account—she claimed she'd intended to turn any profits over to the university, but not even the most gullible gossips believed that. Rumors about the amount withdrawn varied wildly, but two clerks in the treasurer's office said it was $25,000. That settled that.

There was talk about the theft from the locker and Nina's panic. After that, Nina went to the restaurant, perhaps planning to withdraw more money and make profits large enough to hide the lost $25,000. No investment officer showed up. Puzzled, Nina checked the record of received calls on her cell phone, called the number for the dusky-voiced woman, and was surprised to hear a recording invite her to leave a message for Danyelle Travis. Now deeply confused, Nina raced to a computer but failed to find the investment firm's site. She went next to Danyelle's dormitory room, where she learned Danyelle's cell phone had been missing for almost a week.

All that happened Thursday evening. The gossips could only speculate about what Nina's weekend had been like, what desperate alternatives she might have considered before deciding to confess. President Swanson was not pleased—all the gossips agreed on that. He called Danyelle, he called the police, and both Nina and Danyelle spent a good chunk of the morning talking to detectives. At one point, Danyelle burst into tears and had to be comforted by three secretaries.

The four of us listened to all this talk, but we said little. On Tuesday morning, Nina returned to her office and shut the door. On Tuesday afternoon, a fiftyish man in a tan coat came to the adjuncts' office, introduced himself as Lieutenant Mike Ferguson, found Jack Hanson, and walked off with him to have a talk.

On Tuesday night, Lieutenant Ferguson came to my house. "This is just routine," he said when we were seated in the den. "We're looking into this business involving Ms. Nina Dixon. At first, since a student's cell phone was used to call her, we thought a student stole the phone and—well, played a prank. But it looks like the—well, prankster—might be someone who knew Ms. Dixon well, had access to her office and Mr. Hanson's desk. So we gotta wonder if the prankster might be an English adjunct."

Good lord, I thought. At my age, to be suspected of being a prank-ster—couldn't he find a more dignified euphemism? "Are you sure there was a prankster?" I asked.

"No," he admitted. "Ms. Dixon can't show us the letters she says she found on Mr. Hanson's desk, and Mr. Hanson says he never saw them. Did *you* see them?"

"No," I said. "Jack said he got his money through an inheritance, not through investments. I assumed he was telling the truth."

"He was," Ferguson confirmed. "We checked his late second cous-in's will, plus his bank records. And no one can find this web site Ms. Dixon says she visited. We know that last Tuesday she sent an e-mail to a web address that no longer seems to exist, that a call was made from Ms. Travis's cell phone to Ms. Dixon's cell phone Thursday morning, and that Ms. Dixon withdrew $25,000 from the Academic Excellence ac-count that afternoon. That's the only solid evidence we've got. So we're not assuming there really was a prankster. But $25,000 is a lot of money, and the university's eager to get it back—we gotta consider all possibili-ties. Can you tell me anything that might help?"

"I'm sorry," I said. "I can't."

He questioned me for half an hour, and I was impressed by how much he knew—about Nina, about the university, even about our gatherings at Monty's and the fact that Danyelle waited on our table. A smart guy, I thought—and a nice guy, trying to make an uncomfortable situation less distressing for someone he probably regarded as probably innocent. He eased into chat about life as an adjunct, then leaned forward in his chair.

"Tell me this," he said. "I know how hard you people work, how little you make. There must be other kinds of jobs you could get, and the job you've got now can't be what you had in mind when you went to graduate school. So why are you still teaching?"

I thought it over for a moment. "Do you know the story about the elephant keeper at the circus, Lieutenant?"

"No, I don't think I've heard that one. How does it go?"

"A young man went to the circus," I said, "and thought it was the most glamorous, exciting thing he'd ever seen. So he joined the circus, but the only job he could get was as the elephant keeper. For twenty years, all day, every day, he took his shovel and bucket and followed the elephants around, cleaning up after them. Then all the elephants developed—well, a chronic digestive disorder, and cleaning up after them became harder and messier than ever. Every night, the keeper came home exhausted, disgusted, and smelly. After many months, his wife said to him, 'This job's making you miserable. Why don't you quit?' And he looked at her in astonishment and said, 'What? And leave show business?'"

Ferguson chuckled quietly. "Old dreams die hard, huh?"

"If at all," I said. "When a class goes really well—when you feel that you've gotten through to the students, that you've helped them appreciate something important and beautiful and true—not many things in life compare. Even if classes don't go that well often, even if you seldom get the chance to teach things you find important and beautiful and true, it's hard to stop hoping. It's hard to walk away from the possibility it can still happen, at least once in a while."

"I can understand that," he said. "I had high hopes, too, when I started out—protecting the innocent, bringing the guilty to justice. Sometimes, it's worked out that way. Most of the time, it's been a compromise." He grinned. "At least I've had a few pretty good car chases along the way. And at least, when I'm done, I'll have a pension."

* * * *

Not much happened Wednesday. When I got to work, I found a note from Nina on my desk, saying the English adjuncts' meeting would be in Beumler 203, not Cuthbert 107. So I went to Beumler at 10:50, sat between Julian and Inez, and endured Jack's political rant until Nina arrived. Maureen never showed up. When we returned to the office, we found her fuming. She'd waited in Cuthbert 107 until 11:30, she said. Why hadn't someone told her the meeting was cancelled? When we told her that it had been moved, that Nina had left us all notes telling us about the change, she declared she'd received no note, called Nina a nasty name, and got back to grading essays.

Thursday passed quietly. We exchanged details about Ferguson's visits to our homes. He'd shown Julian's daughter a magic trick, read a book to Inez's twins, and arrived at Maureen's house just as she was putting spaghetti on to boil; he'd questioned her while enjoying a bowl of pasta carbonara. We heard rumors that President Swanson had called Nina to his office again, that she might be fired, that he might press charges.

On Friday, when Julian and I got back from our 10:00 classes, we found Nina standing by Maureen's desk, this time not bothering to disguise her interest in somebody else's mail. "Lots of mail today," she said, her tone brighter than it had been all week. "Maureen got a couple of thick envelopes from travel agencies. Is she planning a trip?"

Julian and I looked at each other. "She hasn't mentioned it," he said.

"Oh—being mysterious, is she?" Nina made her tone brighter still as Maureen and Inez walked in. "Hi, Maureen! Your mail's here! Planning a trip?"

Maureen walked over, glanced at the envelopes, and dropped them into the wastebasket. "Ads," she said. "Junk mail."

Nina scooped the envelopes back out. "Ads from two travel agencies in one day? That'd be quite a coincidence. Maybe you won a prize. Open them and see."

Sighing, Maureen ripped the envelopes open. "Must be some new advertising gimmick," she said. "They both say they're responding to my request for brochures about cruises, but I never made a request." She dumped everything back in the trash.

"It's like those automated calls from satellite TV companies," Julian offered. "We get those all the time: 'Great news! Your application for our special one-time offer has been approved!' And of course we never made any application."

That ended the discussion, but it made me uneasy. Later, after Maureen left to teach at the community college, I walked past her desk and noticed her wastebasket was empty. Had she decided to look through the brochures after all?

We got our answer when Maureen returned to put in one last office hour before going to Monty's with us. Shortly after four, Lieutenant Ferguson walked into the office, accompanied by Nina, and headed for Maureen's desk. He lowered his voice.

"Dr. Fahey," he said, "some questions have come up. May I speak to you alone?"

Maureen gave him a puzzled look. "You can speak to me here. I've got an office hour—I should stay available to students. What is it?"

"It's a delicate matter," he said. "It'd be best if—"

"*She's* behind this, isn't she?" Maureen cut in, looking past him to glare at Nina. "She's got some scheme going. Let's clear it up here and now."

He lowered his voice still further, but we could all hear. "If that's how you want it," he said. "Ms. Dixon called me this morning, about the travel brochures. She says you claimed those were junk mail, but she called the travel agencies, and they said you called them Wednesday, saying you'd come into some money and were planning a cruise."

"Nina's lying," Maureen said flatly. "She does that a lot."

He grimaced. "I went to both agencies and checked their phone records. They both received calls from your home, placed between 11:05 and 11:15 Wednesday morning. Ms. Dixon says you missed a staff meeting at that time."

For a moment, Maureen just looked stunned. Then her eyes filled with fury. "This is a set-up, Lieutenant. I missed the meeting because Nina never told me it had been moved. She left notes on everyone else's desk, but she didn't—"

"I did!" Nina insisted, her voice too shrill. "I distinctly remember putting the note on your desk! And I saw you in the ladies' room before you left for your 10:00 class. I reminded you about the room change, and you said—"

"That's another lie," Maureen said. "We never spoke that morning."

"We did!" Nina's face purpled. "And that's not all! Tell her about what Danyelle said yesterday, Lieutenant, about seeing her loitering in the coatroom at Monty's on the day the cell phone disappeared, and about finding an earring stuck to her jacket—"

"That's enough," Ferguson said. "We shouldn't go into that here. Dr. Fahey, Ms. Dixon also says she walked into this office yesterday and saw you looking at something in your bottom desk drawer. When you saw her, you slammed the drawer shut. She's asked me to search the drawer. I don't have a warrant yet, but—"

"Go ahead." Maureen's voice was utterly calm now, utterly cold. "But please notice the drawer has no lock. And Nina has a key to our office. She can get in here any time she wants and plant any evidence she pleases. Be careful about fingerprints."

By now, there wasn't much point in pretending to be oblivious to what was going on. Julian, Inez, and I gathered to watch as Ferguson took things from Maureen's bottom drawer: end-of-semester essays students hadn't bothered to pick up, filled-up grade books, outdated employee manuals. Almost every teacher has a drawer where such stuff accumulates—one might go months without opening such a drawer.

At the back of the drawer, he found other things. There was a manila envelope filled with letterhead for Roth and Cox Investments, with just the firm name and a web address. ("That's the firm!" Nina shrieked.) There was a sheet of paper with three numbers typed on it. ("My God!" Nina cried. "That's the combination to my gym lock!") There was an envelope containing six fifty-dollar bills. ("Oh, Maureen!" Nina moaned. "How could you?") And there was a single earring, a polished jade oval set in gold.

"My ex-husband gave me those earrings," Maureen said. Her voice sounded drained, resigned. "I haven't worn them in twelve years. Does

Danyelle claim she found the matching earring stuck to her jacket? On the day her cell phone disappeared?"

"Wait," Julian said. "That was two weeks ago at Monty's, right? I was with Maureen—so were Amy and Inez. And I'm sure she didn't have those earrings on. I—"

"Thank you, Julian," Maureen said. "But no one who takes one look at you would believe you'd notice what earrings a woman was wearing—certainly not a woman in her fifties. And it was two weeks ago." She turned to Ferguson. "Should I get my coat? Are we going downtown, as they say?"

"That might be a good place to talk," he said, almost apologetically. "Thank you, Dr. Fahey." He cast a look over his shoulder at Nina. "You're coming, too, Ms. Dixon."

Minutes later, Julian and Inez and I stood next to Maureen's desk, alone. "It's ludicrous," Inez said. "Why would Maureen keep those things in her desk, where anyone could find them? Ferguson *can't* be taking this seriously."

"He's clearly skeptical," Julian said, "and clearly sympathetic to Maureen. But a cop can't ignore evidence. And if those calls were made from her house—"

"Maureen keeps a key in a little metal box attached to her drainpipe," I said. "She's had it there ever since her kids were in high school and kept forgetting their keys. *I* know that—I bet lots of people know that. Why can't Nina know that? Why couldn't she have let herself into Maureen's house and made the calls?"

"Because Nina was in the meeting, with us, when the calls were made," Inez said. "That witch! She managed it so she has a foolproof alibi, while Maureen was all by herself in an empty classroom, with no alibi at all."

"If she was really in that classroom," Julian said slowly. "You don't think—"

"Of course not," I said. "If Maureen took the trouble of going home to make the calls, why have the brochures mailed to the office? It's a frame. Nina's scared—the police can't find the money, and she can't prove someone stole it from her. To protect herself, she's got to get the university and the police to focus on another bad guy."

"And she picked Maureen," Inez said. "The logical choice. We're all suspects, because we have access to Jack's desk and Nina's office. But Maureen has the strongest motive because she's in the worst financial shape."

"True," I agreed. "And Maureen's flagrantly bitter, and she has a long history of sparring with Nina and no spouse to stand up for her. She has friends to stand up for her, though. How do we prove the frame's a fake?"

Julian hesitated. "Here's the thing," he said. "The frame's a fake—no argument. But chances are someone *did* set Nina up and steal the money from her, and chances are it was one of us. And I'm sorry to say it, but chances are it was Maureen. All along, she was the most serious about our therapy sessions. To us, it was a joke, but she—"

"We all got wrapped up in it," I said, alarmed at the direction his talk was taking.

"And we all helped plan the crime," Inez said. "If one of us actually committed it, don't we all share some responsibility? Besides, even if we don't know who stole the money, we *do* know Nina planted that evidence. Is it right to let Maureen be framed by false evidence, even if it's for a crime she really did commit?"

"Whoa," Julian said. "That's a tough one. I gotta go back to my undergraduate school, ask my ethics professor what he thinks. And what if we can't help Maureen without planting *more* false evidence? That's not right—and it's risky."

"Criminals have to take risks," I said. "Maureen said that—remember?"

"We're not criminals," he countered. "And if Maureen didn't make those calls from her house, who did?"

"Nina's accomplice," I said promptly. "Maureen said only stupid criminals take accomplices. That sounds like Nina. And I bet I know who her accomplice is."

"Danyelle," Inez said. "Of course. She lets herself into Maureen's house Wednesday, makes the calls, and takes the earrings. Then she tells the police she's just remembered seeing Maureen loitering in the coatroom at Monty's, and just found an earring stuck to her jacket. She didn't tell them that until yesterday—Nina herself said so. Why wait till then unless she had to steal the earrings first?"

"And meanwhile Nina plants the other earring in Maureen's desk," Julian said slowly, "along with the other stuff. But why would Danyelle help Nina frame Maureen?"

"Danyelle's probably as scared as Nina is," I said. "The only real evidence the police have is that someone called Nina from Danyelle's phone. Danyelle could've lied about the phone being lost. She could've set up the whole scam, called Nina with her own phone, and stolen the money. I'm sure the police suggested that possibility to Danyelle. That's probably why she started crying while being questioned."

"Danyelle really *could* have done all that," Inez said. "If she over-heard us at Monty's, that could've given her the idea. Do you think she might possibly—"

"Not possibly," I said. "Danyelle's too clueless to pull all that off. But the police probably don't know how clueless she is—they haven't read her essays. They're probably treating her like a suspect, and she's probably terrified. If Nina came to her with a plan for getting somebody else arrested, she'd jump at it."

"Maybe," Julian said. "But that doesn't help us clear Maureen."

"It might," I said. "Remember the other things Maureen said about accomplices—they make mistakes, they panic, and in the end they make a deal with the police and turn state's evidence. I can see Danyelle doing that. She's the weakest link in a flimsy frame."

"I'm not sure of the metaphor," Inez said, hesitantly. "Do frames have links?"

"I don't care," I said. "The point is, we just have to give Danyelle a push, make her turn against Nina. How hard can that be?"

"Probably not that hard," Julian said, and we sat down to talk it over.

* * * *

We half-expected that Danyelle wouldn't be at Monty's, that Fergu-son had asked her, too, to come downtown—but she was there, ignoring customers and spilling beer as usual. When she saw the three of us walk in without Maureen, I swear she smirked.

"Hey, you guys," she said. "I'll get your pitcher—and three mugs."

"No pitcher today," Julian said jauntily. "Today, we're celebrating. Bring us a bottle of your finest Champagne."

Danyelle blinked twice. "That'd be Andre's," she said.

"Fine." I tried not to sound relieved. What would we have done if she'd said Dom Perignon? "And four glasses—Dr. Fahey's joining us soon. Goodness! That was close!"

"It certainly was," Inez said. "I thought he might actually arrest her. I'm so glad that she insisted he send cops to question her neighbors, and that one neighbor happened to see someone leaving her house Wednes-day morning."

"Yeah, that was lucky," Julian said. "And when that secretary con-firmed she'd talked to her in the ladies' room around 11:15—wait a min-ute." He turned to Danyelle, who still stood behind his chair, eyes less vacant than usual. "Our Champagne?"

"What?" Danyelle gave her head a quick shake. "Oh, yeah. I'll get it."

I flipped my cell phone open. When Danyelle returned with the Champagne, I was chatting busily. "That's great, Maureen," I said. "It's sad she's hysterical, but she deserves—yes, we'll wait for you. What? Sure, bring him along. He should be part of the celebration. If he'd fallen for her lies—but he's too smart for that. How long do you think you'll be? Really? She's that close to breaking? Fantastic." I flipped the phone shut.

Danyelle struggled with the cork; Julian made no move to help her. "So everything's going well?" he said.

"Very well. Lieutenant—well." I made a pretense of lowering my voice. "*He* decided they should all go to—well, to our friend's house. A sketch artist came along to work with the neighbor, and now they've got a good sketch of the person seen leaving her house. And a lab team went through the house and found *more* evidence."

"Fingerprints?" Inez said eagerly. "Hair? Fibers?"

"She couldn't say," I said. "She was calling from a police car, and Nin—well, She-Whose-Name-We'd-Rather-Avoid—was there, too. She says the frame wasn't her idea—the person who *really* stole the money forced her into it. Nin—she was afraid to say no, because this person gets violent."

"Violent?" Inez said, gasping. "How terrifying! I hope Lieutenant— I hope *he* arrests this other person right away."

"And he'll throw away the key," I said solemnly. "Those were his exact words, our friend said. He just has to get—well, our colleague—to break down and name this other person. Apparently, she's within seconds of doing exactly that."

The cork shot out of the bottle, sending a spray of Champagne high into the air, ricocheting off the ceiling, and landing in a full mug of beer two tables away. Danyelle slumped off to get a cloth to clean up the mess. "And a fifth glass!" Inez called after her.

By the time Danyelle got back, we were hunched over the table, conferring in conspiratorial tones. "They really don't have much evidence against her," Inez said. "She admits planting things in our friend's desk, but she's got an alibi for the time the phone calls were made—"

"Unlike this other person," Julian said. "And he or she was seen leaving our friend's house and must've stolen the earrings. So he or she is definitely a thief. It follows that the thief who stole the earrings is the thief who stole the money."

"That's logical," I agreed. "And I got the impression the other earring has already turned up somewhere. He wouldn't say, but—over here, Danyelle. You missed a drop."

"Anyway," Inez said, "this other person's the one in *real* trouble. Our colleague helped with the frame, but she was forced into it. She may talk her way out of jail time."

"Especially since she's cooperating with the police now," Julian said. "That gives her a huge advantage. She can tell the story her way, say the other person masterminded the plot to steal the money from the university, the break-in at our friend's house, the frame, everything. The police are bound to believe the one cooperating with them. They'll pin all the charges on this other—oh, Danyelle, don't go away. May we see an appetizer menu?"

"Right away," Danyelle said, but she was already practically running from the table, already taking off her apron. Moments later, we saw her emerge from the coatroom and leave the restaurant. We looked at each other grimly.

"She's not necessarily heading for the police station to implicate Nina," Inez said. "She could be running home to her parents."

"I doubt it," I said. "She's probably afraid Ferguson would drag her back in handcuffs. And she's used to living in a protected world where any student who makes an accusation against a staff member is automatically believed, no matter how ridiculous the accusation is. She probably thinks the police are as gullible as college administrators."

"And this time," Julian said, "the police wouldn't have to be all that gullible. Danyelle will probably tell them the truth—more or less."

"The truth—more or less." Inez smiled slightly. "That's probably as much as any of us will ever know about all this."

Julian smiled too, also slightly. "Actually, *one* of us probably knows the whole truth. But I'm half-hoping she—or he—never has to reveal it." He lifted his glass. "Here's to Maureen—and to one successful foray into a life of crime."

* * * *

One week later, we were back at Monty's, all four of us, at our usual table, with our usual pitcher of Bud Lite. We had a new waitress, a forty-ish woman who made eye contact and didn't spill beer. Maureen looked wonderful. She'd had her hair done and was wearing a new rose-colored wool dress that subtly accented a figure that, after two children and five decades, was gently rounded but still more or less trim.

"I met with President Swanson," she said. "He's given me back my old job of coordinating the writing center tutors. I won't make nearly as much as Nina did—only one thousand a semester—but I'm glad to have it. And Swanson said he's glad to have someone to step in at short notice, after Nina resigned for personal reasons."

"He shouldn't have let her resign for personal reasons," Julian said. "He should've fired her outright. He should've pressed charges."

"There's no absolute proof she has the money," Inez said. "There's just as much evidence pointing to Danyelle."

"But Nina definitely withdrew a large sum from a university account for her own use," Julian argued. "And both she and Danyelle planted false evidence and interfered with a police investigation—they both admitted it. So why wasn't either of them charged with anything? Why was Danyelle allowed to withdraw from all her classes with a full refund, long after the withdrawal deadline?"

"Because trials create scandal," I said. "And colleges and universities hate scandal. Anyway, Maureen, I'm glad you got the writing center job back."

She smiled at me. "According to two highly-placed secretaries, the dean made a recommendation to the president. Thank you, Amy."

I shrugged. "You're the most qualified person for the job. The dean didn't need my help to see that."

"I feel a little bad about Nina, though," Inez said. "True, she wasn't qualified for her job, and she pushed more qualified people aside to get it. Even so—and without getting into things we don't want to discuss—she probably didn't steal the money. At least, she probably doesn't still have it. So is it right she's out of work?"

"Did anyone force her to read the letters on Jack's desk?" Maureen demanded. "Did anyone force her to withdraw money she had no right to withdraw or plant false evidence? Nina's own vices led her to do all those things. No matter who has the money now, Nina's responsible for what happened to her. Don't waste pity on her, Inez. Don't pity Danyelle, either. She hasn't suffered much, and she needn't have suffered at all if she'd refused to help with the frame. And she's young. Maybe she'll learn from all this."

I shook my head. "Not much chance of Danyelle ever learning anything under any circumstances, Maureen. You know that. You've had her in class."

"Well, I've got news," Julian said. "My wife and I talked it over, and I'm starting law school next fall. Just part-time—I'll still need to do some teaching, pay some bills. But in the long term, being a lawyer makes more financial sense than teaching does."

Maureen looked stricken. "But are you interested in law?"

He nodded slowly. "I'm developing an interest. As of one month ago, I have started to develop a definite interest."

Inez set down her mug. "I may make a change, too. There was an ad in the paper for the new chain bookstore opening in town. I interviewed, and I was offered a job: Twenty hours a week, making more than I do now. And no essays to grade—I'd have more evening and weekend time for my family. Plus the company has a program to help part-time employees make the transition to management when they're ready. The program's specifically designed for employees with young children, the interviewer said. Ironic, isn't it? This big, bad corporation found a way to help parents move into full-time jobs—something our oh-so-liberal universities can't seem to figure out."

"But you'll finish your dissertation, won't you?" Maureen asked.

"Definitely," Inez said. "I enjoy research, and I love literature. I'll have far more time to read if I stop teaching composition. And even if I never use my degree, I damn well want the option of having 'Ph.D.' engraved on my tombstone."

"Well, this seems to be the time for revelations," I said. "Craig and I had a talk, too. I'm not teaching in the fall—I'm taking the semester off to finish my article, maybe start that book. With luck, the article and the book will be so good that next time Phil Hanson teaches an Austen seminar, he'll have to put them both in his bibliography. And we figure if I spend more time clipping coupons, I can save almost as much at the grocery store as I can make teaching three sections of composition. Without essays hanging over my head all the time, I'm bound to be in a better mood."

"Good grief!" Maureen said. "Did this last month traumatize all of you that much? Will I be the only one left? Is this the end of Adjuncts Anonymous?"

"We can still meet here on Fridays," Julian said, "no matter what we're doing during the rest of the week. Let's order another pitcher and seal the deal."

Maureen hesitated. "Actually, I have to go. Mike—Lieutenant Ferguson—and I got to know each other better last Friday, while I was at the station. We're going out to dinner tonight. I'd better get home—he's picking me up in half an hour."

That explained the nicely-done hair, the new dress. Have a good time tonight, Maureen, I wished fervently. Say yes to a second date, and a third. Fall in love with him. Marry him. You're lonely, and he's a smart, decent guy. And he has a pension.

"I should go, too," Inez said, standing up; and then Julian and I stood, and we all looked at each other awkwardly. Then Maureen gave me an impulsive hug, and then I hugged Inez, and then everyone was hugging everyone. It brought to mind the mock-solemn handshakes of a month ago—but this was a happier time, a better time.

I didn't have carpooling duty, so I could go directly home. I pulled into the garage, lugged my essay-stuffed briefcase out of the backseat for weekend grading, and couldn't resist the urge to lift the lid on our ancient freezer, to push aside the bags of peas and corn and pearl onions, to rummage beneath the loaves of bread bought on special, and to pull out the foil-wrapped package labeled "Aunt Susan's Fruitcake, December, 2006." I pulled back three layers of foil. Yes, there it was—$25,000 in crisp, cold bills.

As always, Maureen had been a good mentor. Criminals must take risks, she had said, but only stupid criminals take accomplices. So I'd taken the risk that someone would spot me when I put the letters on Jack's desk and took them away again, when I tacked the note on Nina's door, when I took her combination lock from her gym bag and put my own lock in its place, when I hurried across campus to the old gym wearing the jeans-and-bulky-jacket outfit most of our students wear most of the time, when I took the cash and the note from her gym bag and switched locks again, when I walked quickly back to my car, $25,000 stuffed in my jacket. But I'd taken no accomplices, not even my fellow adjuncts, not even my husband. It was my crime, mine alone—no one to share the blame if things went wrong, no one to keep my secrets if things went right.

If it hadn't been for that damned Austen seminar, I probably wouldn't have gotten mad enough to do it. But now that it was done, I felt fine. No regrets about Nina and Danyelle, no regrets about the university—after exploiting me for sweatshop wages for all these years, it owed me a lot more than $25,000. Maureen had a few uncomfortable hours—I'd never intended that—but she'd been tough enough to weather them, and now she was a little better off than she had been. With luck, she'd soon be a lot better off.

As for me, I had every intention of clipping coupons diligently, of trying to make ends meet on Craig's salary alone. But if we came up short some weeks, I had backup. It never hurts to have a stack of cash in the freezer, just in case.

Of all the stories I've ever written, "Adjuncts Anonymous" draws most directly on my own experiences. Like protagonist Amy, I started my academic career as a full-time, tenure-track English professor, bristling with enthusiasm about teaching and with ideas about the scholarly articles I'd write. After my husband and I had our first child, though, the yearning to spend more time with her tugged at me. And since my husband's only chance at full-time teaching meant moving to another state, I decided to give up my job and try adjunct teaching for a little while. Another child, more moves as my husband's career advanced—"a little while" turned into decades of adjunct teaching, usually only composition, always for low wages, never with any benefits, any job security, or any respect from the full-time members of the departments in which I toiled.

In "Adjuncts Anonymous," Amy remembers a time when she asked the English Department chair to give her a chance to teach a literature course. The chair turns her down because "We can't have a course for potential majors taught by an adjunct—by a faculty wife." Some readers have said that part of the story seems unrealistic, since no department chair would be that blunt, that unfair. It's not unrealistic. It happened to me, word for word, at a fine liberal arts college in western Illinois. And everything the story says about how heavily colleges rely on adjuncts these days, and how much colleges exploit them—that's all true, too. Half an hour on Google will convince you. I know about the crushing financial pressures most colleges face. I understand why colleges feel they have to treat adjuncts so badly. My husband, like Amy's husband, became a dean, so I can see both sides of the issue. But I think colleges have to work harder to address the very real injustices at the center of this light-hearted story.

*The revenge plot the four adjuncts come up with, though—that's pure fantasy. No matter how much I resent the way various colleges and universities have treated me over the decades, I'd never consent to become part of such a plot. Stealing is morally wrong, and that's the end of the discussion. Sometimes, though—over a beer at Monty's, or in a short story—it might be excusable, even healthy, to let ourselves indulge in dreams about how sweet it would be to strike back at those who have denied us our due, and our dignity. "No, no, they do but jest, poison in jest; no offense i'th'world." (*Hamlet, *Act 3, scene 2)*

AUNT JESSICA'S PARTY

(1993)

Carefully, Jessica polished her favorite sherry glass and placed it on the silver tray. Soon, her nephew would arrive. He was to be the only guest at her little party, and everything had to be perfect.

Five minutes until six—time to call Grace. She went to the phone near the kitchen window, kept her eyes on the driveway, and dialed.

"Hello, Grace?" she said. "Jessica. How are you? Oh, I'm fine—never better. Did I tell you William's coming today? Yes, it *is* an accomplishment to get him here. But it's his birthday, and I promised him a special present. He even agreed to pick up some sherry for me. Oh, there he is, pulling into the driveway." She paused. "Goodbye, Grace. You're a dear."

At six feet, William towered over his seventy-year-old aunt. He was a handsome man in his early forties, and as usual he was dressed elegantly and expensively.

"Here's your sherry," he said, shoving the bottle at her. He glanced down the long entryway. "That fat housekeeper isn't hanging around, is she?"

"No, dear," Jessica assured him. "Maria left at five to get Billy from daycare. Go make yourself comfortable in the living room. I'll hang up your coat."

As soon as he was out of sight, she felt in his coat pocket for the gold-plated box he always carried. Moving quickly, she snapped it open, took what she needed, closed the box, polished it with her apron, and replaced it in his pocket. Moments later, she walked into the living room, carrying the silver tray.

"I do love a sip of sherry," she said. "And here's your mineral water. Would you pour for us both? My hands aren't so steady."

Grumbling, he splashed sherry into her glass, water into his. "So," he said, "where's this present? I hope you didn't drag me here for some dumb sweater. You know what I need. You know how slow business is."

I know how many gambling debts you have, she thought. I'm not such a fool as you think, beloved nephew. "Yes, I know. So I got you something special." She handed him a stiff legal document. "Here's your present."

He skimmed the will, then tossed it aside. "So I'm your sole heir. So what? I'm your only living relative—naturally I get your house and your money. Big deal. I need cash now."

She shook her head. "Not unless you acknowledge Billy as your son and help support him. He needs hearing aids. Soon, he'll need surgery, speech therapy, a special school. Maria can't manage alone, and she won't take charity from me. From you, it wouldn't be charity. It would be justice."

William scowled. "Justice? Is it justice that I got stuck with a bum heart, can't have liquor, have to take digitalis every day? I got enough problems. So don't expect me to make everything easy for that kid and his grandmother."

I didn't really expect it, Jessica thought sadly as memories came back. Maria's daughter Angie, only seventeen—William had seduced her, gotten her pregnant, and dropped her, refusing to see her or his newborn son. Heartbroken, Angie had hanged herself, leaving Maria and Billy to struggle by themselves.

"How about it?" William said. "Do I really have to wait years to get my money?"

She looked up. "Not many years. I have The Illness, William."

There was some long Latin name for it, but to Jessica it would always be The Illness, the rare genetic disorder that had haunted her family for generations. There was no cure, only increasing helplessness and long years of agony.

William perked up. "Yeah? You seen a doctor?"

"I don't need to. I know the signs well enough, after nursing your mother for so long." Her voice grew soft. "At the end, the pain was so bad that all she could say was your name. I wish you'd visited her, William. She prayed for it every day. Couldn't you have managed it once, during all those years?"

He shrugged. "I was busy. Look, if you won't change your mind about the money, I'm leaving. Send me your lawyer's name, so I can collect on the will when the time comes."

"Don't worry." She couldn't look at him. "Happy birthday."

When he'd driven away, she sighed as she carried the tray into the kitchen. I tried, William, she thought. I offered you another chance to set things right. She reached into her apron pocket for the ten small, white pills she'd taken from the box in his coat. Carefully, she crushed the pills, poured the white powder into the sherry bottle, and picked up the tray again.

Back in the living room, she reviewed her preparations. The phone call to Grace established that William had come to the house. He'd bought the sherry, his fingerprints were on the bottle, she'd used his digitalis—the method should seem clear, and his fingerprints on the will provided a motive. Probably, he hadn't read it carefully enough to notice Maria would get everything if William couldn't inherit.

Using a napkin, she picked up the sherry bottle and poured a brimming glass. She had some unpleasant moments ahead, but nothing compared to the long agony she'd endure if she let The Illness take her. And nothing compared to the years William would spend in prison, thinking about Angie's suicide, his mother's misery, his own wasted life.

She lifted the glass. "Here's to you, dear sister," she said. "And to you, poor Angie, and little Billy, and my faithful Maria." She emptied the glass in one swallow. "Cheers," she said, and smiled.

Over the years, I've published eight mini-mysteries in Woman's World. When I published the first one, back in 1988, I think the word limit was 1,500; now, it's 750. It must have been 900 in 1993, because that's about how long "Aunt Jessica's Party" is.

Writing a mystery that short is tricky. There's not much time for character development, so I tend to rely on recognizable types, such as the selfish, materialistic nephew and the sweet old aunt—though this particular aunt isn't as sweet as she seems. Most of the interest in a mini-mystery, I think, has to come from the plot. There's just a little time to set up the situation, throw in a dollop of conflict, drop two or three clues, and build a bit of suspense. If you pack all that into under 1000 words, things tend to move quickly, and that can be fun. Most important of all, I think, is the twist at the end. If the twist isn't both believable and surprising, this type of story probably won't work.

When this story appeared in Woman's World, the editor changed its title to "Aunt Jessica's Justice." That's not a bad title. Jessica and William do have a brief debate about justice, and maybe the editor thought "justice" sounds more ominous and is more appropriate for a mystery. But I'm glad to have a chance to restore the original title. I like the contrast between the innocent sound of "party" and the actual birthday surprise Aunt Jessica is planning for her nephew. And there's just a shade of ambiguity. Does "Aunt Jessica's Party" refer to the little celebration Jessica has with William, when she shows him his present? Or does it refer to the private party she has at the end of the story, when she drinks a second glass of sherry and gives her final toast?

THEA'S FIRST HUSBAND

(2012)

She had learned to brace herself against it. It happened whenever they met new people—sometimes at large social events connected to his firm, more often at the charity dinners and political fundraisers he'd grown so fond of attending. They'd be greeting clients from out of town, or sitting down at a table with an unfamiliar couple, or meeting the guest of honor in a receiving line, and that sly look she'd grown to know so well would come into his eyes.

"This is my lovely wife, Thea Hanover," he would say, reaching out to shake hands. "And I'm Edward Hanover." He would pause then, for three seconds. "I'm Thea's first husband."

Usually, people didn't get it. Usually, they'd just look confused, and nod, and introduce themselves. But too often someone—usually, a woman—would be tactless enough, or innocent enough, to press for clarification. "Oh," she'd say. "Then you're divorced?"

That was what Edward always seemed to be hoping for. He'd smile, and the sly look in his eyes would morph to delight. "No, we're not divorced," he would say, and he'd pause again, again for three seconds. "I'm just a realist."

Usually, people got it then. They'd look at her, and they'd look at him, and they'd get it. Most would smile awkwardly and make some neutral remark. But some men would chuckle, and some women would give her a pained, pitying look.

She hated it. She'd asked him to stop, a hundred times. "You make it sound as if I married you for your money," she'd say, "as if I'm itching to move on. People will think I'm a gold-digger."

"It's only my little joke, Thea," he'd say. "Don't worry about what people think." Then, again, he'd pause. "With a man my age, a woman your age—I'm simply saying what they'd think anyway. And I *do* expect you to have another husband someday, when the time comes. You'll still have so much of your life left—I don't expect you to spend all those years alone." He'd turn to her then, and look at her hard. "I also don't expect you to move on too soon, no matter how much you might be itching to. Not considering the way things are settled."

The worst part was that she hadn't married him for his money, not really. She'd married him, more or less, for love.

Even so, almost from the beginning, it had been hard. The first year or so was fine—not exciting, she'd never expected that, but pleasant and companionable, with his big new house to decorate and the fun of having a clothing allowance so large she usually had something left over at the end of the month. As often as he could manage, he'd come shopping with her. He never begrudged her anything, always urged her to get more; he seemed to enjoy buying things for her, just as he enjoyed getting things for the house. But then, for no reason she could see, she felt him drawing away, seeming less pleased with her, less open. Before the second year ended, he was making the joke. Then he started bringing young men home.

Scott Crawford, a junior partner at Edward's law firm, was the first. Edward invited him to dinner but didn't ask Thea to cook, even though she liked to cook, even though she'd started cooking at her parents' restaurant as a teenager and was at least as good as the personal chef Edward now shared with two other senior partners. Clearly, though, Edward didn't want Scott Crawford to see her as a cook. Before he left for the office that morning, Edward gave her instructions. She was to have her hair and nails done and to wear the red silk dress he'd special-ordered from the designer in Hong Kong. She was to wait upstairs until after Edward arrived with Scott Crawford, and then, while they were drinking Scotch in the great room, she was to walk down the broad, highly polished staircase and join them.

She played her part. He won't make the joke tonight, she told herself. It would be ridiculous—Scott Crawford obviously knows him already, so there's no reason for Edward to introduce himself. The men stood by the fireplace; Edward was pointing to the new Picasso sketch above the mantel, and Scott Crawford, glass in hand, was nodding in admiration. When she was halfway down the staircase, both men looked up at her, and Edward swept out his arm to take Thea in.

"At last!" he said. "Scott, this is my lovely wife, Thea." He paused. "And I, of course, am Thea's first husband."

Scott Crawford got it instantly; Thea could see that in his eyes. But he didn't comment, and didn't chuckle, and didn't give her a pained look.

At dinner, Edward told Thea about Scott's charity work. "His mother runs this remarkable foundation, Music Matters. It provides free after-school music lessons for inner-city young people. And on Saturdays, it brings them together for choral and instrumental groups. Scott coordinates the Saturday programs himself."

"That's wonderful," Thea said, smiling at Scott Crawford. He was about Thea's age, and nice looking—perhaps not handsome, not technically, but there was nothing wrong with the way he looked, and Thea felt glad about having him at the table, about being able to glance at him from time to time. "That must be very satisfying."

"It is," Scott said. "Those kids—week after week, they surprise me with what they can do, with how dedicated they are."

"Maybe you'd enjoy getting involved in that, Thea," Edward suggested. "I'm sure Scott could use some help on Saturdays—with making phone calls, and filing, and so forth. You could do that."

I can do more than make phone calls and file things, she thought, but smiled. "You've always said you don't want me to work."

"I haven't wanted you to work for a salary," he said, "since there's no need for that, and it wouldn't be right for you to take a paying position away from someone who *does* need it. But volunteer work—that's perfectly appropriate. After all, you can't do nothing but shop all day, every day."

As if I've never done anything but shop, she thought; as if I didn't work fifty hours a week, more than fifty, until I married you. She smiled again. "That's true."

"How about it, Scott?" Edward said. "Wouldn't you like to have Thea help on Saturdays?"

Scott looked at them, at the senior partner and his beautiful young wife. "Sure," he said. "We're in good shape for volunteers right now, but we can always use more. If Thea's interested, my mother and I would be glad to have her help."

So every Saturday, for the next five weeks, Thea joined Scott in the cramped office of the community center where the choral and instrumental groups met. They were never alone together for long: His mother would pop in often, and so would his sister, and his friends, and the wives of his friends. Usually, they didn't have any particular reason for popping in; Thea got the feeling that Scott had asked them to pop in, that they were popping in to make a point. But she enjoyed those Saturdays, enjoyed doing the simple tasks Scott found for her, enjoyed listening to the music groups practice, enjoyed chatting with the children when there was nothing left for her to do. On the fifth Saturday, when for once she and Scott were alone in the office, he turned away from his computer and smiled.

"How did you and Edward meet?" he asked.

She laughed. It was the first personal question he'd ever asked her. "Oh, I was tending bar at this place in the Flats. And he started dropping by, almost every night. I don't know—maybe he thought it had local color or something, but really it was just a dive. Anyhow, we'd talk, and he was so smart and funny; I liked listening to him. Then he asked me to dinner, and—well, that's how it started."

Scott nodded. "And he was already divorced?"

"Oh, yes," Thea said. "For years and years. Did you know, he invited his ex-wife to our wedding? That seemed odd—it was such a small wedding. But she came, with her new husband. Well, not so new—they've been married for years and years, ever since the divorce. Anyhow, I talked to her after the ceremony. I thought she might be mean to me, but she was nice. She seemed really smart."

He grimaced. "Another slick, over-educated lawyer. The world probably has too many of us." He was silent for a moment. "I've been thinking, Thea. There isn't much for you to do here on Saturdays. You must be bored. How about coming on Thursday afternoons instead? I won't be here—I'll be at work—but you'd be a big help to the administrative assistant, Sharon. You'll like her. How does that sound?"

It sounded a little sad. She'd come to look forward to these Saturdays, to listening to the children play and sing, to spending time with Scott, who was always so nice to her. But she felt this was a good decision; for reasons she couldn't quite understand, she felt relieved. "Of course," she said. "If I can help more on Thursdays, that's when I'll come. I won't come on Saturdays anymore."

But Edward didn't like having her go to the center on Thursdays. After two weeks, he decided it was a bad neighborhood, and sooner or later someone was bound to snatch her purse. That was the end of volunteering for Music Matters. Over the next few months, Edward brought more young men home for dinner, young men who worked for political candidates or charities he supported. Always, Edward offered them Thea's services as a volunteer; always, she found ways to say no. She was irritating him. She could see that, but she felt saying no was the smart thing to do.

Then, one morning at breakfast, Edward put down his newspaper. "You should get a personal trainer," he said.

She pressed down her spoon, easing out another section of grapefruit. "I don't need one. I've got my spinning class, my yoga class, and I go to the club every day to swim and work out on the machines. I weighed myself this morning. I'm eight pounds lighter than on the day we got married." She knew being thin was important, even though he'd never said a word about it, even though she'd always been thin. After he'd started drawing away from her, she'd worked hard to lose those eight pounds, even though she hadn't needed to. She'd thought, somehow, it might help. It hadn't.

"I know," Edward said. "And you look fine. But all my friends' wives have personal trainers."

So this was about having things his friends had. She understood about that. She sighed. "All right. After Andre comes here for his sessions with you, he can work with me."

"No. Andre works with men; he doesn't have much experience with women. And the gym downstairs isn't set up for you—the weights are too heavy. You should have a personal trainer at the club."

Maybe she could use this. "You're right. My sister's wedding is barely three months away—I want to look my best for that. Maybe, if I lose five more pounds before the wedding, you'll think about—"

"This isn't about your weight, Thea." Edward snapped his newspaper back into position. "And it certainly isn't about your sister's wedding. We've been over that. If you feel you must attend, you may, but I have no intention of going. I loathe Buffalo, and weddings bore me. Now, I've heard good things about a trainer named Tony; some of my friends' wives use him. I'll set up a session for this afternoon."

It was settled. At 3:00, she went to the club and had her first session with Tony. He was just her age—thirty-two—and he was magnificent. He was muscular, but not in an exaggerated way. His chin-length light brown hair was streaked with gold, so subtly it must be natural, or at least expensive; and any attempt to find fault with his eyes, nose, mouth, or chin would be silly. They met, five times a week, in a small room near the main gym. When Thea leaned over to touch her toes, his hands rested lightly on her hips, then moved down to close on her thighs; when she reached up to stretch, his hands followed the movement of her body, brushing softly against her breasts. He never said much. He didn't have to. By Monday of the third week, she wore a leotard instead of sweat pants, and she spent half an hour on her hair and makeup before heading for the club.

That was the day when he paused as she stretched, when his hands eased forward to cover her breasts, when he turned her around to face him and put his arms around her waist, drawing her close against him. She put her arms around his neck, tilted her head back, and closed her eyes.

"Excuse me," a man said, opening the door to the small room. He was short and dark and wiry, with sharp little eyes and a jutting chin. "Oops—am I interrupting? I thought I had a session scheduled in here, but maybe not. Say, you're Thea Hanover, aren't you? Hi—I'm Paul

Addison. I'm a friend of Edward's. Gosh—it's been a long time since I've seen you. Can I buy you a lemonade, or a green tea, or whatever they serve in that café downstairs?"

"Fine." Thea backed away from Tony. Paul Addison—the name meant nothing to her, and his face didn't register. But Edward knew so many people; there had been so many introductions over the past three years, often so humiliating that she couldn't focus on the faces of the people she was meeting. Tony looked at her helplessly, then ambled off. Too bad—she'd been so ready, not necessarily for going all the way, though she'd taken note of two decent-looking motels on the drive to the club, just in case. Well, she'd be back tomorrow.

She slipped into her jacket and followed Paul Addison to the café, smiling as he bought her a cranberry juice. "It's nice to see you again," she said, sitting down across from him in a bright orange booth. "I'll tell Edward you—"

"Don't do it, Thea." He took a sip of his pomegranate yogurt shake, winced, and then leaned forward, arms folded on the table. "Not over a jerk like Tony Gleason. You handled the Scott Crawford situation real well—or maybe he handled it, maybe you just followed his lead. But at least you had enough sense to see the situation couldn't go anyplace good. You should've seen that this time, too—it's a lot more obvious this time."

She grasped her plastic bottle of cranberry juice in both hands. Damn, she thought. Damn, damn, damn. "Who are you? How do you know about Scott?"

"Like I told you," he said, "my name's Paul Addison. What I didn't tell you is I'm a private detective, and six months ago your husband hired me to watch you. So I watched you when you were with Scott, and I watch you when you're with Tony. I watch you pretty much all the time when you're not with Edward."

This was it—the disaster she'd dreaded vaguely for months, though she hadn't been able to put a name to it until now. "Bastard," she said, and started to get up.

He grabbed her arm and pulled her back into the booth. "Think about it, Thea. I didn't have to tell you. I could've let you make a fool of yourself with Tony, taken pictures, and collected a fat fee. But I didn't. I decided to help you—to warn you. You know how Edward found out about Tony, why he wanted you to work with Tony? It's not because his friends' wives use Tony. His friends' wives are too smart to go anywhere near Tony. Tony's a whore, Thea. He plays up to rich women—to wives of rich men. He screws them, and then he squeezes them for money by threatening to tell their husbands. One wife stopped paying, and sure enough, her husband found out. Edward's firm is representing the husband in the divorce. That's how Edward found out about Tony."

She pressed her hand against her forehead. Scott, Tony, all the young men who had come to dinner—was that why? But that's so mean, she thought. "He's been testing me," she said. "But why? I've never given him one reason not to trust me."

"You came damn close to giving him a reason five minutes ago," Paul pointed out. "But it's okay. I stopped you before you crossed the line. He never has to know."

"Not if I pay you." Thea started to get angry again. "That's why you stopped me. Instead of paying Tony, I pay you."

"Nah, you don't have to pay me." Paul gave his pomegranate shake another try before pushing it aside. "Edward pays me plenty. As long as you don't actually screw anyone, this job could go on forever. And in lots of ways, it's easier than most jobs I've done. Not in all ways. I'll tell you the truth, Thea. In my line of work, lots of the jobs I do sort of turn my stomach. This one turns my stomach more than most. I hate to tell you, but your husband's a son of a bitch."

"He's not." Ridiculously, she felt tears coming to her eyes, and wiped them away with her fist. "He's nice. At least, he used to be nice. And then—I don't know why things changed. I don't know what I did wrong."

Paul looked at her, for a long time; she thought she saw real sympathy in his eyes. "I don't think it's anything you did," he said at last. "I think it's what he did; I think it's who he is. His mother lived too long. Edward had to wait too long to be rich."

She shook her head. "He's always been rich."

"By your standards, sure," Paul said. "By my standards, definitely. Successful lawyer, big practice—and his first wife made even more than he did. They lived pretty well. And when she left him for another man, she didn't ask for a penny. Lucky guy. But he didn't come into the real money until his mother died four years ago. By then, I think he felt entitled to—well, he's an interesting guy, I've spent lots of time trying to figure him out, but you don't want to hear my theories. The point is, I don't think all this has much to do with you. I think it has to do with his first wife cheating on him, and with him going overboard when he finally got his mother's money, and with him afterwards feeling like maybe he'd been a fool."

She tried to fit all that in with the way Edward had treated her. The money part didn't make sense; Edward had always been rich. And the other part wasn't her fault. "I knew his first wife cheated on him," she said. "I'm sure that hurt him, and I'm sorry. But *I* never cheated. I mean,

Tony, yes, but that wouldn't have happened if Edward hadn't pushed me to—why did Edward do that? It wasn't fair."

"No, it wasn't," Paul agreed. "If you left him, I wouldn't blame you."

She thought about that, not for long. "No, I don't want to leave him."

"I figured you wouldn't. I know about the prenup. If you get divorced, you get just about nothing. If you stick it out, you get just about everything."

"It's not just the prenup," she said, though she had to admit she'd come to love living in that house, and not going to work, and having the clerks in all the stores be nice to her. But it was also not wanting to go to her sister's wedding as someone whose marriage hadn't worked out, after her parents had told her to be careful, after her sister told her flat-out she was making a mistake. And Edward could still be nice, especially when it was just the two of them, at night, when he could still make her feel so pretty and special. "I like my husband—I love him. I want to make things good again."

"So confront him. Don't mention me—just say you figured out what he's been up to with Scott and Tony and the rest. Say you resent it, and he'd damn well better stop."

Confront Edward? No. He'd make her feel stupid—he could always turn whatever she said against her. Or he'd get mad and silent, and that would be unpleasant. She shook her head. "I can't. He's too smart—it'd be too hard." She looked at Paul more closely. "You've been watching me for six months? But I never even saw you before today."

"That's pretty much the goal when you're watching someone." He smiled at her, his sharp little eyes sparkling. "Thanks. You just paid me a nice compliment."

"And you really don't want money from me?"

"No. Like I said, in lots of ways, this is an easy job. Now that I won't feel like I'm setting you up, it'll be even easier. I'll just keep following you around to all the fancy places you go, drinking espresso and every so often taking pictures of you doing nothing in particular. It's safe, it's pleasant, and Edward pays well—I got no complaints."

She thought that over. "It sounds a little creepy."

"A little," he admitted. "But you'll get used to it. So, what'll you do about Tony?"

"I'll never see him again," she said promptly. "I'll report him to the club for trying to take advantage of me. I'll tell Edward—"

"Let's think about this," Paul cut in. "So far, I've been telling him there's nothing going on between Tony and you, that it's all sit-ups and jumping jacks and like that. We're gonna have to account for the change—we're gonna have to work out a narrative. I should take pictures. And you shouldn't be wearing a leotard when I do, and your hair shouldn't look so nice."

Thea blushed. "What should I do?"

He pursed his lips. "Come to the club tomorrow. Wear sweat pants, pull your hair back, don't wear makeup. Tony won't care—it's not the leotard that turns him on. Lead him on a little. When he makes his move, smack him in the face, run out of the room, and go home. When you see Edward, tell him you're switching to another club, but don't say why. Act upset, but just say you don't like this club anymore."

"But you said you want to take pictures," Thea objected. "Tony and I always work out in a private room, with the door closed. How can you—oh."

"Yeah, I've got a camera set up. A bug, too. How do you think I knew right when to barge in? Now, leading Tony on, acting upset for Edward—can you pull that off?"

Thea smiled slightly. "I had the lead in my high-school play, junior year. That's when I decided to drop out and head for Hollywood. I got as far west as Cleveland."

"Then you can pull it off." Paul grinned. "Afterwards, I'll call Edward, show him the picture of you smacking Tony, describe how shocked you were. Maybe he'll report Tony to the club, but I bet he'll let it go—he won't want to come that close to scandal. That should work." He stood up. "See you around, Thea."

"But I won't see you," she said, and felt a little sad. Paul could be crude, and he had strange ideas about Edward. But really, he'd been very nice.

* * * *

The plan worked as Paul had predicted. She enjoyed smacking Tony. At dinner that night, Edward got exasperated when she wouldn't explain why she'd decided to switch clubs. When he came home the next night, though, he gave her emerald earrings. Paul must have done a good job when he made his report, she thought, smiling at herself in the mirror, admiring the way the emeralds complemented the traces of hazel in her eyes. Her matron-of-honor dress was pale green; she could wear the earrings to her sister's wedding, as fresh proof of how much her husband loved her.

She went about her business—shopping, working out at her new club, sometimes having lunch with wives of Edward's friends. It felt odd, knowing Paul Addison was watching her. But it didn't feel bad. It felt almost comforting. Ever since she'd married Edward, she'd often felt lonely. She saw lots of people, but they were all people she knew through Edward. She couldn't really talk to any of them. Paul felt like a friendlier presence, even though she never saw him. My guardian angel, she thought once, and felt embarrassed it had occurred to her. From time to time, though, she found herself thinking it again.

She hoped things would get better with Edward, now that she'd proved herself with Tony—or, at least, seemed to prove herself. He didn't seem any warmer, though, and he still cut her off whenever she mentioned her sister's wedding. The real test, she decided, would be the retirement dinner for Marty Thompson, a senior partner at Edward's firm. Everyone from the firm was coming, and there would be new people, too, Marty's out-of-town relatives. There would be introductions. If Edward doesn't make the joke, Thea thought, that means things are better.

She dressed carefully—the new earrings, of course, and an off-the-shoulder soft black dress with a demurely flaring skirt. She looked exactly the way Edward liked her to look—sophisticated, sexy in an understated way, more glamorous than the other wives but not showy. When she came downstairs, Edward lifted his eyebrows and said she looked nice. Maybe this would be a good night.

At the country club, Marty stood near the door of the banquet room, his chunky old wife standing next to him, wearing some drab powder-blue thing. His out-of-town relatives clustered nearby, along with half a dozen partners and associates from the firm; they all had glasses in their hands. Marty seemed to be handling the introductions himself. So this wouldn't be a test for Edward after all. Thea felt slightly disappointed, slightly relieved.

Marty waved broadly when he spotted them. "Folks," he said, "this lovely young woman is Thea Hanover. And this reasonably well-preserved specimen is Edward Hanover." Marty paused for three seconds. "Edward is Thea's first husband."

All the partners and associates laughed—loudly, without reservation. The out-of-town relatives laughed, too, though some looked confused, not sure of why they were laughing. Edward's laugh was loudest and lasted the longest. Then he shrugged, lifting both hands to shoulder height and spreading his fingers. "What can I say? I can't deny it—I'm a realist. Marty, you son of a gun."

Willing herself to smile, Thea didn't let her shoulders stiffen too much. They all know the joke, she thought. Every single person in this firm knows the joke. Every single person knows it's all right to laugh at me.

Finally, someone else arrived, and attention shifted. She detached herself from Edward and found the bar. White wine, she thought. I should ask for white wine, take one sip, and then hold the glass in my hand until dinner starts.

She asked for a double Bourbon, straight up, and walked to the window overlooking the river. She stared out at nothing and drained her drink. I hate him, she thought. He's a horrible person. I wish he were dead. I hate him.

Someone touched her arm, and she turned to see Scott Crawford. "I was thinking about you the other day," he said. "Remember La'Sheka, that tiny girl who could barely hoist her cello onto the stage? She played a solo at the spring concert—it went very well. Afterwards, she came over to me and said, 'I wish Miss Thea had been here. Miss Thea always liked my music.'"

Coming on such a night, the unexpected sweetness of it made her want to cry. But the last three years had taught her self-control. She smiled. "What a nice thing for her to say. I hope the children don't think I lost interest in them."

"I'm sure they don't think that." He drank some Scotch and looked at her. "How have you been, Thea? How are things going?"

"Oh, fine." She wished she had some new accomplishment to tell him about, some new interest to describe. But she couldn't talk to him about shopping or working out or going to lunch, and she hadn't been doing anything else. She never did anything else. "My sister's getting married in three weeks, in Buffalo; I've been very busy getting ready for that. How about you? Are you handling any big cases?"

He half-laughed. "Nothing very big, nothing very interesting. Music Matters, though—that's thriving. We're thinking of starting two new groups, a string quartet and an a cappella choir. First, though, my mother has to raise money to pay the teachers. Well, if anybody can do it, she can."

She was about to reply when Edward walked over, smiling placidly. "I see you two have found each other. How nice. How's that foundation doing, Scott?"

Did Scott flinch? Probably not—probably, Thea had imagined it. "Very well. I was telling Thea we're thinking of expanding, if we can find the money."

Tilting his head back, Edward laughed briefly. "That sounds like an appeal for a check. Happy to oblige. And if you're expanding, maybe you can use Thea on Saturdays again. How about it, Thea? Feel like doing something useful?"

"No." Was it the Bourbon giving her courage, or the humiliation and anger and hatred? "There wasn't enough for me to do on Saturdays. It was boring. I could go on Thursdays. There's more for me to do."

Edward frowned. "I told you, I don't want you to go to that neighborhood in the afternoons. And on Thursdays, Scott won't be there to protect you."

"It's perfectly safe." She turned her back on him. "Scott, please tell Sharon I'll volunteer on Thursdays again. I'll start this week."

Clearly, Edward didn't like it. But he wouldn't stoop to arguing with her. During the following days, they barely spoke to each other. At breakfast, at dinner, they sat at the table and said nothing beyond routine inquiries and terse responses. As she ate, the sentences that had first come to her as she stood by the window kept going through her mind: I hate him. He's a horrible person. I wish he were dead. I hate him. The words became a mantra; it felt comforting to hear herself think them. Could Edward sense that something had changed, that she hated him now? Thea hardly cared.

* * * *

On Thursday, she went to the community center, helped Sharon in the office, and purposely stayed later than usual, stayed until well after it had started to turn dark. She'd had to park two blocks away from the center, and she felt nervous as she walked those two blocks, feeling the sharp chill in the air, noticing how few people were left on the street, how unsavory those few looked.

And then a man wearing a hooded jacket stepped out of an alley and grabbed her, pulling her into the alley, shoving her hard against the brick wall of a crumbling building. She started to scream, but he struck her in the face, shocking her into silence, and tore her purse from her hand. When she tried to pull away, he hit her again and ripped her coat open, his hand on her throat now, reaching for the braided gold necklace Edward gave her for Christmas. He'll kill me, she thought. After he takes the necklace, he'll kill me.

But someone pulled the man away from her, punching him in the face and the stomach. The man in the hooded jacket punched, too. The other man punched again, snatched her purse back, and let it fall to the pavement. The man in the hooded jacket ran away, and the other man ran after him.

Thea sank down sobbing, too terrified to think about what had happened, clutching her purse to her chest, putting her hand to her throat to feel that the necklace was still there. The other man ran back, slightly out of breath, and crouched next to her, putting his hands on her shoulders. It was Paul Addison, the private detective.

"The bastard got away," he said. "Are you all right, Thea? Did he hurt you?"

She stared at him blankly. My guardian angel, she thought; this time, the phrase didn't embarrass her. "Thank God he didn't get my purse," she said, "or my necklace. Edward would've been so mad."

Paul chuckled. "That's one hell of a thing to be thinking about at a time like this. Can you stand up? Here, let me look at you. You sure you're okay?"

He pulled her coat together and rebuttoned it, smoothed her hair back from her face. She looked at him gratefully. "I'm fine. Thank you, Paul. I'll never be able to thank you enough. And can you please not tell Edward? He'll say it proves he was right about coming here in the afternoon."

He gave her a quick, warm smile. "Edward will never know. But you should pull yourself together before you go home. How about a drink? I know a decent place, not far from here."

"That sounds wonderful." He walked her to her car and gave her directions, and five minutes later she joined him in the bar—just one room, long and narrow and dimly lit, warm with the smells of onion rings and barbeque sauce. She felt instantly at home. Paul sat at a back table; he'd already ordered a double Bourbon for her, a gin and tonic for himself. She sat down across from him, smiling shakily.

"How did you know I like Bourbon?" she asked.

"I know lots of things about you." He took a sip of his drink. "How have you been, Thea? How are things going?"

The same questions Scott Crawford had asked her. But this time, she felt she could tell the truth. "Things are worse. After you showed Edward the pictures of me and Tony, he gave me emerald earrings, and I thought that was a good sign. But then, at this party, he laughed at me—everyone laughed at me, like I'm some big joke. And he still doesn't trust me, and he barely talks to me."

Paul nodded slowly. "Why did you marry him? You didn't love him, did you?"

"I thought I might." She took a long drink. It felt wonderful to be this honest with someone. "I liked him, anyhow. Before we were married, we had some good times. He was funny—not crude, like so many guys, but witty, you know?" She paused and took another drink. "And I was tired—tired of living in crummy apartments and never being able to buy nice things, tired of working hard day after day and still being broke before the end of the month. And I was tired of being with men who said they loved me and wanted to marry me but just sponged off me and then dumped me without paying me back. Edward seemed different—he *was* different. I wasn't crazy about him. But all the men I'd been crazy about turned out to be such losers. I thought Edward and I could just be nice to each other, and it would be all right."

"But it hasn't been all right." He met her gaze directly. "You could leave him. Forget the prenup, forget the money. Just leave him, and find someone who appreciates you."

Was Paul talking about himself? Was he asking her to leave Edward and come to him? For thirty seconds, she let herself think about it; it felt exciting. But she liked Paul but didn't know if she could love him, and she couldn't see giving everything else up, not for a man who might turn out to be no different from the others. She shook her head. "I don't think that'd be smart."

"Probably not," he agreed. "Well, I'm glad I could be there for you today."

"Yes, thank you for that," she said. "If you hadn't been—oh, my God. So you were waiting outside the center, the whole time I was there?"

"No, most of the time I was inside. It gets pretty cold waiting in my car. Besides, I had to keep an eye on you, so I could tell Edward you weren't doing anything nasty."

That made her wince. "But how did you get inside? After the children arrive, Sharon locks the doors."

He shrugged. "Any private detective worth his salt can get past pretty much any lock. And the center doesn't have a security system—not enough worth stealing, I guess. Security systems are tough. The one at your house, for example—I got a look at that one time when Edward had me come over to make a report, and it's top of the line. I couldn't get past that. I'd have to know the keypad code."

Why had he mentioned that? Suddenly, she didn't feel so comfortable with Paul anymore. She finished her drink. "I'd better get home. Thank you, Paul."

"No problem. Say, you're going shopping tomorrow, right? Still looking for the perfect wedding gift for your sister? What do you say we have lunch?"

"That sounds nice. But what if someone's watching?"

"*I'm* the one who's watching. And I'm not telling Edward anything. So, lunch tomorrow?"

He'd saved her purse, maybe much more than her purse. How could she say no? She said yes, and the next day she said yes again, and then they were meeting every day for lunch or drinks. He urged her to talk about Edward, and she told stories about him, laughing at him, not feeling guilty when Paul joined in. "He's so vain about his looks," she said. "And really, for someone his age, he *does* look good. He wants to stay in shape, but he won't go to a club—I think he doesn't want to compare himself to younger men, more muscular men. So he's got all this equipment in the basement, and he works out almost every night, sometimes until after midnight."

Paul chewed on his Rueben. "What sorts of equipment?"

"Oh, every kind. A treadmill, free weights, a stationary bike—"

"Free weights? Those can be dangerous."

"He doesn't use them unless his personal trainer's there to spot for him. His name is Andre. He has the funniest accent; I don't know if it's French, or what."

She told two amusing stories about Andre, but Paul didn't seem especially interested. "Edward seems sorta paranoid," he said, more or less out of nowhere.

"I guess," she said, confused. "He must be, if he's so worried about me cheating on him."

"Yeah, there's that. And that fancy security system. Is that because he has all those paintings?"

"He *does* have a lot," she said. "He likes to show them off when people come over."

"I bet. So, he's vain. I bet he chose his birthdate for the keypad code, didn't he?"

He shouldn't ask that, she thought. I shouldn't answer. But she couldn't help laughing. "Even worse. I suggested using our wedding date—we'd just been married, and I thought it'd be romantic. But it had to be all about him." Stop talking about this, she told herself, though she had an inexplicable urge to tell him the rest. "We can't meet for lunch tomorrow. I'm leaving for Buffalo."

"I know," he said. "I'm going, too—Edward wants me to make sure you don't screw any old high-school sweethearts."

Even at my sister's wedding, she thought angrily. He doesn't trust me to be decent, not even there. I hate him. He's a horrible person. I wish he were dead. I hate him. "That bastard," she said.

"That sums it up," Paul agreed. "But I won't embarrass you—you'll never even know I'm there." He reached across the table, resting his hand on hers. It was the first time he'd touched her since he put his hands on her shoulders after saving her from the man in the hooded jacket. "Do you ever think about it, Thea? Do you wonder what it would be like if you came back from Buffalo and Edward simply wasn't there? Do you wonder how it would feel if you had that whole house to yourself, if you were free?"

For a few seconds, she let herself think about it. Then she shook her head. "That isn't going to happen."

"Of course not," Paul agreed. "So, you said the keypad code had to be all about him. His social security number? The date he graduated from law school? I bet it's really funny. Come on, Thea. I could use a laugh."

Paul's hand was warm on hers. To be free, she thought. No more tests, no more disapproving silences, no more jokes. "The date he made senior partner." She heard herself say the words and felt cold clear through. She pulled her hand away. "I have to go," she said, and left. I didn't tell him the numbers, she thought. He doesn't know when Edward made senior partner. And we were only joking around.

* * * *

That night, she asked Edward, again, if he'd come to Buffalo—not that she'd enjoy having him with her, just that it would feel good to go to her sister's wedding with an escort. But Edward wouldn't give her that small pleasure. She'd have to go as a woman whose husband didn't care enough about her to take her to her sister's wedding. In the morning, she packed carefully—her most expensive dresses, her nicest shoes, the emerald earrings and her other best jewelry in a cloth case she could carry in her purse. Edward was too busy to drive her to the airport, so she took a cab. And Paul will be there, she thought. It would be almost like having an escort—an escort no one could see, but an escort all the same.

At the baggage claim in Buffalo, Thea's sister waited with her fiancé and two cousins. They had balloons and a pink-and-purple welcome sign; when they spotted Thea, Celia and the cousins made a run for her, shrieking, and enveloped her in hugs. The fiancé, whom Thea hadn't met before, held his hand out awkwardly; but when Celia slapped him between the shoulders and called him an idiot, he grinned, embracing Thea lightly and kissing her cheek. He was a mechanic. Celia had told Thea he'd been saving his money and had made the first payment on his own shop. Celia would manage the convenience store attached to it, making the coffee and doing the books.

They scooped Thea up and took her to her parents' house, where her mother was frantically making potato salad for the rehearsal dinner but paused to take Thea in her arms, look deep into her eyes, and say she looked too thin. Her father came in from raking the back yard and insisted on carrying her suitcases up to her old bedroom, where a cot was crammed against the wall. She'd have to share her room with Aunt Maria from Rochester, he said. More aunts and uncles and cousins would be sleeping in the den, the basement, even the dining room. Everything was crowded and crazy and loud and lovely; Thea breathed it in like life. She hung her expensive dresses in her cramped old closet and unpacked her lingerie and jewelry into the beat-up bureau under the mirror still studded with cut-out magazine pictures of actors and singers she'd once adored.

At the rehearsal, everything went wrong. People argued and yelled and stamped in and out of rooms, and in the end it was fine. When they left the church, Thea thought she caught a glimpse of Paul in a car parked down the street; but she couldn't be sure. The rehearsal dinner was, of course, held at her parents' restaurant. Wearing the red silk dress special-ordered from the designer in Hong Kong, Thea tended bar, chatting with old friends, flirting openly with one of the high-school sweethearts who had inspired her husband to hire a private detective. By ten o'clock, she'd kicked off her high heels and put on one of the pairs of the slippers her mother always kept stowed behind the bar. By midnight, almost everyone had gone, and Thea sat at a back table with Celia, eating beef on weck and drinking Bud Lite, confessing how miserable she was.

"Then end it," Celia said. "My God, Thea! You're only thirty-two. That's way too young to give up on love, to give up on happiness. Come home. You don't have to move in with Mom and Dad if you don't want. Wayne and I have an extra room. You can stay there until you find a job and can afford a place of your own. Maybe you could go back to school."

Thea shook her head. "Too boring. Too embarrassing. Too hard."

"Fine," Celia said. "No school. But you can't just keep drifting. Not this time. You can't just let things happen and hope they'll be okay. For once, you have to actually *do* something. Do it, Thea. Walk away and start over."

Could she really do that? Maybe. But something nagged at her. It was much too late, but she went to the ladies' room, pulled out her cell phone, and called Edward.

"Good heavens, Thea," he said. "It's almost one o'clock in the morning. Why are you calling so late?"

"Because I want you to come here," she said. "I want you to come to Celia's wedding. You can find a flight that leaves in time. Or you can leave right now. You can drive here. That'd be better. Please, Edward. I really, really need you to come to Buffalo. I don't want you to stay in Cleveland, not even for the rest of the night."

"That's ridiculous," he said. "Why is this so important to you all of a sudden?"

Because the private detective you hired has been flirting with me, she thought. Because I told him the keypad code, and I think he's going to come into the house while I'm out of town and kill you. But explaining all that would be so hard, and Edward would be mad. "I miss you," she said.

"You must be drunk," he said. "Go to bed. I'll see you on Sunday."

He hung up. She held her cell phone in her hand and gazed at it. I tried, she thought. I really, really tried.

She slept in late the next morning, shutting out Aunt Maria's snores, then went downstairs in her bathrobe to linger at the kitchen table, indulging in a makeshift brunch of eggs and chicken wings, potato salad and bratwurst. Aunts and uncles and old friends came and went; she chatted with them lazily and allowed herself an occasional half-glass of wine. Finally, she went upstairs and showered, blow-drying her hair expertly, slipping into her pale green matron-of-honor dress. She reached into her top bureau drawer and took out the cloth jewelry case.

The emerald earrings weren't there. She stared at the case, picked it up and shook it, probed it with her fingers. Then she grabbed her purse and emptied it out on the bed, shaking it, pulling out the lining. No. The earrings hadn't fallen out of the case; they weren't hiding in her purse; they simply weren't there. All her other jewelry, yes—but the emerald earrings were gone. She looked down at the bed where Aunt Maria from Rochester had slept after Thea had insisted on taking the cot herself. She thought of the aunts and uncles and cousins crowded into every spare space in the house. One of them, she thought. But which one? She couldn't say anything to any of them, not without accusing all of them and ruining Celia's wedding. She'd have to just let it go. When Edward realized the earrings were gone, he'd be mad. She'd have to weather that.

Or maybe not, she thought for an instant. But she shut the thought out, put on her pearl earrings, and got to work on her makeup.

The wedding made her weep with happiness, and with envy. Thea had always been the beautiful sister, and Celia had always been the plain one; everybody had always said that, and Thea had always denied it but known it was true. Today, seeing Celia in her long white dress and lacy veil, holding Wayne's hands and looking so happy, Thea felt Celia was the beautiful one. I want that, Thea thought. I want to be happy like that. When I get to Cleveland, I'll tell Edward, and I'll pack whatever he'll let me keep and come back here. I'll stay with my parents until Celia and Wayne get back from the Finger Lakes, and then I'll move into their spare room and find a job. When they left the church, she looked for Paul again, for the parked car where she might have seen him yesterday. It wasn't there.

Wayne's parents had insisted on splitting the costs for the reception. It was a grand affair at a downtown hotel, with a lavish buffet and a live band. Once, after dinner, Thea thought of calling Edward again. I could tell him about Paul, she thought, and say I want a divorce. Those two things together might make him come here, or at least put him on his guard. But he'd probably say that she was being ridiculous, that she must be drunk. He'd definitely be mad. It's fine, Thea told herself. Nothing's going to happen. Edward's fine. She danced until two o'clock in the morning, kept dancing until long after Celia and Wayne had driven away for their three-day honeymoon.

* * * *

On Sunday morning, Thea ate half a pancake, packed, and flew to Cleveland. She took a cab to the house, called out to Edward as she opened the door, and heard no response. She lugged her suitcases upstairs, called out to him again, and heard nothing. She drew her breath in sharply and sat on the bed for five minutes, her hands clasped. Then she walked down to the basement. He lay on the smooth, sloped wooden bench, the steel bar holding the free weights crushed down on his throat. His pale, dead eyes stared up at her.

She looked at him for a long moment. He actually did it, she thought. My God. She didn't know how to feel. Slowly, she walked upstairs and dialed 911.

That wasn't the end of it. After the funeral, the police came back so often she decided she needed a lawyer. She thought it over for ten minutes before calling Scott Crawford. Yes, he said. He didn't usually handle this sort of case, but he'd take this one if she wanted him to, if the police were making her uncomfortable.

From then on, Scott was with her every time she met with the two detectives who didn't seem to like her very much. Edward had died not long after midnight on Saturday. Yes, the detectives knew she'd been in Buffalo then; they didn't need to see the pictures of her dancing at the wedding reception. But the detectives also knew other things. They knew about the prenup. They'd talked to Andre, and they knew how often he'd warned Edward about never using the free weights unless Andre was there to spot for him. The detectives knew about Tony, too. They'd talked to several people who worked at Thea's old club, and they'd gossiped about Tony's reputation, about how she and Tony had worked out in a private room with the door closed, about how she'd shown up one day in a leotard before dropping out of the club abruptly.

The detectives had also talked to Tony, and they hadn't been impressed. He'd been at a bar that Saturday night, he'd said, until he'd gotten a cell phone call around eleven o'clock, from a man claiming to know what he'd been up to with an ophthalmologist's wife, threatening to tell the husband unless Tony met him at midnight in a park near the Rock and Roll Hall of Fame. Tony had driven there and waited nearly an hour before going back to the bar. The detectives traced the call to a phone booth in Beachwood but couldn't find anyone to confirm Tony had been anywhere near the Rock and Roll Hall of Fame that night.

The detectives also knew Edward had joked about being Thea's first husband, and they knew how upset she'd seemed after people laughed at her at Marty Thompson's retirement dinner. And, somehow, they knew about the emerald earrings. They'd spoken to the jeweler and knew how expensive the earrings were, and they found it odd that Thea couldn't account for them, that she'd never reported the theft. Thea explained about the house being full of relatives, about not wanting to ruin Celia's wedding by accusing people. The detectives took notes but didn't seem to understand.

Scott understood. He understood everything. He shot sharp challenges back to the detectives during all the interrogations, defusing their questions with sarcastic incredulity. After they left, he patted her hand and told her not to worry.

* * * *

Finally, after nearly two months, the detectives stopped coming; after another month, Scott asked her out to dinner, and they had a wonderful time. He asked her out again, and again; once, they had dinner at his mother's beautiful house, and Scott's sister was there and was very nice to Thea. Often, Thea and Scott met for lunch; sometimes, they went to plays or concerts; once, he made dinner for her at his penthouse apartment overlooking the lake, and she stayed for the night. After that, they often spent the night together, either at his apartment or at her big house with all the expensive paintings. She started volunteering at Music Matters on Saturdays again, and she and Scott laughed and talked and had a nice time.

Always, every time her phone rang, she flinched, expecting it to be Paul. He never called. Another three months went by. Maybe Paul got scared off when he saw the police come back so often; maybe he'd decided it would be too dangerous to try to make contact with her. She stopped flinching when the phone rang. She thought she was probably in love with Scott, and that he probably loved her. She was very happy, just waiting for the question. We'll get married in Buffalo, she thought. We'll have the rehearsal dinner at my parents' restaurant.

And then her phone rang, and this time it was Paul. "Hello, Thea," he said. "I've been thinking about you. I've been thinking we should get together."

She was sitting down, but even so she had to grip the edge of the desk to steady herself, to keep the room from crashing down around her.

"Hello, Paul," she said. "Actually, I don't think that would be a good idea. I'm seeing someone else, and—"

"I know about Scott Crawford. I don't think he's the right man for you. Say, did the police ever track down those emerald earrings? The ones Edward gave you, the ones you lost in Buffalo?"

Any private detective worth his salt can get past pretty much any lock, she remembered. Friday night, when we were at the rehearsal dinner, when Paul had been in Buffalo watching her. "No. The police never tracked them down."

"That's good," Paul said. "If they ever showed up in Tony's possession—under a loose floorboard in his apartment, say, or under a tomato plant in the garden at his parents' house, or in a pawnshop where the sale could be traced to him—that'd be awkward. And I'm sure Tony was smart enough not to keep any pictures of you two together, of you in that leotard and him with his hands all over you. It'd be awkward if pictures like that showed up, too. So, let's have dinner tonight. We can meet in that bar where we first had drinks, after I saved you from that man who attacked you."

You set that up, she thought, realizing it for the first time. You set everything up. "I'm having dinner with Scott tonight," she said.

"Break it off." It wasn't a suggestion. "I'll see you at six."

She never had dinner with Scott again. But it wasn't too bad. Edward had thought movies were stupid, but Thea enjoyed them, and Paul did, too; they went to many movies. Even when they weren't movies she'd have picked, it was better than going to dinners where people spoke to her only because she was Edward's wife. They also went to Cavaliers games, and Paul talked about getting season tickets for the Indians next summer. Edward hadn't let her cook for him, but Paul did, and he said her lasagna was the best he'd ever had.

He decided to open his own private detective agency and needed two hundred thousand dollars. She thought maybe that was what he really wanted, maybe he'd leave her alone now. After she gave him the money, though, he moved his clothes into the house. Everything seemed settled. It'll be all right, she told herself. He's nicer to me than Edward was—and if he decides I need to be watched, he'll just do it himself.

He offered to have the wedding in Buffalo, but that didn't feel right to her, not with Paul. They'd do it in City Hall, they decided, just the two of them, and then they'd fly to Florida and go on a cruise. Paul had always wanted to go on a cruise. She thought about buying a new dress for the wedding but decided her light blue suit looked good enough.

On the first night of the cruise, they found themselves seated at a small, round table with a middle-aged couple from Atlanta. Paul reached across the table to shake the man's hand. "I'm Paul Addison," he said, "and this is the lovely Thea Addison." He paused for three seconds, turned to Thea, and smiled. "Thea's my first wife."

I didn't write "Thea's First Husband" until 2011, but I started think-ing about it, and occasionally taking notes about it, for almost twenty years before then. I had two ideas—one drawn from experience, one drawn from a favorite novel—and it took me that long to realize they belonged together.

Long ago, I had a professor who always introduced his wife by say-ing, "And this is my first wife, Joan." With him, I'm sure it was only a joke—he clearly adored her. I wondered, though, if his wife found the joke as funny as he did. Many years later, when I heard the professor had passed away (yes, still married to Joan), I remembered the joke. By then, I'd started writing mysteries, and I thought the joke might contain the germ of a story. But I couldn't come up with anything good, so I just wrote the joke down in a notebook and moved on.

Meanwhile, from time to time, I also took notes about a story based on a situation in a classic English novel, George Eliot's Middlemarch. *Edward Casaubon, an aging scholar, wins the love of beautiful, idealis-tic young Dorothea Brooke (and there you have the origin of the names of the story's Edward and Thea). Casaubon marries Dorothea but is too insecure to let himself enjoy his good fortune: He distrusts her, makes her miserable, destroys her love for him. I was fascinated by the charac-ters and the situation and wondered if I could use them in a mystery. Add a murder, make sure Edward gets his comeuppance, make everything end up happily for Thea—it seemed easy enough. But no matter how often I returned to this idea over the years, no matter how many notes I took, I never came up with anything that felt right, probably because I was too intent on giving the story a happy ending.*

Finally, as I was flipping through old notebooks one day, it occurred to me that I might be able to bring the two fragments of ideas together. My professor's innocent little joke became Edward's way of continually humiliating Thea in public—defusing any scorn people might feel for him by making it clear he knows Thea married him for his money (even though she didn't, not exactly). Although Thea isn't nearly as intelli-gent as Dorothea Brooke, she'd have to recognize the joke as an insult. The more I thought about the situation, the more potentially tragic it seemed—Edward began to seem downright cruel, and Thea began to seem culpably weak and passive for putting up with him. Passivity isn't a glamorous vice, but it's a destructive one. How much evil comes into the world because basically decent people lack the energy and determina-tion to make things right?

I still needed a catalyst to bring the situation to a crisis. So I added a third character, a private detective shrewd and unscrupulous enough to take advantage of Edward's cruelty and Thea's passivity. Then the story's last sentence came to me, and that settled that. After all those years, everything fell into place quickly, including the title. At this point, there was no way for the story to end happily, so I let it play out to what had come to feel like its inevitable conclusion.

A JOY FOREVER

(2015)

Gwen Harlowe had been a florist, my mother said, and had met Uncle Mike when he came to her neat, brisk Beacon Street shop to order flowers for his first wife's funeral. Automatically sympathetic to widowers, she'd helped him choose between carnations and chrysanthemums, between irises and gladioli. Something must have blossomed, for barely six months later he invited us to Boston for the wedding.

Though I was still in college and a long way from being a professional photographer, Uncle Mike had me take the wedding pictures—good experience for me, he said, and less money wasted for him. In some ways, the challenge proved too much for me: I had a hard time finding backgrounds the bride didn't fade into. She was small, quiet, and pale, at least ten years younger than my uncle but no match for his energy. Whenever I posed them together, she seemed diminished. In every picture I took, from whatever angle I tried, she looked like his sandy-colored shadow.

But she adored him. At the reception, she welded herself to his arm, her blushes a shy hint of glow against beige as she gazed at him with joyous gratitude. It was poignant. Even at twenty, I knew it was poignant. When my mother wished them happiness, I choked up. Since I didn't know Uncle Mike well yet, I thought they had a chance.

One year later, I knew better. I spent the summer in Boston, working at Uncle Mike's used-car dealership, so hard up for cash that I often accepted his invitations to have dinner at their house. That's when I learned just how miserable a marriage can be. I sat at their table and cringed.

"I could get a better meal at McDonalds," he said, bouncing his fork against a leathery grilled chicken cutlet, sinking it into a too-soft Brussels sprout. "I could find cleaner bathrooms there, too. You waste hours puttering around in your damn flower garden, and meanwhile you let the house go to hell."

"I'm sorry, Mike." Aunt Gwen's blushes looked nothing like those of the happy bride of just one year ago. These were pained, embarrassed blushes. "I'm trying to make a comfortable home for you. Really, I am."

"It sure doesn't look like you're trying. Remember what you said the first time we talked about getting married?" He raised his voice in a high-pitched, simpering parody. "'Oh, Mike—I just want to make you *happy*. I just want to take *care* of you.'" He lowered his voice again. "But you haven't done it. You don't know how. You spent too many years in that stupid flower shop, fussing over bouquets and boutonnieres and I-don't-know-what."

The flower shop, I now knew, had been the motive for the marriage. The gossip at the dealership was that Uncle Mike had been critically short of cash, in danger of losing his business. Then he met Gwen Harlowe, eager for marriage and owner of a solid little shop with a paid-up mortgage. It hadn't been hard to persuade her to sell the shop, turn her assets over to him, and trade her lonely independence for the glory of being Mrs. Mike Mallinger. Within months, his business was thriving, and she was desperately trying to become an acceptable drudge. She didn't have a penny of her own now. She was utterly dependent, utterly helpless.

It made me feel sick to see one human being so thoroughly subdued by another. At the end of August, I drove away, sure I'd never return. Now, six years later, I was driving back. Mother talked me into it. If I was determined to waste another vacation on another hopeless freelance project, she said, I should stay with Uncle Mike and Aunt Gwen, instead of squandering money on hotels. Since I didn't, in fact, have any money to squander, I gave in. But I wasn't happy. When my partner offered to come along, I said no. I'm all for confronting prejudices and shattering stereotypes. But not with Uncle Mike, not now.

As I pulled into the driveway, I caught my first glimpse of Aunt Gwen. She looked even smaller now, even paler, even quieter. The flower garden she'd cherished had been replaced by sturdy, undemanding shrubs that gave her no excuse for neglecting housework. She's surrendered, I thought. The last symbol of her personality has been plowed under. It was sad, but not surprising.

Uncle Mike, though—the change in him shocked me. He'd always been stocky; now, he was obese. He must have gained a hundred pounds since the last time I'd seen him, and they hung on him flabbily.

"Good to see you again, Chris," he said. "So, what do you think of the lawn? Not bad, huh? And it's all Gwen's doing." He swatted her behind affectionately. Did she flinch? I couldn't be sure. "She took over the yard work years ago. Says I shouldn't have to fuss with that after a long day at the lot. And, by God, she's right."

We walked into the house, where every surface glistened—dust-free, hard-polished, lemon-saturated. Aunt Gwen slipped into the kitchen and then reappeared with a tray: two mugs of beer, a bowl of potato chips, a mound of dip studded with chopped sausage and hunks of hard-boiled eggs. Uncle Mike handed one mug to me, took a long gulp from the other, and scooped an inch of dip onto his first chip.

"Gwen's turned into quite a little cook," he said. "It was rough going at first, but after a year or so—well! You wouldn't believe how many cookbooks she has. She's taken cooking courses, too, and she watches Food Network shows every day. You won't have any complaints about the food here this time."

I didn't. Dinner was overwhelmingly delicious—glazed ham dripping with raisin sauce, baked potatoes buried in butter and sour cream, crispy fried cauliflower, salad with thick Ranch dressing, home-baked cinnamon rolls. Aunt Gwen nibbled at the edges of the feast, toying with her salad, saying hardly anything, watching Uncle Mike.

"So, about this project of yours, Chris," he said. "You're taking pictures for an insurance company calendar?"

"That's right," I said as Aunt Gwen buttered another roll and slipped it onto his plate. "Revere Mutual's putting together a calendar to give their customers. New England scenes—that's the theme. And they're taking submissions from freelancers."

"Is there much money in that?" he asked. Aunt Gwen had carved him another slice of ham. He waved it off half-heartedly but cut into it when she put it on his plate.

"Not really," I admitted. "But the calendar will be distributed nationwide, so it'd be good exposure. It might help me get established as a real photographer."

"Hell, you're a real photographer already." He held out his wineglass so Aunt Gwen could refill it. "Your mom told me how many weddings you handled last year. And you did class pictures for some elementary schools, right?"

"That's not the kind of photography I really want to do," I said, wondering why I was bothering to explain my ambitions to this idiot, and why Aunt Gwen was spooning still more dressing onto his scraps of lettuce. "I want to say something with my pictures."

Uncle Mike guffawed. "Now, what can you say with a calendar picture? Unless it's a pin-up calendar. The Girls of New England. Those pictures say plenty—right, Gwen?" He nudged her with his elbow, almost knocking the salt shaker from her hand. Undeterred, she kept sprinkling his baked potato.

"It's not that kind of calendar." My voice sounded stiff, even to me. "I want to say something about what New England means to me, about my memories of summers at Grandma's house. I'm trying to take a picture for July, and I figure most people will go for trite stuff, fireworks or Paul Revere's house. I want to capture something subtler. I've got all these pictures in my mind—Grandpa cranking up a batch of ice cream, Grandma telling stories in the evening. That's what comes to my mind when I think of New England. Serenity. Security. Contentment. I want to get *that* in a photograph."

Aunt Gwen's hand froze half-way to Uncle Mike's plate, her serving spoon sagging under its load of fried cauliflower. A soft look came into her eyes, and a faint but real smile tugged at her lips. She understands, I thought, and felt glad I'd explained.

"Sounds like sentimental crap." Uncle Mike leaned back to pat his stomach. "Not bad, Gwen. What's for dessert?"

Dessert was chocolate pie—French silk chocolate pie, she said meekly—and it was richer and thicker than any pie I'd tasted before. She took a sliver for herself but carved slabs for us, hiding them under mounds of whipped cream. After taking two bites, she retreated to the kitchen. Moments later, I heard the water running and knew she was washing dishes.

Uncle Mike went back to talking about the calendar. "It's not that I don't like art," he assured me. "Not photographs so much, but I love sculpture. If it's really beautiful, that is. Then it's a joy forever, like Shakespeare says."

Keats, I thought; and it's "as," not "like." But I kept quiet. I understood how Aunt Gwen had been worn down by this man. I just hoped he wouldn't force me to admire the porcelain nude again.

He pointed to the mantelpiece. "Now, *that's* what I mean."

I had to do it. I had to follow his gesture with my eyes, to look at The Thing. It was almost two feet tall, a lumpy ceramic statue of a generously-endowed naked woman sitting, inexplicably, on a tree trunk; and it was painted and glazed in a way too horrifying to describe. Uncle Mike gazed at it with more affection than he'd ever shown either of his wives. "*That's* a joy forever," he said. "I bought it when I sold my first car, thirty-two years ago this October. Blew my whole commission on one statue, and I've never regretted it. If you could come up with something *that* beautiful, Chris, it'd be worth the time."

Aunt Gwen slunk back into the dining room, to cut Uncle Mike a second slice of pie. At least, I thought, she's won some peace for herself.

At least there can't be a repetition of what happened on my last night here six years ago, when Uncle Mike, enraged by an overdone roast, lashed out and slapped her face, hard. I'd gasped; that had been enough to make him glare at me, to make it clear he'd be glad to start on me if I said anything.

That was my deepest reason for hating him. He'd made me stare at my plate and pretend I didn't hear Aunt Gwen's sobs. He'd terrified me and made me despise myself. At least, I thought again, nothing like that can happen tonight.

I was wrong. It happened when Aunt Gwen crept into the den with our bedtime snack: ham and cheese sandwiches, creamy potato salad, triple-decker brownies, two more mugs of beer. Astonished, I stared at the tray.

"This looks great, Aunt Gwen," I said. "But I'm still full from dinner, and I'm not used to eating so late at night."

"Can't go to bed on an empty stomach, Chris," Uncle Mike said. "Besides, Gwen makes the best potato salad in town."

He beamed at her; but as she set down his mug, her hand shook, and some beer sloshed onto the coffee table.

"Clumsy," he said, and smacked her shoulder with the palm of his hand. It was rough, but almost absent-minded. It probably happened often. "Watch the furniture."

"I'm sorry, Mike," she said, and I realized I was surprised to hear her use his first name. It would've seemed more natural for her to call him "Mr. Mallinger."

It felt good to get out of the house early the next morning, while Uncle Mike was still working through his second platter of pancakes and sausages, and climb into my car to begin my quest for the soul of New England. The quest turned out to be tougher than I'd expected. It's not easy to take photographs that radiate serenity, security, and contentment, at least not if you're a stranger in town.

First, I tried a park, standing behind a tree to photograph toddlers at play. I ended up pleading with a policeman and the zealous daycare teacher who'd summoned him, trying to convince them I wasn't a child pornographer scouting for talent. I spent the afternoon approaching senior citizens who scowled when I suggested they whip up some ice cream or gather grandchildren for story hour. What, they wanted to know, was I really up to? Was I selling something? By the time I returned to Uncle Mike's house, I'd begun to think that he might have a point after all, that a life spent taking studio portraits and carefully-posed candids might not be so bad.

His car wasn't in the driveway, so I went to the back door, figuring Aunt Gwen would be in the kitchen. Instead, she sat in a rocking chair on the screened-in porch, humming softly as she made delicate stitches in a large square of linen stretched across an embroidery hoop. She scrambled to her feet when she saw me.

"Dinner's almost ready," she said nervously. "I was just about to go back to the kitchen. I'll get you a beer and some snacks."

"Please don't get up," I said. "I'm not hungry, and I'd love to sit out here with you for a while. I bet we've got plenty of time before Uncle Mike gets home."

I think she liked the conspiratorial tone of the last sentence. She smiled and sat back down. "You came home earlier than I expected. Did you find lots of good subjects right away?"

"No, I got discouraged right away. I don't know if I'll ever find a good subject. I guess part of the problem is that I don't really know what I'm looking for."

"But you do," she said. "You expressed it so well last night. I know exactly what you mean. And I'm sure you'll find it eventually. Sometimes, you can't make good things happen right away. But if you don't give up, if you're patient, you'll get what you want."

"*You're* sure patient." I walked over to look at her tapestry. "That's lovely, Aunt Gwen. Did you design it yourself? Are you going to fill in all that space with those tiny flowers? That takes more patience than I'll ever have."

The design consisted of a mass of flowers—not arranged in a landscape or vase, not forming a pattern in any usual sense, but a joyous profusion ordered by a harmony I could feel but not define. The colors were dazzling, the variety of flowers amazing. No two were exactly alike, and some, I was sure, bloomed only in her imagination, never in any garden. And each flower was composed of dozens of tiny stitches. Each must have taken hours to create.

She blushed—a proud, vibrant blush this time. "I'm glad you like it. I've been working on it for a long time. A long, long time. I take it out whenever I have a spare minute. So I can't do much at a time. But I work on it every day." Her smile hardened. "Every single day. I'll never give up, not till I finish. And when it's done—why, when it's done, it's going to be wonderful."

She sat staring at nothing, silent and motionless. Then she shook herself. "I'd better get to the kitchen. Mike likes his appetizers ready right when he gets home." She gathered up needles, thread, and scissors, placed them in a paper bag with her tapestry, and hid the evidence of her frivolity in the back of a corner cupboard, behind sacks of flour and sugar. "I hope you like Italian food," she said.

I do like Italian food, and I was awed by the dinner: lemon veal scaloppini, baked ziti thick with tomato sauce and mozzarella, roasted onions in a balsamic glaze, sautéed mushrooms, hunks of garlic bread, dusky Chianti. I ate Aunt Gwen's cooking, listened to Uncle Mike rant about lazy employees, and thought of the tapestry hidden in the cupboard. It's her last link to her former life, I thought. Now, those meticulously stitched flowers are the only ones she can have, and even those she doesn't dare show to her husband. She can never display what she's created—their house will be disfigured by his hulking, vulgar statue, not graced by the painstaking work of her hands. I watched her pile more food on his plate and felt profound pity. She has no hope, I thought. She's so trapped that she can't even dream of any escape beyond brief retreats to fields of imaginary flowers.

"So Henderson had made such a mess of the books," Uncle Mike was saying, "that I had to spend the whole afternoon straightening them out. Couldn't even get away for a round of golf. I swear I'll fire the old fool next time." His face flushed clear up to his scalp, and sweat ran down his neck. "Gwen, turn up the air conditioner. It's hot as hell in here."

"I'm sorry," she said, and leapt up to obey.

"I'm glad to hear you still golf sometimes, Uncle Mike," I said, hoping to steer the talk toward pleasanter subjects.

"Yeah, and I've got a great golf cart now. Gwen gave it to me. She saved up for years, always putting something aside from her clothing allowance. It's a beauty—plenty of room for a cooler of beer. Sure beats tramping all over the golf course, lugging those heavy clubs." He gazed at her almost fondly. "She's turned out okay. Not much for looks, but she takes good care of me."

I couldn't believe he'd said it. As a gesture of sympathy, I rose when she did, helped clear the table, and stayed to dry dishes. As I watched her standing at the sink, sympathy overpowered me again. She was barely fifty but looked like an old woman—bent, scrawny, exhausted, her graying hair pulled back in a tight bun. And her drab, shapeless dress had to be at least a decade old.

"You spend so much on Uncle Mike," I chided. "The golf cart, all that food and liquor. Spend something on yourself. Go to a beauty parlor and have your hair cut and styled. Buy yourself some new clothes."

She laughed softly. "Oh, Mike really needs what I buy for him—he really, really does. And I don't care how my hair looks, and I don't need new clothes." Her smile hardened again. "Not yet."

I felt so moved, and so sorry, that I leaned over and kissed the top of her head. "You're too good to him."

"You think so?" She looked at me thoughtfully. "You're a friend, aren't you, Chris? Well, that's nice. It's nice to have a friend in the house. It's handy." She set the last dish in the drainer and dried her hands on her apron. "I do believe everything's ready," she said, more to herself than to me.

My second outing with my camera proved a second failure. When I tried to coax people into posing, they snarled. When I tried to take candids, I got beaten off with canes and purses. Eventually, I shot some pictures of squirrels, trying to convince myself they epitomized New England's serenity, security, and contentment.

It was a miserable day. As the temperature climbed, everyone turned sweatier and surlier. The sidewalks burned, the grass drooped, and even the birds looked damp and listless. Enough, I decided. Tomorrow, I head for Vermont and take pictures of barns.

When I arrived at the house, I saw the windows standing open. No, I thought. Not today. Aunt Gwen toiled at the stove, her dress clinging moistly to her body. The air conditioning, she said, had stopped working several hours ago, and she couldn't find anyone to fix it. So she'd opened up the house to let in some fresh air.

I didn't have the heart to criticize her, but she couldn't have made a worse decision. The air outside wasn't fresh. It was stale, breezeless, hotter than the air in the house could have been. Much better, on such a day, to close windows and curtains against the sun, to hoard the last traces of cool the night and the air conditioner had left behind.

And better, too, to fix a light meal for once. I staggered as she outlined the dinner menu: fried chicken with inch-thick coating; cornbread dressing; mashed potatoes with gravy; corn on the cob, with plenty of butter; biscuits, with more butter; chocolate cake with fudge icing.

"All of Mike's favorites," she said brightly.

Despite the heat, she seemed brisk and cheerful as she fussed among pots and pans. She even hummed. At first, I didn't recognize the tune. Then I realized it was "Tonight," from *West Side Story*. I smarted at the irony of it, at this defeated woman humming a tune so full of hope and romance.

When he got home, Uncle Mike was in a foul mood. He swore first at the air conditioner, then at Aunt Gwen, shouting that he knew damn well she could've found a repairman if she'd tried. I started to protest, but she caught my eye, shook her head, and smiled, placidly bringing him his beer, dip, and chips. As he stuffed them down, he fumed about his day.

For once, he had real reasons to be angry. At noon, his secretary got a call saying a rival car dealer was facing bankruptcy and liquidating his assets. If Uncle Mike got to Quincy right away, he could snap up his competitor's cars for practically nothing. So he drove for an hour through pounding heat and thickening traffic, only to discover that his competitor was not going bankrupt, that he'd sooner die than sell Uncle Mike a punctured tire, that the call had been somebody's idea of a joke. Uncle Mike accused his competitor of faking the call himself, obscenities were exchanged, they shoved each other around the showroom, a police officer was summoned and reprimanded them both.

Uncle Mike ranted about it throughout dinner, eating ferociously, not seeming to notice how many chicken bones and corn cobs towered up on his plate, how much stuffing and potatoes and biscuits and wine plummeted down his gullet. After dinner, Aunt Gwen started to fade into the kitchen. Again, I stood up to help her. This time, she wouldn't allow it.

"No, Chris," she said. "Not tonight. Actually, I'm not going to do the dishes right now. I have to finish dusting the living room first."

Uncle Mike frowned. "Why didn't you get that done during the day?"

"Didn't have time," she said. Her tone wasn't as deferential as usual. She almost shrugged.

Uncle Mike sat at the head of the table, his back to the living room. I sat to his right, so I had a clear view of Aunt Gwen as she got her furniture polish and dust cloth from the kitchen and bustled about, humming "Tonight" again. She dusted the coffee table, the lamps, the bookcase. She dusted the mantel. She lifted down Uncle Mike's ceramic nude, held it in her left hand, prepared to dust the spot it had covered. And she let the statue drop.

The crash was spectacular. Uncle Mike's head jerked. He turned slowly, his mouth falling open as he saw the powdery remains of his treasure—a hand here, a bit of tree trunk there, a hunk of blond hair under the coffee table. His eyes filled with shock, with grief, with rage.

Aunt Gwen sighed. "Oops," she said.

That did it. "Oops?" He stood up, knocking his chair aside. He turned to me, pointing at Aunt Gwen with a trembling finger. "She said 'oops'! She destroys the most beautiful, the most precious thing I own, and she says 'oops!'"

Aunt Gwen looked bored. "It was old anyway."

"Old!" he echoed incredulously. "Yeah, it was old. I've had it thirty-two years—thirty-two years, ever since I sold my first car. Art gets *more* valuable when it gets older, you moron. It was probably worth a fortune by now. And it was a thing of beauty. It shoulda been a joy forever, like Shakespeare says."

"Keats," she pointed out, serenely. "And it's 'as,' not 'like.'"

Uncle Mike's face passed from red to purple. His chest heaved. "Don't you start with me! You little bitch! I oughtta break you in two!"

I'd frozen, but I had to act. "Uncle Mike," I said, standing up. "Calm down. It was an accident. Don't—"

"Stay out of it, Chris," Aunt Gwen snapped. "Sit down." She turned her taunting face to Uncle Mike. "Let him hit me if he wants. If he *can*. Go ahead, Mike. See if you can drag that carcass of yours across the room. Just try to hit me, you disgusting slob."

Roaring, he lunged at her. Before he could get close, she darted to the side. Then she was in the dining room. Spinning around, he charged after her. Sweat poured down his face, his breath turned shallow, and the veins in his neck bulged out, pressing against his triple chin. Laughing, Aunt Gwen raced around the table and back to the living room.

"Can't catch me, can you, Mike?" she said. "You're too slow. And you're as ugly as that stupid statue." She kicked a porcelain arm across the room, giggling when it shattered against the wall. "God! Am I glad to see the last of *that*!"

Uncle Mike stopped a foot away from her, gasping, snorting. The revolt of his slave had shocked him more than the loss of his statue. "You—you—" he started, and grabbed at his chest. His face contorted, and he stared at her. "You," he managed, and crumbled.

* * * *

There were so many people to talk to that night—the neighbors who heard him yelling, the paramedics, the emergency room nurses, the undertaker. At one point, I found myself alone with Uncle Mike's doctor.

"I warned him," the doctor said. "I told him, 'Mike, you're begging for a heart attack. Lay off the booze, the sugar, the fat, the salt.' But did he listen? And I wish he'd never gotten that damn golf cart. I don't think the man ever got any exercise. Some, I guess, working in the yard, but obviously not enough." He shook his head. "He should've learned to control his temper, too. The paramedics told me what the neighbors said. To blow up at his wife because she broke some knick-knack while dusting! The poor little thing. What a shame her last memories of her husband had to be so ugly."

The poor little thing, however, seemed to be doing fine, accepting condolences graciously and giving crisp directions to the undertaker. When we got home, she slipped down to the basement. Moments later, I heard the hum of the air conditioner, and Gwen came back upstairs.

"I thought I might as well tinker with it myself," she said, "and I think I actually fixed it. Help me close the windows, won't you? Then let's sit on the porch while the house cools. We'll let the dishes be. I've got lemonade in the fridge—want some? Mike never cared for it, but I think there's nothing better on a hot night."

I called my mother. Yes, I said, I'd stay until after the funeral. There was so much to do. Tomorrow, Gwen wanted to gather up the things she was donating to Goodwill—Uncle Mike's clothes, Uncle Mike's golf clubs, her cookbooks.

By the time I joined her on the back porch, she was rocking slowly, sewing by the light of an electric lantern. "Come sit down, Chris," she said. "It's turned into a lovely evening, hasn't it? I do believe the heat will break tomorrow."

I settled down on the porch swing. "You'll have more time for sewing now," I said.

"In the evenings," she agreed. "Of course, I'll have so many other things to do, too. Tomorrow, I'll get my hair cut and buy some decent clothes—for the funeral, and so forth. Then I'll see about selling the business. Perhaps I'll call Bill Morgan."

"Bill Morgan?"

"Yes, he owns a lot in Quincy. He was one of my late husband's competitors. I hear his business is flourishing, and he's thinking of moving to a better location. Then I'll look for a florist's shop—a bigger one this time, with a greenhouse." She gazed at her tapestry. "But I won't give up my sewing. Some day, this will look just lovely over the mantel. So I'll work on it every chance I get—little by little, day by day, until it's finished. That's the way to get things done."

"Gwen," I said, "may I get my camera?"

That was the picture that got me my first sale, that won me my first award, that gave me my start as a freelance photographer. Gwen laughed at the thought of being a pin-up girl at her age, but she was a good sport about it, even when the picture attracted so much attention that the company decided to use it every year, as its perennial July scene.

She's sitting in her big pine rocker, on her screened-in porch, sewing her delicate fantasy of flowers, her hair pulled back in a bun, her faded cotton dress soft in the lantern light. I take some credit for the composition of the picture, for working in the glass of lemonade on the wicker stand, the apron hanging on a hook near the door. But I can't fool myself. It was Gwen's face that made the picture famous, made everyone agree my camera had captured the soul of New England. Serenity. Security. Contentment.

You can get a copy at any Revere Mutual office.

In most of my stories, I work hard at being mysterious, at trying to keep readers in the dark as much as possible for as long as possible. I don't want readers to figure out where the story is headed—I want the ending to come as a surprise.

Those weren't my goals in "A Joy Forever." I think the story's more fun if readers realize what's going on long before the narrator does. In the first dinner scene, for example, Gwen's actions are more amusing if readers understand what she's up to. The narrator clearly doesn't *understand, and I think his (or is it her?) confusion adds another layer of humor—but that works only if readers can see how clueless Chris is being.*

The story does have a few twists at the end, but they don't involve the basic plot. Mostly, they involve the three works of art in the story—Mike's porcelain nude, Gwen's tapestry, Chris's photograph. Each work reflects important things about the character with whom it's associated. Mike likes to quote (and to attribute to Shakespeare) a line from Keats' Endymion: "A thing of beauty is a joy forever." In a sense, these three works of art sum up the conflicts in the story. Which ones are truly things of beauty and sources of joy? Which will last "forever," and which will be consigned to the oblivion it deserves? I've got to admit I'm pleased by the way the three come together at the end of the story, after Gwen has completed yet another "thing of beauty" that will bring her lasting joy.

Just for fun, I drew some character names from George Eliot's Daniel Deronda: *Gwen Harlowe is named after Gwendolen Harleth, and Mike Mallinger is named after her husband, Henleigh Mallinger Grandcourt. Gwen's personality bears absolutely no resemblance to Gwendolen's, but the two women's marriages are similar in some respects, and there are other similarities, too. I can't explain further without spoiling the plot of* Daniel Deronda *for those who haven't yet read this wonderful novel. Those who* have *read it will understand why I gave Gwen and Mike these names.*

PUBLICATION INFORMATION

"A Joy Forever," *Alfred Hitchcock's Mystery Magazine*, March 2015. Nominated for Agatha Award for Best Short Story.

"Adjuncts Anonymous," *Alfred Hitchcock's Mystery Magazine*, June 2009. Nominated for Derringer Award for Best Long Story, Short Mystery Fiction Society.

"Aunt Jessica's Party," *Woman's World*, July 6, 1993.

"Death in Rehab," *Alfred Hitchcock's Mystery Magazine*, May 2011.

"Death on a Budget," *Alfred Hitchcock's Mystery Magazine*, February 1998.

"Honor among Thieves," *Alfred Hitchcock's Mystery Magazine*, July/August 2000.

"The Listener," *Family Circle*, August 1995. First prize in national suspense-writing contest sponsored by *Family Circle* and judged by Mary Higgins Clark.

"Night Vision," *Alfred Hitchcock's Mystery Magazine*, Mid-December 1991.

"The Shopper," *Creatures, Crimes, and Creativity 2014 Anthology*, Intrigue Publishing, October 2014.

"Table for None," *Alfred Hitchcock's Mystery Magazine*, May 2008.

"Thea's First Husband," *Alfred Hitchcock's Mystery Magazine*, June 2012. Nominated for Agatha Award for Best Short Story. Nominated for Macavity Award for Best Short Story. Named to list of Other Distinguished Stories in *Best American Mystery Stories 2013*.

www.ingramcontent.com/pod-product-compliance
Lightning Source LLC
Chambersburg PA
CBHW020756250626
47155CB00003B/1100